Northdale

Northdale

Robert L. Nelis

Copyright © 2016 Robert L. Nelis

All rights reserved.

ISBN-13: 9781534636354
ISBN-10: 1534636358
Library of Congress Control Number: 2016909701
CreateSpace Independent Publishing Platform
North Charleston, South Carolina

Dedication

*To my wife Sheila.
When you accepted my proposal
I told you our life together would have
highs and lows like a roller coaster.
You stuck with me for 41 years.
I could not have ridden the bumps
without you.*

Homecoming

―

KING HENRY OF ENGLAND SIGNED the last document, slid it across the table to his First Chancellor, and asked, "Is that the end of it? I need a glass of wine."

"One last thing, Prince Edward's friend, Sir Rupert, asked for a short interview. He said he wants to ask a small favor that will not cost you anything."

Henry smiled. "Sir Rupert seems to be very solid young man who does not spend time pushing himself forward like numerous less talented knights seem to love doing. A free favor? Send him in."

Rupert entered the office and made the correct courtly bow. With a friendly tone in his voice, King Henry said, "Sir Rupert, what can I do for you?"

"Your Majesty, it is a five-day trip from here at Red Ford to my home in Lincolnwood. I have not been home in four years and request permission to ride ahead of your retinue and reacquaint myself with my family."

"I've already dispatched a herald yesterday, but you have my permission. Pass on my personal salutations to your father and mother—we are old friends."

After closing the king's door, Rupert raised his right hand, make a controlled shout, and then ran to the stable. Prince Edmond found him preparing his war and pack horses. "Rupert, you lucky dog, you get to flee this slow-moving horde. How about letting me dress up as your squire and taking me along?" They both laughed.

"Look, Edmond, if you left without permission, the king would hand both of us over to the cook with orders to skewer and slow roast us." They laughed again.

"Will your family be glad to see you?"

"All, I believe, except my older brother. All my life, he never stopped trying to impress on me that he would be the future earl, and I would not be noble. I heard he is married, so I cannot guess if this will make him more obnoxious or less."

As Rupert led his horses out the gate, Edmond said, "Ah, Rupert, you forgot one thing. As the Crown Price I cannot be skewered and cooked, but you certainly can be." They smiled and waved farewell.

Sir Humphrey had spent most of the day working with two peasants repairing a stone wall when the barony's designated runner raced up to him. "The king's herald just arrived, and Lord Cuthbert requests your immediate presence."

"What news did the herald bring?"

"Well, sir, you know they won't tell me anything, but her ladyship started running around, talking about Rupert's return and the king's visit."

With unnecessary force, Humphrey tossed the stone he was holding onto the ground. "Rupert is coming?"

The runner responded, "That is what I heard, my lord."

Not a muscle moved as he stared across the fields at Lincolnwood's castle. He stood motionless for over a minute; the runner looked at the peasant workers with a puzzled expression, and together the two workers shrugged their shoulders.

Humphrey slowly turned to the runner and with an irritated-sounding voice said, "Tell my father I will directly come." The messenger turned and ran toward the castle.

He looked at the two peasant helpers and said, "Keep stacking stones until dinner, and I'll meet you near the drawbridge tomorrow an hour after sunrise." He then picked up his tunic and began walking quickly toward the castle. One worker gave a look at the other and raised his eyebrows; the other smiled and waved his hand in the gesture indicating they should slow down. Their productivity dropped as soon as the earl's son could no longer see them.

By the time he reached the castle, Humphrey's pace was one notch below a stomp. He ignored everyone while passing over the drawbridge and through the courtyard. His sister Mary stepped out of a side door, saw him, and yelled, "Humphrey, did you hear? *Sir* Rupert is coming home!"

Humphrey stopped dead in his tracks and looked at Mary. With an incredulous facial expression, he said, "Did you say 'Sir'?"

Mary had run up to him. With a big smile, she said, "I don't know any details, but the herald said the Count of Flanders had knighted him." She hopped up and down with that news.

Humphrey's face looked like stone. "Are you not glad?" she asked.

He looked at her wirh a very serious facial expression. "I must talk to father. Where is he?"

Mary stepped back from him and, with a questioning look, pointed to the main door. He strode away.

The earl stood looking at several papers on the desk when Humphrey entered the library. He looked up with a smile that disappeared when he observed Humphrey's face.

"Father, can we talk?"

Obviously, his elder son was troubled. With mild concern he said, "Of course, son, what is bothering you on the day we receive great news?"

Humphrey returned to the door and closed it. Cuthbert asked, "Son?"

Humphrey walked up to the opposite side of the desk. "Father, Lincolnwood cannot support an earl and a knight. You know that! You have said the barony cannot be divided into pieces and still remain viable! I don't know how, but now Rupert is a knight?"

The earl actually flopped back into his chair and looked at his elder son for a moment. "Humphrey ... Humphrey, what did you expect? We sent Rupert off as a squire to a court knight. I hoped to be the one to knight him, but we will find out what happened."

Humphrey leaned over and placed both hands on the desk, "Lincolnwood cannot afford to pay the costs of a roving knight. How will he be supported?"

The earl now slowly stood up, put his hands on the desk, and looked directly at Humphrey. "You are the heir to Lincolnwood, and you will be the next earl. But I am still alive and will make the decisions." He stood straight up, and Humphrey followed him. "I don't know the answers, but many alternatives always exist." He then walked around the desk, stood next to Humphrey, slapped him on the arm, and said, "Come, eldest, let us enjoy the youngest's return after his four-year absence." He smiled.

Humphrey turned his head away from his father, waited a moment, and then with an absolute minimum of warmth said, "I will celebrate, but this topic must be discussed."

Cuthbert grabbed his son's arm, and together they began to walk toward the door. With a beaming smile the earl said, "But not now."

Humphrey opened the door of his living quarters and with a very firm voice yelled, "Philippa?"

His pregnant wife sat near the window, sewing baby clothes. When she saw her husband's face, she asked the servant girl to leave.

He impatiently waited until the door closed. "Did you hear that *Sir* Rupert is coming home?" He made the word "sir" into a sneer.

She rose, went to him, and put her hands on his chest. "What does this mean for us?"

He twisted away from her, walked over to the window, and looked out. "My father said a long time ago that he would not divide the barony between us." He faced his wife. "His lordship just said he planned to find alternatives."

"What does that mean? Are we protected?"

A pillow had fallen to the floor, and Humphrey kicked it. "I cannot guess yet, but you and I must put pressure, carefully, whenever we can."

Philippa took her husband's hands and vigorously nodded her head in agreement.

Rupert rode over Lincolnwood's drawbridge at middle afternoon, two days later. No one paid much attention to just another visiting knight. He dismounted and tied the reins to a post. Mary was walking in the courtyard and looked at the new arrival.

She screamed when she recognized Rupert. She ran over to him and jumped on him for a sisterly hug. "Rupert! Rupert, you are home. I did not recognize you at first. You are so grown up. Last time I saw you, you were just a boy. You looked so scared when you left. You look like a man now. You don't look scared anymore. I'm so glad to see you. Mother and Father …"

Rupert had put his hand over his sister's mouth. "Mary, stop talking." He gave her another hug. "Where can I find everyone?"

She put her arm around Rupert's and tugged him toward the main door. She also let out an unladylike yell. "Rupert is home!"

Lord Cuthbert and Lady Elizabeth sat in the great hall, discussing decorations for the king's reception. They heard Mary and reached the main door just as Rupert did. Elizabeth threw her arms around his shoulders and started to cry. "You've been gone so long." He looked over her shoulder at his father, whose face radiated happiness.

"Yes, mother, I'm home."

He disengaged from her and walked over to his father; they embraced with sound slaps on each other's backs. His father then placed his hands on Rupert's shoulders and pushed him to arm's length. Looking over his son, he said, "You have grown into quite a man, thank God." Rupert took his mother's arm and walked into the castle. The lord called for wine to be served in the great hall.

They sat around one end of the large wooden banquet table and questions and answers flew. Rupert could hardly keep up with producing a steady flow of information. Mary's question about a wife stopped the conversation. Rupert smiled, sipped his wine, and looking at his father. "No one yet and no prospects either. Who wants to marry a new and poor knight?" They all laughed.

Humphrey and Philippa entered the room. With a very polite smile, Humphrey said, "Welcome, brother." Rupert rose and they exchanged the customary greeting between men—right hand grasped the other's right arm just below the elbow. Rupert then faced Philippa and made the proper courtly bow. With a controlled smile, she curtsied. Cuthbert directed them to the table and gestured to the servant to pour two more glasses of wine.

Cuthbert then looked at Rupert. "You just said knight, explain the circumstances."

"It is a fairly long story. Do you want to hear it now or make it dinner's entertainment?"

Her ladyship said, "No long story now. Too many questions exist. Tell about the Low Lands where the king sent you to fight."

Rupert spent a long time describing the Flanders and Holland countryside. He included many interesting descriptions of the landscape and amusing social customs. After an hour, Rupert asked to take some time to bed his horse and take a bath.

Humphrey dryly observed, "Rupert, here the servants care for your horse."

Rupert smiled and slightly shrugged his shoulders. "Ah…old habits. Squires and new knights don't have such assistance." He stood up. "Where do I sleep?"

Elizabeth, also standing, said, "We designated an apartment for you, assuming that you would come home someday. The houseman will show you." She waved her arm, "David."

Philippa, smiling, stood and added, "It is not one of the main quarters, but it is very nice." Rupert waved as he turned to David.

He put his arm around David's shoulders, and as they walked to the door, he said, "David, you old fart. I see your wife has not yet run you through with her kitchen knife!"

Humphrey looked at his wife and shook his head.

At the dinner's conclusion, Rupert said, "I'm having a hard time adjusting to this wonderfully cooked food. When campaigning, as a squire you eat whatever walks, even cats."

Mary wrinkled her face. "That is disgusting."

After general laughter, Cuthbert said, "Now tell us about your knighthood. How did it become bestowed on you?"

"Well, when I arrived at court, the instructor knights had assigned everyone to a training schedule. We took instruction in etiquette, schooling, arms, and horsemanship. New squires also had to serve at court functions; this gave us a chance to observe correct behavior. After two years, we were appointed to a specific knight whose responsibility was to sharpen our fighting skills. Sir Mortimer of Cornell undertook my training.

"Sir Mortimer possesses almost all the traits expected of a court knight. His clothes and other fittings were beautifully made; he demonstrated very smooth social skills; and he possessed and demanded of me perfect court deportment. He also showed great skill in using weapons and jousting. I learned a great deal from him. Squires were not allowed to joust until they were older, so I just kept handling his horse and equipment during jousting activities.

"The Duke of Flanders had asked the king for assistance in suppressing a rebellious baron in the Hainaut area of the Low Countries. For a payment in gold, the king had offered one thousand men organized into ten companies. A knight was appointed to lead each company and Sir Mortimer received one.

"The fight occurred because one of Hainaut's barons married the duke's youngest daughter. As a dowry, he gave his new son-in-law a castle, Mont Haven, located on the Flanders and Hainaut border. Apparently, the duke failed to mention his daughter's problem before the wedding. The young lady suffered some sort of fits and often had to be tied into her bed for her own protection.

"Obviously, the young baron did not view this as a happy marriage, and he began an affair with a young widow lady. He then decided to divorce his wife and announced that he planned to marry his attractive and fully-functioning mistress. The duke could not stand for this situation, and he ordered a considerable armed force to take up residence in Mont Haven. The baronet in charge of this unit informed the young baron that he would protect the duke's daughter and prevent the divorce."

Cuthbert raised his cup. "An angry duke and an ungrateful son-in-law. I can see the problem."

Mary asked, "Was she pretty?"

The assembled group all smiled, and Rupert shook his head. "I never saw her, and no chance exists for a lowly squire to ever be directly involved. What I tell you comes from campfire gossip."

Philippa inserted herself. "Tell us more from a *squire's perspective*." Everyone looked at her, but Rupert ignored the comment and continued.

"Well, the Low Country nobles do not like the French court, in general, and, in particular, the Duke of Flanders. They did not want a French military unit stationed directly on their border, so they told the duke that its presence violated the not friendly, but at least respectful status quo. They demanded the duke remove this force or they would attack, thus the mobilization of the forces.

"As Sir Mortimer's squire, I went with the company when it marched to the Battle of Brigmort. The two armies lined up on opposite sides of a large field whose sides were forested. Our company had been stationed as the far right unit. As we advanced, the field narrowed, and we were forced into the woods.

"The Hollander commander apparently expected this and had assigned some troops to guard his left flank. They waited in the forest and set up a trap into which my company stumbled. The enemy quickly surrounded us. We were hard-pressed on all sides.

"As the trap closed in, Mortimer and his horse bolted out of the woods. We were left in a very precarious situation."

Humphrey sat back in his chair. "He abandoned his company?"

"Brother, I can only relate what others reported he told the Duke after arriving safely behind our lines. He asserted the noise of the fighting and the men yelling frightened his horse." With shake of his head, Rupert added, "Lost control was his excuse, but I think the pristine knight lacked the courage to use his weapons in actual, potentially fatal encounters." Wrinkled brows and concern registered on the faces of those at the table.

"As I watched, it became clear to me that it was only a matter of time before the Hollanders were going to capture or kill all of us. So standing in the middle of a closing circle, the spot where Sir Mortimer had stationed himself before leaving, it became obvious to me that we must force ourselves out of the confinement. I could tell by the sound of the fighting that the thinnest rank of the surrounding force stood on the battle side of the encirclement."

The men and ladies at the table all were leaning forward with arms on the table.

"I cannot tell what came over me, but I started yelling to rally around me and then charge toward the battle side of the trap. I guess my company's men sensed that no other choice existed, and they followed. We broke though the surrounding force and popped out onto the field. The Hollanders were in the process of pushing our army back. We came out of the woods behind their formation. Not knowing what else to do, I ordered that we attack the back of the enemy's ranks.

"The Low Country generals organize their infantry units with four ranks of fighters. When we hit the Hollander's rear line, they turned to face us, and our momentum pushed them into the third rank, toward the front. These men turned around, but could not actually use their weapons -- no room to swing them. The second rank's men became aware of the fighting taking place at their front and rear. The Hollander unit's formation became completely disorganized, and it began to retreat into the next unit in line to its right, which subsequently became disorganized.

"The Duke of Flanders observed the Hollander's left disorder and decided to take advantage of it. He ordered his reserve corps to throw its weight at the disorganized units."

"So," Humphrey said with a slightly disbelieving tone, "your action created a victory for the duke?"

Rupert nodded his head. "It was a combination of the reserves' vigorous attack and the trouble we caused. The Hollander's left flank dissolved, and that allowed the Duke's men to attack the flank of the Hollander center. In about two hours, their whole army retreated."

Cuthbert and Elizabeth sat back in their chairs. Mary shouted, "Good for you."

"After the battle, my friend Prince Edmond, who had been sent by the king to learn battle tactics, told the duke that a squire who happened to be the son of an earl led the successful charge. I received a summons from the duke. When I arrived at the celebration, he vigorously welcomed me and thanked me for the brave attack that turned the battle. He next called the assembled host to witness, told me to kneel down, and on the spot knighted me."

Cuthbert slammed his fist on the table. "Good boy, good boy." All, except Humphrey and Philippa, raised their glasses in toast.

Humphrey leaned in and said, "But you cannot be a knight without all of the trappings, including a suit of armor, a war-horse, all the clothes, and equipment."

Rupert turned, looked at his brother, scratched the back of his head, and with a wry smile said, "Well, Humphrey, the winning army has the choice of the loser's weapons. This sounds bad, but a number of Holland knights suddenly had no need for their armor, horses, or equipment. The duke granted me first choice."

Mary piped in. "Why didn't they want their possessions? It seems unfair to take it if they fought at the request of their lord."

Rupert looked at her, raised his hands with palms toward her, and said, "Well, Mary, they were dead."

She shot back in her chair, saying, "Oh, that is terrible! Your armor came from a dead person?"

"Well, he had no need for it, and it doesn't rot away. I bet many knights accumulated their trappings this way."

Philippa asked, "Don't most knights' estates pay for their weapons and such?"

"That, Philippa, I do not know. But the man I chose wore a metal-filled vest. At first I thought it was some new form of chain mail, but I discovered it was a cloth vest into which someone had sewn a layer of gold coins." Smiling, he added, "I have been able to purchase needed items, including repairing the hole in the armor's breastplate."

That comment brought out a roar of laughter from Cuthbert.

Humphrey stood up and extended his hand to Philippa, who then stood; neither of them smiled. Looking at Rupert, Humphrey said, "Your story exhausted my pregnant wife. But I must pass on my congratulations to you, Rupert. You earned your knighthood." They left the room.

Lady Elizabeth asked, "What happened to Mortimer?"

Rupert shrugged his shoulders. "Well, I was told that after making it back to camp, he settled his fractured nerves with a huge amount of wine. I believe other people shared my estimation of his courage because I never saw him in the duke's company again. Later, in London, I did pass him in the street. He wore his fancy clothes, but he ignored me."

Mary, using a halting voice, asked, "Rupert, did you have to kill other soldiers?" No sounds were made by the other people sitting at the table.

"Sister, a real battle is completely different than the tournaments you have seen. Men are not trying to gain applause or prizes; they are killing each other. I killed one French knight by stabbing him in the neck with the only weapon Mortimer would let me carry, a short-handled spear. The man thrashed around on the ground for a few moments before he died. It was horrible to see. I took his sword and fought in the general melee where I hacked and slashed in every direction. I'm sure I killed others." He took a drink of wine. "I hated it. Blood, bodies..."

Cuthbert cleared his throat. "Listen, that is a sorrowful subject on which to end this happy dinner." Smiles returned to the two ladies sitting at the table. "Let us to bed and we can hear more stories tomorrow."

As they all stood up, Rupert said, "Well, Father, if I ever fight again, it will have to be for a good reason."

Elizabeth and Mary gave Rupert a hug, and Cuthbert slapped him on the back. Cuthbert asked Rupert to go hunting with him and Humphrey the next day.

At breakfast, Elizabeth and Mary asked many questions about the eating habits of the French and Low Country people. The conversation was humorous, even Philippa laughed.

Mary asked about identifying Prince Edmond as a friend. "Well, we both attended the same squire training, with one difference." He took a mouthful of eggs. The three ladies' faces projected curiousity. He smiled, "The instructors did not use a stick on Edmond—they broke several on me." They all laughed. "We became friends and helped each other survive squire training. I consider him a good companion. You will meet him in a few days."

Mary asked with a mischievous smile, "Is he good looking?"

Rupert responded, "He does not look like the ass of a horse."

War-horses do not serve well on hunts because they are very large and restless. The three nobles rode domestic horses as did Lincolnwood's forester, Robert. Several other servants rode along, and one drove a cart carrying various weapons since different prey required different armaments. The cart also functioned as a conveyance for any hoped-for carcasses.

As they rode, Cuthbert asked Robert about prospects. "My lord, the summer's heat has driven most sporting animals into the deep forest. I have not seen a deer in weeks, nor any boars."

Looking over at his sons, Cuthbert said, "Well, it is a nice day for a country ride." They smiled.

While moving along, Rupert noticed Robert's son, Rorik, among the servants. They had been inseparable playmates before he'd left to begin squire training. Rupert pulled his horse back to ride next to his old friend. "Rorik, you old nut thief," he said, starting a long and laughter-filled conversation. Humphrey looked at the two and then looked away with a slight shake of his head.

When reaching the wood's outer fringe, the party deployed. The three nobles with bows stood in the middle, about twenty feet apart, and the servants extended in a semicircle about one hundred feet from the left and right sides of the hunters. One servant walked behind, carrying the boar spears, because these very aggressive animals required more than arrows to bring them down. The knights also each carried a short sword in case a boar got too close. The servants wielded short sticks to literally beat the bushes in order to scare out game.

Even with the servants beating the bushes, no game could be roused, so at midday the party stopped on a small hillock to eat. Cuthbert waved his arm at the surrounding woods. "It is good we made this hunt so I can tell the king not to waste any time trying it. Not paying for a grand effort will save me some money." The three smiled.

When finishing a piece of lamb, Rupert said, "Rorik told me that he and his father cleared about a one-acre site deep in the woods. It now supports thick grass and attracts deer." The other two looked interested. "The problem is that it's almost a two-hour ride, and the deer appear in the hour just after sunrise and one just before sunset. We would have to set up a camp to take advantage."

Humphrey sat forward. "We better not tell the king about that opportunity, or he will insist we pay for a camp large enough for all of this attendants. Agreed?" He looked at both his father and Rupert.

Cuthbert shook his head in agreement. "I think we will save that opportunity for a purely family outing."

After a moment of quiet, Cuthbert looked at Rupert. "What was the outcome of your little war?"

The humor left Rupert's face, and he threw the bone he was holding as far as he could. "Father, it's unbelievable. The Low Country lords met in a great tent with the French and made a deal. The addled lady would be confined in Mont Haven for the rest of her life. Its revenues would pay for her care. The bishops agreed the Hainaut lord would be granted an annulment due to the lady's inability to perform her wifely duties. He would be allowed to marry his new woman. The French would keep a very small company of troops at the castle, just to provide protection for its inmate. In compensation for the theological services and ruling, the local bishop would be given title to Mont Haven when the woman died."

Humphrey said with some spirit, "You mean the troublemaker basically got what he wanted. That is ridiculous. He should have lived up to his bargain."

Rupert stood up, took a few steps, and then turned, and with a very angry voice said, "In the end everything remained almost the same as at the beginning. Only the bishop seemed to make a profit. He will receive a steady income source." He picked up a stone and threw it. "Almost twenty knights and four hundred men died in the fighting for what in the end proved meaningless." His voice became hard. "On the ride back to England, I've thought about this quite a bit. The whole thing was *disgusting*. As I said last night, if I ever fight again, it will have to be for a very good cause."

His father made a harrumph sound, and Humphrey asked, "So we won't be able to send you on the crusade everyone seems to be talking about?"

Rupert laid back on the grass. "I've already fought for church and country. I don't need to travel several thousand miles to fight in a war whose church-sanctified goals, as far as I can discern, probably hide ambitions for individual self-aggrandizement." He turned on his side and looked directly at his brother. "You are welcome, Humphrey, to take up the holy cross any time you choose."

For a few moments the two young men stared at each other. The lord said, "This is a subject for another day. I think we should forget hunting and find some cool wine."

As they prepared to mount, Robert walked up to Rupert. "Thank you, sir, for my son's wedding gift. We never expected such a large gift."

Rupert slapped him on the arm, "Anything for my old playmate. I hope he experiences great joy with the young lady."

As the three nobles rode side by side on the way home, Humphrey said, "What did you give that servant?"

"A gold crown so they'd have the money to set up a household."

Humphrey stopped his horse and, with an effort to control his anger, said, "You *gave* him a whole gold crown?"

Rupert also stopped and with a very firm face said, "I obtained the money from a dead knight who fought in a useless war. I think it should be used for higher purposes, and my old friend's wedding is perfect." He then spurred his horse into the lead.

Humphrey asked his father, "Do you believe it? When our family faces a huge expense we can hardly afford, to host the king and his retinue, he gave a gold crown to a servant."

Cuthbert looked at Rupert riding away, and then back at his older son. "I suspect fighting for your life alongside the common soldiers, without even minimal armor, might alter a person's views a bit. Let's give him some time."

The next two days were filled with a flurry of activity for every member of the household, no matter rank. The king expected each earl to entertain him and his horde with the best available of everything. This expectation comprised one of several vassal obligations every earl bore.

Despite the obvious costs which would take several years to recoup, Cuthbert and Elizabeth wished to make the king's visit special. Servants cleaned parts of the castle that very rarely received any attention. Barrels of wine and ale arrived. Fresh and preserved food had to be available at all times. Linens were cleaned and folded. The servants trained in their respective duties. Activities were arranged for the lord and ladies as well as all of the visiting servants. A wandering minstrel show arrived and its performers were given special space. A hunt to be attended by a legion of nobles and dignitaries was organized. The visit usually lasted two weeks and Lincolnwood prepared for the siege. David's nerves became stretched almost to the breaking point.

The local earl also had to organize a jousting tourney. Neighboring knights and barons actually looked forward to it. The king's presence gave prestige to the contests, thus making their honors very desirable. The winners received the awards from the king's hand. Humphrey had developed considerable skill in the sport and he itched to show off. The king always included in his retinue several first-class jousters just to spice up the contests: the awards constituted their only source of income. The locals desired to test their skills against these top fighters.

Humphrey knew that a knighted person who'd never received jousting training could, with all honor, decline to participate. While standing in front of several family members and neighbors, he asked Rupert to join the contests. The latter looked at his brother and responded that after killing several men, including a knight in a battle, he could not stir interest in jousting.

Cuthbert also made two arrangements with the nearby abbey. First, he contracted for its choir of nuns to sing. His donation paved the way, but knowing the king's tastes, he insisted the nuns sing religious songs only at morning services. A repertory of modern songs had to be used during the night festivities. The abbess, recognizing the future implications of pleasing the king, discovered several of her nuns had previously worked in taverns, so several bawdy drinking songs were added to the program.

Second, different levels of chastity existed at the abbey. For some women, the vow included a little flexibility. Two ladies, who by birth or circumstance possessed courtly manners, were assigned to provide companionship for the king. Tradition required that these ladies sleep with several nobles in addition to the king to avoid any possible paternity claims. The ladies received a nice gift from anyone with whom they socialized that was, of course, split with the abbess. Etiquette required the ladies to be housed above the servants but not with the nobles. Etiquette also demanded they be treated with all due courtly respect without any public recognition of their duties.

The King's Visit

King Henry preferred to travel in his coach. However, he knew he could not inspire his subjects by arriving while sitting on cushions, so two miles from Lincolnwood's castle, he mounted his war horse which was draped in his royal colors and insignia. The retinue's knights and nobles, riding their decked-out horses, immediately formed a mounted escort. Trumpeters preceded the company. The runner, stationed about a mile and a half down the road from the castle, saw the approach and dashed back to announce the arrival.

What followed had been dictated by generations of courtly manners. Lincolnwood's knights formed an escort line leading from the far side of the drawbridge into the castle's courtyard. Lord Cuthbert, wearing his finest robe and earl's crown, waited at the base of the main door's steps. Lady Elizabeth stood five paces away. Humphrey and Philippa stood two steps up, and on the top step Mary stood next to Rupert.

The king dismounted, handed his reigns to a squire, and waited until his nobles and knights strung out behind him in the shape of a V with him at the point. He stepped over to Cuthbert. The earl and his entire household knelt down.

Using his commanding voice the king said, "Lord Cuthbert, my loyal vassal and friend, arise!"

Just Cuthbert rose. "I and my entire household welcome Your Majesty, and we are greatly honored by your visit to Lincolnwood. We will provide all that you require." They then made the traditional hand and arm shake.

Turning to the rest of Lincolnwood's people, the king said, "Arise, loyal subjects." All did. The retinue did not move when the king walked to Elizabeth. "Countess, it pleases me to again see you. Your mother's beauty is reflected in your face. She was such a great lady."

Elizabeth curtsied to the compliment and said, "Thank you, Your Majesty. You are absolutely welcome to our house."

The king stepped up to Humphrey and Philippa. He bowed and she curtsied. "It is good to see the future earl and countess, and I understand a little one is on the way." Philippa blushed. "If you don't already have a name picked out, I suggest Henry." The king laughed and the two expecting parents followed his lead. The king turned to his old friend and then back to the two. "Cuthbert contains much honor and is a distinguished name."

Philippa said, "Your Majesty, we will pray on the name."

Smiling, the king next walked up to Mary and Rupert. "Tell me, my new knight, who is this beautiful flower you are standing next to?" Mary went bright red.

"Your Majesty, may I present my sister Mary?"

She curtsied.

The king turned and said, "Cuthbert, you are lucky she carries her mother's looks instead of yours." The lord and the king laughed, and this time Elizabeth blushed.

It was David's turn. He stepped out of the doorway's shadow and said, "Your Majesty, would you care for some refreshment?" While bowing, he gestured toward the great hall.

The king entered the hall, but the family formed a receiving line on the steps. Each of the attending nobles and knights lined up in order of rank and then introduced themselves, as did the family members. When finished, all hurried into the great hall. Having already removed his hat and gloves, the king sat on a raised chair and held a glass of wine. A general reception occurred. The servants had covered the table in food, pitchers of wine, and mugs of ale. Most travelers get hungry: the food disappeared.

After about an hour, the king rose. "Lord Cuthbert, let us talk privately." Cuthbert pointed to the library door and the two entered it.

Humphrey stepped onto the dais and shouted, "Gentlemen and ladies, dinner will be served after vespers."

When the door closed, the two gave each other a hug accompanied by slaps on the back. "Henry, you old gold robber, what have you been doing?"

"Me? I have been saving England from evil influences. I should call you a whore's son, but I knew your mother, and I would not insult her. By looking around, I observe that you have been spending your time on building your estate."

They laughed and sat down with a pitcher of wine between them. It was drained and another called for as they swapped information about their respective situations. Subjects ran from international politics to jousting news.

The king stood and tossed his robe onto a table. "It is amazing that even the southern nobles seem content to remain quiet."

After finishing another glass of wine, the king continued. "As for domestic tranquility, the queen remains very happy and a delight to live with, a rarity in most royal households. Edmond seems to be accepting grooming for the royal seat, and my daughter married a Midlands earl. His family provides strong political support. The marriage is agreeable, they already have a son."

"Well, the main family strain I face is the rising friction between my two sons."

"Rupert reflects a true compliment to you, Cuthbert. He performed very well in France. I might have knighted him myself if Count Simon had not beat me to it."

"Yes, but Humphrey has proved adept at managing all of Lincolnwood's affairs. He deserves to be the next earl. But what to do with Rupert?"

Without much enthusiasm the king asked, "How about the crusades?"

"Well, he has developed an unusual attitude. He fought very well, but the experience apparently took the shine off military campaigning. He says now that he will only fight for a good cause. He seems particularly suspicious of church causes."

Smiling, the king replied. "Cuthbert, because we are old friends and alone in this room, I can say Rupert demonstrates good sense." They laughed as they clinked glasses.

After draining his, the king said, "Let me think on this. I might have an answer, but I need the advice of my chancellor, Old John. He is now soaking up your wine."

One of the serving ladies approached Elizabeth. "My lady, the king requested a third pitcher of wine." Elizabeth raised one eyebrow as she looked at the closed door. "I will take it."

After a knock, the door opened, and Elizabeth said, "Your Majesty requested another pitcher?"

Both men looked surprised when they saw the pitcher's bearer. Elizabeth closed the door and said, "I will not be happy if you two old farts get drunk before my carefully prepared banquet."

With a smile the king said, "How dare you call your king an old fart!"

"Henry, I've known you for thirty-five years. Out there, we play formal games; in here I'll call you anything I want. And, if you are not careful, I'll ask if your parents were married!"

The king slapped his knee while letting out a roar of laughter. After catching his breath, he said, "Cuthbert, your wife is always charming. Elizabeth, how did I let you get through my fingers?"

She put the pitcher on the table and said with a big smile, "My skimpy dowry, and I like Cuthbert's fingers." The men smiled. "Henry, tell me about the queen, but before you speak, know that each of you will only receive one more glass of wine."

The king responded, "Cuthbert, we require a woman's control."

The three sat and rehashed family doings for fifteen minutes.

Cuthbert put his empty glass on the table. "Henry, if you and I don't stop drinking wine, we will not be polite at tonight's banquet." They both needed their respective chair arms to stand up.

Lincolnwood served meals on a regular schedule. At dawn, the servants placed food on one of the great hall's tables and replenished it at midday. People came to eat what and when they chose. Wine and ale were available all day. Dinner required a banquet and one occurred on each night of the visit. They started after vespers, about sunset, and lasted until the drunks fell asleep. On the days of major outside activities, such as the jousting, the servants set up outdoor tables and served on the same schedule. An additional meal was served at the end of tournaments because the combatants usually were ravenous and very thirsty.

Convention required a fixed table arrangement in the great hall. The dais table faced the main room from in front of its only fireplace. It was raised approximately one foot higher than the floor. The king's chair rose another six inches above the other chairs on the dais. With a gap between them and at right angles to the dais, two other long tables extended the length of the hall.

Seating also adhered to strict convention. Sitting at the main table were the king, two visiting earls, the prince, the host earl and his wife, and special guests, if seats existed. The abbess and Mary qualified as special. The visiting and house knights sat at the other two tables in strict rank order. These tables also held the two companion ladies and the king's numerous traveling officials.

When Rupert arrived for the first banquet, he saw Humphrey and Philippa standing near the door. He approached and asked, "Where do I sit?"

Showing a tight smile, Humphrey said, "You are a very short-tenured knight so you sit at the far end of the knight's table."

"But should not a family member sit at the front table?"

"Sorry, brother, tradition dictates that the front table is reserved for nobles or soon-to-be nobles. No matter what, you are just a knight."

Rupert looked at him without emotion. His squiring experience had taught him the court's etiquette rules, and he understood the ranking. Only Philippa's smirk proved slightly irritating. He nodded his head and moved to his place.

On the first day of the jousting, Rupert went to the stable and attended to his war horse. Prince Edmond found him there. "Rupert, you're not entering the joust or the standing sword fights?"

"Come on, Edmond. You know I cannot joust, and I have had my fill of sword wielding. I just don't see the point of doing these things for sport."

"But look, this is an elimination tournament, so on the first day, all of the rookies get thrown off their horses, so you will fit right in!" He laughed.

Rupert tossed the curry brush on the floor and with some force said, "Edmond! You know well my feelings, so don't pester me."

Edmond smiled and walked around the horse. "This is a great animal. Will it obey only you, or will it take commands from a new rider?"

"When I acquired him from his previous owner, he adapted to me from the first."

Edmond finished his circuit of the horse. "You and I are about the same size. How about lending me your armor and horse so I can take your place in the first round?"

"I thought the king forbids your jousting because you are the heir. In fact, I believe he is very firm on this point."

"Look, Rupert, my friend, I practiced jousting with my trainer in London without the king's knowledge and Lincolnwood offers an ideal opportunity. I really want to try my hand, and this could be my only chance." He put his hand on Rupert's shoulder. "Please. I can only gain true knowledge of this sport by participating in it."

Rupert leaned back against the stall wall and looked into Edmond's eyes.

"Please."

Rupert stood erect. "I'm risking my head for this deal, so when you become the king you'd better make me a noble."

"It is a deal."

Surprise filled the family members as they watched Rupert enter the tourney. His first opponent held many jousting honors, so they winced as they watched the clash. Rupert was tossed off his horse and landed ten feet away from the fence that separated the combatants. A squire ran out and helped him stand up. Rupert waved to the assembled crowd and limped off the grounds. Cuthbert shrugged his shoulders when Elizabeth shot a questioning look.

The king leaned over. "I thought Rupert did not joust."

Cuthbert shook his head, "It is a surprise to me, Your Majesty."

Shortly before the banquet, Rupert and Edmond walked along one of the castle's corridors. Edmond limped. They turned a corner and almost ran into the king.

Using a command voice, he said, "Sir Rupert, I thought you choose not to joust."

Rupert was surprised and a little flustered. "Your Majesty, I don't." No sooner were the words out when he realized the mistake.

"Prince Edmond, you seem to be limping."

"A horse in the barn kicked me, Your Majesty."

The king stood still and gave an evaluating gaze at each of the young men. He actually began tapping his foot.

"Sir Rupert, do you know what chaos would occur if I did not have a male heir? And do you remember you swore an oath to protect the Crown?" Turning to his son, he continued. "Edmond, a horse's kick sounds like a stretch of the truth." He paused a moment. "A king can survive having a slight deformity, but a major one only invites contests for the crown. Do you understand that?"

"Yes, Father."

"Sir Rupert, you will meet with me and your father just before midday tomorrow. We will have things to discuss." The king waited until the two had backed to the wall, and then he strode past.

Edmond peeked around the corner to ensure the king was out of hearing range, and then the two burst into laughter.

In the intense social climate that existed at the castle, everyone seemed to know the king was angry. Starting at breakfast, everyone avoided Rupert and he did not see the prince anyplace. When Rupert arrived outside the library's door, Edmond stood there.

Edmond pointed at the door. "I've also been called down here."

Rupert respectfully knocked and a loud voice responded. "Come in."

One library table had been pulled into the middle of the room, and the others had been pushed against the bookcases. The king sat in a middle seat, Cuthbert at one end, and king's Chancellor at the other. The king pointed to the spot on the opposite side of the table from him.

The king yelled, "No one has the right to endanger the stability of the monarchy, absolutely no one." He slammed his fist on the table. "You two put the future king's health and even survival at risk! Do you know what would happen if, my prince, you had been severely injured or killed? Did you even think before putting the heir to the throne into a joust?"

He pounded his fist down again. "Edmond, you in particular have the responsibility to keep the crown from falling into chaos. And you, sir knight, have a responsibility to assist the prince at all costs." He picked up his empty wine glass and threw it across the room. "What were you two thinking?"

No one spoke. The two young men projected very guilty faces. The king stood up and walked behind his chair. "The southern nobles always itch to gain power using French assistance, and the middle nobles tolerate me, providing I have strength. Only the northern nobles, like Cuthbert, remain consistently steadfast. Without a strong and healthy king, civil war will break out all over England! Weakness breeds rebellion."

He picked up the chair and then slammed it down. After walking back to the table, he leaned over, placed both hands on it and gave the two an absolutely fierce look. He yelled, "Do you comprehend what I am saying?"

Neither young man moved. He then stood straight up, looked at the ceiling and hissed, "Jesus Christ save us."

Henry sat down. "There will be consequences. There must be, so the whole court learns the lesson." He turned to the chancellor. "Prepare an order to the dean of Oxford's law college and tell him that Edmond will be studying law for two years." He pointed at his son. "When you come out of school, you will assume the duties of the chief magistrate and hear all the law cases in and around London."

Edmond took a small step forward. "Your Majesty, you know that I don't like law and lawyer's work."

"Silence. You are to assume true responsibility. There is no discussion."

"Chancellor, draft an appointment for Sir Rupert. Make him sheriff and king's protector of Northdale. The appointment is for four years."

Rupert looked shocked because negative rumors about Northdale were widespread.

"Include that if the term is not completed, he forfeits his head! Also include that I delegate to him the authority to control all of that district's affairs."

Cuthbert kept looking at his lap. Henry looked at the chancellor. "Have those orders and Sir Rupert's commission prepared before we leave in two days. Also, provide a separate letter to the dean saying the instructors may use the stick on the prince."

The king stood up. "Now, get out of my sight!"

The two scurried out. The king sat down and looked at the door for a moment. "Cuthbert, get me some wine."

When the earl brought a fresh pitcher and three glasses, the king began to smile. He then turned to the chancellor, "Don't write the letter about the stick." While the man scribbled notes, the king and Cuthbert exchanged direct looks.

The chancellor stood. "Your Grace, I must begin to prepare the documents." The king waved him away.

When the door closed, Henry asked, "Too harsh?"

Cuthbert shook his head. "He is my son, but the two of them acted stupidly."

They both sat quietly and sipped the wine.

The king put down his cup. "I really need someone to administer Northdale. It actually may solve your problem. Rupert will have something to do."

"Henry, I've heard hard things about that place."

"The last person I sent there was the nephew of the bishop of Canterbury. The man's grandfather had divided the family estate into little pieces so all decedents could own some land and gain income. However, the land's revenue proved too small to provide funds equal to this little shit's lifestyle."

Cuthbert slapped his chair's arm. "I've never heard that before." The two smiled.

"I offered Northdale to him, and the possibility of income attracted him. The archbishop insisted I elevate the boy to baron, and I did it."

The earl injected a thought. "It is good to have high-ranking friends."

The king ignored that comment. "So the little shit went up there and lasted about six months. Then he came home crying about the place lacking any value. Something to do with Norsemen attacks, cold winters, and the lack of any income-producing enterprises. So now I have the archbishop shopping for an appropriate new estate for his new baron and Northdale without a leader. What a pain in the ass."

He took another drink and looked at Cuthbert. "Look, old friend, your son is young enough to take on a hard challenge. In fact, with his practical attitudes, I think he might succeed."

"If the Norsemen don't kill him." The king shrugged his shoulders.

SARA

THE EARL OF SHEPARDLAND SAT at his desk reading the agricultural summary from his last harvest when his wife, Countess Osburth, burst into the office. With a loud and very agitated voice she said, "Roland, she did it again!"

He put his papers onto the desk and looked at his wife. "What did Sara do this time?"

The countess had reached the desk and put her hands on her hips. "That visiting knight, Sir Elford, left at sunup."

Having heard this before, Roland just crossed his hands, placed them on the desk, and watched with mild amusement.

"Apparently, last night they had a conversation about the relationship between husbands and wives. The thick head told her he would never use a whip on his wife, but the flat of his sword might get a workout."

Roland let out a grunting smile as he leaned back in his chair and looked at the ceiling.

"You might think this is funny, but it is not. The servant told me she jumped up, pulled a sword off the mantle, and challenged him. Elford, thinking it to be a good time to show who would run the household, drew his, and they fenced!"

"She didn't hurt him, did she?"

"Roland!" She raised her hands to shoulder height and turned a complete circle. "They fenced for ten minutes, and then Elford stopped. According to the witnesses, he was sweating, and Sara smiling. He sheathed his sword and walked out!"

"My dear, you know Sara must be handled carefully."

The countess walked to the door then turned around. "You cannot ignore the inheritance of this earldom forever." She slammed the door.

Roland had married a beautiful young lady, Beatrice, third daughter of an earl. They had moved to Shepardland and had been very happy. She'd given birth to Mark and, a year and a half later, Sara. Not having any other playmates, Mark and Sara had exclusively played together. Running, climbing, wooden sword fighting, archery, and the skills of a woodsman had dominated their lives. Mandatory school had taken half of every day, but the professor they'd imported seemed to find great joy in the children's energy. He spoke Latin and Greek to the children, and they had slurred both into a language of their own.

When Sara was almost ten years old, a sickness called the flux had struck Shepardland. Most everyone living in the castle and on its grounds had become ill. The disease had taken Beatrice and Mark.

The deaths hit Roland hard. In response, he'd bent over backward to make Sara's life happy. Once, when learning that a visiting tutor had struck her, he knocked the man across the study before chasing him out of the castle with the tip of his sword. He'd only required her to attend morning classes, and given her the rest of the day to pursue what she enjoyed which mainly meant playing with several servants' sons and the ten men-at-arms the earl employed.

Five years after Beatrice's death, the earl had married Osburth, the widow of a knight who had captained a company of mercenary soldiers. Jousting and military affairs had consumed most of the knight's interest. Over the years, many warring lords had hired the force to strengthen their positions. Osburth and the knight had consummated their marriage on many occasions, but his attention did not lie in a bed. As part of the knight's payment, Osburth received room and board; thus, for almost fifteen years, she'd never actually had her own home. The knight died while fighting in France.

Roland had been lonely, and Osburth sought a man who offered a normal life. Their first child had come two years after the marriage, and it proved to be a very difficult delivery. Matilda, the child, was healthy, but Osburth had hemorrhaged severely. The doctor had applied simple logic. If she moved her lower abdomen it bled, so he'd prescribed bed rest until this phenomenon ceased and told both parents another birth would prove fatal. Roland loved her and absolutely did not want to lose another wife. They refrained from future intercourse.

Because a wet nurse and several servants tended to the baby and mother, Sara never received the instruction in baby care a healthy mother normally would have given. Osburth had convalesced for almost a year, increasing activities in very small increments. This allowed Sara to continue unabated with her school and tomboy activities.

The inheritance problem revolved around the fact that, being the oldest, Sara retained first claim on the estate. If she married, her husband would receive the noble title. Matilda's future would depend on whomever she married. However, Matilda's prospects remained uncertain because Sara did not seem capable of attracting a man—amazing considering the estate. If Sara never married, then Matilda's husband would receive the title and the land. Such a dowery would make Matilda a avery attractive prize and cause considerable interest in other noble families with an eligible a young man. Settlement of matters totally depended on Sara.

Young women generally married in their late teens. Sara, at twenty-four, had already been passed over, and this fact lessened her desirability. In addition, her reputation for horsemanship, archery, and swordsmanship raised many questions. No established family would consider her as acceptable for one of its offspring. A steady stream of impoverished knights came to woo and, to a man, all left. She told her father each time that the man was stupid, incompetent, or not manly; some were all three. "Mad Sara" became her informal nickname.

That night Roland and Osburth sat alone eating dinner. "My lord, you simply cannot keep ignoring the problem Sara causes." Roland stopped eating and lifted his wine cup to his mouth to hide his smile. "Matilda nears marriage age and what prospects does she have? Either offering a title and earldom to a solid, noble family or, if Sara marries, then she will go to a low ranking noble with very limited income. It is not fair to your second daughter to let Sara's future be unresolved."

"Osburth, I have heard your concern. But Sara is a grand girl and not mad like everyone says. Let us give her a little more time. Remember, this estate is a handsome prize so the right man may yet appear." The countess looked away from her husband so he could not see her very disgruntled face.

Osburth's sister, Countess Blanch, visited once every two years. Most sisters form a true sorority and take delight in protracted opportunities to talk about everything. Court gossip, marriages, deaths, inheritance problems, noble title changes, and land swaps comprised the grist for enjoyable conversations.

In addition, Blanch traveled with her daughter, Adela. It became a friendly rivalry between the two sisters as to which daughter showed the most correct courtly manners. Both ladies spent considerable time instructing their respective protégées in such proprieties. The two girls' advancing skills provided a source of pride for both women.

They abandoned their efforts to instill etiquette when it came to Sara. Although she had mastered the basics of womanly manners, she showed no interest in perfecting them. Sara told her stepmother and step-aunt that other things attracted her interest.

Shepardland's castle contained a private outdoor courtyard that, by tradition, only the noble ladies used. It gave them a place to freely discuss sensitive subjects about which men should not hear. While lunching with Osburth, Blanch asked, "What are you going to do about Sara?"

Osburth put down her food and shook her head. "She is Roland's project and out of my control. He lets her do whatever she chooses. I would certainly corral her if allowed."

"How does Matilda get along with her?"

"The problem is that they like each other. Matilda would like to participate in some of her sister's activities, but I keep them separated as much as possible. However, I cannot move around enough to watch my daughter at all times, so I suspect they do get together."

"And the inheritance?"

"I need a drink before answering that." Osburth filled both wine glasses. "Sara regularly chases out men before they make any attempt at wooing."

"Maybe it's the smell of horse sweat." Both laughed.

Osburth looked up at the sky for a moment, "As our daughters approach wedding age, we must begin to consider alternatives for them. But Sara's antics cloud the future. I don't know what rank Matilda's future husband should hold. Ought I give her away or look for someone to take charge around here?"

Both took a sip, and then Blanch put down her glass and leaned toward her sister. "Have you spelled the facts out for your husband?"

"He will not discuss it with me. I've tried, and he flat-out told me not to bring up the subject."

"Well, when the time is correct, I will bring it up."

———

The next day, the mothers assigned Matilda and Adela an afternoon of sewing. The task concerned completing a new quilt. While eating the midday meal, Sara had told the girls that today the weekly cheese-making would occur. When told neither had never observed it before, Sara smiled and said, "Well, you will see it today." After checking to ensure the two mothers had settled into the ladies' courtyard, Sara walked to the sewing room and signaled for the two to follow her.

They could not participate in the messy cheese-making process wearing their nice dresses so Sara had the girls change into peasant ones in the stable. Then the three walked to the cheese barn located at the village's edge.

Tasks for the work included stoking the cooking fire; adding the vinegar to the fresh milk; starting the process by adding some of the last production's cheese; and stirring—lots of it. Once cooked, many hands were required to pour the mixture through a number of cloth strainers in order to separate the curds and whey. Finally, the ladies helped pile rocks on a wooden frame that pressed the results into cheese. They were tired, smelly, and smiling when they returned to the castle.

Unfortunately, at mid-afternoon Blanch had decided to check on the girls' sewing progress. When she found the room empty, her yells triggered a somewhat frantic search that produced the nice dresses stored in the stable. Guards waited at the drawbridge and then escorted the three into the ladies' courtyard.

Osburth stood up and, without even trying to control her anger, yelled her demand that Sara explain.

Sara, projecting a quiet innocence, said, "Well, my ladies, your daughters will probably someday hold the rank of baroness or countess like you do. They should know something about the life requirements of their future subjects."

Blanch now jumped to her feet. "Sara, they are our daughters. They follow our directions and not your unladylike lifestyle that should not be followed by any decent woman!"

Sara open her mouth to respond, but then stopped and just stared at Blanch. "The girls are not hurt, and they learned something today." She smiled, turned, and walked out.

A red-faced Osburth shouted after her, "We will discuss this with Lord Roland tonight."

At dinner, stone-faced Blanch and Osburth attended without either of their daughters. Sara sat with a pleasant smile. Roland noticed the cool atmosphere and asked, "Where are Matilda and Adela?"

Both Osburth and Blanch simultaneously exploded in heated comments on the cheese event. A wide-eyed Roland sat back in his chair while trying to sort through apparently inappropriate actions. Sara calmly ate dinner.

When the accusations wound down, Osburth finished by saying, "We scrubbed the girls with stiff brushes to wash off the smell and then sent them to bed without supper."

Roland took a deep breath, took a drink of wine, and then faced his elder daughter. "Sara, Osburth and Blanch are correct. They are responsible for their daughters. Here, you are granted an almost total independence, but limits exist. You must adhere to their wishes. Understand?"

With a twinkle in her eye, she responded, "Yes, my lord."

Roland immediately put his wine goblet to his mouth to hide a smile, but his eyes still projected it.

Sara rose and said, "I beg your pardon to leave. I think dinner would be more agreeable tonight if I depart." Neither lady looked at her. As she passed out of the dining hall, she stopped at the kitchen door. "Please, I need a piece of cheese and some bread."

She opened the girls' room door and smiled at the two chagrined youngsters. "Never tell your mothers, but here is dinner." They nodded their heads and smiled.

Two days after the cheese-making incident, Shepardland held its first formal banquet in honor of the visitors. The head table offered seats to the earl, the two countesses, the three daughters, and the two lead knights. The table formed the top of a T in the castle's main hall. Numerous generations of earls had added touches to this room. The vaulted ceiling rose two stories, and the walls were covered with dark wood paneling reaching from the floor to about ten feet up. The builders' portraits, along with those of their wives, adorned many places on the walls. The earl's family traced itself to one of William the Conqueror's favorite nobles. A mandatory cluster of crossed swords hung over the room's walk-in fireplace. A large shield showing the earldom's coat of arms centered on the sword cluster. On the wall over the main door hung a bearskin, although no one alive could tell of its origin.

The dinner produced a very jovial atmosphere. The quantity of reasonably good wine may have provided the lubrication. Sara's hunt that day yielded the fresh venison. Osburth had hired two French chefs, and they routinely produced delectable accompaniment to the deliciously prepared meat. Conversation was light and humorous.

One of the knights, sitting at the long portion of the T, rose and lifted his glass. "Toast to Lady Sara, whose clean shot beat mine to the heart of the deer." With a cheer, all raised their glasses. The first toast generated many more salutes for the host, his generous wife, and then for almost everyone else at the table.

The earl stopped the parade. "To His Majesty, the king." All stood and completed the toast.

When everyone was sitting again and general conversation had begun, Blanch leaned toward Sara and with a loud voice asked, "Lady Sara, have you yet become engaged?" The discussion at the head table stopped.

Nobility had just begun introducing eating forks. Normally, men and women ate with their fingers. The only table utensil was a knife. The men carried knives attached to their belts. With these, they both cut meat and often stuck a cut piece on to the tip and put it into their mouths. The servants placed a medium-sized kitchen knife at every woman's place. The women were expected to cut food into small, ladylike pieces and then eat them with their fingers. Ladies never used a knife to place food in their mouths.

The whole assembly looked at Sara. With slow deliberation, she placed a piece of meat into her mouth and took a half-minute to chew it. She looked at her aunt. "My Lady Blanch, I have three responses to your inquiry. First, if your concern is for my future happiness, I'm grateful for your interest. Second, if your inquiry concerns my seeming lack of current suitors, it is absolutely none of your business. But third"—she pounded her knife handle onto the table—"if you are concerned about the inheritance and wondering if any of your relatives may anticipate receiving some portion of it, then tomorrow I will go to the stable, shovel a large pile of horse manure, and plop your ass into it." She stuck her knife into a piece of meat and then put it into her mouth.

The room was dead quiet. Even the servants stopped moving. Blanch raised herself in her chair and opened her mouth, but before she could speak, Roland let out a roar of laughter. The other men followed; it was, after all, a rare occasion when courtly ladies used such language. The two countesses' faces turned bright red, and the two younger ladies put hands over their mouths to hide snickers.

When the laughter died down, conversation on other subjects began again. Sara showed a beatific ladylike smile for the rest of the evening.

The next morning, the countesses met in the ladies' courtyard for a morning snack. The banquet's conversation foreordained the first topic. As soon as the servants were out of earshot, Blanch said, "Osburth, do you believe what your stepdaughter said to me last night? And that is in addition to encouraging our daughters to perform peasant work. What will you do about it?"

"Blanch, I've already told you that Roland controls her. You are welcome to ask him to get an apology, but I would not anticipate obtaining one."

Blanch sat back in her chair. "*Disgusting*! The whole situation is disgusting!"

"Look, sister, my husband will not bend on this subject. Sara is just wild, or mad, as everyone thinks."

Pointing a finger, Blanch replied. "Convent! After Roland passes, you should ship her to a convent. And remember there are different types of convents; some are for holy ladies serving God and some lock all doors, gates, and windows. With a substantial donation, an abbess of one of the latter will be glad to constrain a madwoman."

"Sister, how could I do that? She is my stepdaughter."

"Osburth, your daughter's economic future is at stake. I know your husband has another daughter, but your concern is your daughter." She was pointing at Osburth. "You have to find a way to guarantee her future support. Absolutely no question on the subject!"

"How could I get Sara into a locked convent?"

"I've seen it done before. You obtain a certificate of madness from some official, a noble with jurisdiction or, better yet, a bishop. Then you make a financial arrangement with several knights to take her. It's simple, actually."

Osburth sat and ate several bits of an apple while looking at the table. She looked up, "I know our local bishop despises her. He thinks she defies church leadership's dictates on the proper role of women. He would be glad to sign a warrant."

Blanch said, "You get a bunch of knights to forcibly escort her by offering them a small piece of Roland's lands. You don't have to give huge chunks, just enough to offer the possibility of an income stream. You would be amazed at the willingness of even faithful men-at-arms when it comes to a revenue source."

Osburth stopped a piece of apple halfway to her mouth. She gave Blanch an intense stare. "Even our own long-term supporters?"

"Absolutely, and they get another advantage."

Osburth's facial expression asked the question.

"Because the bishop declares her mad, her testimony cannot be used against anyone. So the knights can take her in several ways." With a smiling sneer, she added, "I think it serves her right!"

Osburth dropped the apple piece and knife.

First Trip to Northdale

Rupert decided to visit Northdale in late June. He wanted to experience the environs before winter set in. He researched any source of information that could be found on the place. The North Atlantic formed Northdale's north and west boundaries, the south boundary was formed by the River Ibix, and the east boundary by a long, high ridge of what the locals called mountains. Only goats utilized the ridge's slopes. The district was divided by the River Downs, and it attracted Norsemen. It produced limited agricultural products and some dried salmon.

The Norsemen could spend weeks rowing and sailing to England. The Downs River offered fresh water and the opportunity to stretch one's legs on dry land. Therefore, for some Viking chiefs, Northdale had become the first stop on their annual excursions. Pillaging always occurred, as the Norsemen held much pent-up energy to start acquiring treasure. Northdale's residents learned to simply run into the far hills and wait out the intrusion. They also began to tie up several cows so the hungry invaders could satisfy themselves and, after a rest, launch their aggression against more rewarding targets. Unfortunately, each year, despite cautions, the Vikings almost always captured some of the locals. The men were killed, the women used, and the children taken as slaves.

Informally, a man who used the title of squire made the day-to-day government decisions. He owned the most land and, considering the relative economic structure, claimed to be the richest person in Northdale. Of common background, his forefathers had adopted the title of squire and because no alternative existed, it had simply stuck.

The North Atlantic held the most influence over the district's weather. Although the temperature never reached subzero, the stiff, moist wind chilled any living thing to the bone. Any visitor would testify to the unending cold. The inclement weather forced the residents to curtail animal husbandry. Grazing land existed every place, but ordinary grass could not be harvested and stored for the winter. This limit on feed forced residents to maintain small herds. Meat, cheese, and milk always remained at a premium.

The people had taught themselves to catch and dry some of the abundant salmon that annually surged up the Downs.

However, by the time the Norsemen reached Northdale, they had lost any interest in dried fish because that comprised seagoing food rations. Once in a while, a band of invaders would burn the fish supply just out of cussedness. Most years, they simply ignored the undesirable stuff. The dried salmon became Northdale's only export. During the winter months, the English ate dried meat and grain products. The fish offered a different dining treat, thus a market existed. Every year, several traders made the trek up to Northdale. They brought wagons full of trade goods and left loaded with dried fish.

Due to the need for farm animals to wander about, searching for suitable grass, Northdale residents did not cluster into one defensible community as almost all the rest of the European people did. Instead, the majority of folks lived in two- or three-house groups scattered over the hilly areas. The only village, named Northdale, contained agricultural support operations and a very limited number of artisans. Its population never rose above five hundred.

No mineral assets existed. The Downs provided fish, but no valuable mineral of any sort had ever been found. The local saying was, "If you could count rocks, we would all be rich." Timber grew in wind-protected hollow pockets on the slopes of the ridge and along the Ibix. It was considered scarce. Every few years the baron of Hollingsbrook, the barony that abutted Northdale's southern border, would complain about the obvious logging occurring on his side of the Ibix. Because the Ibix valley and river sat almost ten miles from his estate house, his men-at-arms never could stop the clandestine logging. He repeatedly wrote to the king, requesting compensation, but none ever came.

―――

The departure preparations proved quite pleasant. Humphrey and Philippa's collective attitude changed. Rupert would no longer be a threat to them and their unborn child. Philippa, an accomplished seamstress, even made a pair of double-layered wool leggings for Rupert. His mother collected a huge pile of things she knew he would need. Based on his research, Rupert decided practical, almost survival, items should be taken. Frilly things would come later—maybe.

Cuthbert asked to meet with Humphrey and Rupert to settle financial contributions. Over wine, and while sitting at the library's main table, the discussion occurred. Cuthbert asked, "What do you need, Rupert?"

"Father, at this point I only require two pack horses to carry my trappings. I don't really know what is needed, but I will take a small supply of a few basic items like a pot, frying pan, and warm clothing. Of course, my weapons and armor will also go."

Humphrey leaned forward. "Before we settle, could you list all that you expect?"

Cuthbert said, "I suggest——"

Humphrey cut him off. "Father, we need to hear his expectations."

Rupert looked at Humphrey and then leaned forward. "You are the heir to this land, estate, and income. I have no legal claim to any of it. If I ever run into difficult financial times, I hope you might spare some money. That is all I ask. I now have about half of the gold recovered from the dead knight, fifty crowns or so, but at this point, I have absolutely no idea of the expenditures Northdale will require." Rupert smiled. "If I begin to starve, I hope you could send some scraps."

He sat back in his chair. Cuthbert smiled. Humphrey looked very serious.

"Brother, are you asking for a yearly allowance?"

Rupert shook his head. "The king expects me to go up there and succeed. I will try. Several have failed before me, but they might have all been courtly popinjays who lacked any clue as to accomplishing goals with the assistance of working peasants." The other two sat without moving. "I really want to see Northdale and find its potential. I suspect I will be fine. But if I fail, then a little cash will spur me on to another opportunity."

"I ... uh, we cannot offer you a yearly income," said Humphrey.

"Father and Brother, all I need now is a bag of pennies, a big bag, because I doubt the Northdale people often see gold crowns. I need two packhorses and the supplies they carry. And, once in a while, a traveling professor who knows something about farming comes here. I probably could use his advice so could you pay his expenses to go up there? I believe these requirements are very cheap."

Cuthbert firmly placed his glass on the table. Both sons looked at him. "Here is the offer. You take the two horses and the trappings you need. While I am alive, I will send you five gold crowns a year. Once gone, Humphrey must decide if Lincolnwood can afford you. We will give you the bag of pennies. You are always welcome to visit, and I have no damned idea about a farm professor."

Cuthbert raised his glass, "A toast to the deal." Humphrey's glass hid the victorious smile he had on his face.

A young man leaving home for a protracted separation occurred almost continuously all over England. Society accepted it as a fairly common phenomenon. Cuthbert and Elizabeth threw Rupert a going-away party the night before he left which neighbors and family members attended. It was fun. As a present, he asked his father for three extra swords, two long bows, and one hundred arrows. He received them all. Attendees drank a considerable amount of wine. Rupert spent the night carrying around a glass of wine, but no one saw it refilled. In the morning, Elizabeth, Mary, Cuthbert, and Humphrey saw him off. Some tears occurred as they wished him well.

Rupert rode his war-horse and pulled the supply horses, now three, tethered to a lead line. He estimated it would take two weeks to cover the one hundred and fifty miles. The king's commission carried certain privileges, one of which required castles, estates, or abbeys to give him food and lodging. The distance between such facilities ranged from fifteen to twenty-five miles and Rupert scheduled his trip accordingly. The necessity to unpack and then repack the supply horses at each stop required an hour. One of Lincolnwood's peasants showed him how to correctly use a packsaddle and the practicality of putting the same material in the exact same place on the same horse. He mastered the tasks.

Hosts and hostesses actually enjoyed the surprise visit. It was not uncommon for a single knight to travel alone and add interesting topics to mealtime discussions. But Rupert's appointment to Northdale proved something out of the ordinary to talk about. Most people had heard rumors about Northdale that they eagerly retold. Rupert calmly absorbed all of the talk, but his squire experience at court had taught him that most rumors contained only a grain of truth. He considered the information with reasonable skepticism.

The baron of the second-to-last castle Rupert visited had talked with the last person to hold the Northdale post before he arrived in the district and again, six months later, upon his hasty withdrawal. "The young baron went up there with the assumption that everyone wanted to help him establish a functioning barony as he defined it. He called the whole town to a big meeting and laid out his requirements. He generated no enthusiasm and no cooperation! On his way out, he said, 'Northdale people are stupid'."

Rupert's routine response was, "That is interesting. I'll take note of your comments."

The Baron of Hollingsbrook, Northdale's southern neighbor, expressed concern over the wolf pack that inhabited the dense forest located in the northern five miles of his land. The road to Northdale ran directly through it. He offered to send a company of archers with Rupert to fight off any animal attack. He added, "You know, Sir Rupert, the Ibix River runs through a two-and-one-half-mile-wide valley. Bluffs exist on both sides of this depression. I own the south two miles of the valley, and Northdale's side is about one half a mile. However, your inhabitants frequently cross the river at the road's only ford to hunt deer and take logs from my land. I cannot afford to pay for a squad of troops to patrol the valley so all I ask is that you stop these intrusions."

"My lord, that is very interesting. I certainly will think about it. Having never been there, I don't know yet the situation or how the people conduct themselves."

With a hardy laugh, Hollingsbrook shouted, "*Good luck!*"

The next day, Rupert and the archer company made it to Ibix without mishap. Gravel and small rocks, interspersed with small patches of grass, comprised the shore. The spring floods annually scoured its banks of any vegetation except for the short, hardy grass. They camped for the night and ate fresh venison. In the morning, after a cold-meat breakfast, all wished him luck, watched him cross the ford, and waved before heading home.

The Ibix, except during the spring flood, was a very shallow river. Salmon didn't inhabit it. The ford at this time of the year measured only six inches deep, an easy cross for the horses. Rupert stopped on the Northdale side and examined the geography. The bluff was about forty feet high, and it ran unbroken as far as he could see in either direction. The road utilized the only break in this solid face. The break looked like a tributary leading off the main valley, and it was about thirty feet wide. It rose at a steep but manageable angle to the top; wagon ruts testified to this fact. When entering the bottom, it seemed as if a rider was confined in walls of stone. While riding to the top, Rupert said out loud, "Why hasn't anyone built a fortified gate here?"

Once on top, Rupert entered a dense forest. One of the archers had said it ran for ten miles, an almost full day's ride. He passed several fairly open glens in which only grass grew. The archer had also told him that the Downs valley started about two miles from the village. When he reached the crest at the valley's edge, he dismounted and began to pace back and forth across the road while looking down into it. He could see the top of the keep and some smoke rising from scattered locations. After about ten minutes, he walked over to his war-horse, patted it on the neck, and said, "Well, good friend, into the fight we must go." He mounted and started the descent.

The flat portion of the valley extended about one and a half miles from the river. The land on both sides of the road contained fields of grain crops and what looked like vegetable beds. The outermost residences were nothing more than small, one-story stone cottages and, as he rode into the village, he observed most of its buildings were no bigger.

The keep dominated the skyline. Previous lords had built a square, three-story high stone structure. Small, glassless windows pierced the stone walls at the second- and third-story levels, and at the top a wall was built for archer-firing positions. A six-foot-high stone wall encircled the keep. Only a large, open wooden gate that did not appear attached to its own hinges provided access. As he approached, several people gave him quick glances, but no one spoke to him.

After entering a courtyard through the gate, he could see the keep's almost church-sized front door. It was open. Assuming a very shallow ramp leading to the door provided access to a stable, Rupert rode into the keep. He stopped his horses when he saw that he had entered a room that contained a large fireplace and, against one wall, two massive tables. Two of its walls supported ten-foot-high wood paneling, and two large candle chandeliers made of rough iron hung from the ceiling. No ornamentation or portraits hung anywhere. The room looked and felt like a main hall and certainly not a stable. He dismounted and led the animals out into the courtyard. After tying his horses to a hitching post, he walked around the keep. Opposite the main gate, two sheds had been erected against the back wall. A short inspection revealed stable stalls in one and nothing in the other.

Rupert returned to the animals, unpacked them, and carried the supplies into the keep. Its front doors, upon exercising, worked. They could be closed, but not latched. A fairly large flock of pigeons infested the fortress. The keep's courtyard supported a thick grass cover, so after hobbling them, Rupert let the horses feed. He noticed two people looking through the open gate at him. He casually waved at them, but they quickly walked away.

Strapping on one of the short swords, he walked through the village square that faced the keep's gate. He strolled into one of the four streets that emptied into the square and found a small boy, "Where can I find the squire's house?"

The boy obviously had not seen many persons dressed in knightly tunics. Without speaking, he pointed down the street. The building was larger by four times than the local peasant houses and supported a second floor. A six-foot-high stone wall that a wolf could not climb surrounded it. A six-foot-wide gate finished off the wall, and it hung on hinges.

Rupert looked for a few moments at the closed gate and said to himself, "I will wait until he comes to me." He smiled at the boy, reached over, and rubbed his hair. "Thank you."

As Rupeert walked back toward the keep, a girl approached. "Are you the new lord?"

She wore a plain brown, coarse cloth dress, had curly black hair, looked to be about eight to ten years old, and smiled from a pleasant, freckled face.

Kneeling down to her height, he said, "I guess I am. Who are you?"

"I'm Joanna. Who are you?"

"I'm Sir Rupert, the new sheriff, and I love beautiful little girls like you."

She smiled and then asked, "What is a sheriff?"

"Well, it is my job to carry out the king's wishes."

She started to run off, but then she turned and said, "Good-bye."

In the early evening, Joanna passed the squire on the street. She told him about meeting a lordly-looking man who said he was the new sheriff.

"Damn, the king sent another fool up here. Why doesn't he just leave us alone and let me run things? Where did you see him?"

"Walking near the square."

As he walked to his house, he said aloud, "Well, I will just outlast him like all the others. I will be here long after this one leaves."

When he reached a location from which he could see the keep, he stopped and stared. Again he spoke, "It's odd that he did not demand that I see him." His face showed contemplation as he stared at the keep for a few moments. "We will meet tomorrow!"

When the squire approached the keep's front door, a great deal of yelling and swearing could be heard. A large number of pigeons flew out of the main door. "Devil's spawn, devil's bastards!" This was followed by a reverberation of, "Shit bags!"

When he entered the room, a man wearing peasant clothes stood on a ladder, attacking the pigeons' nests with a long sapling tree. The person had left a few leaves at the end of the stem and used them to wipe the birds' residue from the beams and ledges. He yelled, "*Disgusting!*"

When Rupert climbed down, he saw the stranger. The man was about five and one half feet tall and had a very stocky build. A few white strands streaked his brown head and beard hair. "Hey, would you please close those doors? I don't want the goddamned things to come back." The squire complied. "I'm Sir Rupert, the new sheriff."

"I am Squire Theobald."

Rupert walked back to the ladder and moved it a few paces. "Please don't mind, but I have just one more section to wipe off. You can look at my commissions if you want. They sit on that table."

The squire walked over to the table and put three fingers on the formal documents on which royal wax seals had been affixed; he slid each one around a few inches. Rupert yelled from the ladder top, "They are in Latin, and I'll tell what they say if you want."

"Well, Sir Sheriff, Latin finds little use here."

Rupert jumped off the last two steps. "That is great. I've never liked the stupid language, but scribes write all formal documents in it." He walked over to the squire. "I'd offer to shake your arm, but mine is now disgusting and it would be an insult to touch you with it."

The squire's rather frozen face did not crack a smile, and he looked back at the documents.

"One document appoints me sheriff and the other the king's protector of Northdale. All of the Latin gibberish just means that I hold the same authority as a baron would." With a big smile, he said, "The king judged me not worthy of that rank."

Squire looked up, then leaned over and spat on the floor. "Do you have a list like all the others had?"

In Lincolnwood, spitting on the main hall's floor occurred, but relatively discreetly, and not during face-to-face conversations. While looking at the spittle, Rupert asked, "Do you spit on your floor?" Then without waiting and with a very level voice, "What list?"

Rupert walked around the table to stand opposite the squire as the latter answered. "Every one of the king's appointees comes here and hands me a list of the things he wants the people to do, how they should act toward the noble, and what projects they should finish." He was looking directly at Rupert.

"Did things get implemented?"

"I would get done what I could."

Rupert looked toward the fireplace for a moment and then faced the squire, leaned in, and placed both hands on the table. "Well I don't have a list, but I already see things must be accomplished. I plan to ride all over Northdale to inventory other needs. I will tell you what is to be undertaken, and, squire, I will expect they are completed. Are we clear?" They gave each other very hard stares. Rupert stood, walked over to a nearby chair, drew his sword, walked back, and dropped it on the table. "Are we clear?"

Squire stepped back with a shocked look. "You draw a sword on an unarmed man?"

"No, squire, I'm trying to make a point. If I ever draw a sword on you for business purposes, you will know it. Look, I'm obviously not yet familiar with Northdale's needs, but this much I do know—everyone must work together, especially you and me."

"That has always been the problem. All you young lords come up here to fix Northdale. What makes you think anything needs to be done? We've gotten along before you and will after you!"

Rupert walked around the table and looked up at the remaining flock of pigeons flying around. He looked at them for thirty seconds and then back at the squire.

Squire followed Rupert's gaze to the birds and then returned the eye contact. "So, sheriff, some things do need to be done, but things the people need, not things you impose."

Rupert smiled. "Deal, my friend squire. You will help me inventory suggestions and seek ideas from the residents. I've worked and fought with people like Northdale's, and I respect their skills and energy. I don't intend to impose objectives unless they are necessary to meet my duty to the king." He smiled. "He's not expecting too much. But you and I have a responsibility to help people make their lives better. I intend to meet that obligation and hope you will participate.

"And let me add, squire, you don't know me, but I'm not a pompous ass of a lord. I am not at all opposed to getting my hands dirty." He turned around and began to roll up his commission papers. "I don't want any bird shit on these."

Squire crossed his arms and watched. After finishing, Rupert turned around and looked questioningly at him. "Well, sheriff, you sound different from the last few lords who strutted around, yelled orders, handed down work to be done, and demanded servitude. You will find that I very much want to make better the lot of Northdale's people. So let us see how this plays."

Rupert walked over and stood directly in front of the man. "Squire, what I say now is an appeal for your cooperation and not a threat. If you cannot see your way to put your effort into helping me, then I hold the authority to require you to leave. It is your choice."

Squire's eyes became like ice as he glowered at Rupert. He did not move for almost a half-minute, and then he slowly turned.

"I'm telling you the truth when I say I need your help." Rupert raised one hand, palm up, waist high. "Let me know what you decide. When out in the public, you should address me by title, but when we are alone, please call me Rupert."

Without turning back to Rupert, the squire said, "You call me Squire." He used a very stiff stride as he departed. After picking up a jug of wine, he went to Father William's cottage.

The priest pointed to the table and two chairs in his rectory hut. Squire rubbed his forehead with his left hand and said, "We've got another bossy noble. I need some wine."

After pouring two wines and sitting down, Squire repeated Rupert's comments.

William asked for a second glass, and then said, "Well, the two of us will just have to wait out another dumb king's appointment." They clinked glasses. "But I must tell you that the king's protector document you described gives him the power to kick you out, and he decides what assets you can carry with you."

Squire yelled, "Shit!"

William tapped his glass on the table. "But wait, you have alternatives."

"Yeah, leave or kiss his ass!"

Shaking his head, William said, "No, no. You can say no, and then leave with the small amount of gold I think you have accumulated, or you can agree to help."

"William, that is a damnable choice."

"Squire, you miss the point. A difference exists between agreeing to carry out a program and actually doing so. It could take a year or more before this sheriff figures out that you are undermining his plans. So then, he kicks you out. It's the same loss you now face, and a chance exists he will have left by then."

This time William filled the glasses and they clinked them.

The next day, after deciding the pigeon fight would take some strategic planning to win, Rupert took a walk around the village. Rumors had flown through it, so the residents gave polite nods to him. They were all dressed in unpretentious, utilitarian, heavy woven cloth of various shades of brown. The women wore one-piece, loose-fitting dresses tightened at the waist by a leather belt. The men wore leggings and a tunic cinched by a belt; some had small knives hanging from the belt.

The houses were small, stone cottages. All had one front door and one window located next to it. Each roof was made of thatch and one wall included a chimney. One universal rule seemed to exist: all were painted white. Several two-story buildings existed. In them the artisans kept shops on the first floor and lived on the second. The shops provided leather necessities, general merchandise, and wood products.

At one corner, Rupert saw three children playing. He approached. "Hello, children, I'm the new sheriff." They just stopped playing and stared at him. "I guess you will tell me the truth if I ask you a question?" They just looked at him. "Do you know anyone who can ride well and knows most of Northdale's land?"

They gave each other quick glances, and one boy faced Rupert. "Eleanor rides fast."

Not expecting a woman's name, Rupert could not help his surprised look. "Where can I find her?"

All three simultaneously pointed up an adjacent street. One girl said, "Last house."

At the door, Rupert called for Eleanor. A woman in her mid-twenties with dirty brown hair, dressed as the others, opened the door. "Who wants her?"

"Sir Rupert, Sheriff of Northdale and a person seeking a woman who is reported to be a good horse rider."

"What for?"

Rupert smiled and crossed his arms. "Is this the hospitality of Northdale? I'm here to offer a job, and you won't even tell me if you are Eleanor."

She now crossed her arms, tilted her head slightly to the side, and said, "Two things, how much does it pay?"

"A penny a week."

She raised one eyebrow. "Second, the cursed Norsemen took my only horse. I think the bastards ate it!"

Putting both hands on his hips, Rupert asked, "Saddle too?"

She now put her hands on her hips. "One learns how to hide things from them. You need to learn that."

"I have two horses you can ride, so come to the keep at noon with your saddle."

"Where am I going?"

"You are going to show me Northdale's lands." Her face registered disbelief. "The horse is fast." He turned and started to walk toward town.

She took a step forward and smiled. "My name is Eleanor." Rupert waved his arm.

The fact that she wore men's leggings under a tunic that extended only to her knees did not cause the looks—it was normal for her—but the fact that she carried a saddle did. Several people stopped and cast curious looks.

Once in their saddles, Eleanor said, "Northdale has two roads. They both follow the Downs up to the waterfall at the mountain's edge. One road is on the south side and the other on the north. A ford lets us cross at Mary's Sorrows Falls. It is a full day's ride up to the falls; we cannot make it today."

Rupert commented, "Curious name for a waterfall."

She turned her horse in a circle. "Some priest decided it should remind us of the tears Mary shed after Jesus got killed."

They rode up the south road. After seeing several clusters of one-room cottages, Rupert stopped at one. The residents were shocked into silence by a noble's visit. Eleanor's positive head shake encouraged their answering his questions about their well-being.

They stopped two more times and Rupert asked the same questions. The last homemaker offered them carrot soup. Rupert surprised them by sitting on their bench and eating with relish; nobles never did that either. As they mounted, Eleanor whispered that he had just eaten the family's daily ration. Rupert dismounted and gave the hostess a penny. She was very surprised again.

Because it was late, they headed back to Northdale. Eleanor asked, "Are you really listening to these people?"

He stopped his horse and Eleanor did the same. Rupert nudged his until it stood sideways in front of Eleanor. Smiling, he said, "Questioning the motivation of your royal sheriff can cost you your head." His facial expression became serious. "I am measuring the problems they face and the spirit they have." He turned his horse down the road. "We've walked them all day; let's exercise them." He spurred his horse. Eleanor looked at him for a moment and then, with a grin, did the same. Her packhorse seemed to like its light load and matched the war horse's pace.

That night, people came to Eleanor's house to ask about the new sheriff. She answered all questions in the same way: "I don't know what he will do, but he is not like the other ones."

They rode to Mary's Sorrows Falls the next day. Rupert made sure Eleanor slept in a residence on one side of the

Downs and he on the other. The trip resembled yesterday's. He stopped often and asked people questions. Rupert decided to carry provisions so as not to impose on the hungry people and bought anything he and Eleanor required with pennies. The people responded to his inquiries, and he picked up much information.

Over the next few days, Eleanor showed Rupert the good and bad points of Northdale. The Downs' mouth at the ocean, the salmon-catch area, and the seaside cliff edges. The sheriff now knew the location of arable land and dense forest. While traveling around, he stopped to meet any residents they encountered, and he listened to their remarks. Eleanor's presence, being one of their own, seemed to encourage their expression of concerns.

After the last day, he made an offer. "Eleanor, if you care for my horses, you can have free use of them, even the war-horse."

With a very large smile, "Deal," she said.

Rupert next sent for the priest, Father William. He was an older man with very white hair. Northdale certainly did not represent prime theological territory. Rupert never discovered what ecclesiastical crime caused a distant bishop to exile William to Northdale.

Rupert sat at the desk when William walked into the main hall and, without any introduction, asked bluntly, "Why are you talking to all of those people? Trying to stir something up?"

Rupert looked up and spent several seconds evaluating the man. He decided to repay curtness with curtness. "Father, I'm Sheriff Rupert, and I will require your services." The priest just stood still. "Two Sundays from now, I want to have a meeting of Northdale's people, and I need you to take down notes on what transpires."

"You do know, sheriff, that it is your responsibility and mine to lead these people and not to be swayed by some common grumbling."

Rupert stood up, walked around the front of the desk, and rested his butt on its edge. He gazed at the priest.

Father William added, "They are good people, but need firm direction."

Rupert stood up and walked over to the priest. "I disagree and my voice counts. I'm sure you can write in Latin, but the notes must be readable. Can you write English?"

William's face expressed indignation. "Of course I can."

"Good, two Sundays from now, you take notes. Oh, you may also start the meeting with a Mass if you choose."

"If I refuse?"

"Well, you can refuse to say Mass because I hold no authority over church matters, but with the civilian business, I can require you to take notes. And if you prepare unreadable notes, I will proclaim an order forbidding anyone from selling or giving you wine or ale. Goodbye, Father." The sheriff stood and gave the priest a very hard stare. With a stony face, William turned around and walked out.

Three days later, a servant delivered a note from the priest. In English, he stated that Mass could only be celebrated in a church, but he would take notes.

Rupert purchased a cow destined for the winter culling; servants cooked it in the main hall's fireplace. He also found a cask of ale. About two hundred people showed up for the meeting. A lot of happy conversations were heard. The people truly liked the opportunity to eat free food while talking to neighbors.

After walking among the folks and making a show of trying to remember names, the sheriff went to the main table and asked for quiet. "Father William, will you step up here?" After the priest held his quill over paper, Rupert began.

"Folks, this meeting is to give me an understanding of the problems you face and, more important, which ones to attack first. What is a big problem up here?" No one spoke. Rupert waited about fifteen seconds. "Come on, nothing bad will happen if you speak up." No one spoke. "All right, let me start. I've heard a lot about the Norsemen. Anyone want to say something?"

A dam burst; voices erupted. Rupert finally stood on the table and yelled for speakers to take turns. It took almost two hours to work through a reasonable, descriptive list. The list contained the following:

1. The Norsemen kill many men, rape women, and steal children—they always seek children because they can be sold at a high price.
2. To keep the Norsemen from pillaging everyplace, the squire requires one cow to be offered up every time they come. In some years, ten different clans of Norsemen arrive, thus costing a cow each time.
3. The Norsemen invasions require that everyone flee with anything of value, so everything had to be movable. This means nothing, like high quality workshops, can ever be constructed.
4. The squire requires everyone to escape when the Norsemen come; there is no armed resistance.
5. An impossible circle exists with the livestock. Not much grain can be grown in Northdale, so very little can be stored. The animals have to be culled

every fall to a very small number. Herds can't not get large enough to supply surplus meat, milk, or cheese.
6. There isn't enough land to grow grain. Only grass is plentiful, but the sheep and goats also have to be culled
7. Is is too hard to get enough wood to keep houses warm. It is very cold in the cottages and children die because they get sick from the cold.
8. There is no chance to learn a trade because so few tradesmen exist.
9. There is very little money to fix things like the roads and drainage. This work is done only when an individual undertakes a project to protect his own property.
10. The squire requires one Saturday a month for work on roads and river bank projects
11. The church doesn't care about people's problems.

The list-making had to stop for a very practical reason—Father William ran out of paper. Rupert thanked all, invited them to feast, and directed the priest to make four copies of the list. He made a closing statement. "I will study this list and see if I can come up with some solutions. Eat and drink more." A general hubbub ensued. He slapped the priest on the back. "Nice job, William."

Surprise always favored the Norsemen. When they suddenly appeared, Northdale scrambled to remove itself. The suddenness of the attacks drew Rupert's first consideration. If the residents had enough warning, they might have time to carefully evacuate or possibly offer some resistance.

Because Squire had, for years, required the men to report once a month to work on a public project, Rupert called the monthly work force to meet the next week. He surprised everyone by insisting women also report. Squire appeared at the main hall to ask which project the sheriff planned to undertake. The sheriff did not answer, but told him to attend because he would direct a work project.

When gathered on Saturday morning, Rupert told the group that Northdale needed a warning system to alert the village about approaching Norsemen. He wanted an observation post built on the high north bank of the Downs overlooking the coast. It needed to be rain resistant because starting in a week it would be manned twenty-four hours a day. This caused quite a verbal stir among the people. One shouted, "We have too much work to do, sheriff. We cannot spend all that time watching the water." Rupert anticipated this complaint. "That is why the women will also take turns watching." That stunned them into silence. "Squire will supervise the outpost's construction and will spend the first rainy day in it as a test." The people seemed to appreciate the fact that a superior would now have to pull his own weight. Many smiled.

"But that is not all. The lookout will contain two people, one to watch and one to run to the keep if danger approaches. One thing I learned in France is you do not want approaching forces to know they've been seen. That is why the women will carefully cut a pathway through the brush and trees that leads from the outpost to the keep. The path must be hidden so the Norsemen do not see our messengers. Eleanor will supervise this task." The women instantly started talking at once.

"Squire, take my two packhorses into the woods and pull out the trees needed to build the lookout. But do not cut down the dead and dry ones. Those are to be made available for this winter's heat." The faces showed some appreciation for this last comment.

Rupert faced Squire. "Do you also want to assist me in selecting a site?"

"No, Sheriff, this is your doing."

"Six men need to volunteer to dig. The rest will cut trees. Eleanor, you come with me, and, women, fetch things to cut small trees and brush."

The crowd came alive, a cacophony of talking yelling, and directions occurred. Rupert noted the presence of some spirit in the folks, except for Squire.

The six diggers, Eleanor, and Rupert picked the outpost's site. The outpost's back wall would be dug into a small, existing berm. One window would face north, one south, and the door, west. After the excavation started, Eleanor and Rupert traced a good location for the path. It zigzagged around fallen trees, large live ones, dense bush groupings, and several ditches; anyone running on it would not be seen. By mid-morning, the women were at work. By noon, the men finished the lookout's foundation, and, conveniently, the wood began to arrive. The day's end saw the walls up. Eight men eagerly offered to come back the next day and finish the roof and door. Harsh weather required the window shades be made of leather. Rupert asked how to finish the roof. The men looked at him as if he were stupid. "We have sod up here, sheriff." Laughter followed and Rupert joined in. Several women also agreed to return and complete the path.

Two days later, Rupert summoned Squire to the main hall. "I need a schedule of the people who will man the lookout. Two at a time for a twenty-four-hour shift. Women should alternate days with men, but we should not mix men and women." Squire made a questioning facial expression. "Come on, Squire. For obvious reasons. Also, include my name, Father William's, and yours."

Squire pulled in his chin and sputtered, "Father William will have church business to attend to, and it takes almost all of his time."

"I think Jesus would approve of his helping to protect the people from the ravages of the Norsemen." While laughing Rupert added, "Or, if you choose, I can tie the priest to a stake when they come, and he can pray them away." Squire did not find any humor in the comment. "We start tomorrow. Tell me, Squire, in your experience, when do the fall's incursions cease?"

"They seem to stop in mid-November; I suspect the seas are too rough to return home after that because all of their booty makes the ships ride low in the water. Sir Rupert, I must tell you I don't believe women should take a turn watching. They should be at home."

Rupert stood up, walked to stand in front of Squire, and with a firm but pleasant voice said, "Squire, Northdale does not have enough men to protect itself. It must be an effort by all adults. Besides, they might like to sit without work for a day." Squire shook his head in disagreement. "No questions on that subject. Please extend the schedule until mid-November and remember: on the first rainy day, assign yourself to watch." As it turned out, once started, the women really did enjoy the chance to spend twenty-four hours free of domestic chores.

A day later, Rupert sat at the main hall's table when Squire entered the room. His face projected rock hard determination as he strode up to the table.

Using a hard voice, he said, "Sir Sheriff, I'm beginning to think you plan to fight the Vikings next time they attack."

Rupert intertwined his fingers and placed his hands on the table. "Absolutely."

Squire's faced tightened, and his voice rose in volume. "You young lords come up here and think you know everything, but you don't have any idea of the true situation."

Rupert grimaced. "Squire, tell me what is on your mind."

"I've been dealing with Vikings for years, and you have no such experience. The only way to survive their assaults is to flee into the hills. To fight them means a slaughter of my people!"

Rupert slowly stood up and walked around to the squire's side of the table. His face now became resolute. "They are my people, also, Squire." He raised his voice. "Don't forget that!"

Squinting his eyes, Squire pointed at Rupert. "Have you ever lost your only means of work? Have you had your house burnt down? Have you ever seen family members killed before your eyes?" He took another step closer to Rupert. "Have you ever had your wife and two children stolen from you and forced into slavery?" He began to yell. "I have seen all of these things and lost my family. And the worst pain comes from not ever knowing what happened to your loved ones; you think up all sorts of horrible ends for them. That pain stopped me from starting another family." The squire was really yelling. "No one should face the same situation again, so we run to the hills." He now raised both hands with clenched fists. "*You, Sir Sheriff, don't know shit!*"

Rupert paused for a moment. His red face reflected the conflict between true information and the insulting manner in which it was delivered. Without speaking, he took the time to walk around to his side of the table. He leaned forward, placing both hands on the tabletop.

"Look, Squire, the Vikings will continue to steal Northdale's assets unless we do something." He raised his voice a notch. "Past losses cannot freeze our reactions. If we sit still, many more people will feel your pain." He slapped both hands on the table, and then he stood straight up. "Action must be taken. and it is my responsibility to take it." He yelled, "*Do you understand?*"

Both men stood looking at each other without speaking. Rupert lowered his voice. "No other way exists, so this discussion ends." Again, Squire said nothing. "If you cannot help me, I cannot have a disgruntled public official living in Northdale, and you must leave. It is your decision."

Squire looked disgusted, faced the door, and walked out.

First Raids

Two weeks after the lookout was completed and manned, one of the observing woman burst into the main hall. "Three boats on the south horizon."

Rupert had been reviewing money affairs with Squire. Both ran out the door. Squire said, "If they are rowing, it will take two to three hours, but if the wind is behind them, we have just about an hour." Looking at the runner, he asked, "Which way the wind?"

"From the south."

Rupert pointed at the village. "We have one hour. Sound the warning. We've all practiced this event, so let's get moving!" He ran inside to get one of his four swords, the only ones in the whole district.

Despite past experience with such attacks, the town's people spent valuable time scurrying about, gathering up belongings. Rupert had prepacked his belongings, so with the aid of only one servant, his possessions moved to the hills. Both he and Squire ran all over the community, yelling at the people to get out. They met three times to ascertain progress, and at just about one hour, Squire left last. Rupert and six men began to observe the Vikings.

The Norsemen used the Downs twice a season. In the spring, they landed to get fresh water and meat. It took three to four weeks to row and sail to the northern parts of England, so the crews required fresh food and a chance to exercise. The spring raids concentrated on supply gathering.

From experience, the Vikings knew that Northdale held no treasure. In the past, the Vikings greatly enhanced the fiscal return of a season's raiding by taking slaves. Northdale's young boys and girls were prime, but men and women under the age of twenty-five also attracted a fair sale price. Slave-taking did not occur in the spring because securing and feeding them would have greatly encumbered the summer's treasure campaign.

The fall's return trip provided the best opportunity to pick up and transport slaves. The Norsemen also required subsistence supplies for the travel home, so the chief would split his crews into two teams, one to concentrate on quick searches for available slaves and the other to gather fresh food and water.

Squire, Eleanor, and many other residents had explained this reality to Rupert. He knew that getting the people out of reach formed the primary goal, followed closely by the necessity of removing any possessions. The latter had, in a backward way, trained the Vikings that nothing of value existed, and they tended not to burn Northdale's buildings.

One problem always existed. The Norsemen did not come from a unified government. Chiefs and numerous nobles could and did launch raids. Viking kings usually organized large-scale assaults on major cities like Paris, but the division of spoils often became rather thin when hundreds of ships were involved. However, no Norse law required association with a big raid, and if a lesser royal remained confident in his ability to resist the king's calls, he could make more money leading his own raids.

Vikings built several different-sized boats. Some carried twenty to thirty men while others, more than fifty. Three of the latter size entered the Downs. The river's width only allowed four ships to enter under the power of oars. Another could be towed into the river if the four ships' oars had been stowed.

As expected, Northdale tied out a cow. The flotilla's commander immediately sent a contingent to butcher the animal. Most of the other men began filling water barrels. Eight men started the search for slaves. They ran through the village and its environs seeking potential captives; they found none.

Norsemen divided spoils on a sliding scale. The most prestigious members of the crew received larger portions than the least important. Thus, four of the lowest-ranking crewmembers asked the chief if they could try and scrounge up some spoils for themselves. The chief gave permission with one condition. "We sail at dawn; be back or be left behind."

The four raced off the boats and up into town. Finding nothing, they assumed the villagers removed their possessions from Northdale itself, so they decided to walk up the south road. After an hour's hike, they stopped at a cottage in which nothing of value existed. The next cottage they came across contained a kitchen with two valuable items: a large block of cheese and a five-gallon keg of wine. The four immediately realized that if these two items were carried back to the boats, the property division system would leave them with no more than a small snack. They eagerly resolved to eat and drink all of it. After about two hours, the four inebriated men passed out.

Rupert and his six men remained hidden to observe the Norsemen's activities. After the large group of fighters finished their slaving sweep, they saw the four men begin their search. Rupert sent one member of his squad ahead to set out the wine and cheese. While the four Vikings concentrated on gorging themselves, the sheriff and the other men arrived.

The Vikings had taken the precaution to wedge the door shut with one of their battle-axes but had failed to secure the window. To avoid any noise, Rupert and three men took off any metal attachments to their clothes and then climbed through the window. One of the outside men handed four tree axes through it. The tree ax made a very quick business of killing a sleeping man. Three were dead with one stroke; the other required two.

Northdale acquired four swords, three battle-axes, one spear, and four Viking shields. Two metal and two leather helmets complemented the other weapons. A treasure for Northdale!

Rupert ordered the removal of all traces of the incident. He assumed that if the Vikings found any evidence of harm to their shipmates, many buildings would be burned down, possibly the whole village. The bodies would be thrown into the ocean at low tide, the armor hidden, and the kitchen cleaned of all food and blood traces. In an hour, the cottage appeared empty and unused.

At the next dawn, the Viking chief swore several oaths at the missing men. He ordered two of his fastest runners to search the village and its immediate environs. They ran through the village, shouting the names of their shipmates, and they actually ran to the south road's second cottage. Finding no trace, they reported back. The chief slammed his hand on the railing. "Horse shit! Cast off!"

That night, Rupert organized a celebration, a victory celebration, the first one anyone could remember. He placed the captured weapons on a table located in the center of the main hall. Ale flowed. For a people who long felt victimized, the party made them experience some hope. It also stirred a very rudimentary feeling of unity. Toward the end of the evening, people began to dance around the table.

After about two hours, Squire approached Rupert with a serious face. "Sheriff, do you really think the swords, battle-axes, and shields will allow us to stand up to the next invasion?"

These words could not wipe off Rupert's happy look. "Squire, we will experience many more evasive encounters before we are prepared to mount a face-to-face defense." He picked up a mug of ale. "But it is a beginning. Man, do you understand? A start!" He slapped the man on the arm, and with a broad grin, Rupert said, "Let me buy you a drink!"

In the early fall, a female watcher ran into the keep and screamed, "A boat from the south!"

The alarm yells made everyone pack up and leave. They were much quicker the second time.

For the previous two months, Rupert had been training some men in the art of sword fighting. Because of their lack of metal swords, the men trained with wooden ones. However, with the recently acquired Viking weapons, the sheriff organized a six-man squad that carried three swords and three battle-axes. Rupert made it absolutely clear that under no circumstances were they going to fight experienced Norsemen warriors. But he knew from his Holland fighting experience that the simple act of carrying weapons somehow injects a bit of fighting spirit.

The sheriff's squad, once it reached the observation post, began to evaluate the boat's threat. One of the men said, "Sheriff, the boat is not moving very fast." Another added, "Look! The sail is only half raised."

Vikings built boats with only one mast. A crossbeam held the top of the sail, and it was raised to the mast's top by several pulleys. The approaching boat's sail looked to have been lifted to the height a standing man could reach, or about halfway up the mast.

The boat did not follow a direct course. It wandered back and forth in a general direction. The first man asked, "Is it even coming here?"

Rupert suggested, "Seems to be switching in different directions, but still aiming at the Downs' mouth." The squad and the two women lookouts studied the boat for almost an hour.

One of the women said, "Sheriff, I only see one man at the tiller." As the boat got closer, someone said, "The tiller man looks flopped over it."

Rupert motioned for everyone to get low. "This could be some weird trap, but I agree: no one works the oars or sail. It could be a trick to get us to expose ourselves so those bastards know our location. Stay out of sight."

A sandy beach existed on each side of the Downs' mouth. The boat grounded itself on the north side. The man at the tiller slipped to the deck, and none of the others sat up. As they watched, the south breeze carried a strong, filthy stench. A few men on board seemed to roll over on their rowing benches, but none stood up.

Rupert looked at the youngest member of the squad. "Charles, leave your weapons and run down there and look. Don't stop. Just look and run back up here." The young man nodded his head while putting down his weapons. Crouching through the overlook's grass, he ran down to the beach and up to the boat. He looked in quickly, and all the observers could see the disgust on his face as he ran back.

"It stinks. Shit, piss, vomit all over the pace. The men are lying in the filth. They all look sick. They couldn't swat a fly."

Rupert pointed at two other men. "Take a little time and look over the situation. Leave your weapons. Signal if Charles is correct."

The two crouched, running to the boat. When they arrived, they stood up and slowly walked around it. One of them waved for the squad to come down. The women accompanied them.

A stinking scene waited. The men had obviously contracted a sickness. Vomit, diarrhea, and piss covered most interior surfaces. Almost all of the men seemed to be moving, but only barely. One clearly dead man sat amidships. The tiller man had either passed out or died. The crew numbered about thirty men, one young boy, and two tied-up people—probably slaves. Rupert walked the length of the boat, twice.

After the second review, he stopped. His face showed contemplation. One of the battle-axe carriers said, "Let's kill them all. They can't fight."

For a long moment Rupert viewed the very eager-faced squad members. "No honor exists in killing sick opponents. None whatsoever. We actually might accomplish some peace by taking care of these poor souls." The Northdale people looked surprised.

Turning to one of the women, Rupert asked, "Joan, what do you think about this sickness?"

"My mother always said when someone has the shits, they need to drink lots of water."

Charles had also been walking back and forth. He pointed. "I see two open and empty water barrels."

The sheriff walked over and looked at the two barrels. The squad stood without moving. Turning to them, he said, "Charles take up your weapons and run to the other men's hiding places. Get about twenty men down here, fast. Tell them to bring some wood planks, so we can carry these men."

He pointed at the other woman. "Name?"

"Marta."

"Marta, you go up and get about ten women to start making a mutton broth. Joan, get up to the observation post and bring down the water bucket and its dipper. The rest of us will find a line and tie that boat to the nearest tree after we pull it out of the water as far as we can."

They still just stood in place. Rupert clapped his hands. "Move!" They almost jumped into their assigned tasks.

The remaining five men pushed and pulled the boat fifteen feet onto the beach. The boat's bowline reached one of the shoreline's old oak trees. Rupert asked, "Where are we going to put thirty men?"

One of the men said, "The biggest spaces are the keep's main hall or the church."

Rupert put his hand over his mouth and rubbed. "Other choices?"

Joan had returned and, after hearing the question, injected, "There is an old, unused barn on this north shore. No one knows why it was built; its odd location keeps anyone from using it."

Rupert raised an eyebrow and shot her a questioning look.

Joan answered his gaze. "It's not real nice inside, but it will do for our smelly guests."

Northdale's residents fell in to the task. The barn was swept, and with some effort, the men were moved into it. They were all spoon-fed water and liquid broth. Rupert proclaimed two orders: Viking weapons were to stay on the sand next to the ship, and absolutely nothing was to be taken. The man at the tiller and four others were actually dead. After their armor was removed, they were tossed into the ocean. The ladies noted that the boy required some tender care. He was carried to one of the near cottages. The two presumed slaves were unshackled and carried to a different cottage.

It took twenty-four hours for the water, broth, and sleep to begin reviving the Norsemen. Men were awake for short periods, but remained extremely weak. Only Rupert carried a sword when visiting the sick barn. Two guards stood at the door.

In forty-eight hours, the Norsemen were speaking to each other and expressing uneasiness. Their chief kept telling them to remain calm. After all, it was a good sign that women attended to them.

One of the younger men, after receiving some broth from a woman, said, "Thank you," in English. When she asked, he explained that he had been abducted from someplace in England when he'd been about eight years old. The Viking who'd purchased him had lost his only son and offered to adopt Estrid, formerly John. For obvious reasons, he'd accepted and was now a full-fledged Viking. He offered to translate, as this was often one of his duties.

Rupert brought a table and three chairs into the barn. He asked Estrid to get the chief to sit at the table and to take a seat himself. After the sheriff sat down, several Vikings stood, somewhat unsteadily, behind the chief. Introductions followed. The chief's name was Sweyn. He wanted to know three things: where was his son, when would they get their weapons, and what happened to the boat?

The sheriff explained the boy had been taken to a warm house under the special care of a Northdale woman. The chief could see him when he felt he could walk. Sweyn slammed his open hand on the table and demanded to see him. Rupert told him that he could do so as soon as he'd finished answering the other questions. The weapons had been stacked next to the boat and must stay in the pile until the Vikings left. The boat had been beached, and it would take the assistance of Sweyn's crew to clean the filth out.

Rupert added, "We found five men to be dead; four in the boat and one at the tiller."

The chief's face was sorrowful as he turned to his men. "Haakon is dead." They immediately frowned. Estrid explained that Haakon was second in command and a father to everyone.

Rupert then leaned over the table. "We have no intention of harming you. Once you are well enough, you will be free to leave. No one will take anything from your boat. While you are here, we expect you and your men to honor our peace. Weapons are to stay on the ground. My healers say you should be fit in about four more days. Do you agree?"

Sweyn looked at half his men still lying on the floor and then back to Rupert. "How do I know this is not some trap?"

Smiling, Rupert said, "If it was, you all would already be dead."

The chief pursed his lips as he spent a few moments pondering that statement. "I agree."

As Rupert stood, the chief asked, "The boy?" Rupert waved his hand in a come-with-me gesture. Sweyn, Estrid, and two of the more stable fighting men slowly walked to the boy's cottage. Disease had hit him hard, probably due to the fact that the boat's water supply ran out the day before landing. Despite his Norseman lineage, the Northdale women had hovered over the boy. When he saw his father, the boy smiled and made a weak wave of his hand. Sweyn gave a large smile to his two followers and then a strong nod to Rupert.

As the days passed, the Vikings began to eat more regular food and gained strength. Northdale men and the Norsemen tilted the boat onto its side. Each crewman stored his belongings in a chest, which also served as his rowing bench. These were removed, cleaned and stacked on the beach. Then all of the men grabbed buckets and spent hours throwing clean water at the filth-encrusted boat's interior. On the day before the Viking's departure, Rupert provided a cask of ale and a cow for slaughter.

After the last night's meal, Sweyn requested a meeting with Rupert to settle their debt. Sweyn, his son, and Estrid sat at one side of a table, Rupert and Squire on the other side. The latter's face remained hard throughout the meeting. Several Vikings stood behind their chief and a number of Northdale's men and women behind the sheriff.

After filling all the mugs on the table with win, Sweyn said, "You people have been very fair with us. You had the chance to kill us and take all of our possessions, including that beautiful boat. My men and I have decided we should repay you."

Rupert sat back in his chair and nodded his head. "My people have been raided every year. This must stop. Your crews need food and water after sailing here and before sailing back home. Would it not be better for you and us to begin trading with each other rather than fighting every year?"

Sweyn clearly was surprised by this idea, but not at all displeased. A considerable discussion occurred over what items each party valued. The Vikings required a safe harbor to trade for supplies both in the spring and fall. They had discovered that taking wine back produced large revenues. It proved too demanding to haul wine all the way from the raided sites, but it would be opportune to purchase it at their last stop. They proposed trading furs and gold for wine and dried fish.

Rupert agreed to the safe harbor in exchange for furs on the inbound trip and gold for wine on the outbound. There was one rule; he insisted that the Vikings never tell anyone from whence the gold came. That brought a laugh from all the Norsemen.

After the second mug of wine, Sweyn asked, "What is fair for helping us now?"

Rupert put both hands on the table. "We need two things. First, this district cannot afford weapons; we request the weapons and armor from the five dead men. Second, our religion will not allow slavery, so the wrath of our God will descend on us if you take the two slaves; they must stay."

Sweyn looked at Rupert. "I must talk with my men." The gathered Vikings formed a tight circle and much talk occurred. Squire glanced at the sheriff and raised his eyebrows.

The Norsemen suddenly stopped, and Estrid asked, "What happened to the bodies of our dead?"

"We buried them in the sea." After translation, this comment generated another round of conversation. After five minutes, the chief returned to the table.

"One of the dead was our sub-chief, Haakon. Viking tradition holds that his rank deserves a burial in a special place in our homeland. Because his body is at sea, his armor must come and be buried. We agree to give you the other four sets.

"As for the slaves, we understand a helpful act should not result in the wrath of your gods. You can have the slaves. Besides, this trip proved very profitable."

The chief noted the curious looks on the faces of the Northdale men.

"We found a small abbey that had been raided so many times it only had two gold candle sticks and one cup. But while searching the room with all of the books, Haakon began pulling at the shelves. One moved and behind it was a door!"

The listening Vikings made an approving grumble.

"Behind the door, the abbey had hidden a great quantity of gold items. Other raiders completely missed them. We did well."

The Norsemen continued making appreciative noises.

"My men wanted to offer you one other thing. Our boat divides the treasure into one hundred parts. The boat gets twenty-five, I get fifteen and Haakon would have received ten. The remaining fifty are divided equally among the crew. That is why I have no problem recruiting men for my small raiding operations. Each crew member will get about one and one-half pounds of gold."

This large amount got the Northdale residents to mutter in disbelief.

"Haakon's share must pay for his funeral, but the men believe you should take the other four men's shares."

Rupert first turned to Squire; they exchanged a long, serious look. He next turned to the Northdale people, and they registered pleasure. He slowly faced the chief and made a very slight nod.

"Do those men have wives and children?"

Sweyn rotated to face his men, and after a minor consultation among them, he twisted back and said, "Three of them do."

"Northdale does not want a family to starve, so we will only take the share of the man with no family."

That brought total surprise to Sweyn's and Estrid's faces and silenced the Vikings. The chief slowly stood up and roared his approval; his crew amplified it.

Rupert and the squire also stood, and when Sweyn extended his arm, the sheriff seized it. Squire turned away.

The next morning, the chief and sheriff, along with Estrid, walked to the boat just before it shoved off.

"You know that I am only one chief. Others will have no respect for anything you and I agree to. You will be raided again. My ship has the sign of the ram on the sail. You will always know us."

Rupert nodded.

"You now have four more swords, shields and battle-axes to help defend yourselves."

Rupert stopped, scrunched up his shoulders. "I know the sword but have no experience with battle-axes."

Sweyn let out a big laugh. "Next year, I will bring one of our old warriors who now spends his time training young ones to fight. He will stay the summer. And one more thing: I want everyone to know that the gold we give you came from our homeland."

Rupert, with a big smile, extended his arm and vigorously shook the chief's arm.

Mid-November saw the end of raiding season and the rather frenzied preparation for winter's onslaught. Herds required culling; meat, drying; and grain, storing. From mid-summer on, the men began to chop firewood. Rupert's war horse possessed the muscle to pull heavy trees, so Rupert and the men selected large dead ones and dragged then into the square. Several men pointed out that Hollingsbrook's woods contained many prime, dead—thus, dry—trees. The sheriff smiled. "Not this year."

On the last day of November, Rupert asked to meet with Squire. "I'm going to visit my father's castle for Christmas. I plan to return by early spring, before the Vikings get here."

Squire tilted his head down, but rolled his eyes to express doubt. Seeing his expression, Rupert added, "I will absolutely return. How could I miss the spring invasions?" He laughed; Squire did not.

"Because you are still here, I assume you plan to work with me?"

With a resigned look on his face, Squire said, "Yes."

It was a rare warm and sunny November day. Rupert put a table in the keep's courtyard. He and Squire prepared a schedule for the next three or four months. "Are the folks willing to continue training in winter?"

"Sir, they crave something to do in winter."

The sheriff directed the wooden sword fighting should continue and that volunteer women should take up archery. "The main hall is big enough to set up targets."

Squire did not hide his surprise at the idea of women being archers. "You cannot be serious. You expect women to fight?"

"Look, Squire, we have maybe one hundred men who could fight. That is not enough to chase a small Viking scouting squad. We must find new and different methods to protect Northdale. One hundred women archers could make quite a statement."

With an incredulous face, Squire said, "You still plan to make a stand-up fight?"

Rupert dropped his quill with some force as he stared at Squire. "I don't think these people should spend the rest of their days scrambling from invaders. I don't know the correct strategy, but something must be done. We will have to experiment until we find the right one."

Squire sat back in his chair with his mouth open.

"We've talked about this before and my decision is final. And don't go running to Father William. If you go in screaming, he will come out condemning."

That comment did bring a controlled smile to Squire's face.

Next Challenge

Rupert enjoyed the ride to Lincolnwood. Several of the nobles along the route, experienced with the history of Northdale's governance, asked if Rupert planned to quit so quickly. After ten days, he arrived at Lincolnwood. He sensed immediately that somehow he had changed. He understood the place was now his former home.

Cuthbert and Elizabeth were delighted to see him. Mary ran into his arms. Humphrey shook arms, and Philippa remained pleasant in a courtly, prescribed manner. Their new son, John, looked very healthy.

Mary told him that several aunts, uncles, and distant cousins were to join the Christmas festivities. The number of family members guaranteed a large and jolly party. The banquets matched those in the past. Rupert sat at a low-prestige position, but as an appointed sheriff, at a position higher than his former entry-level knight's seat. He told his parents that the wine's quality exceeded his memory and tasted much better than anything available in his district. He made sure to drink his fill.

One of the most interesting conversations occurred when the men drank port after dinner. Rupert began to explain the Norseman invasions and asked for suggestions. Even Humphrey, with his limited military experience, participated in the almost two-hour exchange of ideas. The conversation did not produce any final answers, but generated interesting alternatives. One unanimously expressed opinion stood out—women could not be archers.

An interesting spinoff of the military conversation occurred two days later. The whole castle not only knew of his woman-archer idea, but found it humorous. At breakfast, one of the distant female cousins mentioned a noble's daughter named Sara who was reported to be a huntress of some renown. In fact, many people called her mad because of her horse riding and hunting skills. Rupert stopped eating during the description.

Later, he asked his father about this Sara. "Her father, Roland, is an old fighting comrade. We shared a tent during several of the king's campaigns. I've heard rumors about his mad daughter, but I don't put stock in gossip. You know how everyone exaggerates any exceptions to the normal rules."

"Do you think she might be happy in Northdale?"

Cuthbert was sitting at his desk. He crossed his arms and gave his son an intense gaze. "You interested in finding a wife?"

"Father, only a special woman could survive up there. Many hardships exist. No courtly lady could tolerate it."

"Well, Rupert, sitting in this room will not answer your question. It's a five-day ride to Shepardland, and I will write an introduction letter for you."

Some English Januarys are almost livable. Rupert made the journey in five days. His first impression of Shepardland's castle was of decline. Maintenance had clearly been forgone. Its courtyard contained a fire woodpile whose cutters had been extremely slovenly in stacking. A wagon leaned against a wall to prevent its falling over because of a missing wheel. All of the exposed door wood needed painting, and two of the three hitching rails had fallen down. No recognition or challenge occurred when he rode in.

After getting off his horse and tying it to the one standing hitching rail, a servant girl walked out a side door. "Girl, step over here." She hesitantly did so. "Please inform the earl that Sir Rupert, son of Cuthbert of Lincolnwood and Sheriff of Northdale, seeks an audience with him."

The girl looked surprised and questioning at the same time. She nodded her head and, without speaking, went toward a different door. While waiting, Rupert continued to evaluate the castle's status.

Hearing footsteps, he turned and saw a young woman with a smile approach.

"A sheriff, or should I say, one of the king's lackeys. I mean, your official position is to carry out the king's directives."

She wore a dark brown, leather dress that showed considerable wear and dirt. A few strands of black, wavy hair escaped some sort of yellow cloth hat. Her twinkling eyes were blue, and she stood straight with her hands on her hips.

With his hand on his saddle, Rupert turned and made a disbelieving face. "Be careful. A sheriff holds king's authority to hand out punishments."

"Like cutting off my head?"

Rupert now crossed his hands at his waist and leaned back against his horse. "In your case, it would be cutting off your tongue." He smiled and turned to his horse and began to loosen the cinch strap. While doing so he said in Latin, "I don't want to continue to talk to a horse mother."

The girl looked surprised and responded in Latin, "Better to be the mother of a horse than the ass who rides on one!"

"Girl, I do not come to spar with the likes of you. Please tell the earl I'm here."

In French she responded, "You would get severely hurt by sparring with me."

The humor was gone when he led his horse by the reins to the girl. "Please take the horse to your stable and feed him." He handed her the reins.

She took the reins and said, "This animal looks like a fine war horse. Obviously, it is too good for you." She dropped the reins.

Sword training had given Rupert quick, physical reflexes. He grabbed the girl's collar, turned her around, and picked her up by grasping her ass. She let out a scream and started to flail with her arms and legs. He took the blows to the body and ducked his head out of danger. The nearby horse-watering trough received her body with a splash.

Sara jumped to a standing position and yelled, "You son of an alehouse whore!"

Rupert, with a big smile, said, "No. My mother is a charming and well-mannered lady. This place is small, so I bet the earl now knows I'm here." He led his horse back to the hitching rail and then walked to the castle's main door. As he walked, he heard words to the effect of "shit head" and "pompous asshole" along with several local variations. He did not see the servant girl who ran to the trough to give the woman assistance.

Earl Roland had arrived at the main door just as the splash occurred. He did not look pleased, and Rupert did not know at whom the displeasure was directed.

"My lord, I am Cuthbert's son, Sir Rupert, the sheriff of Northdale."

Roland's face lit up, "My old friend Cuthbert's son. Welcome, welcome. Please come in and take some wine." He raised his hand and pointed to the interior. As they walked, he turned to look at the wet woman. Without letting Rupert see it, Roland 's furious frown clearly transmitted his displeasure with her.

The earl's study contained one table. All its walls supported eight-foot-tall, crammed bookshelves. A large south-facing window provided ample light. Generations of artifacts sat atop the highest shelves.

Affably, Roland filled him in on his family's history, local politics, and estate management. Rupert did the same.

"Tonight, at banquet, I will ask you to tell us the reason for your visit. My family loves to be involved with visitors and hear news from other locations."

"Thank you, my lord. May I ask for care for my horse? I seemed to have trouble obtaining it this afternoon."

Roland cleared his throat as he stood up. "Yes, yes, sorry about that. No doubt a misunderstanding. Your horse will be tended."

As a servant woman showed him to his quarters, he asked, "Is there a servant woman here who speaks Latin?"

"If you mean that silly language priests speak, only Lady Sara speaks it." When the lady closed the door, Rupert said aloud, "Oh shit." He decided to respond to Sara at tonight's formal introduction in the manner that reflected how she'd treated him.

Answering a knock at his door, Rupert opened it to see a very large man standing there. He was last least five inches taller and wider than the sheriff and his muscle structure told of great strength. A mop of black hair covered his head, and it matched a closely cropped beard. His brown eyes did not waver from whatever he looked at and his expression was all business. He carried no weapon.

"Excuse me, sir. I'm Oloff and I would like to speak with you about Lady Sara." Although surprised, Roland stood back from the door and waved his hand into the room.

"I don't ever talk to you nobles, but I think you must know that the earl assigned me to guard Lady Sara when she was only ten years old. She acted wild, so he wanted me to keep her from getting hurt or letting anyone hurt her. I have been watching her every day for the last fourteen years."

Rupert shook his head. "From my short introduction to her, that must have kept you very busy."

Oloff did not show any humor. "I must tell you that I am trained on most common weapons. However, battle-ax is my specialty. You should know that before I tell you if I had been in the courtyard today, I would have stopped you from throwing Lady Sara in the trough."

At first, Rupert squinted at Oloff; he did not answer for a moment. Then with a very slight smile, he responded. "Well, next time I will be sure to watch for you before I throw her into the water." Oloff did not move or take his direct stare off Rupert. "Tell me, Oloff, will you stop her from saying insulting things?"

Without breaking his direct stare, Oloff slightly nodded his head. "She says things that should be left alone, but I can tell you her heart is good—very good."

"Then let me tell you something, Oloff. I am fairly familiar with weapons and their use." He gave Oloff an intent look to transmit the message. "However, I have absolutely no intension of harming her in any way. Quite the opposite, in fact. But her mouth needed a little cooling off today."

"Sir Sheriff, I hope you never feel the need to do that again." He turned and walked to the door. Without any facial change, Oloff said, "Good evening."

At the banquet, Rupert's rank entitled him to sit at the main table; that caused him an internal smile. He sat with Roland, Osburth, Matilda, and the castle's head knight. In addition, one empty chair existed. After sitting and introductions, Rupert asked, "I heard you have a daughter named Sara. Is she to attend?" With the exception of Roland, people sitting at the table snickered.

Matilda, with a smile, said, "She had a problem this afternoon, and her hair is still wet." Even Roland joined the table members' restrained laughter.

After a round of wine and the first course of soup, Sara walked in wearing a bright green formal dress. Courtly manners required every male below the rank of earl to stand; Rupert and the other knight did so. Roland said, "Sir Rupert, I believe you have already met my daughter, Sara."

He took a moment to evaluate her attitude then he made the correct slight bow and said, "I'm pleased to meet you, Lady Sara."

She ignored him as she walked to her chair. Then, just before sitting with an almost-dismissive side-glance, she said, "And I you, Sheriff." Rupert could not help noticing that she cleaned up very nicely into courtly ladyship. Oloff quietly entered and stood against the far wall.

Roland started the conversation by relating the wars Cuthbert and he had endured. He described some of the funny things that always occur in a military campaign and some of the things the two instigated. Osburth and Matilda described their day's activities and interesting local news. Sara said nothing.

"Now, Sir Rupert, please tell us of the cause of your visit." Everyone, even Sara, directed his or her eyes at him.

In a small, isolated society outside news provided a very welcome break from the normal local chitchat. Rupert began by describing his appointment as sheriff and Northdale itself. Without dwelling on the bleakness, he offered to bring its list of goals to the next night's dinner. He then warmly described its people and their struggle to restore hope. Last, he explained how the place's physical beauty could not be ignored. He looked forward to returning and seeing sunsets over the ocean and how daytime sunshine created sparkles in Mary's Sorrows Falls.

The earl asked, "How do you plan to defend the place?"

"That brings me to the reason I visited you. You see, Northdale does not have a very large population, and the Vikings bring more men to attack than I have to defend. One tactic will be to teach the women how to become effective archers." That comment caused considerable pause. Sara actually dropped her food-cutting knife.

The knight was first to comment. "You mean you want to arm women?"

"I do not have a choice. It will take about one hundred men trained in sword and battle-axe and another fifty to one hundred archers to mount sufficient resistance to encourage the Norsemen to seek easier targets. If we don't, then the invaders will continue to trample any efforts I make to improve my people's lives."

Rupert turned directly to Sara. "I've heard that you are an accomplished archer. I would like to see you in action and discuss how I can train my local women." That sentence contained enough subject material to require everyone to spend at least a minute to absorb it.

Sara looked pleased when she put her elbows on the table. "I saw your horse, and it can keep up with mine, so I will be glad to take you shooting. Afterward, if you are still interested, we can talk."

Matilda found the subject to be almost humorous. Osburth was perturbed. Roland let out a small breath. He would later tell his wife in private, "At least she did not challenge him to a duel."

"Tomorrow at dawn we will hunt deer."

Rupert raised his glass. "Just wake me up."

A light breakfast awaited him when he got to the main hall. Sara said, "We eat a light meal so as not to be slowed by a full stomach."

Rupert smiled. "As a soldier and squire, I became accustomed to moving on an empty stomach. Where are we going?"

"If your horse is vigorous enough, my forester saw a herd of deer about two miles from here." She had not smiled yet.

The stable servants had saddled the horses, and Sara, Rupert, two of the castle's knights, the forester, Oloff, and two servants mounted and began the chase. They rode the two miles before Sara stopped and dismounted.

"The deer will hear us coming, so we must move quietly." Everyone walked carefully for about a half an hour, before Sara said, "We will return to the horses. I don't think we surprised any game."

When mounted, they began to ride deeper into the forest. Suddenly, the forester whispered, "Lady Sara!" He was pointing. Two deer could be seen walking across an open glen in the forest. Without a moment's hesitation, Sara spurred her horse and charged the deer. While they ran, she put the reins on the horse's neck, held the bow with her left hand, and notched an arrow with her right. Rupert and the others followed her. Just as the deer reached the forest's edge, Sara stood in her stirrups and shot an arrow. It hit a tree branch and bounced wide of the target. Rupert, being the closest to Sara, heard her exclaim, "Damn!"

The group looked around for more deer, but none could be found. Sara rode up to Rupert. "Well, the horses cannot chase into wild forest, so we must quit for today."

"Lady Sara, it may have been a miss, but it was marvelous seeing how you attempted it."

She gave him a truly pleased smile. "We can try on foot tomorrow."

The next day, they started even earlier in order to be near the deer tracks at early dawn. A servant held their horses as Sara, Rupert, and Oloff snuck into the woods. Rupert carried a bow, Oloff a battle-axe. After they had selected an advantageous blind, Sara whispered, "The only problem occurs if a wolf pack finds us first." With his face showing agreement, Rupert nodded.

After sitting until two hours past full sunrise, Sara said aloud, "Not today, Sheriff. Maybe we need some of your prisoners to chase them to us."

With a pleasant smile, Rupert said, "I don't have a jail." Sara responded with a pleased look.

As they walked back toward the horses, Sara suddenly stopped. "This is not good; notch an arrow." Rupert looked around and could see nothing. Sara hissed, "Wolves!" Oloff took the ax from its shoulder strap and crouched.

Most people considered forests to be dangerous places. The word *evil* often became attached to *forest*. Many things could befall a traveler, but wolf packs were not only common but also very dangerous. When given the opportunity to catch a meal, the hungry animals became very persistent hunters.

Sara pulled out three arrows, stuck them into the ground, and notched another. Rupert, still not seeing any animals, put one into the ground and notched one. She pointed with the tip of her bow in a circle motion; the pack had surrounded them.

Sara's first two shots sent animals screaming. Rupert's first missed, and the second hit. The persistent pack circled them and moved in again. Sara shot two more, and Rupert missed again. He took out his sword and Sara continued to shoot. Two animals got close enough for Rupert to dispatch them. The beasts also seemed to misjudge the length of Oloff's battle-axe. The weapon claimed several more wolves. Sara's accuracy executed three more. The pack retreated.

She quietly, but very firmly said, "No time to retrieve arrows—let's move!" Rupert did not need coaxing.

When they found their horses, all three needed to catch their breath. The servant looked very relieved to see them. Sara said, "The pack will not venture into open fields, usually."

With his eyebrows up, Rupert said, "Usually?"

Looking Rupert in the eye, she replied. "Only when they smell really good meat. I think we should ride."

They stopped for a midday meal of wine and cold meat. While sitting, Rupert said, "Sara, that was incredible, you really can shoot."

She looked at him, "Thank you, but I must warn you that swords are usually too short to be effective against wolves.

Oloff's ax proves effective, so maybe you should learn to use another weapon."

"Battle-ax, I have no interest. But that brings me to the main question: how can I teach my women to shoot like you do?"

Sara leaned against the tree under which they were sitting. "Bring me up there." She let out a strong laugh, and Rupert followed with a little less enthusiasm. She then began a discussion of how to teach women to be archers. The conversation became long and entangled in details like the size of the bow and adjusting the force required to pull it. The servant asked, after an hour, "Cannot we go?"

At dinner that night, the adventure with the wolves provided another interesting break from the typical dinner conversation. Rupert's comment registered with the group. "Sara prevented the wolves from making a meal of me."

After the next breakfast, the two sat at the table and renewed the archery subject. This time, Rupert started to take notes, in English. Having only one sheet of paper, he filled both sides to their edges. He finished the archery discussion by commenting, "You have convinced me that Northdale women can become effective archers."

Sara responded. "Women are quite capable with training and practice. You could still use someone like me to lead them." Rupert nodded then filled his cup with ale.

"What is on this list you keep mentioning?" Rupert had just happened to place it in his pouch that morning and pulled it out. While explaining each one of the goals, what caused them, and what steps were necessary to accomplish them, he did not notice Sara's fascination.

The next morning, Matilda spent time with Rupert talking about her interests. She seemed very involved with the feminine side of the castle's life and was strongly in favor of supporting the church's efforts to control theological thinking.

After two hours, Sara stopped by and offered him the chance to try shooting again. With all polite apologies to Matilda, he jumped at the chance.

That afternoon, he sought out Roland. "I have one more piece of business to discuss with you."

Roland waved his hand. "At dinner, my boy, the whole family is involved with anything that impacts Shepardland's life."

Rupert attempted to disagree, but the earl insisted on drinking some wine and exploring Rupert's views on jousting. He only veiled his disappointment when the latter explained his distaste for the sport.

Many Changes

In about the middle of dinner, Roland said, "Sir Rupert has some business he wishes to discuss. Proceed."

Rupert had been unusually quiet up to this point. He put down his knife and looked at the earl. "Your Lordship, I must return to my district by early spring, so I do not have time to take all the typical steps." His throat went a little dry, so he took a sip of wine. "I need to find a wife."

The room buzzed with comments. Both sisters sat frozen.

"I would like to marry Lady Sara, and request your permission."

Matilda put her hand over her mouth. Osbruth let a very small smile cross her lips, and Sara stood up and immediately rushed out of the room. Everyone remained speechless.

After taking another sip, Rupert continued. "Your Lordship, I have a very limited amount to offer. I am the crown-appointed sheriff, but my district is very poor. If I succeed there, the king might move me to more lucrative places, or he may just let me stay in Northdale. My father's estate will go to my brother, so I will never become an earl like you. Being a knight and sheriff may be the sum of my advancement. And more, I happen to like my people and want very much to help them for a long time."

Roland looked at Osbruth. "We will talk on this tomorrow."

Rupert asked to be excused, and it was granted. As he got to the door, he could hear the conversations immediately address marriage.

Once in the corridor, he saw Oloff. He walked right up to him. "Oloff, when Sara needs to sit and think, does she have a special place?"

Oloff stopped and looked long at Rupert; an evaluation obviously took place. His face still transmitted a business approach. "If you go into the south garden and walk to the farthest wall, you will find a cluster of benches." He waved his arm in the correct direction.

She was sitting on one of the benches, and she turned when Rupert approached. Her face was not mad or happy, just neutral. "How did you find me?"

"A voice told me you like to think out here. Sara, I did not want to say those things in public, but you know that I must ask your father first, and he insists on taking all subjects to the whole family."

"You are different than the others who came sniffing after my inheritance. You seem to think that I must leave here and undertake an adventure in an uncivilized place. Is that the sum of it?"

Rupert opened his mouth, then stopped, and nodded his head.

Sara looked up at the stars. She said nothing.

"Sara, you are a fascinating woman. I am sure we would enjoy each other. And more important, I think you are the type of person who will see Northdale's difficulties as a challenge. It will be tough, and not at all courtly. Even the church assigned an old fool as priest, and when he moves on, there is little chance of replacement. But it is a wonderful place with people who need our leadership. And one last thing to consider: castle life is boring. Northdale will actually be fun—very fun.

"I should add some facts about me that may make a difference in your decision. I'm not a courtly lord. I don't joust or strut about in fancy clothes. I work with the peasants and actually fought once beside them. I treat them as people. If you want an ordinary nobleman to marry, then I am not the right person."

"You experience resembles mine. After my brother died, my playmates were the children of the castle's staff. We had fun for several years and I often would play at one of their residences. The differences between our respective family status came after I had eaten a number of meals at my friend's house. Her mother asked my father for a food contribution to cover my expense. An explosion occurred—he was furious. From then on, the other children could only play with me in the castle. He kicked the woman, her husband, and, my friend out of Shepardland."

Rupert added, "You cannot make a lord mad."

"Oh no, I make some nobles mad all the time and don't care. But when my friend's family left I was really upset. But as I grew older and reflected more on the incident, I became aware of the luxury we nobles held when compared with the plain folk. They work hard, but with very few luxuries and sometimes little food. That is why I treat the commoners with respect. I know how their efforts make Shepardland succeed. My receptivity to the people causes my father to smile, but upsets Osburth. Of course, that is not all bad." She laughed.

Sara took a deep breath, looked at the stars, and then turned to him. "Please leave me alone. I have much to consider. But you should know, I'm impressed that you asked." She retuned her gaze to the stars.

Rupert stood up and slowly walked away. He got near the entrance to the garden and almost bumped into Oloff. They looked at each other, and Rupert nodded to him. Oloff returned the gesture.

In the morning, she found her father taking a walk near the garden. Sara pointed at a bench and said, "We must talk, alone."

He smiled at her, and they walked into the garden.

"Father, I'm confused. I actually think Northdale sounds interesting. But it means I give up everything I'm used to, and I will give up my ability to choose whether or not to act more ladylike."

"What about the young sheriff?"

"I told him last night that he was not like all the others who were sniffing around my inheritance and basically holding their noses when it came to me. He seems to like me for who I am and does not care about my inheritance. He even seems to like the things about me that make others think I'm mad."

"I know his father is a fine man. Often that characteristic passes to sons, but not always. In this case, I sense it has."

She looked down at the ground. "I think I could really like him."

They stopped at some benches, and he sat down. "Let's get the hard part over. If you marry him and move to Northdale, it means that you will give up any claim on Shepardland. If you did not marry, I might have been able to divide it between you and your sister, but that takes law bending and there is no certainty it could occur, especially if objections arise."

"No objections? I bet a bunch of people, including the bishop, would object to me getting any land."

Roland slapped her knee. "Sara, you are correct. If you choose to go, then Matilda will become a prime marriage target, and Osbruth would be made happy."

Sara crinkled up her face. "I'll be glad for my stepmother."

He turned now to Sara and took one of her hands. "Daughter, what is important? I want you to be happy after

I'm gone. I don't know if Rupert will give you luxury, but I suspect he will try very hard to make you happy. A difficult tradeoff: pick a disagreeable husband, but gain a steady income; or an unknown future with someone who makes you happy. If you leave here, I will try to give you some income, but once I'm gone, whoever controls this place will no doubt stop it. But on the positive side, you might just not care."

Sara leaned over and gave her father a hug. "Thank you. I need to walk a bit." She moved away. Roland smiled.

At breakfast she saw Rupert. Because no one was in hearing distance, she asked. "Why so fast?"

"The church banns take three weeks. I must begin the return journey then."

Sara waved good-bye and left without other words. She mounted her horse and, with Oloff, rode off.

Castle residents pretty much stayed away from the sheriff the rest of the day. He rode some and spent a number of hours in the castle's good library.

At dinner that night, Sara arrived late. She sat and concentrated on her meal. She did nod to Rupert when she came in, but that was all. Everyone focused the conversation deliberately on small talk.

Just before the meal ended, Sara rose. "Listen, everyone, you should all hear this." She then turned and faced the sheriff. "Sir Rupert, I am glad to accept your proposal of marriage. We will post the banns this Sunday."

It would be hard to catalogue the numerous, different reactions to this announcement. Sara simply walked out of the room. Rupert made a controlled smile.

The next three weeks simply spun with activity. When the bishop heard, he insisted on performing the ceremony himself. He wanted the deal to rid himself of Sara sealed tight. Osbruth, after dashing off a message to her sister, dove into preparations that included the banquet, the guest list, and the intricate protocol of seating order. Matilda just seemed to have fun. Roland appeared increasingly pleased.

The more the engaged couple discussed Northdale, the more they became immersed in its requirements. The pending gifts generated the thinking. Sara announced that, instead of frills, she wanted practical items that would assist in the district's development. She asked for books, cooking utensils, and even farming equipment. She confronted her stepmother and insisted on receiving bolts of sturdy cloth instead of numerous courtly dresses and other fancy clothes.

Rupert, Sara, and Roland along with the senior knights held a meeting on weapons. Northdale did not own enough. The experienced knights strongly suggested that the shorter swords, then considered very old fashioned, be given. The practical reason concerned the years a person needed to master one of the currently popular long swords. The armory could provide twenty short swords, and Rupert readily agreed. As for shields, the older, full rectangle ones, descendants of the Roman era, provided less flexibility, but created a good blocking wall. Chain mail's cost proved too expensive for most military units, so none would be provided.

Other raw materials discussed included leather and metal. Northdale had no source of metal, except imported items. As odd as several people noted, the bottom layer of material in the wagons going to Northdale would be scrap iron. The district could only tan a very small amount of leather, so it was requested as a gift. Wedding guests were asked to scour the countryside for fabricated metal products, such as hinges and construction brackets.

Northdale needed men—not enough lived there to accomplish much in terms of development and industry. Rupert asked the earl if he could recruit men to emigrate. The earl said, "Well, second and third sons face military service, the rare chance to marry into some land, or poverty. I think some might accept a chance to obtain their own land."

Six men volunteered. However, when screened for alcohol consumption, only four passed inspection. They would function as the teamsters for two wagons.

Oloff requested a meeting with the earl. "My lord, as you know I've watched over Sara for almost fourteen years. It would be very hard for me to see her leave. She is your daughter, but if you are not insulted, also mine."

Roland stood up. "You will leave everything you now know. I don't think Lady Sara will come back here." Oloff nodded his head. The earl walked around his desk up to Oloff and put his hands on his shoulders. "I would be grateful if you continued to watch over her."

Departure of one heir required a settlement of the estate. Roland asked to meet Sara, alone. The earl explained that Matilda's future husband, whoever he was, would inherit the estate. He would probably be raised to rank of baron, thus Matilda would remain in the nobility.

Being the wife of a knight entitled her to be addressed as "Lady," but she would not be considered nobility. She would always, when attending formal banquets, have to sit below her own sister.

"Father, there are many to which I would object, but I love Matilda and I would never mind sitting below her. Besides, I must have someone to throw food at." He laughed.

Finally, he would give her a cash settlement of one hundred gold crowns and each year would send her another ten. After he died, Matilda's husband would make the cash distribution, if any. He would give her two wagons and the horses to pull them and her favorite hunting horse. The wagons would be filled to capacity with the requested materials for a dowry.

Roland gave his daughter a loving, fatherly look. "Sara, you know I love you dearly, but this separation settlement is all that I can afford."

Roland stood up and walked around to her. She stood and they hugged. "Father, you have given me more things that are far more valuable than objects. You let me be myself and supported my unusual habits. Your love has been demonstrated in numerous ways, and although you are going to give me a handsome dowry, it will never compare with your love."

He then reached under some papers on the table and pulled out a sheathed sword. It was medium sized. An intricate, gold latticework decorated the leather sheath, and the hilt was gold. "This was given to me by my father when I was young and not quite big enough to use one of the long swords. I think you should have it." He smiled. "I don't think Matilda will have use for it."

Crying, Sara gave her father another very tight hug. She then strapped on the sword and walked out.

Rupert sat eating when Sara and Roland strolled up. When he saw a strapped on sword, he rose. "A sword?"

With a large smile, she replied, "If you ever again get ideas about a water trough, you better reconsider." They all laughed out loud.

Four days before the wedding, Sara and the sheriff went riding. They returned late and put the horses in the stable before dinner. After the evening meal, both went out to the stable to curry their horses. The two animals stood next to each other, and Sara and Rupert discussed many items as they brushed the far side of the animals. They simultaneously walked in between them. Due to the horse's closeness, Sara and Rupert inevitably pressed against each other. Rupert dropped his curry brush, turned around, put his hands on Sara's hips, and spun her around. He kissed her, and without any hesitation, she kissed back. One of the stable hands had earlier that day spread fresh straw. Sara and Rupert found it to be perfect bedding on which to loose their passion.

That evening, one stable hand came to make a nightly check. Oloff stepped out of the dark and informed the person that the sheriff and Lady Sara did not want their animal care disturbed. When the two lovers finally left the stable, Oloff stood unobserved in the dark with a big smile on his face. No one in the castle thought anything unusual about Sara caring for her horse or talking to another about the subject. She and Rupert found reasons to discuss animal care on the next two nights.

Osburth clearly wanted the wedding to be a grand statement of Sara's departure. She had acquired a dress appropriate for a royal court dance or wedding. She planned to give it to Matilda, but the opportunity to marry off Sara inspired her to ignore Sara's request to avoid frills. It was blue and trimmed with red ribbons and a yellow sash. Sara relinquished all objections because she really liked the dress.

However, due to the short three-week notice and the existing practical travel restrictions, the number of attendees remained small. All who came enjoyed an excessive banquet and thoroughly fun dance. The bishop could not help smiling all the way through the marriage ceremony held in the castle's chapel. Before the event, Sara told everyone she just wanted to have fun. She did. The wine she and Rupert consumed caused them both to sleep soundly through their wedding night.

It took a week to pack the wagons, and organize the horses. On Monday, departure day, Matilda and Sara cried. Osburth teared-up, as did Roland. The four men's families also participated in a difficult family separation. Rupert could not wait to start, and by mid-morning the wagon train left.

At first, getting the horses to work together caused some delays. They made only about ten miles. The wedding dowry included a tent, but because this February produced mild weather, the party slept under the stars. With smooth roads, they traveled twenty-five miles the next day.

On the third day, a young man stood on the road. "I would also like to go to Northdale." He explained he was the Shepardland candlemaker's second son. Sara knew his father. When asked the reason for not leaving with the train, he turned to the nearby bushes and made a come-here motion with his hand. A young woman stepped out.

"Her father sold Agnes to a Denton merchant, but she did not want to be forced to marry the man. She wishes to marry me. I followed her there, and we escaped before the marriage took place."

Rupert and Sara looked at each other. The facts presented several real moral conflicts. Sara looked at the girl. "Your father sold you?"

"Yes, Lady Sara, for a horse and wagon."

Sara twisted in the seat to face Rupert. "Well, my Lord Sheriff, is slavery allowed under the laws of the church?" He shook his head. "Has the young man stolen something of value?" He shook his head. Sara took a quick look at the two and them back at the sheriff. "Does the sheriff have jurisdiction in the county of Denton?"

Rupert asked, "How far does Denton extend?"

The young man said, "The border is the Sax River, almost a day's ride."

"Are you being hunted?"

"I'm sure the merchant knows she is missing, so we could be."

Rupert looked at Sara, scratched his head, "I have no jurisdiction there or the responsibility to enforce rules." He then turned to Oloff. "Can you find a place for them under the tarp? And you two keep completely quiet if anyone comes along." Sara reached over and gave Rupert's arm a warm squeeze.

About an hour later, four armed men approached on horseback. The leader stepped his horse closer to the wagons. His horse, armor, and embroidered tunic clearly indicated nobility. In addition, he oozed cocky, noble self-confidence from his facial expression and body language. Using a commanding voice, he said, "We are searching for a thief."

Rupert dropped the reins and looked around at his party. "You see us and you do not see a thief."

"Well, fellow, I will search your wagons."

Rupert stood and, using his commanding voice, said, "To whom am I talking?" The tone and look on Rupert's face made the man turn his horse in a circle.

"I am Sir Gismore, son of the earl of Denton, and who might you be?"

"Sir Rupert, Sheriff of Northdale, and the wagons contain my wife's dowry." With an absolutely flat, business-like voice, Rupert stated, "They are not to be searched."

Oloff, riding the warhorse, came alongside Rupert.

Gismore turned his horse around again, and with a sneering facial expression and voice, he said. "I heard about your marriage to Mad Sara."

Rupert put a restraining arm across Oloff's waist. He then bent over and picked up his sword from the wagon's floor. "Sir Gismore, I will let your first insult pass, but you will now make a proper address to my wife."

The earl's son seemed to be taken aback; he almost never heard such defiance. He looked at Rupert and then at Oloff as he slid his battle-ax out of its sheath that hung on his saddle.

Rupert continued. "Or, Sir Knight, you will die today on this spot."

The other four Shepardland men stood on the ground near their wagon. They all held swords. Rupert had shown them how to stand in a ready-to-fight crouch. He had told them they would not actually sword fight until he taught them how, but he wanted any trouble makers to be fooled by a threat of readiness.

Gismore looked back at the four men and turned his horse around again; he clearly was evaluating each side's strength.

Rupert looked past the knight and addressed his three men-at-arms. "You three have not made any insult, so you can choose to live or die here." Sara now stood with her sword, unsheathed.

The knight shot a quick glance at his men, who did not look happy, and then he faced Sara. His faced clearly showed disgust while with a sugar-smooth voice, he said, "Good morning, Lady Sara." Gismore dragged out the pronunciation of each word to thinly disguise his anger at being forced to be polite. He then made the correct courtly bow for a mounted man.

Sara made the correct return bow and said with a pleasing voice that transmitted graciousness. "Sir Gismore, I am so pleased to meet you."

He then rode his horse to Sara's side of the wagon. He saw Rupert pull his sword slightly out of its sheath. With a complete lack of warmth, Gismore asked, "Will you be long in Denton?"

With her charming smile, Sara responded. "Your land is quite beautiful, but we must push on to reach Northdale. But thank you for the kind invitation."

The knight's face showed considerable anger when he looked back at Rupert. Then he jerked his arm in a follow-me gesture for his men and galloped down the road. Oloff slid his ax back into its sheath, and Sara did the same with her sword.

Rupert yelled, "Let's put on some speed, I want to cross the Sax River and be out of Denton before tonight." He sat down and leaned backward over the seat and patted the tarp. "You two did very well keeping quiet." After taking up the reins, Rupert said, "Our next encounter with that bastard might not end so well."

They pushed on and camped about a mile past the river. Sitting around the campfire after eating, Sara looked at her husband. "Would you have killed him?"

"No, Sara, I would not have had to. I believe Oloff already planned to split the knave in two." Sara looked at her protector, and he, with a tight smile, nodded his head.

Lincolnwood

After several nights of camping, Rupert guessed that Sara would like a clean place to sleep. They, therefore, began to exercise his status as a king-appointed sheriff. The hosts always extended hospitality and welcomed interesting conversation topics. Sara's reputation attracted an audience anyplace they stopped. While on the road, she wore common-folk clothes with the exception of the sword. Once given a chance to clean up, she would appear at banquet wearing one of her nice day-to-day courtly dresses without benefit of the sword. When asked about it, she would always tell listeners that it was "for killing vermin."

When they crossed Lincolnwood's border, Rupert ordered one of the men to ride ahead on Sara's horse and announce their pending arrival. The news triggered a flurry of activity, and both Cuthbert and Elizabeth awaited when the travelers pulled into the courtyard.

Sara told Rupert, based on his own description of his family, that no purpose existed in pretending to be a courtly lady. It simply did not match her true behavior, and she would inevitably miss the mark. So she decided to just be herself. She saw no reason to change her traveling clothes or to hide the sword.

Rupert's father and mother had heard of the marriage and truly looked forward to meeting their son's spouse. Her physical appearance made a reserved first impression.

"Earl Cuthbert and Countess Elizabeth, may I present my wife, Lady Sara?" Custom dictated that the lower-ranking person made a proper bow, and Sara did.

"My lord and lady, thank you for inviting me into your home. And thank you for raising a wonderful son."

The last comment did not fit custom, but it brought Elizabeth forward, and she extended her hand to Sara. "Lady Sara, I've always wondered whom my son would marry, and I'm glad he chose you. May I introduce you to Lord Cuthbert, my husband?" Again the exchange of formal bows.

Cuthbert then walked over to Rupert and gave him a firm hug. He then ordered the stable hands to take the horses and wagons under care and to find accommodations and refreshments for the other party members. As they walked into the main door, Cuthbert noticed Oloff. "Who is this?"

With her pleasant smile, Sara explained. "My lord, this is Oloff. He has been my protector for over fourteen years. He stands near me at all times."

Cuthbert shot an inquiring look at Rupert, and he, with a smile, nodded his head in agreement. He also leaned over to his father and whispered in his ear, "But not in the bedroom."

After a small snack, the travelers were escorted to their quarters for a chance to rest and clean up before banquet. Oloff retired to the servants' lodgings.

Sara put on her wedding dress and the sword. At their apartment door, Rupert wrinkled his eyebrows. "My wife, the sword?"

Sara looked at him. "Would you rather I not? I don't know if any vermin exist here." Rupert just looked at her. "All right." She took it off.

Nearby neighbors had been invited, and they almost filled the hall. Sara and Rupert made the introductory rounds with smiles and very pleasant talk. When they came to Humphrey and Philippa, Rupert said, "Lady Sara, this is my brother, Sir Humphrey, and his wife, Lady Philippa. They will someday be the earl and countess of Lincolnwood."

With a big smile and no bow, Sara said, "Brother and sister, how nice to meet you. I have been very fortunate to marry your brother." The address broke all formal requirements. Humphrey stood stiffly, and Philippa actually took a small step backward.

After a moment to recover, Philippa, without a smile, said, "We are glad to meet you Lady Sara." Rupert extended his arm, and Humphrey grasped it.

Just before the dinner, Cuthbert made an announcement. "I know that seating arrangements normally take certain precedents, but I ask all of you to forgive me when I take my son and his new wife to the main table. I want to get to know them." Humphrey and Philippa exchanged sharp looks.

The banquet talk became dominated by Sara and Rupert's description of their brief courtship, Shepardland, and the trip. They left out the part about the young man and his woman, but they did relate the confrontation with Sir Gismore. It caused some laughter.

Cuthbert said, "I've never liked his father. Always one to be political rather than do things."

Sara silenced the room when she asked about the opportunity to hunt. She raised her eyebrows and looked around the table. "I don't know about Lincolnwood, but at home, I always try to enhance the table with fresh fare." Still there was no reply.

Rupert added, "Sara is an excellent hunter and archer. She once saved both Oloff, the man standing over against the wall, and me by killing ten wolves that mistakenly thought we were their next dinner." Again, the comment froze tongues.

Cuthbert cleared his throat. "I would be glad to try for some deer tomorrow, if you would be ready at dawn."

Sara leaned back in the chair and raised her glass. "Absolutely." And with a big smile, she added, "When offered the same opportunity in Shepardland, your son responded, 'Just wake me up'."

The general conversation began again, and the newlyweds participated when appropriate. Humphrey and Philippa restricted their participation. Sara and Elizabeth seemed to get quite involved.

When back in their apartment, Sara said, "You father and mother are charming; Humphrey and Philippa are a bit frosty."

Rupert climbed onto the bed. "They are very impressed with their future rank."

Smiling, Sara said, "Your rank suits me just fine," and then she jumped on him.

Lincolnwood's hunt differed in one main aspect from Shepardland's: Cuthbert ordered out some servants to beat the brush and chase deer toward the hunters. It still required considerable skill to bring down a deer, and Sara impressed them all. She made her fatal shot while standing in the stirrups of her moving horse. The fresh meat, shared by the main house and servants, justified the effort.

Rupert announced that due to the threat of late spring Norsemen attacks, he only had one week to visit. Elizabeth and Cuthbert arranged to spend considerable time with their new daughter-in law.

Two days before departure, Sara sought out Cuthbert in his study. After knocking to gain entrance, she said, "My lord, I have a small matter that needs attending."

Cuthbert looked up and with a smile. "Is the door closed?" Sara glanced at it then back at the earl and nodded her head. "Good, when we are alone can we drop the formal language. You can address me as Cuthbert."

Sara looked surprised. "You know the courtly manner traditions irritate me, but you remind me so much of my father, I would like to address you as such."

Cuthbert folded his fingers. "Agreed. Now what matter do you wish me to address?"

"Well, Father, you may have noticed a young man and woman in our party. Their marriage arrangement requires a little formalization. Do you have a priest who could perform the ceremony tomorrow?"

"My son, a sheriff, allowed a casual relationship?" He laughed out loud as did Sara. "I will arrange a marriage tomorrow, just after breakfast."

Sara found the two sitting in the visiting servants' quarters. "Mark and Agnes, you will be married tomorrow just after breakfast." Both looked surprised, and immediately stood up. "But, Lady Sara, we have nothing to support ourselves."

"Well, Sir Rupert believes Northdale holds opportunity for all. You will find something." She straightened up to a formal posture. "No questions, I cannot have you flaunting the church when I enter Northdale."

The wedding turned out to be enjoyable. The servants hurriedly put together wedding presents and cooked a special little meal. The following dance became a departure party for the servants. Dancing did not fit well with Rupert, but Sara dragged him out, and to his surprise he enjoyed it. They never heard Philippa's negative comments about frolicking with servants. Sara and Rupert also gave the newlyweds one gold crown.

Rupert always became restless when facing a trip. He could barely sit still for the Mass and departure breakfast. Hugs and tears followed. Even Philippa seemed moved. After the departure, when walking back into the castle, Elizabeth put her arm through Cuthbert's arm. "I think he married the right lady." Cuthbert made a vigorous nod.

Several Lincolnwood couples and four single men asked to join Rupert and Sara's group, and so the wagon train now numbered four wagons. Even though the men did not yet know how to use their swords, Rupert, as before, had them all strap one on. The ladies declined, but Sara showed hers off at any chance.

Having had enough formal, courtly life, Sara insisted the group camp for the week it took to reach the Ibix. Manners required they stop at Hollingsbrook for one night because gentry neighbors needed to be introduced. It was dusk when the wagon train approached the Ibix River. Rupert insisted on sleeping in Northdale, so he ordered a slightly risky night river crossing.

The climb from the riverbed through the road cut into the cliff face took several hours, as horses from one wagon had to be attached to other wagons in order to provide additional pulling power. Once in a grassy campsite, Rupert could not hide his delight at being back in Northdale. His smile almost looked frozen in place.

The next morning, Sara's restlessness came to the fore. "Rupert, I want to take Oloff and ride ahead into the village.

I just want to get the feel of the place." Not knowing the interesting consequences and now knowing his wife's firm intentions, Rupert agreed to push on with the wagons and asked that Sara not scare anyone. She laughed, waved, and trotted off.

Sara's Introduction

Bright sun created a beautiful day. Sara donned more formal clothes to make a good, first impression. She and Oloff enjoyed the ride through the spring forest up to the small ridgeline that overlooked the village of Northdale. They dismounted and surveyed the scene. They could see cottages, gardens, farm fields, and the keep. Sara looked at Oloff. "Well, Rupert described the keep correctly. It looks nasty." They exchanged smiles and then mounted again.

As they approached the buildings, they clearly heard the noise of a crowd emanating from the center of the village. With a humorous look on her face, Sara said, "They know I'm coming and are celebrating!" They spurred their horses and galloped into the central square.

It was far from a reception party. A woman's arms had been tied to the top of a post in the middle of the square. She had been stripped above the waist, and the crowd counted out loud each whip stroke as it hit her back. The galloping horses caused the crowd to turn and look at the intruders. As Sara nosed her horse into the square's center, the whipping stopped, and the crowd actually stepped back. It obviously wondered about the nobly dressed woman, riding a horse, wearing a sword, and accompanied by a very large man who held a battle-ax.

Squire and Father William stood near the post. With a slightly angry voice, Sara asked, "What is going on here?"

Squire adjusted his shoulders and asked very firmly, "Who are you and what is your business?" At that moment, a small baby laying in a basket at the feet of the whipped woman started to cry. The woman also cried.

Sara's anger became mixed with astonishment. "I'm Lady Sara, wife of Sir Rupert, sheriff of Northdale, and you fellows have not answered my question. What is going on here?" She dismounted and handed the reins to Oloff.

The host of villagers now looked amazed. She walked directly to Squire. Confrontation crackled in the air. He stepped back again. "Punishment for having a baby out of wedlock!"

"You publicly flog a woman for that? On what authority?" She placed her hand on her sword.

Father William took a step forward. "It is God's will that she be punished. The church condones this action."

Sara drew her sword slightly out of its sheath and then pushed it back in. "I don't recall that Eve or Mary received a whipping." Father William's eye widened at this comment. She stepped near the post and walked around it. "What is the punishment?"

The priest held up his Bible. "Twenty strokes."

Sara walked around the post again. The woman's head was hanging down. "If law and tradition requires twenty strokes for not being married, that might be fitting. How many has she received?"

Squire responded, "Eleven."

Sara stood in front of the priest, "It is twenty, you say? Then the man should also receives twenty. Forty strokes seem high, does it not?" Squire and Father William shuffled their feet. Sara looked around at the crowd and asked, "Where is the father?"

Father William straightened himself. "The church held the trial, and the man testified to the woman causing him to succumb to sin."

Sara lost her restraint when she screamed. "What! I know breeding, and I know that it takes two to make a baby.

The guilty man testified against the woman. What absurdity is this?" She now pulled out her sword. The woman at the post looked up.

She pointed the sword at the priest. "Father, twenty strokes may be fair punishment for creating a baby out of wedlock as long as it is shared between the guilty parties. *Where is the man?*"

The crowd began buzzing at this statement. Father William spoke loudly. "That is not Northdale's or God's law. Women cause the sin." The crowd's muttering became much louder. Oloff dismounted with his battle-ax.

With a bright-red flush testifying to her emotion, Sara again yelled, "Bring the man here!" She pointed the tip of her sword at the ground in front of her.

The crowd began to smile and laugh. A corridor in the crowd opened, and it led to the alehouse door. Several men ran inside and with a bit of a scuffle dragged out the man. He continued to struggle until tossed at Sara's feet.

Sara raised both hands over her head. "If the woman got eleven so should the man!" The crowd began to cheer. She turned to Squire and pointed at the man and then at the post. Neither Squire nor Father William moved. She then looked at Oloff who walked next to the post. He pointed at three bystanders and the post. While they stood the guilty man up, he cut the woman's bindings. She fell into his arms.

Oloff carried the women a few feet from the post, took off his tunic, and wrapped her with it. When the three crowd members finished stringing up the man, Oloff yelled, "Baby." A woman of the crowd picked up the baby's basket and carried it to Oloff. He then tossed the whipped woman over his shoulder, took the basket under his other arm, and walked out to the edge of the crowd.

Sara pointed her sword at the man. "He gets eleven." Two men from the crowd grabbed for the whip. With a big smile, one of them delivered a stout eleven.

When it was finished, Sara walked over to the priest and again pointed her sword at him. "Father, never tell me again that a woman bears responsibility when two people engage in sex." She looked away from him as she sheathed her sword. Turning back to the priest, she pointed a finger. "Never. Do you hear? Never." The crowd cheered.

Rupert heard cheering as the wagon train approached the village's center. He turned to one of the teamsters and said, "Sara made a good impression."

The ruckus caused by Sara completely caught Rupert by surprise. It would be hard to describe the overlapping social concerns. The crowd liked what they had seen. They also wanted to welcome their sheriff and his impressive new wife. New immigrants had to be introduced and accommodations found. The wagons' contents needed to be stowed and dinner cooked. Squire and Father William stomped out of the square.

By the time Rupert and Sara entered the keep's main hall, Oloff had pulled a table into the middle of the room. On blankets, Eleanor lay face down while he cleaned her lash wounds.

Eleanor's head lay on the end of the table to which Rupert walked. "Eleanor, what happened?"

She rose up on her elbows and, without any apology, said, "Well, Sir Rupert, things happen and sometimes babies come."

Sara approached and pushed Rupert aside. "Can we do something for you?"

With a smile, Eleanor replied, "Thank you, Lady... uh, I did not catch your name. I just got whipped for having a child out of wedlock; so things must get better from here." She made a soft snicker.

With a stiff smile, Rupert's bride said, "I am Lady Sara, and you demonstrate much courage. Do you want to marry the father? I can arrange that instantly." She smiled at Rupert, and he nodded his head.

"Marry the bastard that testified against me? I could never do that to my daughter."

Oloff had finished applying strips of clean cloth to the whip marks and closed his tunic to cover her bare back. "Have no fear, Lady Sara, I will take care of this lady and her baby."

He rested his hand on the table as he spoke. Eleanor studied him for a moment and then reached over and gripped his arm with her hand. Although not known at the moment, it turned out to be a lifelong match. Oloff gave the guilty man a choice, leave Northdale immediately or die. He chose the former. Oloff would also announce that the baby, Ann, was to be considered his daughter, and he would meet any man who claimed differently. None ever did.

Settled Life

Life in Northdale settled into a fair routine. Rupert and Sara trained the people in fighting techniques, but it would take time to develop the necessary skills. Residents began to believe in the district and its sheriff. Community projects and a pride in Northdale grew. Farming improved, as did animal husbandry.

The military situation experienced a transformation. At first, Northdale followed past tactics: retreat, quickly, into the hills. The Vikings would land, seek treasure or slaves, burn a few buildings, and then leave. They acquired very few assets. With more trained archers and swordsmen, Northdale began to allow the sacking of the village, which had been stripped of any valuables, but Norsemen's forays into the hinterlands resulted in their deaths. The invaders would, of course, launch retaliation against the Northdale forces, but they could never find anyone to punish.

The ultimate disincentive came when some Northdale men and women learned how to swim. Tactics dictated feigning with an armed demonstration to attract Norsemen fighters. The standard Viking military thinking required chasing any opposition forces. Their troops would run after disappearing Northdale forces; meanwhile, its swimmers would set fire to the invaders' boat or boats and set some adrift by cutting mooring lines. These efforts made Northdale simply too big of a risk; a boat's value far exceeded any profit from raiding the place.

While some raids continued, trade with some Vikings chiefs began to rise. Sweyn and Estrid spread news of their agreement with Northdale; other chiefs began to perceive its appeal. In spring, they exchanged pelts for food and wine. In fall, the summer's successful raids provided gold for wine, food, provisions, and medical care. Because of the harbor's limited size, Northdale never accommodated large fleets. However, chiefs commanding single boats or small fleets found it reasonable and profitable.

Northdale, for its side of the trading enterprise, spent the winter and spring months preparing provisions for sale. It also opened trading partnerships with small, coastal boat captains. In exchange for the furs, they delivered wine before the Viking's fall return trips started.

The willingness of Northdale to care for sick Norsemen created a whole health-related service. When boats made return voyages in the fall, they stopped in Northdale to drop off injured men. For a realistic price, Northdale took the wounded men and nursed them to health by the time the boats returned in the spring. Rupert ordered the repair of the barn in which the original sick crew received attention. Every fall, between six and ten men were in the hospital, now called North House. Care of a wounded Norseman stopped fellow crew members from assaulting Northdale or its people.

Two interesting side effects occurred because of the North House. First, the recovering Vikings became restless, so Rupert established a fighting school. As promised, Sweyn brought fighting instructors every spring and took them home in the fall. The recovering men handled winter instruction. The Norsemen trained Northdale men in the arts of sword, battle-ax, and battle tactics. During the third year of North House operations, one of the Viking English translators, crippled by a fall from a scaling ladder, arrived. He declined the offered return trip and became, in effect, the head of all-male training.

In addition, the women's archer corps' skills reached a surprising level of military proficiency. Sara observed that the men needed to prepare fields just when the salmon ran. She once heard of a tribe that fished with arrows. She decided to utilize the annual salmon run to develop archery skills. Women were trained in the use of bow and arrows. Strings were attached to arrows and together proved effective in landing fish. The female archers developed skill at hitting moving targets.

Sara expanded the women's role. As the captain of the women archers, she established mandatory training. Women quickly learned the critical role they played in Northdale's defense. They also learned that underperformance or improper performance quickly earned Sara's public and humiliating rebuke. Girls entered the corps at ten years old and never left it. When called to participate in repelling invaders, the fishing skills delivered a fearsome toll on Norsemen from arrows fired by concealed markswomen. Archery generated new pride in the women.

Sara also caused a second social shift. One evening, while sitting on the bed with Rupert, she asked, "Do you remember the man named Robert whose bull killed him about eight months ago?" Rupert looked up and nodded. "Well, I met his very unhappy widow today." He continued to watch her, recognizing a stone block was about to fall. "The cause of her despondency is that, at twenty-eight years old, no available men exist. She will never have any children."

Rupert scratched his forehead. "Solution?"

"The men in the North House are men, and they are here. Why not take advantage?"

Rupert dropped both hands into his lap. "Are you suggesting that our unattached women make babies with the Vikings?"

"I prefer to describe it as making little Christians who would otherwise be fathered as little pagans in their homeland." Rupert just stared. "We could appoint any interested woman as an undernurse and let her so serve until she becomes pregnant or, if it becomes popular, rotate every month."

He stood up, walked across the room, and then turned. "You are suggesting fornication with pagans." Sara nodded her head. "How could the sheriff and his lady ever condone such things?"

With very pleasant smile, Sara said, "Just don't recognize that it happens. You appoint the nurses with a rule that they currently cannot have a child under three years old." Rupert shook his head as he walked to the edge of the bed. He wrinkled his brow as he looked at Sara.

"Besides, we would avoid any future incidents." Rupert raised his eyebrows in a question. "Warriors with renewed health will for sure someday grab an unwilling woman. It's bound to happen, and you know it. Rape is punishable by death, so you might face breaking all of the Viking treaties."

Rupert put his right hand on his forehead. "So blond-hair babies, creation of good Catholics, and international peace;

that's all on the table in exchange for possible theological condemnation."

"You grasp the concept." She laughed.

"Well, as lord of Northdale, I should be inspecting all ongoing activities. So that means I should inspect all of the ladies."

Sara jumped to her feet and, with both hands, pushed Rupert onto the bed. "Does this lord of Northdale know that I not only have a sword, but also know how to use it to cut meat?" They both roared with laughter.

She now stood at the bed's edge. "Think about all of the pleasure we would be encouraging."

With mock seriousness in his face, Rupert said, "Ah, Sara, what excitement are you talking about?"

Sara dropped the last of her outer garments on the floor and jumped on Rupert.

She kissed him. He put his arms around her and flipped her flat on the bed. After some spirited horizontal persuasion, a smiling Rupert said, "Yes, we should encourage pleasure."

After about five years, Viking raids completely stopped. Trade in wine, furs, and supplies along with healthcare became standard interactions with the Norsemen. The Vikings changed their trading transportation from the longboat filled with fighting men to the cargo ship called a *knarr*. It required a ten-man crew, relied on a single large sail, used oars only for maneuvering, and carried approximately twenty tons of goods. This ship's storage capacity produced far higher profits than that of a longboat. Sweyn appointed Estrid to captain a knarr, and eventually he bought his own.

Northdale settled into a profitable existence. It even developed a currency. It constructed a smelter that converted Viking gold from unknown sources into small ingots whose weight exactly matched the king's crown coins. Of course, when the king found out about the Northdale ingots, he cracked down. Annually, the royal minters arrived to smelt official gold crown coins. They imposed a ten percent fee payable to the king's treasury for the service!

Not all of this activity went unnoticed by the rest of the kingdom. Father William repeatedly sent letters that described Northdale's activities to his superiors or any interested persons. Some of the ruling class enjoyed reading and circulating these documents. Resentment grew. The church and numerous nobles considered the Vikings to be pagans, murders, and bandits. Trafficking with them equaled treating with the devil himself. Trade with Norsemen that would eventually become normal, at this time generated anger. The fact that Northdale's activities remained very small scale and that the Crown received in effect ten percent of the profits seemed to mollify any general resentment. In addition, the king informally let the court know he had no interest in correcting Northdale. However, English society considered Northdale and its people to be dirty.

THE SCHOOL

THEIR FIRST CHILD, MICHAEL, WAS almost five years old when one evening Sara made a proposal to Rupert. "We need a school so Michael can learn to read and write. I think Oloff's daughter, Ann, is six, so she could also start. We could offer the chance to learn to read and write to all Northdale children, boys and girls. Mary is only three, but she and the child I'm carrying will also eventually need a school. Both of us read to Michael and Mary, but that does not quite qualify as an education."

These comments required considerable consideration; Rupert sat looking at his wife. He then picked up a glass of wine. "All boys and girls who desire an education, even common folks?"

"Of course!"

Rupert stood up, walked to the fire place, rubbed his forehead with one hand, and then said, "You will be absolutely contradicting the commonly accepted ideas about schooling." He looked at her smile, "Maybe you enjoy that fact?"

Sara went over to Rupert, put her hand on his cheek, and said, "You know me very well."

"I suspect our holy priest will strongly object. I've only heard of the church supporting the education of female nobles and nuns."

"Rupert, dear, all the more reason to start educating them!"

Sara proposed that she would begin the teaching and then draft Father William to teach Latin. When the school attracted a number of children, Northdale should hire a professor.

"I told you once that I found you fascinating; this never stops. A school is a grand idea." He pulled her up by her shoulders and kissed her.

Responding to Lady Sara's request, Father William entered the keep. Sara sat at one of its tables. "Ah, Father, please sit down." She pointed to the opposite chair.

"Good morning, Lady Sara. How can I be of assistance?"

"Assistance is what this meeting is about. Sheriff Rupert and I intend to open a school, and although we can read and write Latin, we want an expert like you to teach that subject."

He smiled. "Some people absolutely must learn to read and write. Michael and any of your future children should learn in order to carry out their duties. The classes will be small and quite manageable. I will be glad to assist."

"Wonderful. Your help will be greatly appreciated. However, I hope the classes will not be small. I intend to offer school to any child who wants it."

William's pleasant facial expression turned to wrinkled questioning as he leaned back in his chair. "You mean common boys as well and noble ones?"

"Yes, but not only boys—girls also."

The priest's face turned red. "It is not a women's place to read and write. The church settled that years ago!"

"Father, I can read Latin and have studied the Bible. I never found a restriction on women's education" With a slightly raised voice, she added, "Never!"

William stood up. "As a woman, you do not have the capacity to understand the church's sacred teachings. Women should not be trained to read and write!"

Sara now stood up. "Father, I don't happen to have my sword with me, but I have warned you before about degrading women. The sheriff and I will not accept your attitude."

William pushed his chair aside and began to yell. "You are actually sinning. I will never cooperate. If you proceed, you are condemning your souls."

Sara's face had turned red. "If you find this an insurmountable problem, perhaps you should leave Northdale and find some less challenging parishioners in some other place!"

William spun on his heel and stomped out of the main hall. Sara sat down and put her forehead in her left palm. "Damn!"

When he arrived home, William's sixty-five-year-old body did not take well to the full-scale rage. His muscles were stiff and shaking, his face bright red. He knew that he would never find another posting, and Lady Sara's ideas defied all of his lifelong beliefs. He picked up his chair and threw it against the wall. Twenty minutes later, his heart gave out. He staggered to bed and died quietly.

Most of Northdale's residents came to the funeral. Afterward, they enjoyed a reception that quickly turned into a party. Rupert and Sara performed their official mourning duties and then enjoyed the party.

Sophia Stream's parents, Northdale's harness makers, were intelligent, although they could not read or write. They remembered Father William's rambling sermons and often sat around the table discussing the obvious contradictions contained in them. When Sophia asked about the source of the priest's opinions, her father explained that the priest and no one else could read the Bible. So his interpretations could not be disputed. When they confronted Father William with his inconsistencies, he had always reacted with anger because he alone knew the word of God.

Sophia asked if she could attend the school that Lady Sara had recently announced. Her parents smiled and readily agreed, but only if Sara accepted her.

The next day, Sophia walked to the keep by herself. In Northdale, everyone knew everyone else, so children could walk unescorted. When she entered the keep, she asked a servant if she could speak to Lady Sara and was directed to the table in the main hall.

"Lady Sara, I would like to attend your school, if I could."

Sara dropped her quill, clapped her hands, and said, "You are welcome. It will be fun. It will take work to learn to read and write both Latin and English. Do you want to try?"

"I think it is unfair that some people can read and others cannot. I really want to learn."

Sara motioned Sophia to come close and then gave her a hug. "You have the right attitude, and we look forward to putting you in school. My son, Michael, and Oloff's daughter, Ann, may be the only ones at first, so you will get lots of attention. Let us go to the kitchen and see if the cook has some cake."

Holding hands with Sara, Sophia skipped to the kitchen.

Most Northdale children lived on family farms where they made significant contributions to the farm's output. They simply lived too far away from the center of the village or could not be spared from farm chores. Also, some skepticism existed over the value of reading and writing for peasant folk. The first school opened with five children.

In time, as more children were born, the class became bigger. Sara told Rupert it needed a professor, because she simply could not do all of the class preparation.

Rupert sent messages to Lincolnwood, Shepardland, and nearby districts, inquiring about any available professors.

Lord Humphrey read the letter and laughed out loud. "My brother envisions teaching Northdale peasants how to read and write. Philippa, can you believe that?"

"What does he request. Money?"

"No, my dear, he seeks an available professor who would be willing to go up there."

Philippa wrinkled her face. "Didn't the Earl of Throwbridge just discharge his?"

With a big smile, Humphrey said, "Yes, something to do with his wine consumption and habit of inappropriately touching women."

"I think he would be a perfect candidate for your brother. Can we forward a message that we are sending him one?" They both had huge smiles. "I will send a message to my brother and also the ... qualified professor himself." Smiles turned to laughs.

Professor Stephen Hazelwood weighed about three hundred pounds. His short beard and bushy eyebrows had turned white. He combed his long white hair directly over the back of his head, and it reached his collar. His cheeks and nose turned deeper shades of red in direct relationship to the amount of wine he drank. His brown eyes darted around when in any conversation, but he projected the image of a learned man. He owned one flamboyant academic red robe, and he knew how to strut in it.

He decided to take full advantage of the fact his reputation had not preceded him. He resolved to work hard at running the school. He told his Throwbridge housekeeper that he expected success in Northdale that would translate into better jobs elsewhere.

Stephen found his introduction to Lady Sara and Sir Rupert to be quite pleasant. He agreed to concentrate on Latin and English and pounded the table to show approval of Sara's comment, "Greek is a stupid thing to waste time on." He was surprised that all social levels could attend school, and he expressed his skepticism. Sara assured him that her teaching experience showed that success or failure depended only on the child's abilities and drive. They agreed on compensation and housing. In a side comment, Sara mentioned how the girls would like him.

"Lady Sara, did you say girls?"

"Why, yes, Professor Hazelwood, the class actually has different levels based on age, and girls make up at least half of each tier."

"But only some nuns and high-ranking noblewomen learn how to read and write. I have never taught girls. In fact, I believe the church discourages and in some places outright bans the practice."

"May I call you Stephen?" He nodded. "You will find Northdale a semi-forgotten place as far as the church is concerned. They consider trading with Vikings the same as trafficking with the devil. Our priest died, and no bishop will send a replacement even from the ranks of drunken, ignorant priests. So we make our own rules up here. Our administrator, Squire, marries and baptizes people."

Rupert interjected, "We have no one to hear confessions." Sara and he laughed. Hazelwood made a pained smile. Rupert continued. "However, I will hear any confession you wish to make anytime." They laughed again.

With a smile Sara added, "One more thing: Northdale has more women than men. So the firm rule up here is if you grab, you marry, even if at sword point." Rupert also smiled, and Hazelwood forced one.

That night in his house, Stephen sat pondering the situation. A bottle of wine helped get his brain wrapped around the ideas of commoners and girls going to school. Knowing he had no alternative, he said out loud, "Well, I better give this a go."

Class started a week after his arrival. Twenty-five students attended. The eldest children he estimated at about ten years and the youngest about seven. He wore his robe, and it impressed the children. He described the schedule and rules of his class, and they seemed eager to get going. He became surprised by the skill of the older children to both read and write Latin and English, definitely something to build on.

The first trouble came in the second week. Hazelwood always carried a stick that had two purposes: first, to point out items and, second, to provide judicious whacks to lagging students. Society approved the latter use, and most schoolboys understood the consequences of underperformance.

He set up a vigorous Latin declension exercise in which the students had to quickly recite verbs forms. If they stumbled, it had been his practice to hit them on the back with the stick. It always proved amazing how much Latin a good whacking produced. From the older children's group, Mary, the sheriff's daughter, stumbled on a verb. Stephen made a quick decision. Boys and girls in this place were treated equally, so he hit Mary. After doing so, he walked to the front of the room, turned around, and was startled to see Sophia, Ann, and Mary approaching him with drawn daggers. He would later learn that in their ninth year, all Northdale girls received a dagger that their dresses concealed.

Sophia said, "Professor, no one hits us."

Stephen, in an alarmed voice, yelled, "Sit down students, or I will use it again."

The other two girls stepped to either of his sides. Sophia walked up to his front and placed the point of her dagger on his belly. In Latin she said, "I think you better reconsider your next step, Professor."

Stephen stood frozen. He did not know how to handle the situation.

After gently poking him with her dagger point, Sophia said, "You will put down that stick and walk with us to see Sir Rupert." He complied. Using a variety of sounds, the rest of the students expressed humor.

They found Rupert sitting at the main hall's desk. When called, he turned and could not conceal a slight, amused smile. "What have we here?"

Mary stepped to the front, "The professor hits students with a stick. We don't like it."

Rupert roared laughter. Stephen cast a completely disapproving facial expression. The girls' showed dead seriousness. One of the other students had run to tell Sara, and she walked in at this moment. She struggled to suppress a smile.

With a smirk, she looked at Rupert. "Husband, what it the meaning of this?"

"Professor Hazelwood likes to hit students with his learning rod. When I attended squire training, instructors broke several on me."

Sara looked at the group. "Ladies, please return to the classroom. Sir Rupert and I will deal with this."

Ann replied, "My Lady, we will go back, but if the professor ever hits me, my dagger will find its mark."

Sara shook her head and waved the girls to leave. "Stephen, let's sit at the table and have a glass of wine." Behind Stephen's back, Rupert gave Sara a hug around the shoulders.

Hazelwood drained his first glass and refilled it. Sara waited and then said, "Stephen, rules are a little different up here. Women form part of the defensive corps. They are trained to defend themselves. You see, if you ever do hit Ann or any of the others, they will use their dagger."

Stephen's hands began to shake.

"Boys don't carry daggers, but most of Northdale's women do. We are very careful, but predators have gotten loose up here. We never know the place, time, or location for evil designs. More than one assailant has learned the hard way that Northdale women are ready."

Stephen drank his second glass. Rupert leaned over the table's edge. "Look, Professor, new situations arise, and you as an academic have seen how thinking changes over the years. So, if you choose to stay, you simply must adopt new ways to encourage performance. You would actually find experimenting to be very interesting."

He was into his third glass when he looked both Sara and Rupert in the eyes. "You mean you condone what just happened?"

Rupert looked at Sara, and she responded, "Stephen, you just have to understand us. We will not keep you if you cannot figure a method to teach without beating students."

Stephen stood up, "Please tell the students that class is dismissed for today and tomorrow. I need time to consider alternative methods."

When the girls reached the classroom, Michael put his arm around Sophia's shoulders. "You showed courage, girl." She beamed.

Stephen entered his house and looked around. The ten-by-ten room contained a bed, one table, and one chair. A fireplace occupied one of the far corners. Plain, rough gray wood planks covered the walls. One window faced the square. Two shelves attached to the wall over the table held cooking pots and a few plates, glasses, and eating utensils. He walked into the middle of the room and turned around in a circle.

"So this is it; I'm at the bottom and have no place to descend." He poured a glass of wine and sat on the hard bed, thinking for over ten minutes. He sat up. "Look, you old fool, they want something different, and I really have no choice. It might even be interesting to try new techniques."

When class started two days later, Hazelwood did not carry a stick. In the beginning, he stumbled around trying to find positive motivation, but by trial and error and the realization that a piece of cake encouraged enthusiasm, he began to inspire learning. He actually would stay in Northdale until his death. He became beloved, as many teachers can.

Sophia made peace with Hazelwood because she soaked up everything he taught. Other children, like Michael were smart, but learning just fit Sophia. The professor always sought new books because she devoured them. He actually began a book-exchange program with a local abbey and several other estates just to keep up a fresh supply.

He also found, charmed, and married a widow. She always remained impressed with him because a professor is an imposing person. Her adulation made him a very happy husband.

Prince Edmond's Visit

Three years after Hazelwood arrived, a scruffy-looking herald entered the main hall where Rupert and Sara sat in front of the fireplace. Using his formal voice, the herald said, "His Royal Highness Prince Edmond will arrive in two days. He will be accompanied by two knights."

Sara looked at Rupert. "We heard months ago that he had undertaken a grand tour of earldoms. It must be our turn."

"I did not think he would fit this small place into his agenda. So, Sara, you must begin grand preparations immediately."

"Let me think, Rupert. Two days, this kind herald said. I will begin preparations in three." They laughed.

"Herald, please visit our kitchen and then, tomorrow, leave to tell the prince he is welcome."

As Edmond dismounted, Rupert said, "Only two knights? Is that because a horde of angry husbands is chasing you?"

After taking off his riding gloves, Edmond said, "I'm glad to see you are still impressed with my high rank." Edmond turned to Sara. "So you are the lovely lady who married my old friend. I am very interested in meeting you." He faced Rupert again. "Actually, my retinue chose to stay in Hollingsbrook when they learned of your Spartan lifestyle up here. I'm actually glad to be rid of them."

"I know this is not proper etiquette, but Lady Sara would you mind escorting me past this dull sheriff and into your castle?" He put his arm through hers.

"My Prince, if the rumor is true, then you need a woman to control you." Laughter came from all three.

Rupert turned to the two accompanying knights whose faces expressed disbelief at the informality of the interaction with the prince they'd just witnessed. "Gentlemen, we have wine and food inside." He gestured for the later-introduced Sir Clement and Sir Peter to follow.

As they reached the door, Oloff's daughter, Ann, ran out, along with Rupert and Sara's son, Michael. When they stood in front of the guests, "Prince Edmond, let me introduce the daughter of my marshal, Ann, and my son, Michael. Children, say hello to the prince."

After they did, Ann asked, "Are you really a prince?"

With a big smile, Edmond crouched down on one knee so he could look into the children's eyes. "Yes, I am."

Ann said, "Oh." She grabbed Michael's arm, and the two ran off.

Edmond laughed. He stood and said, "God, the informality is wonderful." He looked at Sara and Rupert's questioning faces. "The Earl of Winchester organized a formal children's introduction ceremony for me. It must have been fifty children of the local nobles and dignitaries who were presented. With the mandatory Mass, it took three hours. The only thing I prayed for during Mass was for the whole thing to be over." They all laughed.

Oloff, Eleanor, and Squire attended the evening meal. Edmond explained that the king sent him to tour the majority of England's earldoms so he could familiarize himself with their physical assets, noble's viewpoints, and people's conditions. After York, he traveled to the west coast and planned to visit England's whole length before returning to London. The king also required he write a journal that described his observations. His retinue included several scribes who labored on that task.

"Well, Edmond, please include a glowing description of my wife." The two laughed, but Sara blushed.

Toward the end of the meal, Rupert said, "Tomorrow's occupation will be brush cutting." Edmond gave him a questioning look. "My forester found that if some of the nasty and entangling undergrowth can be cleared off the forest's floor, the sunlight seems to make the grass grow. Deer feed on it, and we on them. I'm taking a crew of twelve workers out."

Edmond looked at his two knights, and said, "That does not sound too inviting."

With a pleasant face, Rupert said, "Oh, Edmond, you are one of the twelve." The Northdale people controlled their smiles.

"What!"

"You need honest exercise, and work is required if you plan to eat here."

"Rupert, you are telling the heir to the throne of England that he must work like a peasant and chop weeds?"

Nodding his head, Rupert said, "But don't worry. Your work will also provide meals for your two knights so they can rest."

Both men stood up, and Edmond picked up his glass of wine and gulped it down. Onlookers could see the obvious amusement that existed between the two old friends. "When?"

"Breakfast is an hour after sunup. An hour after that."

Edmond deposited his glass on the table. "Damn. My two knights also just volunteered to come."

An hour after breakfast, Oloff, Rupert, Edmond, his two knights, and ten Northdale men began the task. The men each picked up a curved long knife that proved very effective on the snarled brush. At midday, the crew ate lunch. Edmond sat with the Northdale men, and Oloff and Rupert with the two knights. The men talked about agriculture, weather, a pending wedding of one of the men, and techniques to keep a wife happy. Oloff and the two knights discussed advances in weaponry. The laughter and gesticulating showed the prince and men had much more fun. He would again sit with them during the next two workdays.

Only Sara and Rupert ate dinner with Edmond that night. He described his wife, Princess Joanna, the daughter of the Duke of Portsmouth. He first saw her after their fathers completed the marriage negotiations. She looked very frail, but had proved to be very vigorous with all of her responsibilities. Their first child died at birth, but Joanna expected another by the time he returned.

Sara stood up. "I will refill the wine pitcher while you two men discuss your wives' vigor."

Edmond watched her walk to the kitchen and then noticed Rupert's fond facial expression as he also watched her. "Your wife looks very accomplished."

Rupert smiled. "Like yours, she has enthusiastically performed her duties."

"I see."

"Wait, wait, wait, my Prince. Your appreciation must be left to *visual* only."

"As a vassal of the royal family, you should share your assets with the crown." He snickered.

"As a fellow squire, you know misconduct gets punished with a stick. If you do more than look, I will use something much more deadly than a stick." They both laughed. "And I might add, she is very competent with a sword."

Edmond raised both hands in a gesture of surrender. "I hear you."

Sara returned with a full pitcher. Edmond left the hall to relieve himself. She leaned over to Rupert and whispered, "I heard that last exchange when I stood at the door. I plan to enthusiastically reward you tonight for your manful defense of my honor." Rupert grinned.

When Edmond returned, he said, "I do have a problem with socializing with women while on this tour. The local lord usually provides fair companionship. However, rules exist."

Both Rupert and Sara raised their eyebrows.

"To avoid any succession claims, I must be content with a married woman. That leads to all sorts of negotiations to settle any favoritism claims. If none are available, then I must only enjoy a lady after one of my retinue has socialized with her. It is embarrassing to ask other men about a socialization."

"Ah … Edmond, what do you expect us to do?" asked Rupert.

"Well, you have a local priest who periodically sent letters to the king that describe alleged permitted activates up here. The king stuffs them into a never-visited things-to-do file, but I always read them just to keep track of you. The letters always contain reference to fraternization with Vikings. How does that work?"

Sara answered. "Listen, Edmond, very carefully. In Northdale, strong punishment exists for any man who makes an uninvited grab of a woman. Records exist of our Northdale court-issued penalties. But we do not take note of consensual grabbing that, as you well know, happens whenever men and women interact. The North House is staffed all day by two unmarried women nurses. We choose them because it avoids any possible conflict with irritated husbands. Maybe Father William knew things because of the confessions he heard, but Rupert and I have no knowledge of anyone's rampant sexual romping."

"But, Sara, cases of an unmarried woman giving birth must exist. Do you not require some atonement for that?"

"When I arrived, our local and recently departed priest required a twenty-lash whipping of an unmarried mother—right in the square. It took the tip of my sword to convince him to stop that practice."

Rupert said, "Edmond, we have more women than men living here. And I have important issues to deal with.

There is simply not enough time to pay attention to trivial matters. I let the people themselves handle the births."

Sara leaned back in her chair, and Rupert now spoke, showing a very controlled facial expression. "Your responsibilities include inspecting activities of your subjects, so I will issue you a pass to inspect the North House. I suggest you take some wine to reward the nurses' demonstration of medical practices."

Smiling as he spoke, Edmond said, "Rupert, I will conduct my inspection responsibilities. And, by the way, do you need a new priest?"

Sara and Rupert looked at each other. Sara said, "Edmond, our lifestyle does not exactly fit traditional church views. We need either a very flexible one or none at all. No urgency exists."

As Edmond stood up at the meeting's end, Rupert put his arm around Edmond's shoulders. "We only need to take corrective action if we become aware that a situation exists. You cannot be located someplace else at breakfast time. It is served one hour after dawn. *Be here.*"

Edmond would inspect North House on three evenings.

After the dinner on the last day of his visit, Edmond asked to meet privately with Sara and Rupert. They met in the sitting room on the second floor.

"Listen, you two, and this is not a prediction of imminent action, but someday I will be king. As such, I probably will be able to grant you a larger estate. And before you say anything, I have not forgotten my deal to make you an earl someday. My question is, do you want me to assign you to a much bigger territory?

"My offer is not all altruistic. A fool named Gismore now sits as the Earl of Denton. Do you know him?"

Sara and Rupert smiled, and he said, "Just after we were married, a small confrontation occurred; Gismore did not show correct courtesy to 'Mad Sara'. He begrudgingly chose to be polite rather than face my sword."

"Ah, well, his thick headed attitudes keep stirring up the middle nobles. He preaches that they should be receiving a larger portion of England's tax revenues and actually has risen to become an informal spokesman for a number of other middle nobles. I might need an ally to assume control of one of those earldoms and try to counterbalance Gismore. Interested?"

Sara and Rupert had only given this topic passing consideration. They simply had too much to worry about in Northdale. Both sat without moving.

"Well?"

"Edmond, I can say that we have never considered leaving here. We—"

"Stop, my friends! Your hesitation is one of the reasons I admire you. Never have you transmitted the unending desire to accumulate more of everything. Almost all other nobles never stop scheming for increased wealth. As far as I can remember, you have only sought things that could improve your people's well-being."

Sara and Rupert fixed their eyes on each other for a good half minute. Then Sara faced Edmond. "You know I've held the reputation for being mad, so this answer may reflect that point. Something important happens here, and that in itself makes Northdale most interesting. Rupert's unusual ideas started this community's resurgence, and it is very rewarding to keep the progress going. I don't believe anyone else's attitudes could produce the same results, and if you assigned a typical, thickheaded noble here all progress would stop. I believe we would feel guilty of desertion if we left now." Rupert made a grunt as he nodded his head.

"Damn. Over fifty earls exist, and I bet no more than two or three would express similar sentiments. The offer remains if you ever change your minds. And remember, I may be forced to order you to address a problem in the middle earldoms." He raised his glass in a salute.

War Service

It was almost ten years before the first royal draft arrived. King Henry had been succeeded by Edmond, Rupert's old playmate. He ruled with equality and fairness. However, revenue-splitting caused tremendous resentment among the southern nobles. The geographic location these men held provided considerable trade opportunities with France. Trade produced crown taxes and the king controlled the revenue dispersal. The king openly bought the middle and northern counties' loyalty by funding abbeys, road improvements, and castles. The generators of the taxes reasoned that they should receive the lion's share and the middle and northern nobles a pittance. Push came to shove. After years of simmering, the southern nobles enlisted France's help and then attacked the king.

King Edmond called upon his middle and northern noble vassals to provide support. Although not large, Northdale received a summons to help. Rupert organized a one-hundred-man contingent; eighty carried swords, battle-axes and shields, while twenty men hefted bows. Women performed most archery tasks, but the lack of weapons made some young men take up archery, often taught by their mothers. Rupert knew that the military establishment would never, ever accept women, so none were included in the contingent.

As preparations continued, Rupert knew he needed to settle one factor. He found Sara sitting at her worktable. He walked up next to her. "Sara, we must talk."

Recognizing the serious tone, she turned her chair to face him. Rupert put both hands on her shoulders. "Sara, Michael must come with the expedition; I will appoint him as my squire."

She jumped to her feet and moved to the back of the chair. "Rupert, do you know he just turned sixteen? All sorts of things can happen to him, including simple sickness. He is way too young to fight!" She had been holding a book in her hand and now she slammed it down on the table.

He looked at the floor and shook his head. "Sara, the boy will lead Northdale someday, and his only experiences in combat are with the tactics we once used on the Vikings. It is simply not enough. He must witness large military efforts just so he can base his future decisions on this knowledge. If not, some king can call him to battle, and he will have no way to evaluate sound tactics. And I can tell you from my time fighting in the Low Lands, military operations must be seen and felt. They cannot be absorbed through writing or verbal descriptions."

Sara held the back of her chair and began to tear up. "But he is my oldest child. Cannot this education wait several years before taking chances?"

Rupert also looked unhappy. "I will be in command, so I can guide him and protect him. In the future, he might join some eager battle commander who leads his command to destruction. I want to be the one to teach him sound military operations."

Sara walked away and then turned. She was plainly crying now. "I see he might be a future sheriff, but it hurts to let him go, hurts so much." She walked over and hugged Rupert.

He held her at arm's length. "You can choose to help protect him by sending Oloff with Michael. Oloff will stick with you for life. You might ask him as a favor to help shield your son. You decide, but our Northdale forces that stay here may require a commander, and Oloff is it."

She discussed the subject with Oloff. Together, they reviewed alternatives. Finally, Oloff stood up. "Sara, it is Rupert's job to take care of his son. With the troop away, Northdale, including our children, could be in danger. I think a fighting commander needs to stay and organize a defense, even if it is just your archers." Sara looked at the ground and nodded.

When Rupert told Michael about his appointment as squire, Michael started to jump about. Youthful enthusiasm eliminated any concern about potential harm. He was ecstatic. As preparations progressed, he threw himself into the thick of the work. His only major disappointment came when Rupert told him not to pack a sword; Rupert ordered him to exclusively learn, observe, and perform typical squire duties. In front of Sara, Rupert specifically commanded him not to get into any fighting.

After that exchange and when alone in their bedroom, Sara asked, "Will he restrain himself?"

Rupert tossed his tunic on a chair and looked directly at her. "In truth, Sara, he will stay out when I can watch. At his age, I would have gotten into the thick of things because all young people know they are immortal." They held each other very tightly when they got into bed.

The night before the departure, Sophia found Michael and dragged him from the crowd. When alone, she faced him and, with tears running down her cheeks, reached over and kissed him.

"Sophia, I—" She put her hand over his mouth.

"Michael, you must come back. You make my life here possible." She spun around and started to run off.

Michael yelled, "Sophia, I will come back. You can count on that." For the first time, a sobering incident counterbalanced all the preparations' excitement.

The Northdale contingent looked like a mob—no uniforms and no military formations. Because Northdale gathered weapons from any source, swords came in long and short sizes. Shields displayed even more inconsistency: wooden Viking, current French, and fifty years' worth of English designs. Other than Rupert's, no real armor or chain mail existed. Some men wore leather jerkins with small metal plates attached, but most wore plain leather. Over the years, the Vikings had paid for goods with helmets gathered from all over Europe resulting in an international conglomeration.

Rupert, himself, added to the image. His twenty-year-old armor did not match the current gentry-favored fashions. His original war horse sired three large animals, two of which earned their keep as community draught animals. The one he now rode had never been trained in combat requirements. Its viability as a battle horse remained suspect. In addition, the sheriff's experience in France suggested that a noble riding while his men walked negatively impacted their motivation. So Rupert only rode his horse for about an hour a day. Michael, of course, walked.

It was customary for the noble in charge of a military unit to pay for food and lodging as well as a salary for the soldiers. Rupert could not afford to pay wages, but the Northdale men were willing. They had never engaged in a battle; past fights with Vikings resembled skirmishes. They knew the experience provided a great training opportunity. Besides, it gave them a chance to see land, communities, and women that were completely different from those in Northdale.

The battle would be fought at Middledale. As typical, both armies encamped near each other while organizing and gathering strength. The king's servants erected two tents, and together they became the central source of activity. The large tent functioned as a great hall, including a fire pit in its center. Formal and social gatherings occurred in the large tent. The small tent served as living quarters and the place where top commanders planned strategy. A gathering of many earls, barons, and knights required banquets and dances. At one of these affairs, a sentry entered and announced, "A horde of totally disorganized men just arrived from Northdale." King Edmond's smile reflected interest in meeting an old friend; other smiles transmitted a dismissive evaluation.

Rupert put on his best tunic and entered the meeting tent. Michael went with him. Custom dictated that he walk directly up to the king, kneel, and offer his sword. The king stood. "Sir Rupert, Sheriff of Northdale, you have honored my summons as a loyal vassal. Welcome." No one else said anything. "How large is your troop?"

Rupert now stood. "We are small and poor, so I brought my best one hundred men. I hope, my lord, that we can be of service." Deprecating comments could be heard all over the tent.

Smiling, the king pointed to a tall, well-dressed man, "The army's marshal, Sir Perry of Kent, will direct you to a campsite and assign appropriate duties. When settled, please come to my tent for a glass of wine."

"Before I take leave, I would like to introduce my squire and elder son Michael whom you actually met years ago when he was quite young."

Edmond looked over at Michael. "He is a fine-looking young man. Luckily, Rupert, he reflects your wife's fine appearance." Both men laughed; Michael blushed.

They made the required bow and walked over to the marshal who stood as tall as Rupert and wore a red tunic covered with gold-thread decorations. Anyone who approached him instantly recognized his air of command authority.

―――

When a guard opened the tent flap, Rupert walked in. The king stood up and, "Old friend, I'm glad you have come." Two knights sitting at a table wrinkled their foreheads at the informal greeting.

Rupert extended his arm. "My fellow squire." As the two laughed, the king shook Rupert's arm.

The king turned to the other men. "Please leave us. Sir Rupert and I have some old memories to recount."

Rupert watched the others leave and then turned to the king. "How the hell are you? It looks like this pending fight is a big sprained leg, again."

The king laughed and waved his hand at the table. "Get a glass, you son of a horse thief."

They spent half an hour retelling old stories, catching up on people they knew, describing their current family lives, and discussing Northdale news. Finally, they discussed the current military situation. The king also inquired about Michael. "He is a fine young man. Takes his homeland and squire duties seriously." They similarly discussed the king's son, Richard.

They only stopped when the marshal intruded. "Sorry, Your Majesty, but military placements must be discussed before tonight's meal."

That night, Rupert attended his first banquet. Being an actual king-appointed sheriff entitled him to sit above plain knights, although several tables sat between his seat and the main dais. The men seated near him carried on a friendly conversation, and as usual, Northdale's life attracted interest. Michael stood along the tent wall with the other squires.

After finishing the sit-down meal, the men stood with glasses of wine and intermingled. Bishop Steven Blackwood saw Rupert and asked in a voice loud enough to attract a number of listeners, "Are you Northdale?"

Rupert faced the man and raised his glass. "Quite so."

"You traffic with Viking devils, yet stand among honorable and holy men!" The immediate area went dead silent.

Rupert first put his glass down and, with a completely straight face, stared the bishop directly in the eye. "My Lord Bishop, I have always faced two choices. Either be completely overrun by pagans and enslaved or make some accommodation so my good Christian people could survive."

"You left out the alternative to stand up and fight," said an overweight noble who had pushed through the crowd. The man wore a beautiful gold-thread embroidered tunic showing a complicated crest.

The man looked vaguely familiar; Rupert crinkled his eyes. "Do I know you?"

Contempt dripped from the man. "I'm Gismore, Earl of Denton."

Taking a moment to collect his thoughts, "Well, my lord, since the last time we met fifteen to twenty years ago, you have not changed. Your mouth still runs faster than your brain."

"Gentlemen!" said the king.

Blackwood addressed the king. "Your Grace, this man traffics with the swine that despoil churches and kill priests."

Turning his back on Gismore and Blackwood, Rupert said, "Your Majesty, no one offered to send troops to assist in Northdale's defense. None came from Denton and this bishop commands a troop of soldiers, but never offered assistance." Rupert cast his glance around at all of the assembly standing in a small circle surrounding this confrontation. With a hard, accusing edge to his voice, Rupert continued, "It is easy for men like these two to talk of fighting the devil when they are safe in a castle or abbey. We, on the other hand, had to stand up to Vikings without even owning enough swords to arm all of my men."

"Silence!" yelled Marshal Perry. "All of us will shortly face an enemy and have a chance to do plenty of fighting. Put aside your squabbles, and I mean now!"

The king, now standing, said, "You are correct, Marshal."

Gismore raised his left hand while sneering at Rupert. "Your Majesty, I hope for God's grace to descend on the justified and give us a chance to thrash those French-loving bastards!" A cheer went up from the assemblage.

The king and Rupert exchanged hard looks. The marshal had waved at servants, who now quickly filled ale mugs.

As the group returned to socializing, the king passed Rupert and in a very muted voice said, "Stay calm, friend." Rupert nodded his head.

Humphrey of Lincolnwood marched in with the last addition to the king's force. Two years before, Cuthbert's death initiated Humphrey's elevation to earl. When Rupert saw him, he rushed up to his brother. "Humphrey, how are you?"

Humphrey looked around at the persons within hearing and then back at Rupert. "Sheriff Rupert, I am the Earl of Lincolnwood. You will address me as 'My Lord'." Rupert's eyes widened, and he tucked in his chin. Without moving, Humphrey stood with a disapproving facial expression.

"I guess, My Lord, things change and not always for the better."

"Things will be fine, providing you remember rank."

Rupert's eyes were very sad. "Well, I wish you well in the upcoming battle. If I don't survive, please forward my regards to Philippa and your four children." He turned around and moved off.

Events began to move quickly. Heralds moved between armies and passed insults along with scheduling arrangements. It was agreed to hold the formal pre-battle meeting one week after Northdale's contingent arrived. The pre-battle meeting conformed to rather strict social customs. It had to occur approximately halfway between the respective armies, be held under a tent, and keep insults to a minimum, even though some could be hurled. Both sides brought their senior commanders, and everyone stood except the king.

The southern nobles presented a list of demands centering on the king's surrendering control over tax revenue generated by their holdings. The king not only rejected the proposition, but also reminded the nobles of their sworn fealty to him. Both sides passionately described broken commitments as justification. In the end, they all agreed to battle on the following day.

The king, marshal, and five senior nobles, including Gismore, met to establish battle order, command structure, and position assignments. The king assigned Marshal Perry to command the right side of his line because it faced the fearsome mercenary Brittany Legion. This fighting unit had never lost any battle. The king estimated his best officer should stand against the best unit the southern alliance commanded.

After it was decided who should direct the left and center, the king, recognizing this was Gismore's first major battle, assigned him to command the reserve with the duty to reinforce any weak positions caused by French advances.

When the meeting concluded, the marshal came out to the gathering of lesser commanders and read their assignments. Northdale drew the assignment of building a roadblock that crossed behind the line's right. Northdale would actually not participate in the main battle.

Rupert pushed his way to the marshal as the marshal left the meeting. "Sir Perry, we are to guard a road and that is all?"

The marshal looked at Rupert. "If the enemy decided to slip a contingent around behind us, it could be a catastrophe. You must block the road long enough for us to send a larger force to repel any such move. It is important!"

"But we could end up sitting all day."

The marshal put his hand on Rupert's shoulder. "I've been told that you fought in France a number of years ago." Rupert nodded his head. "Then you know formation fighting. A loose cluster of men would simply be slaughtered and thus leave a hole in our line."

He moved directly in front of Rupert and made very hard eye contact. "Correct?" Rupert moved back a step, eyed the ground, and nodded his head in the affirmative. The marshal straightened up. "End of discussion." The marshal walked off.

―――

Both armies served breakfast and a pint of ale to their men. The battle commenced an hour later. Rupert's roadblock had been located where a road passed through a small, but dense tree line. The trees provided protection for his flanks in case an enemy chose to attack. By walking about two hundred feet, Rupert could see through the trees and observe the battle's progress.

About an hour into the battle, the sound of many horns blowing was heard just at the edge of the king's right line. Rupert saw that the men wearing the Brittany Legion's distinct bright blue uniforms with broad silver edges were actually a ruse. The real legion, wearing a blue tunic lined with gold stitching, had not lined up in the battle formation, but had, instead, stayed in the tree line out of sight of Edmond's commanders. When Perry's line pushed forward, the fake legion tactfully retreated so that Perry's line passed in front of the real legion. At that point, the real legion burst out of the trees and attacked Perry's exposed far right. This caused a partial collapse of the English line.

Rupert could see the pending disaster pass in front of him as the real Brittany Legion pushed the English right. Watching, he surmised that the southern nobles could care less about the road his men blocked because they had already sprung their big surprise. He went back to his men.

"Does anyone see any messengers coming from the king or marshal?" No one had seen any. "Listen, men, I participated in a very similar situation in Holland. We hit the back of a strong formation and caused it to crack. We can do it again, here." He searched the men's faces and found eagerness. "Let's go. We cannot fight standing here!"

Just before jumping off, Rupert grabbed Michael by his leather tunic. "You are not to touch a sword—do you understand me? I promised your mother that you would not join the battle, and that vow cannot be broken. Clear?"

Michael said, "Yes, Father."

When the Northdale unit reached the edge of the tree line, Rupert paused. "Look, men, we need to attack that unit in the blue tunics; they are about to crush the right wing. Don't make any sound, but run like hell down to their back line, and cut the hell out of them! Archers, wait until the sword men engage and then shoot the nearest blue tunics. All understand?"

The men displayed controlled smiles. Rupert drew his sword and started the charge.

The Brittany Legion did not recognize the attack on its rear lines until eighty of its men were cut down. In combination with the archers, it took only two minutes to cut down about forty more legionnaires. With the shredding of the forth line accomplished, the third turned to fight, and it backed into the rear of the second line. The second line's main responsibility was to fill the place of any downed soldier in the first line. Because it now had to fight in two directions, it could no longer perform its job. The legion's solid structure began to weaken.

Sir Sigmond of Lions commanded the side of the legion under Northdale's attack. He stood about six foot four and carried a legendary six-foot sword. The sword had a name, "Reaper," because of the death it caused. He saw the weakening of his command and charged. The first swings of Reaper claimed two Northdale men, and people began to back away from Sigmond.

Rupert realized Sigmond could stop Northdale's progress, so he confronted the big man. Reaper made two strokes, and Rupert ducked both. As he would tell people in the future, "I remembered an old forester in Lincolnwood who told me that when facing a bear, one should dive to the ground to miss the claw swing, then chop at its knee to disable it."

Rupert followed the forester's advice, and his chop at Sigmond's knee hit hard enough to cause it to give way. Apparently Sigmond's beautiful armor makers never considered it necessary to protect a knee from a sideways sword blow. The big man dropped to one knee, but as Rupert approached, he stood up. He made one swing, but the injured knee offered no support, and he crashed to the ground. Rupert stepped on Reaper to keep Sigmond from lifting it again. Rupert yelled, "Yield, Sir Knight."

Sigmond looked out his helmet eyeholes and said, "I would rather die that yield to trash like you!" Twenty years of tree chopping in Northdale gave Rupert the muscle to cleave Sigmond's head with one stroke.

From his position behind the English right, Marshal Perry observed the legion begin to falter. He spurred his horse over to a contingent of the reserve. Its commander, Sir Archibald, told the marshal that Gismore split the reserve into two units and posted one each behind the right and left lines.

The marshal, in an agitated voice, asked, "Where is Gismore? It was obvious an opportunity existed once the mob of Northdale men struck that damned legion."

Sir Archibald pointed at the king's tent. "Lord Gismore spends his time around the king's tent."

Marshal Perry made a quick look at the king's tent and then ordered Archibald to throw his reserve into the fight. "I take full responsibility!"

With a loud shout, "Yes," Archibald led his men on a charge.

The death of its esteemed leader along with at least another two hundred casualties, the collapse of the first line, and an energized English counterattack caused the legion to crack.

For the first time in history, it fled the field. Its retreat caused the southern nobles' left line to waver and then retreat.

The English left and the southern right seemed to be evenly matched. Neither side pushed the other. The southern commander had placed his least experienced troops in the center. He surmised the strong left and right lines would bolster the center's courage. However, when the left side began to waver, it took only fifteen minutes for the center's troops to panic; they became a rout. Within one hour, the king's opponents began a general retreat. The battle was over.

Northdale lost fifteen men, a pittance by the standard of most army units, but a major blow to a small one. Rupert and his men spent time carefully retrieving their fatalities. Another six men had been injured, but crusty, old, battle physicians predicted they would recover. Getting all back to camp took most of an hour.

Rupert saw blood splashed on Michael's tunic and demanded to know its source. Michael said it came from carrying the dead and wounded.

When Rupert and Michael arrived at the king's meeting tent, the celebration had reached a very loud level. As he approached the dais, both the king and the marshal stood.

With a huge smile and a very happy voice, the king said, "Sir Perry tells me that your surprise attack on the legion saved his line and, therefore, the day for me. Thank you, Sir Rupert, for great service to the Crown." The tent had become quiet.

Rupert bowed his head. "King Edmond, I'm glad to serve an old friend."

"Serve, bah. How can I repay you?"

While walking up to the tent, Rupert and Michael had discussed the possibility of this question.

"Am I free to ask?"

"Sir Rupert, what would you like?"

"I would like three things. First, make me the hereditary earl of Northdale. Second, allow my men to each pick up two swords and shields along with other fighting equipment. And, third, let me recruit men from the defeated army to emigrate to Northdale."

The king smiled at Rupert's modest list. "All granted without any hesitation." There were clear murmurs emanating from the other nobles. "I will have my chancellor draw up the necessary decrees, and I will elevate you in two days."

"Pardon my insistence, Your Majesty." He turned and looked at the faces of the other nobles. "Could you make me a noble right now before some of these folks behind me spend a lot of time lobbying?"

Actual gasps could be heard. However, the king asked a servant for his sword and faced Rupert. "I remember a deal you and I made a long time ago. Kneel right here."

Rupert did so.

"In recognition of the magnificent service rendered to the Crown today by Sir Rupert, I dub him Earl of Northdale, and this title will be hereditary, so it can be passed to his heirs." He tapped Rupert on either shoulder.

"Chancellor, prepare the decree." Most, but not all of those present, started to clap and cheer.

When Rupert stood, Marshal Perry said, "Who was the small man who prevented a French knight from attacking your back just after you dispatched the ugly giant?

"Small man, Marshal? I don't know of whom you speak."

"He wore no armor and only carried a battle-ax. He trapped the knight's sword between the ax's blade and the spear-point on its shaft and then used the ax's pole to strike the knight on the head. The knight stepped backward, but not far enough to keep the next ax swing from crushing his head. That man saved your life!"

One of the captains standing in the group added, "He still swung the ax at the end of the fighting. I saw him."

"I will ask my squire, Michael." He waved to his son.

As Michael stepped near Rupert, the captain yelled, "That's the man who saved your life!" The nearby men cheered. Rupert's mouth was open.

"Sorry, Father, but you said no sword. Oloff and I have long practiced with an ax, which you did not forbid." Rupert grabbed his son in a mighty hug.

The king yelled, "Gentlemen, we have here a squire who, without armor, took on a French knight, killed the bastard, saved his father's life, and then fought the rest of the battle and helped rout the French line! What say you?"

Lord Humphrey raised his arm. "Knight him!" By sheer acclimation, the assembly concurred.

The king pointed to his front. "Kneel, Michael." He the dubbed him and said, "Rise, Sir Michael of Northdale." It could have been the wine or the exuberance of victory, but the crowd really started cheering.

The king pulled Rupert over by his shoulder and whispered in his ear, "You now owe my son a favor." Rupert looked him directly in the eye. "You know I'm always good for it." A rock hard commitment had been made.

When the noise quieted a bit, Rupert stood, raised both arms, and with a big smile shouted, "Your Majesty, can I buy you an ale?" Laughter by most of the crowd followed, as did many congratulations.

Words cannot describe all Rupert's emotions when he again hugged the now Sir Michael. "I wish to tell our soldiers, so I will see you later, Father."

Earl Rupert passed among the crowd and found his brother. "Humphrey, you old horse jockey, it pleases me that you did not get hurt."

Humphrey's face clearly showed him struggling with a new rank reality. "I'm also glad for your deliverance, brother." They clinked ale mugs.

"Thank you for your leading Michael's knighthood acclamation."

Humphrey smiled. "We should keep promoting the family." They clinked mugs again.

Gismore had claimed, just after the battle's conclusion, his reserve saved the day. He happened to say it loud enough for Marshal Perry to hear. The Marshal directly faced Gismore and, with a very firm voice, said, "Bullshit, bullshit."

He then walked away, and Gismore realized most of the assembly agreed with this viewpoint. He spent the rest of the celebration standing near the tent wall and, with rising hate, watched the celebration and Rupert's honors.

The next day, the king's herald invited Lord Rupert to dinner. It was very welcoming and relaxed. The king, with glass in hand, said, "Perry, Rupert is one of the few men who, in private, can call me Edmond. You see, we trained as squires together."

"Perry, I, of course, was a better student than Edmond." Edmond threw his wine at him.

Both Edmond and Perry wanted to know why Rupert decided to attack the legion. The conversation covered the battle at length and then moved on to funnier topics. The wine helped the changes in topics.

Edmond said with a big smile, "You must be very proud of your son."

"You have met my wife, Sara. She is a formidable woman and commands my archer corps. I promised her Michael would not participate in the battle. I have some explaining to do." Both Perry and Edmond laughed out loud.

Rupert drained his next glass of wine and told Edmond. "Remember, I will always offer you or your children protection if ever necessary."

Both other men smiled. Perry pointed out, "This fight should settle disputes over crown authority for years. No one will be stupid enough to break the peace. Thank God." They all raised their glasses.

Perry put his glass down with a little force. "You know, Edmond, there will be a fight over spoils and an execution list."

The king slammed both hands on the arm of his chair. "You would think everyone would be happy with victory and not start trying to cut up the carcass." He looked at his friend. "Rupert, you only asked for simple rewards, no money or land grab. I wish all nobles followed your example. How do you suggest I levy punishment and then divide up the spoils? Before you answer, remember that some of those lords out there expect big rewards. Take that coward Gismore, he absolutely lusts for big booties."

Rupert stood up and walked to the table and filled his glass. His face was serious when he faced the king. "Edmond, this sounds weak, but I don't think it wise to kick a man when he is down."

Edmond raised his right palm toward the tent's ceiling and almost hissed, "God, I wish it was that simple."

"Well, Edmond, that is why you have all the gold."

They talked almost another hour and then a slightly-wobbly king said, "I have a present for you. I ordered the delivery of the big knight's armor, sword, and shield to your camp. You have earned it, and besides, it will reflect earl status. But you will need a new helmet." They all laughed. "Michael will also receive the armor of the knight he killed, but he will also need a new helmet." They raised their glasses yet again.

"Look, Edmond, thank you for making me an earl, but I think some of the other boys out there did not like it."

Edmond put his hand on Rupert's shoulder. "Northdale is much smaller than most earldoms, so your appointment is different. However, when I consider the complainers, I have only one response: Let God show them swift access to hell."

When Rupert entered his tent, he found Michael passed out, drunk. Apparently, the Northdale men insured that he celebrated when he'd gotten back to camp.

The king paid all the soldiers a half-crown. The treasury cut half-crown coins into four *eights*. The smaller coin became the market medium of exchange. Any military encampment offered numerous pleasures with women, drink, gambling, and just rough play. Northdale's men took full measure of these opportunities without anyone getting seriously hurt.

It required four wagons to hold all of the newly acquired military equipment. Rupert and Michael delivered several threats of discipline to motivate the men's packing efforts. However, distracting as military campaigns can be, the men became restless for home. It would be a two-week trip. The wagons only carried enough food for the first week. Food levied on the good king's vassals would provide the rest.

Twenty men volunteered to emigrate. Rupert and several of Northdale's soldiers pushed them into a circle. "You are welcome, but you must remain aware of the rules. We don't know you, so we will be watching. The laws of Northdale are generally the same as you would find in any

Christian community. The discipline is a little different. We view breaking the law as choice. If you choose to violate a law, you will be kicked out of Northdale for minor offenses and executed for major ones. It is simple and your choice."

Rupert decided Sara should prepare Northdale for the return. He sent a dispatch by courier.

Sara yelled, "What is this?" when she saw the message addressed to "Countess Sara of Northdale." After reading it, she called together Oloff, Eleanor, and Squire.

In the dispatch, Rupert requested the families of the fifteen causalities be notified before the troops came home. He proposed Northdale should throw a joyous party for the returning men, but fairness required the families of the deceased be informed first. He described accepting twenty emigrants and asked Squire to arrange living and working conditions for them. He finished by announcing his elevation to earl and the knighting of Michael.

Sara hit the table with her fist. "He promised to keep Michael out of the fight!"

Oloff said, with a big smile, "Sara, he not only has Rupert's blood, but also yours." He then raised the first of several congratulatory glasses of wine accompanied by numerous jokes about Sara's new rank.

The next morning, Sara, Oloff, and Eleanor each took five names and rode to personally tell the families. They met in the main hall afterward; all three were depressed.

Eleanor said, "My God, that proved most painful." All three got sloshing drunk that night.

Just before they entered the village, Rupert insisted the men line up in some order. They did not have to march, but he wanted them to look like a proud unit. He and Michael rode their horses at the rear of the procession. He patted Michael's leg. "This is not about us."

The families mobbed the men and all hint of a formation dissolved as soon as they reached the square. A two-day celebration began.

Rupert and Michael did not get shorted on hugs; Sara and Mary provided plenty. Oloff and Eleanor also contributed. Many jokes about "Sir Michael" flew as he walked through the crowd, searching for Sophia. He stopped at the far end of the square to continue looking. Her arm reached out between two houses, grabbed his shoulder, and pulled him into the dark for a heartfelt and private welcome.

Intervening Years

Peace reigned for another five years. Northdale's commercial niche became firmly established. It catered to the smaller Viking traders while the larger ones exchanged goods at the larger English port cities. The North House continued to profitably operate because, despite peace, drunken sailors did get into battles with each other and authorities. In addition, accidents with rigging, boats themselves, and harbor maneuvers seem to frequently occur. The number of children with bright blond hair increased.

Rupert and Sara raised three children, Michael, Mary and Alfred. A fourth, Elizabeth, contracted fever and died. Oloff and Eleanor had Ann and two boys, Garf and Eric. They also lost a daughter, Maud, when a boat accidentally crushed her against a dock.

Before Sara's father died, he sent a German architect to Northdale after the architect had bragged about designing an effective farmhouse. The building had a low-pitched roof, and two stories. The animals wintered on the lower floor and the family lived above. It seemed odd at first, but the animal's body heat actually helped warm the living quarters. Of course, animal waste required daily removal. If some of the side or back walls could be covered with earth, then the houses became even warmer. The prototype proved very effective, and Northdale's farmers adopted it wholeheartedly. If funds existed, Rupert issued construction grants.

In addition, breeding techniques improved. The impregnation of cows occurred in late fall and gestation occurred during the winter. The new births occurred in spring, so the little animals had great opportunity to eat their way to adult size. Northdale's meat supply became large enough to manufacture dried sausages for trade with sailors.

Development required wood. Rupert made an attractive gold offer to the Earl of Hollingsbrook to purchase the southern half of the Ibix valley. The offer settled long-standing irritation caused by Northdale's harvesting desirable trees. Despite being generated by devils, the gold sealed the deal.

One last change, Rupert's children noted that most people had two names, but they had only one. They approached Rupert and asked him to adopt a surname. Several weeks of very humorous name creation occurred. Mary held for the Latin *regula* meaning "ruler." Michael liked Latin *fortis* meaning "brave". Alfred, the youngest, liked the English word "horse." In the end, "Northdale" seemed too long, and Rupert and Sara agreed simply to North. Oloff's family chose Watcher as its last name.

Education Gained at York

Sara sat with Rupert after dinner. She leaned back in her chair and said, "I have an idea."

Rupert grabbed both chair arms as if he was about to be thrown and said, with a broad smile, "We have women warriors, North House, and a school. What is this idea?"

She returned the smile. "I happened to be talking with Sophia, Ann Watcher, and our Mary, and they inquired about the nature of court life. They simply have not experienced it. In fact, they have never seen it."

"Sara, you personally know it's nothing but little, puffed-up people spending hours of time keeping track of vague pecking orders."

"True, but the girls should experience it once. They may, in their future lives, be required to interact with courtly manners. I suspect other courtly people will virtually dismiss our ladies as peasants if they could not display proper etiquette, and I want our women to stand up to them and prove their quality.

"Besides, Mary is the daughter of an earl; Sophia is probably the smartest child here; and no one messes with Ann, because she is the daughter of one fearsome fighter. They don't receive any challenges here. They must go someplace where they have no such advantages and test themselves against a much broader social mixture.

"That is why I want you to write the Duke of York and ask if our three could spend six months learning court manners."

"Sara, I have a rule that you fight the fight you must and avoid those you will lose. I have already lost this one. True?"

"Earl Rupert, you gain wisdom as you age!"

When the girls arrived in front of York Castle, they did not move. They stared, frozen. Northdale's keep would simply be a little guard tower here. The wagon driver asked, "Are you ladies planning on getting out?"

As they climbed down, a lady walked up. "Are you the three Northdale girls?"

"We are."

"I am Lady Adela Radcliff. My title is Lady-in-waiting to the Duchess of York."

Sophia pointed first at herself, "I am Sophia Stream, this is Ann Watcher, and Lady Mary North." They all smiled.

"Girls, I understand you come to York to learn something of courtly manners. First lesson, when introduced you must always curtsy to the higher-ranking person. And remember: almost everyone you meet here is higher ranking."

"Oh." They all curtsied.

With a smooth tone in her voice, the lady-in-waiting continued. "Hum. I can see we need a little work. But, please come with me and I will show you around this castle, the places you are allowed to go, and to your room." The building's size and beauty left them breathless. The colors, tapestries, furniture, and rugs could never be matched in Northdale.

At the end of the tour, they entered a small room on the third floor. It contained three beds, one table, two chairs, and one clothes cabinet. One small window faced north, and the walls were plain, gray masonry. Someone had delivered their belongings.

"Several other girls from various parts of the duchy are also here for a similar purpose. You will all meet tonight before banquet. One will come here earlier to explain basic banquet etiquette."

They smiled and said thank you.

"Girls, the curtsy rule applies when a higher rank person leaves your presence." They did so, and Lady Radcliff raised her eyebrows as she closed the door.

They were told to put on their best dresses for the banquet. With great excitement, they did, and they discussed what they expected to see. One of the other visiting girls escorted them to the main hall and sat them at the end of the farthest table. During the walk to the dinner, the other girl gave a brief description of the manners the three were to use. Speechlessness would never be an attribute assigned to any of the three, but they were struck dumb by the sheer pageantry. It was well that no one spoke to them, for they would not have been able to respond. The top-dignitary entry ceremony almost took as much time as a whole Northdale dinner. Not knowing what to do, they stood and sat when everyone else, except those at the dais, did. They clapped, laughed, and prayed in concert with the group.

Once a week, the banquet ended with dancing. This one just happened to be that night. The three were astounded, watching the dancing; they had only seen rough neighborhood jigs in Northdale. The music, the flow of the dancers, the twirling dresses simply backed them against a far wall. They were transfixed. When another visiting girl led them to their room after the evening, they remained silent. After the door closed, they erupted with comments and stayed awake, talking far into night.

Their informal status resembled a lady-in-waiting-in-training. They were not servants, but held no status of any sort. Life quickly developed a schedule. Ladies-in-waiting practiced etiquette to gain proficiency at it. They rehearsed correct speaking, learned correct dancing, tried embroidery, painted, played musical instruments, supervised servants, ensured proper wardrobe care, and discreetly carried messages.

The three began to get bored. However, they recognized the importance of mastering etiquette and showing deference by rank, because no one would talk to them if they did not. Embroidery did not come easily for them because they never experienced it at home. Recognizing gross inability, the trainers assigned them to folding cloth and sitting quietly. Slowly, they began to skip these classes and were not missed. The same occurred in painting and music instruction; Northdale's girls knew they could not conquer these skills in a few months. They did remain involved in wardrobe care; ladies-in-waiting were expected to manage the noble's clothes. The three remained fascinated by the accumulation of clothes they knew they would never personally experience. Once it became known that they could read, no literate noble lady would ever trust a message to them.

Dancing, however, drew their intense concentration. They drove the instructors to distraction with constant requests for dancing lessons. The three practiced, practiced, and practiced some more. By the end of the first month, they'd reached acceptable proficiency. The dances required considerable physical effort. Most young ladies would participate in half of the dances in order to maintain proper ladylike composure. With unhidden enthusiasm, the Northdale three participated in all of the dances.

Lord Rupert included one unusual clause in his message to the duke. The Northdale ladies had to be given one day in which to continue to practice his required skills. So on Fridays, they rode, hunted, practiced archery, and utilized the massive library—activities never undertaken by other visiting girls. They began to have more time on their hands as they skipped the useless classes. Lady Radcliff ignored them because she considered them untrainable. The library and archery range absorbed the open hours.

Once, when all the girls sat at a mandatory etiquette-training lunch, one of the other visitors asked the three about their life plans. Mary North talked about making a contribution to the success of Northdale. No reaction. Ann talked about being involved in a great fight and leading her troop. Stunned silence. Sophia smiled. "I plan to marry an earl." Ann and Mary exchanged knowing looks with each other. The female members of the castle's society, however, decided this answer showed the Northdale ladies' preposterous overreaching. The girls learned about gossip's speed in an enclosed community!

Mary North met Heescome Airlie at the archery range. She was shooting during the time that some of the young knights also used the facility. The skeptical men quickly became aware of her skill.

One stepped forward. "I don't know your name. How about a bet?"

"Mary North, and I accept; what is the wager?" Heescome looked at his companions and then at Mary. The three other knights began to snicker.

"If I win, you will bring me a fresh strawberry cake."

Mary smiled as she tapped her bow's tip on the ground. "And if I win, you will dance twice with me at the next banquet."

The other men laughed out loud because full knights, even junior ones, never danced with low-ranking ladies.

It proved short work for Mary. To the surprise of the men, she clearly won.

As they left the range, the defeated archer said, "I am Heescome Airlie, third son of its earl."

Mary, with a mischievous smile, said, "Well, no wonder you took my wager. You won't be able to deliver my prize."

Heescome's face registered surprised denial. Before he could speak, she added, "You third sons disappear into a celibate monastery or an army campaigning in a foreign country." She started to laugh. He hesitated, and then also laughed.

He shook his head. "I will dance with you on Friday night." She stuck out her hand to make the wrist-grasping handshake. He first looked at her hand with a questioning smile and then shook it.

As the knights walked away, Heescome said, "She is really different."

One of the others said, "She is one step above a peasant and maybe half Viking!"

Sophia discovered an interesting feature of the castle's architecture. Almost every large room contained a small balcony that provided seating for women who came to watch men's activities on the floor below. By accident, she stumbled onto the balcony overlooking the castle's head professor giving a history lecture in Latin. She began regularly attending and certainly did not have to fight for a seat with other women. Ann and Mary would attend for stimulating subjects.

Heescome asked to ride with the three on their Friday morning hunts. Mary agreed, on one condition. On his honor as a knight, he swore not to repeat anything he heard. The riding and hunting proved enjoyable, but he became captivated by the unorthodox viewpoints the three expressed. He roared with laughter when they constantly poked holes in the posturing of York's people and traditions.

As the months progressed, attitudes began to shift. When the three arrived at York, its informal society considered them pretty, country relatives requiring coaching. As the Northdale women continued to demonstrate considerably different skills and interests, comments and corrections became much sharper. The initial benevolent attitude disappeared. The gossip circles made derogatory comments, and even the Duchess asked about the departure of this somewhat disruptive element.

Three factors contributed to the new attitude. First, the dancing: Heescome's dancing with Mary invited a large number of young knights who were eager to show their abilities. Ann and Sophia provided perfect partners. Heescome informally staked claim to Mary North. Other women, especially the marriageable ones, did not like the attention focused on the few.

Second, before Sophia came to York, she had developed a great appreciation for the Roman historian, Pliny the Younger. She loved his work because of its literary beauty. While attending one of the lectures, she could not hold back as the professor completely misinterpreted the author. She stood and in Latin challenged his interpretation. Caught by surprise, the teacher actually debated her. The attendees found the discussion humorous and later hilarious because Sophia proved her points.

That night at banquet, one of the young knights called on the professor to explain the problem he had in lecture that day. He stood, cleared his throat, and declared that a completely uneducated woman, who did not understand Pliny the Younger, had spoken with improper decorum. He sat down without ever looking at Sophia. Mary North and Ann pulled her back into her seat as she rose to refute the comments. The banquet guests began humorous mutterings among themselves, but no one asked her to speak.

Third, Ann decided to hunt alone early one Friday. She downed a large stag, field stripped it, cut it into quarters, and rode back with them to the kitchen. The head chef was delighted with the meat, as the night's banquet would be large and the duke loved the way he could prepare such meat.

At the banquet, the duke called for the chef and, when present, complimented him on the excellent fresh venison. He inquired about the hunter. The room fell quiet as the chef searched for and then pointed at Ann. She arose and the surprised duke began a polite round of applause.

One of the young knights called out, "Which man helped you bring in the carcass?"

A furor of comments arose when Ann yelled back, "Why would I need the help of a man to do that?"

Two weeks later, Sir Luke and two of his companion senior-squires, men who would be elevated to knighthood within months, decided the Northdale girls showed some spirit. It would be fun to grab them and teach them what real men were like. After banquets, it was common knowledge the three often wandered in the formal gardens because, as they told people, nothing like them existed in Northdale. The men found the girls near one of the far walls.

"Well, ladies, it is time you met real York men." The girls stood shoulder to shoulder with squinted eyes. Luke pointed at Sophia. "I'll take this one. You split the others." It surprised them when the girls stood solid and did not begin to shrink back or turn to run.

They were more surprised when the three charged. Luke's cheek was sliced open, one man's forearm sliced to the bone, and the third's abdomen was sliced from navel to side. Only the fact that he turned sideways at the last moment saved him from a direct stabbing. The three girls did not look back as they walked away.

When the duke convened his weekly commanders meeting in the library, the men sat around the largest table in the room. The usual attendees included the chancellor, head knight, captain of the men-at-arms company, the bishop or his representative, and some invited knights. Talk proceeded through the routine agenda items and always reserved the last discussion for new or interesting subjects.

The duke pointed at the head knight. "George, I asked you to look into the hunting accident that injured one knight and two senior squires. Your results?"

George shifted a little in his seat. "My lord, it seems it was a hunting accident." His face had a slight smile.

The duke crossed his arms on the tabletop. "George, rumors are flying all over this castle. How about your telling me the truth?"

George cleared his throat as he looked at the captain and the bishop before facing the duke. "It might be true that the three men decided to force their affections on the three Northdale women. And it might be true that no one knew that all of the women from there carry daggers. And it might be true that the women cut them up."

The duke put one hand over his mouth and started to chuckle. "Three of our best! No wonder the Vikings started to leave Northdale alone!" He slapped his hand on the table. "Chancellor, one of those three is Rupert's daughter; I cannot tell them apart. I want to meet with her now."

Being Friday, the ladies practiced at the archery range. One of the chancellor's assistants walked up to them. "The duke wishes to speak with Lord Rupert's daughter. Immediately!" Ann and Sophia smiled and pointed at Mary.

"I guess I'll be back," said Mary with a grin.

The duke and head knight sat in chairs, each with a glass of wine. As the library door closed, Mary walked directly to them. "My lord?"

The head knight set his glass on a table. "Are you Rupert's daughter?"

She put her hands on her hips. "I am Lady Mary, Rupert's daughter."

The duke leaned forward in his seat. "Mary, I seem to have a problem, and as a noble woman, you and I should discuss it." Mary's face expressed a humorous and mild surprise. "Three of my men seem to have had a hunting accident."

"My lord, they should be more careful."

"That is true, but it is also possible they attempted to force affection on three women."

Mary again smiled. "Well, that is a violation of knightly vows and a sin."

The duke grunted and assumed a business like expression. "It is also rumored that some women carry daggers concealed in their dresses."

Mary reached into the covering fold of her dress and pulled out her dagger. "You mean like this one? Don't all women carry these for protection from uninvited affection?" Her face projected complete innocence.

The duke put his glass down and looked at his head knight and shook his head. Then he turned to look at her again. "Lady Mary, let me explain the complications. If a knight attempted affection on an unwilling woman, it is a violation of his vows, and I would convene a court of honor to determine whether or not to hack off his spurs. The other lesser ranking men would face a court and could be subject to severe physical punishments. This is all complicated by the fact that all three come from families that give me strong support."

Mary sheathed her dagger and looked up. "Well, my lord, if rumor is correct, the hunting accident left some physical punishment, so you need not impose any."

"Look, Lady Mary, at such trial, the offended woman must testify. If the character of the woman could be attacked the defense will be sure to do so."

Mary looked concerned. "But if the woman is honest, good, and truthful what would be the problem?"

The head knight did not change his mild scowl, but the duke's face softened. "Lady Mary, character includes a history of trafficking with the devil Vikings. Anyone involved is tainted."

Mary said, "Oh," and shook her head.

The duke added, "Devil traffickers could be completely repudiated, and their description of the incident totally disregarded. In fact, guilt for the incident might be attributed to the woman for utilizing devil enchantments to entice an innocent, God-fearing man."

Mary again said, "Oh."

The duke leaned back in his chair. "Do you have a suggestion?"

Mary stood still for a few moments and then walked over to the table holding the wine pitcher and glasses. "Thank you, my lord, for offering me some wine and a seat." She poured a glass and then sat in the empty chair. The head knight's eyebrows rose in anger. The duke made a fatherly smile.

"I can think of one alternative. I will announce that my father summoned us to return posthaste for Northdale business. We will leave on Sunday, after Mass of course."

The head knight looked at the duke. "No courier has arrived in the last three days."

Mary smiled at him. "Really, Sir Knight, sometimes a little flexibility in memory is required."

The duke burst out into laughter. After a moment to stop, he said, "Lady Mary, I will draft a letter to your father telling him how enjoyable you three were and that I am sorry to see you depart, and it will be the truth. A wagon will be ordered and escort knights assigned. I will pay for all costs related to your trip."

Mary placed her glass on the table, having taken only one small sip, stood up, and smiled at the duke. "My lord, I must begin packing immediately. I beg your permission to leave."

The duke stood up. "Mary, your father should be very proud of you."

She made the required courtly bow, and the duke stood to return it with one reserved only for high-ranking ladies.

Heescome found Mary North. Sophia and Ann left them alone. "Mary, you are fascinating, and I have become infatuated with you. Can you not stay or at least come to another estate where we can learn more about our future?"

Mary picked up his hand. "Heescome, Northdale people are different than your world. The last few months should have clearly identified this point. I don't fit here and never will. I think you are truly the best person I've met and I am interested in you, but nothing can proceed until you come up to Northdale and experience its lifestyle. If you can stand it, maybe we could continue seeing each other. But you may find it like I found this place. Nothing will progress."

They talked for more than an hour. At the end, Heescome said, "I will visit you in Northdale after my military obligations are fulfilled."

"Please, it would cause me great pain to know how much backstabbing gossip would occur if you saw us off tomorrow.

I know you wish me and my friends well, but please do not see us off."

He kissed her hand. "Lady Mary, good-bye."

Only Lady Radcliff attended their departure. She did not try to conceal her pleasure at their leaving.

Papal Dispensation

Typically, the selection of popes resembled a blood sport. Powerful and rich families formed coalitions with lesser families in attempts to gain the papal crown and its associated revenues and patronage.

The abbot of the Fourth Cross Monastery was Antonio Rossi. His family lost the last papal contest to the Gambino coalition. Over several hundred years, the abbey had acquired a large wine production operation. It provided very desirable revenue.

The new pope needed to provide rewards to his supporters; the Abby of the Fourth Cross's revenue offered a perfect prize. Three methods to open the abbot's seat existed. First, troops could show up and simply evict the incumbent. Second, trumped up charges, generated by torture, could be leveled and harsh punishment meted out. Third, the abbot could be promoted to a higher post. The only unacceptable option would be to demote him, then allow him to remain at the abbey.

Opportunity arose when the Conference on Christian Institutions' head cardinal gave the pope, almost as a joke, a report on an English earl who horded gold given by Vikings, practiced odd religious customs, employed armed women, and encouraged sexual contact with pagans. The pope recognized the almost comical and very unusual activities by an obscure nobleman could justify an investigation.

Abbot Rossi could not conceal the surprise and pride caused by receiving a scroll signed by the pope himself. He would become a papal Legate a latere and be assigned to represent the pope on a special project. The appointment carried ambassador rank, including a handsome stipend and authority to take required action after the investigation. A copy of the Northdale report accompanied the appointment documents.

Rossi considered the legate role as great recognition of his faithful abbey administration and a great compliment. His extended family saw through the glitter to the basic points. Revenue would be substantially cut, and being exiled for at least two years would keep the abbot from participating in any future power recovery efforts.

Assuming the title Lord Rossi, Papal Legate, he took almost ten months to reach Northdale. His new stature required generous welcome by nobles and bishops through whose jurisdictions he passed. The trip itself provided much enjoyment to Rossi, his assistant priest, and one servant.

The Ibix guards checked Rossi's credentials and then let him pass. It was late fall when he arrived at the keep. Squire arranged sleeping quarters and told the Lord Legate that Northdale only held one banquet a month, so the formal recognition celebration would wait two weeks. The delay in recognition caused a slight irritation, but Rossi attributed it to Northdale's backward social life about which many nobles and bishops had warned him.

Just as the legate settled in for dinner, Lady Sara, wearing one of her best court gowns, swept down the stairs. She also wore her countess tiara. When he saw her, he wrinkled his brow because he had only seen women dressed as servants walk up the stairs.

"Lord Papal Legate, I am Lady Sara, Countess of Northdale. We are honored to receive such a distinguished guest." It was a narrow courtly etiquette matter of who should bow to whom; Sara chose to flatter the legate by first bowing to him.

"Lady Sara, I am pleased to meet you." He held out his ring for her to kiss and received the first of many surprises to come when Sara shook his arm.

With a radiant smile, Sara said, "The dinner is served. Lord Legate, would you care for some wine? We purchase it in France."

Antonio had anticipated making an introductory speech that clearly laid out the charges to be investigated. Somehow, the unexpected graciousness of Lady Sara sidetracked his intentions. "Thank you, Lady Sara. I would enjoy some good wine and dinner, but most of all your wonderful company."

After everyone sat, Rossi rose. "I believe grace is in order." Sara waved her hand in a gesture to proceed. Although he used a very common prayer, only he and his assistant repeated the words.

Events outside Northdale's borders fascinated Lady Sara, and due to the scarcity of news sources, she continuously pumped the legate about the status of countries, royal families, papal business, and new ideas circulating in the civilized world. The dinner lasted almost two hours, of which Antonio spent the largest part discussing Lady Sara's interests.

Lady Sara also asked if he carried any books, as they were very hard to obtain in Northdale. She admitted her Greek had waned, but Latin or French texts would be very welcome. Rossi again looked surprised and turned to his assistant. The young man said he'd brought a history of the Roman wars written in French. In return, she invited them to utilize Northdale's very limited library.

Toward the evening's end, the legate became serious. "Lady Sara, the pope sent me on a mission, and I must speak with Lord Rupert."

"Ah, Lord Legate, Rupert is currently near the head of the Downs River, the one that runs through our village, supervising the construction of several farm buildings. I know he regrets any delay this causes, but he will not return for three more days."

"Cannot you send for him?"

With a smile and a shake of her head, she replied, "No."

"You do not understand, Lady Sara. I have been sent here by the pope himself. I must begin my work."

Sara crossed her hands on the table. "My Lord Legate, winter approaches and the farm buildings must be completed. He cannot stop now. But our farmers tell me that tomorrow's weather will be sunny and dry, so you and I will take a riding tour of Northdale."

Antonio opened his mouth to speak, but Sara raised her hand to him. "Breakfast is one hour past dawn, and the horses will be ready one hour later." She stood up and courtly manners required Rossi to also stand up. "Good night, Lord Legate."

Northdale's quiet atmosphere proved soothing, and despite the accommodation's rather crude quality, Antonio slept way past dawn. When he approached the breakfast table, Sara made a welcoming gesture. "Did you sleep well?"

"I think Northdale's air agrees with me."

With a nod, Sara said, "Most visitors come to that realization."

Both clerics enjoyed the breakfast's hardy cuisine. The day's first surprise occurred when Sara stood up. The Legate had never before seen a lady wearing a knee-length skirt with leggings covering her lower legs. Seeing his face, Sara smiled, "Lord Legate, the riding up here can be difficult and cold; women riders always wear leggings." She could only guess at the meaning of the look the two clerics shot at each other.

Once on the horses, Sara introduced Oloff as her companion and protector.

Antonio questioned her. "I did not think you required protection."

She turned her horse so she could look directly in Antonio's eyes, "Attacks come from many places, my lord." She circled her horse and began the tour.

The tour started in the nearby farms and took several hours. They dismounted so Sara could show them the improved house/barn design. The Downs' rapids were next, the location of the salmon catching. She explained the process. Several women archers demonstrated their shooting skills on targets towed up the rapids. The clerics commented on their shooting ability. Next was the wharf. No ships were present.

"Is this the place the Viking ships come?"

With an innocent face, Sara responded, "Yes."

Oloff suggested the Downs' lookout as the final stop. He explained the guard watch lasted twenty-four hours, and that the system, on many occasions, proved its value as no surprise intrusions occurred.

"The guards find the sea's beauty intoxicating, except when storms rage." He and Sara laughed. "One more point: every adult, including the women, takes a shift manning the lookout, even Lord Rupert."

The legate and his assistant had become almost numb to new revelations, but this one caused them to wrinkle their brows.

When the party returned to the keep, Sara waved her hand at the pitcher of wine sitting on the main table. "Please refresh yourselves." She looked at Oloff and, with a smile, added, "We should all rest and wash off the horse smell."

Once in the legate's room, both clerics expressed the need for rest. Then they began to inventory all of the completely and sometime foreign things they had seen. They did not rest.

At dinner, Antonio said, "One thing we did not see today is the hospital or rest place offered to Vikings."

Eleanor, who attended this dinner, responded, "Oh, your lordship, neither Lady Sara or any other woman may enter that place without Lord Rupert's pass. He usually only allows the appointed nurses to enter." Sara nodded her head.

The following day, Sara and other residents made excuses based on tasks to be accomplished. The legate and his assistant took the opportunity to begin writing. At the evening's pleasant dinner, Sara introduced her children. The legate had a fondness for children, and the three put on a good show. She also told him Rupert would be home for the next dinner.

At the start of the third dinner, formal introductions were exchanged between Lord Rupert and Lord Legate. Rupert restricted conversation to the farm progress and fall preparations. Sara, Oloff, Squire, Eleanor, Sir Michael, Mary, and the assistant attended. The young Alfred did not attend because his addiction to constant motion usually resulted in an early bedtime.

After several hours, Rossi stood up. "Lord Rupert, I have been sent by the pope himself to investigate some reports on Northdale and your activities."

Rossi made his pent-up speech and related, in Latin, that the pope had sent him to investigate allegations of trafficking with Vikings, women serving in the army, and sexual relations with the Vikings. He wrapped his speech in large, official-sounding words that he thought transmitted the seriousness of the issues.

Rupert listened without any reaction except a slight smile. When the legate finished, he translated the content into English. Sara chipped in language corrections when necessary. Humor crept into the faces on the Northdale people.

In English, Rupert said, "Well, my Lord Legate, let me start with the most easy response. No record is kept on the personal relationships of unmarried women. All married couples are required to remain monogamous. However, you must remember that people will do things they choose. You will find the same truth in any place you go. In fact, I believe if you tried to make a list in Rome of all persons having relations with each other, you would run out of ink!"

The Northdale people laughed out loud. The legate smiled and the assistant grinned. Rupert did not mention that he had ordered all blond children to be moved far up the Downs.

Rupert went on to explain the reality of fighting Norsemen with Northdale's small military force. He also described the Vikings making pagan slaves out of Christian young people. To protect the community, he'd adopted military tactics fitting the problem; and they had been successful. The Vikings decided to trade rather than invade—less death and equipment damage. However, the situation was not fixed. At any time, some chief might decide to raid Northdale. Unless the pope would send a troop of soldiers, Northdale must continue to defend itself.

He then outlined the commercial exchange. The Norsemen bought food and wine with gold. The gold came in the form of little chunks, so no one knew its source. One other service Northdale offered was to tend to sick or injured Vikings. They were housed in the North House through the winter, and they usually recovered by the spring when the Vikings returned. "The Norsemen realized the value of our assisting their incapacitated sailors, so North House helped end violent attacks."

That did it. Rossi jumped up, "You give succor to the pagan despoilers of the church! They are the *devil's horde*, and it violates church rules to help them recover so they can continue their despoiling ways. I insist on seeing this North House! Lady Sara would not show it to me, and I know she was hiding something."

Rupert looked pained. "Lady Sara is not allowed to go into North House, and only the assigned nurses can enter. That is my rule, and it is enforced!"

A good deal of theological debate ensued. Rupert pointed out that the Good Samaritan gave help to someone who was not of his religion; therefore, helping sick Vikings was consistent. Rossi claimed, as papal legate, he held the overriding theological knowledge, and it supported him as he denounced Rupert's points that differed from approved church doctrine. No conclusion could be reached, but at the end, Rupert agreed to show the North House.

After breakfast, they rode to North House. It had seven occupants. Two were near death from injuries. One straddled the line of improving or declining. The other four's injuries continued to heal and, thus, they would sail in the spring. One, Vissvald, was the son of a powerful chief, almost like a prince.

When they entered, Rossi and his assistant projected disapproving facial expressions, clearly indicating that no matter what they saw, their opinions were fixed. It did not help that Vissvald, who had been warned about the pending visit, walked right up to the legate and greeted him with a loud Viking welcome and extended his one uninjured arm. Rossi shrank away from the hand as if it gushed poison.

Vissvald then laughed and patted Rupert on the shoulder as he returned to his cot. The condition of the three bad cases aroused no Christian pity in either cleric.

Outside, Rossi said, "Lord Rupert, you are committing a sin by giving aid to these despoilers of Christians and churches. I will inform you of my finding at dinner tonight." The two clerics rode back to the keep by themselves.

Rupert and Sara went back into the North House to explain to Vissvald the problem everyone faced if this papal representative caused church retribution.

At dinner, the legate remained quiet while the others talked of local matters. Lady Sara even tried to liven things up by describing the French author's views on Caesar.

Finally, Rossi rose. "Those pagans defy God's will and commandments. You, my lord, sin by giving comfort or aid!" He pounded his fist on the table. "There can be no questioning my decision. I possess the pope's authority to settle things. Therefore, you must execute those seven men in order for you, personally, and all of Northdale's people to regain the church's blessings. If you do not comply, I will excommunicate all before I leave." He then looked for Rupert's reaction.

Rupert did not stand. He simply reached for a glass of wine. "Well, Lord Legate, that is very serious. I will give you my answer tomorrow morning." He then took a sip of wine and looked the legate straight in the eyes.

Antonio obviously expected some cowering, and began to shift his weight from foot to foot. Rupert showed no discomfort. Rossi signaled to his assistant and left the main hall.

Once the legate left for his room, Rupert said, "Sara, you keep an eye on those two. I don't want them leaving the keep for any reason. Oloff, you and I will visit Vissvald."

They sat with Vissvald and one translator. Rupert explained that if Northdale received papal condemnation, all sorts of problems could happen. The pope or some bishop might authorize an army to purge the land of this impurity. The harbor might be burnt down and closed. They also, for sure, would close North House.

Vissvald talked about the convenience offered by Northdale's port. It actually offered a badly needed respite after crossing the sea. He also raved about the benefits of the care offered here to the injured. He wanted to know what the pope would expect to settle things. With some clear regret, Rupert told him about the executions. Vissvald laughed. He then stood and walked around the room for a few moments. "Could we fake the executions?"

They all offered different ideas, but each stumbled on the same point: Rossi would want to see bodies. Vissvald made the final suggestion. Vikings would kill the three sickest men. The four healthy ones could hide, and somehow a body switch could be arranged to fool the fool. Together, they hatched a plan to convince the legate that the executions occurred.

"If any of your people find out, will they not take revenge on us?"

"No, I know my father and other chiefs will see the plan's logic."

The next morning before sitting for breakfast, Rossi walked straight up to Rupert. "What have you decided?"

Rupert stood. "It is about time you got here. The executions started this morning because the Viking tradition requires them at dawn. Let us go to North House. You can eat later."

Three bodies lay in a wagon in front of the door. They were wrapped in their bedclothes. Rossi demanded they be unwrapped so he could see them. He almost stomped inside to observe the other beds. All four had fresh bloodstains on their padding. "Where are the four bodies?"

"I must ask Captain Rodger; he oversaw the executions."

Just as Rupert spoke, an empty wagon rode up to the North House. Captain Rodger drove.

"Rodger, what happened to the other four bodies?"

"My lord, the cart takes no more than four. The tide is right, so I took them down to the beach where they washed into the sea. My plan is to take the others now. Should I stop?"

Rupert explained to Rossi that Northdale never buried the bodies of invaders. "We keep the land pure."

Rossi actually smiled when he took one last look at the three. "They are pagans, so sea burial is quite appropriate. You have done well. I will prepare a complete report to the pope describing how you exercised your Christian duty. I will also give you a dispensation on the other subjects because you rose to the challenge and accepted God's directions." He then turned to Rodger.

"My son, did you personally oversee this execution?"

"Your lordship, I oversaw what was to be seen."

"Kneel!" The legate asked to borrow Rupert's sword. "The pope's authority includes elevating knights, so in honor of your outstanding performance, I dub thee Sir Rodger of Northdale."

He tapped Rodger Cartwright on both shoulders. "Rise, Sir Knight."

Everyone congratulated him and simultaneously kept their faces turned from Rossi to avoid revealing the great subterfuge. As they walked back, Oloff put his arm on Rodger's shoulders, "This means any girl you marry will be a lady. Good hunting!" Rodger hid his grin.

Rossi kept his word. He wrote and copied for Rupert a formal papal dispensation from all charges. He documented how the Lord of Northdale had recognized his duty and removed seven pagans. He could not keep his pride out of the document; he wanted full credit for arranging seven Vikings' executions.

The night after Rossi left, Rupert and Sara offered a grand party. Sir Rodger sat at the head table, and every one gave him mock tribute. He took it with good humor, but at any future formal occasion he would insist on being called "Sir."

Rossi expected great praise when he returned to the Vatican. He had sent the dispensation ahead so it could be reviewed before he arrived. The opposite occurred. The pope was furious that Rossi assumed the authority to grant a broad papal dispensation and order executions while failing to curtail women's obviously incorrect activities. He also fumed over elevation of a knight. It was solely his prerogative to grant such honors, as he had discovered this practice produced considerable personal gifts from wealthy families. The pope ordered Rossi to be confined in the abbey located at Italy's southernmost tip, and if he ever left the confining walls, a warrant existed for his execution. Because of Northdale's relative obscurity, the pope decided not to bother with all of the formal, time-consuming, and expensive requirements to reverse Rossi's mistakes.

One other event occurred as a result of Rossi's visit. Cardinal Tonti held authority over the Vatican office which had the responsibility to assign territorial control to bishops. Having discovered that Northdale actually sat in no diocese, he ordered the Bishop of York to assume responsibility. York's bishop wanted no part of Northdale because no manpower existed to undertake controlling what he considered to be the semi-barbarians. In a letter to the pope, he politely refused the assignment and considered it void unless he received further direction.

Cardinal Tonti long followed one strict administrative rule: all work by his assistants must be completed by noon of Friday so his appropriate relaxation could occur. To show a clean desk by the deadline, an assistant realized low priority documents could be slipped between two boards at the back of the main bookshelf. Three hundred years later, during an office renovation, workers discovered about one hundred documents hidden behind the bookshelf boards. The Bishop of York's was among them. Northdale never went under the authority of any bishop nor received another priest.

Invasion

Court intrigues never quite settle. King Edmond fell off his horse and broke several ribs. He contracted pneumonia while bedridden, and the resulting coughing lead to fatal hemorrhaging. Prince Richard was only fourteen years old when crowned. History shows that when a young king is crowned, tremendous pushing and shoving occurs over who directs the government and controls taxes.

King Edmond's settlement decrees after the Battle of Middledale had caused very hard feelings. Rather than executing them, Edmond had allowed the leaders of the rebels to be exiled to France for an eight-year term. Other than several small parcels granted to knights whose job was to police the southern nobles, he did not extract lands, castles, or titles. Edmond did impound a large portion of the southern nobles' income that he then distributed as compensation to the middle and north nobles who had expended resources for the Middledale battle. Even Northdale received twenty-five gold crowns each year. Some of the middle nobles, led by Gismore, continually complained that the southern nobles' relatively light punishment denied them sufficient reimbursement.

The inveigling came to a head when Gismore and fellow midland nobles decided to replace the young King Richard. They kept their plans well hidden from the court, thus denying the king time to rally a strong army to stand at the Battle of Denmore where the middle nobles triumphed. However, King Richard escaped. The middle nobles could not elevate one of their own to be king while the legitimate heir still lived.

Richard and his court wished to flee south because the southern nobles despised the victors. However, the middle noble's military units occupied all of the roads leading southward. Richard fled north. Due to his inability to access London's capital or the treasury, his court's size decreased the farther north he moved. Eventually the king, three chancellery officials, and two knights crossed the Ibix.

Rupert's long-standing promise to protect Prince Richard came to fruition. In September, one month after Richard reached Northdale, the herald arrived.

The message was simple—deliver up Richard or face invasion. The wording actually contained many insults revolving around accommodating the rapists of churches and trafficking with devils. The church, represented by Bishop Blackwood, included its formal blessing of the incursion, thus sanctifying any action taken by Gismore to smite the devil worshipers. In effect, any invasion would become a small crusade.

Rupert responded, in formal Latin, that his vow to protect the king and his heirs went back to Edmond's father, Henry. He could not hand over the king. He requested to hold a meeting of all England's earls so a settlement could be reached.

In late October, the herald carried the reply. The standard personal insults now accompanied a direct ultimatum—deliver the king or face a spring invasion. Rupert escorted the herald into the courtyard, threw the document on the ground, and then pissed on it. He kindly provided a leather bag so the herald, as he returned it to Gismore, could avoid touching the now-wet document.

Two days after Christmas, Rupert convened Northdale's first war council. He invited Sara, Oloff, Eleanor, Michael, Squire, King Richard and his two knights. After reviewing the documents—the contents of which everyone already knew—he asked for an estimate of the enemy's strategy and timing. A great deal of ideas flowed, but in the end, consensus held that Northdale did not offer much booty for an invading army. Gismore's army could harvest cows and destroy a small-scale trading operation with Norsemen, neither of which offered cash. Rupert spent, every year, the trading profits on public improvements and subsidizing farmers' enhancements; so no large treasury existed. The real prize for Gismore and Blackwood would be the enhancement of their future political moves. Therefore, all doubted a large attacking army would be mustered.

Even Squire agreed that no alternative existed, but to fight. None of them expected to see a merciful Gismore. In addition, although no direct threat had been made, they assumed Gismore would have, with the church's blessing, a free hand to subjugate Northdale's devil supporters. All sorts of ramifications were imagined.

Rupert then made assignments. Sara would command the archers and Oloff the foot soldiers. A mobile headquarters would function under Squire and the king. Rupert would retain overall command.

"Each of you will require captains to lead contingents to which you must assign tasks you cannot oversee," Rupert said. He looked at each one of them. "I could appoint them, but you must be comfortable with their skills, so select your own captains. I want to point out that leaders in battle must be skillful, but it's extremely important that the troops also respect them."

Silence existed for a few minutes. Sara turned to Eleanor. "I want you for one captain and ask if you have a suggestion of another."

Eleanor contemplated her answer, watching her fingers as she rubbed them on the table. She looked up. "Sophia always shows her skills, and that girl has fight in her. Everyone knows it."

Sara wrinkled her brow and looked at her son. "Michael?"

Rupert leaned forward to get a good look at Michael's face. "Michael, is that a problem?" He vigorously shook his head.

Oloff leaned in. "Good, because Michael should be one captain. The men already like him. The other good one is Sir Rodger Cartwright. Command by two local knights will sit well with the troops.

"They are appointed. I want to add that our other children are, in my opinion, too young to be leaders. I don't want it to appear that we are pushing unqualified family members to command troops. Our respective children, obviously other than Michael, will take regular positions in the ranks."

"Rupert," Oloff said, "I think our other children Alfred, Mary, Ann, Garf, and Eric should be runners. The young ones don't tire, and they can get through the brush with less noise. We will need at least six more to make sure messages get to the command center and back."

Sara looked at Eleanor, and then she said, "I think I speak for Eleanor. Ann is actually older than Michael. She should be in the ranks. Our Mary knows how to shoot very well; she should also serve in the ranks. Appointing them as runners would give the appearance we are protecting them from the risky service that others face."

Eleanor injected, "I agree."

With a smirk, Rupert said, "Well, then, I must agree. Correct, Oloff?"

With a smile, Oloff responded. "Domestic peace requires it, Lord Rupert."

Rupert poured a glass of wine. "The last appointments will, again, be up to you and your captains. For small tasks, you will need squad leaders. I suggest you pick out ones who could someday be captains."

Michael, with a very straight face, added, "I will tell Sophia about her appointment and responsibilities."

Rupert shot a quick look at him and then at Sara. With a quiet smile, she nodded her head.

They then dove into strategy. All agreed Northdale could not survive a full-scale battle, so the tactic used on Vikings would be employed: attack and withdraw followed by the same, again. Also, all resources, especially food, would be removed. Without a food supply, Gismore would starve or be forced to ship in supplies, thus providing great targets for ambush.

As with the Viking wars, Northdale would cut hidden walking paths through the woods that extend all the way to Hollingsbrook. They would provide scouts the ability to move unobserved. If time existed, several paths would also be cut to provide advantageous shooting positions for the archers.

Sara and Oloff would begin vigorous training. Considering the sword and shield supply, about two hundred men could be fitted out. Sara claimed one hundred and fifty archers. The general public would begin to move valuables into the high woods before the snow melted. The military training would extend to men and women who might not be ready to join the main fighting, but who could be drafted as replacements if necessary. Squire would organize arrow manufacture.

Finally, scouts would set up hidden observation posts at Hollingsbrook. It was assumed Gismore's and Blackwood's overconfidence would keep them from being secretive. In fact, it was assumed they probably counted on a dramatic show of force to intimidate Northdale.

As they walked out of the meeting, Rupert put his arm around Sara. "Is there something going on between Michael and Sophia?"

Sara stopped and, with raised eyebrows, gave a disbelieving look at her husband. "My love, among your many faults, add that you are obviously blind." She laughed and he smiled.

Baron David of Hollingsbrook expected he could make a profit out of the situation. He hoped the virtual dictator of England, Earl Gismore, planned to stage any army on his estate—clearly a potential revenue. He had always remained friendly with Rupert, but not close. No scruples held him back from hosting Gismore. No practical alternative existed, either.

Gismore and Blackwood arrived shortly after Christmas. Their retinue numbered twenty-five and filled Hollingsbrook Castle. It included Gismore's oldest son Hugo, knighted a year previously, and his youngest child, Gilbert. The earl employed a small core of heralds to seek other noble's support for the holy invasion. It turned out that the response did not produce a huge army; the other nobles could not believe

Gismore would require anything more than a police force to take Northdale. By spring, twelve hundred men had arrived and seven knights had volunteered.

Gismore held, and paid for, nightly banquets. The pending smashing of a weak opponent inspired some spirited bragging. Wine and ale kept up the spirits. As each new knight arrived, the feeling of invincibility increased.

At the final banquet before their departure, Gismore stood up on the head table and announced, "We move tomorrow and should subdue the devil traffickers within a month. The only thing stopping us will be the lack of wine!" He held up his glass, and the assembly roared its approval. "We will prevent the Viking traders from ever returning to the dirt pile north of the Ibix." Another cheer rang out.

As the party continued, Gismore and Blackwood left the room to meet privately with Sir John Macabe.

When the door closed, Gismore asked, "Well John, did the patrols report any activity?"

Sir John stood six feet tall and sported a thick black beard. His bright blue eyes always appeared to be penetrating anyone with whom he spoke. Gismore had appointed him as the campaign's marshal due to his well-known, fierce love of fighting. He wore a chain mail shirt and a plain, but rather dirty leather tunic.

John pointed at the table. "I need some ale." He threw his gloves on the table before grabbing the mug.

Blackwood, after pouring himself a glass of wine, said, "John, results?"

"I cannot find the bastards to fight. You remember a month ago, when we sent out the first patrol it simply disappeared; we never found a trace of it. Ten men were on that patrol. Since then, every time we send out another, the damn woods are full of unseen archers. I've never completed a patrol without losing at least one man, and on top of it, they have no respect for the horses. Almost every patrol also costs at least two. Shit!" He chugged his ale.

"Have you chased the archers?" asked Gismore.

"You know we have, and the results are the same: they don't stand to fight, and yet I often lose one or two more men. I don't chase them anymore; I just have my own archers shoot into the woods at shadows. Damn it, if I ever get my hands on one of those cursed archers, I will personally cut out his intestines!"

"You know that I am a man of the cloth with no military training, so pardon this question, but you have not found the location of the enemy? In fact, it sounds like you might not have any knowledge of them."

It was Gismore's turn to fill his glass. "Only one road leads into Northdale, and if I remember, they don't have more than about two hundred men.

Gismore sat in one of the four chairs and indicated Blackwood and Macabe should also sit. "The Northdale rats possess only one option, defend along the one road. Therefore, we have no problem knowing where they are. John and I just hope they make a fight of it, so the butchery can start."

Blackwood persisted. "Have you told the other commanders that we do not have an exact fix on Northdale's positions?"

Gismore and John looked at each other, and then Gismore drained his glass. "Look, Bishop, I see no need to tell them. We have only had a problem with some enemy patrols. Besides, we only lost about twenty-five men, and that number could be matched by those lost to the whore disease." The two soldiers laughed; Blackwood winced out a half smile.

The earl rose to his feet, "We should find a herald and send a message demanding a meeting with Sir Rupert."

Macabe raised a finger. "He is an earl."

"He is a bloody asshole. John, I hope you cannot wait to cut his nuts off." John raised his fist in confirmation.

The herald reached the top of the road cutting though Northdale's cliff. An armed man stepped out of the brush and drew a sword. "Halt! What is your business?"

"I am a herald and by the king's authority am free to transport messages between parties in a dispute. Please direct me to Earl Rupert."

"Well, Sir Herald, you will wait here, and we will contact His Lordship."

"Soldier or guard or whatever you claim to be, you cannot interfere with the duties of a herald. I travel with the king's protection. I am to see Earl Rupert."

Sir Rodger Cartwright put the tip of his sword in the ground and crossed his arms on its hilt. "Herald, hear me clearly: either you get off that horse and wait or you will fall off it dead. It is your choice."

The herald's face transmitted complete disgust as he turned his horse around. It changed to surprise when he saw two archers standing behind him. Rodger said, "We can offer you wine or ale—again, your choice."

Rupert, Oloff, Michael, and Squire stood in the trees observing the interaction with the herald. Oloff faced the other two. "I don't trust that bastard Gismore. He talks like a noble man, but he is just a shit pile. To make himself look good, he would try sneaky tricks in a minute. He will try to kill you."

Squire nodded his head in agreement. "Let me go as your representative."

"Thank you two, but the herald will invite me to a conference. It is a required step before any major confrontation. I must go, and I will take Michael. But it seems we should be very cautious. I agree with Oloff's view of Gismore. The site must have easy access and offer sufficient protection."

They agreed on a small clearing about two hundred feet back from the ridge on Hollingsbrook's side of the Ibix valley.

"Oloff, you get the archers infiltrated through the woods surrounding the open area. But remember, they must evaporate whenever Gismore's troops search for them. Clear?

"Squire, you go back to the village and put on your best tunic and ask Lady Sara for one of mine and one of Michael's. We will set the date for three days from now. Oloff, you and Sara will take the archers and try to pick off invaders each night. An army experiencing its first march is usually quite disorganized. Numerous targets will exist." All agreed.

As they ate dinner next to a campfire, Sophia looked worried. "Michael, you are for the meeting tent and I'm into the woods. Please be careful."

"Look, Sophia, the only thing I fear is some hotshot archer mistaking me for the wrong side." Smiling, she hit his arm with her bow. "Mistress, you cannot strike a knight of the realm, but you can promise to take care of yourself." When departure time came, they rose and exchanged a kiss and a very strong hug.

The tent sat in the designated clearing. Gismore, Blackwood, and seven knights gathered on the Hollingsbrook side of the central table. They'd already had two glasses of wine by the time Rupert and Michael rode up.

Rupert and Michael strode into the tent with very deliberate steps. With a completely emotionless face, Rupert stated, "I am Earl Rupert, and this is Sir Michael of Northdale. What business do you have here?" He gazed at each of the men.

Gismore did not bother to stand. He put down his glass and placed his hands on the tabletop. "You devil traders have no business protecting Richard. *Hand him over!*"

"Interesting." Rupert first turned to his son and smiled as he looked back at Gismore. "Definition of devil should include people who break their fealty vows, should it not?"

"You!" Blackwood's self-righteous voice boomed. "You, almost peasant, cannot interpret holy dogma."

Rupert put his hand on his sword and the other in his belt. "You are dressed as a bishop, so you are Blackwood. How can the church, with your blessing, condone a royal usurper?"

Gismore jumped to his feet and, with unhidden disgust, said, "My dear lord, I will stuff those words down your throat."

Rupert again turned to Michael and they exchanged mock frightened looks. "Well, let's cut the bullshit. If you invade Northdale, you face three punishments. First, when you depart, you will leave all metal objects including all weapons behind. Second, you and your men will become prisoners and stay for one year to repair any damage. Third, you must walk out and leave your horses and any other livestock." With a big smile, Rupert finished. "I will enjoy seeing you, Gismore, cleaning out my stables."

Gismore put both hands on the table and leaned forward. "I will enjoy cutting your balls off."

"You and your men will be truly sorry for entering Northdale." Rupert spun on his hells and strode out just as he'd come in.

Gismore faced his knights. "What a horse's ass."

―――

Gismore's army made only five miles the first day. It hunkered down in a lightly forested area. On this night and for the rest of the campaign, Gismore placed his and Blackwood's tents in the center of the camp and surrounded them with the bishop's troops, the other knights, and his personal bodyguard.

Rupert had doubled back, once out of sight of the invaders, and joined Sara and Oloff. They chose one of the newly arrived contingents under Sir Tagmore's command for the first large attack. Fifty archers crept close after dark and fired. Approximately twenty-five men were hit. Tagmore ordered twenty-five men to give pursuit. Only five injured men returned. The captain reported being surrounded by archers and swordsmen once they'd penetrated the woods. Tagmore ran to Gismore's tent and related what happened.

"Of course, you stupid man. Sending troops into the woods at night invites disaster."

The next day the army progressed to the south side of the Ibix. Arrows fired from the top of the bluff on Northdale's side could not reach this campsite. The following day's commanders meeting established a strategy to cross the river and assault the narrow bluff cut through which the only road ran. They surmised it would be heavily defended.

Attackers planned to fabricate mobile wood barricades behind which squads of men could be protected from arrows. The men would also hold their shields over their heads. The barricades would be lifted and slid forward a few feet at a time, thus giving their archers time to shoot at Northdale's archers. In addition, fifty men on each side of the road would climb the bluff face and chase off its defenders.

The barricade construction took two days. Some unit commanders ordered their men to dig trenches to protect their positions. After Northdale's archers took another twenty men that night, Gismore ordered the completion of a ditch around the whole camp. He also created a flying squad of his own archers. Wherever Northdale attacked, this group unleashed retaliatory arrows. The second night's loss of another twenty men caused an order to extinguish all campfires providing light by which attacking archers located targets.

Rupert and his staff saw all the tree cutting and woodworking. They suspected Gismore of constructing ladders. Still, one hundred Northdale infantry troops and seventy-five archers were divided into two ranks: one to be stationed on each side of the road cut. The infantry collected a considerable number of good-sized throwing rocks.

After inspecting their positions, Rupert, Oloff, Rodger, Sara, Sophia, Michael, and Eleanor met at the bluff's edge. Eleanor asked, "Can we hold them?"

They watched Rupert as he kicked a stone off the edge. "If we had another five hundred armed men, maybe. I mean, even if they just try and run their men up the road, we don't have enough arrows to get them all."

They all stood quiet, thinking. Oloff put his hand on Rupert's shoulder. "So we hurt them for some time and then melt away."

Sadness clouded his face as he gazed at each of them. "We don't have a choice. This is the best defensive position in the whole district, but we just don't have the manpower to hold it."

Sara tapped him on the shoulder with her bow. With a smile, she said, "Or women power."

"I will wave a red flag when it is time to withdraw. Sara, Eleanor, and Sophia keep a watch for my signal. Agreed?"

Sara put the tip of her bow on the ground. "I can tell you that archers don't want to remain when the swordsmen retreat!" She was smiling as she looked at each of the commanders. "Would you folks get to your posts? I want to talk to Rupert."

When they were gone, she dropped her bow on the ground and gave Rupert a strong hug followed by an equally strong kiss. They exchanged several verbal expressions of love along with several more kisses.

"Sara, please take care of yourself, no risky maneuvers. Do you hear? I want to grow old with you."

"Do you think I'm tempted by dangerous positions?"

"I know it, so please be careful."

"Listen, hero boy, an army cannot succeed with a dead commander, so listen to your own advice. Understand?" They held hands until they reached the main road. One more hug and they both turned to their respective duties.

Sophia signaled Ann to crawl over. "Someone should check on Rodger's dispositions. Go and be back in fifteen minutes."

"I cannot do anything in fifteen minutes," whispered Ann. Smiling, Sophia made a fist and shook it.

Gismore moved the barricades across the river before dawn. Northdale's night archer team reported the movement of large objects, but they could not identify them.

As dawn broke, the assault began. Rupert's team had not prepared fire-arrow supplies, so none could be launched. The attack proceeded slowly, as the barricades had to be moved and the bluffs scaled. Northdale forces repelled the two scaling parties, but arrows and rocks only slowed the barricades. It took an hour before Rupert raised the red flag.

Gismore and his commanders were ecstatic. He stood in the middle of his captains. "We only lost thirty-five men while breaching a great defensive position. Moreover, we now know Northdale does not have a large army. This should be a very quick campaign." He raised his mug setting off a loud cheer from the captains.

The attackers found a small clearing about five hundred feet down the road, and they set up camp. From this date onward, the troops always dug a defensive trench around the camp. The digging guaranteed slow marching progress because the army could only move about six hours before entrenching again. As a reward for all the digging, Gismore made sure ample wine supplies reached the men and commanders.

After about an hour of trenching, the first arrow hit a victim. Gismore's army lost about five men a day to the archers' arrows. However, he accepted this loss rather than pursuing into the woods and suffering greater causalities. His men took all sorts of personal safety precautions; no one used a latrine standing up.

The next day's progress equaled the last's day progress. Orders required the men to finish the trench before evening meal. That fact provided motivation. Cooking meals inside movable walls prevented light from shining out, but also proved to be a great inconvenience to the men.

On the third day out, at the intersection of the main road and a rutted farm access road, the scout horsemen came across a grumbling old man who constantly talked to some unseen person or persons. When one of the men dismounted and walked over to Simon, he started yelling about the stupid sheriff taking everything including his stash of twenty barrels full of wine. He then continued to mumble to his invisible companions. Not knowing how to interpret the old man's ramblings, they took him to Gismore, enduring much yelled abuse along the way.

Simon presented an eccentric image to Gismore. He had no teeth and followed the habit of cutting his hair with a dull knife, so tufts of it stuck out at different lengths. In short, he looked very shabby. Simon also did not stand up; he preferred to squat. Bathing never appealed to the man—he absolutely stank.

Gismore addressed Simon in a commanding voice. "Old man, what is it that you have told my men?"

"Oh, a fancy lord." He turned to one of his invisible friends. "Do you see the fancy lord? Always the same—wants to yell and demand things."

"Old man, what about the wine?"

Simon stood for this harangue. "Mighty sheriff took all my wine, twenty casks. I keep and sell a little to make food money, but now I starve." He squatted and looked at an invisible friend and pointed. "That is what the mighty sheriff did."

Gismore looked at two of his companions and raised his eyebrows while shaking his head. One of them said, "If the mighty sheriff took your wine, where did he put it?"

Simon looked at one of his invisible friends off to the right and then at another off to his left. He then gazed at the questioner. "I sit at the road to keep them from taking a full wagon out. In a house up the road about five miles." He faced the invisible friend to his left. "About five miles. Right?" He then looked at the ground and began doodling in the soft dirt. "He agrees—five miles."

Gismore waved to his assistants, and they all moved away. Sir John de Burghton, one of the captains, had watched the interview. When out of earshot, Gismore said, "Well, John, what do you think?"

Burghton gestured with his hand to the others. "Please leave us." When they were alone, Brighton continued. "Gismore, we are running out of food. These Northdale devils leave nothing for us to eat. But the men will be temporarily content with half rations if we can supply them with wine."

Gismore nodded his head in agreement and then looked back at the mumbling old man. Gazing at John again, Gismore spoke. "I think that old man is crazy, but even the addled sometimes grasp truth. The wine sticks firmly in his mind."

"Well, shit, Gismore, it is only five miles. Let your son, Hugo, take two hundred men and four wagons up there and see what he can find. Besides, giving your son a little independent command will be great confidence building for him and his troop."

Gismore examined the small farm road, and his face showed contemplation. He put his hand on John's shoulder. "Northdale only has about two hundred men, and they have never shown any desire to initiate a full confrontation, so give orders for the excursion."

After learning of his new assignment, Sir Hugo ran up to his father. "Thank you for giving me this opportunity. If any wine exists, I'll find it."

Gismore stood directly in front of his son and gave him a hard eye-to-eye stare. "Don't take any chances. If anything seems odd, turn around and get back here. There is never any disgrace in making strategic moves that save your men's lives. Do you understand?" Hugo nodded and ran to his horse. The company moved out after the midday meal.

After the troop departed, Gismore saw Sir Adam de Yealand and called him over. "Look, Adam, my son Gilbert and yours, Theobald, have proven helpful in accomplishing their responsibilities. From my observation, they both also seem to be learning military skills very fast. I saw them in the sword practice area, and they handled their weapons very well. Agreed?"

"Gismore, the boys have become very involved in this campaign and all of its activities. And I agree they seem to be taking assigned responsibility seriously. I think they don't want Hugo to feel too superior." They both laughed.

"Well, Adam, I wonder if we could ask the other knights to approve knighting these two. I know they are young, but I can name others who were elevated at this age, including our soon-to-be-dead king."

With a very pleased facial expression, Yealand said, "They are boon companions, and they should be elevated."

"And the knights' reactions?"

"Despite those damned archers, the men sense victory very soon. You are the cause, and you might soon be picking yourself as the new king. The men will support you. Gladly, I must add."

That evening, Gismore, Blackwood, and most of his knights sat talking and drinking wine after dinner. Sir Adam attended. Gismore addressed him. "Adam, your son and mine are about the same age, twelve." Adam nodded his head. "The two of them could be knighted. They are young, but old enough to be dubbed. After all, our friend Richard over there was knighted when he was twelve."

Yealand said with a big smile, "I believe they are old enough and have shown considerable responsibility in carrying out duties on this campaign. Do the other knights agree?"

Gismore and Blackwood gave the group hard facial expressions. Tagmore raised his glass. "I agree and, as knights, both will gain battle experience that carries credibility."

The others expressed their support, except Sirs Henry and Ranulf who remained silent.

"Blackwood, tomorrow night will be the vigil. Will you make the necessary preparations?"

"Of course, my lord." He faced the group, "I will need two sponsor knights to nominate the candidates." Tagmore and Macabe jumped to their feet, spilling wine as they did so.

When everyone left the tent, Gismore grabbed Blackwood's arm. "I know the prospective candidate is required to stay up all night during the vigil. When I was dubbed, the vigil provided time for the person to meditate on the twelve vows. But I doubt Gilbert and Theobald can stay up all night. Have one of your priests use a rod on them for a while, but we will have to allow some sleep. Just make sure they are up before dawn."

"Do you two fathers have a sword, shield, and spurs for each?"

Gismore waved his hands around the tent as if showing its contents. "We are in a battle camp, so fancy things don't exist. We will paint their crest on new shields when back in civilization. Swords are plentiful, even if they must be surrogates for their yet-to-be-acquired dress ones. As for spurs, we will find someone willing to loan us two pairs."

Blackwood slapped Gismore on the arm. "It will all be arranged. I even happen to have a copy of the twelve vows they will take. It will be available to them for study during the vigil."

Blackwood sent for the two boys and informed them of the pending knighthood and explained its requisite ritual. Both expressed extreme excitement, both verbally and in body language. Because their rank would soon rise, both strode, not walked, out of the tent. Blackwood, with a fatherly smile, shook his head.

The assistant priests erected one unused, small tent. Into it, they placed a table covered with a decorated altar cloth, numerous candles, one crucifix, and two makeshift kneelers with pillows for the knees.

The relatively truncated ceremony started at dusk with a Mass and blessing of the swords, shields, and spurs. The candidates were then given a meal and escorted by the sponsors to the chapel tent. Blackwood stood before them and read the twelve vows of a knight.

1. To fear God and maintain his church
2. To serve the liege lord, or other placed in authority, with valor
3. To protect the weak and defenseless
4. To give succor to widows and orphans
5. To live by honor and for glory

6. To despise pecuniary reward
7. To fight for the welfare of all
8. To avoid unfairness, meanness, and deceit
9. To speak the truth at all times
10. To respect the honor of women
11. To never refuse a challenge from an equal
12. To never turn the back upon a foe

Gilbert and Theobald loudly proclaimed that they understood the responsibilities of knighthood. Blackwood then gave a short lecture on the power of the vows and that divine retribution would follow if broken. Should the candidates be false, the minimal punishment would be eternal damnation! He then instructed them to study and understand the written copies of the vows which he placed on the kneelers.

Blackwood had already told his two assistants to take turns watching the boys. They should be regularly hit with a stick to keep them focused. At midnight, they could sleep on the floor. Servants contributed a bucket of water so the assistants could wash the boy's faces in the morning to give the appearance that they'd stayed up all might.

In the morning, all of the knights, Blackwood, and Earl Gismore entered the tent. Both candidates placed their hands on a Bible and swore to uphold the twelve vows and to give their allegiance to Gismore. The earl then tapped each on the shoulder with his sword, and one of the sponsors attached spurs to the knight's boots. When completed,

Gismore announced, "Gentlemen, I give you Sir Gilbert and Sir Theobald." The host cheered and then headed into a celebratory breakfast.

Sir Hugo and the wine-searching company stopped at every farmhouse along the little road and made two universal findings: there was nothing of value in them and no wine casks existed. They reached a farm at the five-mile distance at about dusk. The men were hungry and tired. Spirits immediately shot up when searchers found two large wine casks. By poking into every nook and cranny and tearing up floorboards, they increased the haul to eighteen.

The company captain approached Sir Hugo. "One cask has already been breached, and I suspect more will go tonight. I suggest you formally give two more with the condition that no more are opened."

"All right, but before any more is consumed, the men must put the fifteen remaining into the wagons. And post a guard."

With a big smile, the captain replied, "I will, but I bet all of tonight's guards will have a cup in their hands."

Observing the increasing inebriation, Sir Hugo decided his responsibility required him to stay sober and alert. Just after dark, he took an empty wooden box and placed it near the road. The men had been pissing anyplace they could stand, and he wanted some separation. After two hours, he took off his helmet and chain-mail shirt for comfort. The arrow entered his left temple, and he was dead when his body hit the ground.

Most of the Northdale's forces and commanders had observed the advance of the wine seekers. Only twenty-five archers had been left near Gismore under the command of squad-leader Marta Posley. Their job was to keep up the normal arrow shots so the main force did not become suspicious.

Leaving any extra weapons or other metal objects that could make noise, the Northdale soldiers stepped among the passed-out enemy. The number of troops almost equaled each other. Rupert signaled by opening a shielded lantern to emit a short burst of light. It was over in fifteen minutes. Only about twenty-five of Gismore's men were able to stand and form a hopeless defense. Northdale's men showed no interest in quarter; none was given. It lost three men in the fight.

Pointing at Oloff, Rupert said, "You know what to do with these bodies. Anything of value, keep. Throw them into the wagons."

Oloff nodded. "Then into the ocean." Rupert slapped him on the arm.

The wagons transported the bodies to the shore; the ocean's tide took them out. It took five trips with the four wagons. The encounter replenished Northdale's armory with a windfall of weapons and equipment.

After the elevation ceremony, the main army remained in camp the next day, waiting for the wine contingent. Concern began to show by nightfall. Gismore decided to send a ten-man, fast-riding scout squad out at dawn to get an answer. The results were unexpected, but definitive. About half-mile away and still within sight of the army, a hail of arrows cut down all ten men and horses.

One interesting camp development occurred during this waiting day. As Burghton made his daily tour of the defensive works, he came upon a company that had piled cut brush along the top of the earthwork. Upon inquiry, the company's captain dragged over a crusty old solder. "Well, my lord, when I fought in the Crusades, the Sarsens had good archers. So we piled up brush to stop the arrows."

"Come on, man," Sir John said as he walked up to the man. "Brush cannot stop arrows."

"Begging your pardon, sir, some get through all right. But the archers cannot clearly see any targets, and most important, the branches of the brush knock the arrows off target." By nightfall, brush mounted all defensive works.

Commanders Meet

AT A COMMANDERS COUNCIL THAT evening, Gismore asked for suggestions from the nine knights and some captains. Sir Tagmore proposed Gismore send to Rupert a herald carrying a message requesting another council. The purpose would be to pry information directly or indirectly from Rupert as to the condition of the wine-seeking force.

It took time for the herald to find Lord Rupert. He told the herald to wait until he could summon his commanders. They all agreed it could do no harm at this point to talk again; the invaders now knew Northdale's obvious tactics. The herald did not return to Gismore until dusk.

Gismore's staff set up the meeting tent on the road, first thing the next day. The men and table stood in the same positions as the last meeting. Rupert and Michael arrived as before.

Rupert strode up to the table, dropped his riding gloves on it, quickly scanned the assembled reception group, and fixed his eyes on Gismore. "Purpose?"

Gismore said with a sneering smile, "Well, Lord Rupert, do you not practice correct manners?"

Rupert smiled, picked up his gloves with his right hand and slapped them against his left. "Gismore, I practice manners with people worthy of them. I ask again—purpose?"

Gismore now stood up. Anger clouded his looks, "You have seen that you cannot stop my army, so I will run over Northdale. Once completed, I cannot leave a noble or any of his family alive to reclaim the land." He glanced at Michael. "Nor can I leave any captain who might wish to take up future revenge. However, if you surrender Richard, I will withdraw immediately."

Rupert was now controlling his anger. He turned to Michael and, with a dead flat voice, said, "Did you know that we are losing a fight?"

Michael looked surprised and said, "No, my lord."

Rupert turned back to Gismore and, again, scanned the faces of his commanders. "Gismore, you have lost almost a quarter of your men, you have dwindling food supplies, and I know no supplies have gotten through to you. In fact, we quite enjoyed the wine from your last caravan." He made a face showing great pleasure.

Sir Tagmore, with hand on hilt, stepped forward. "You are an insolent bastard."

With a mildly curious glance, Rupert said, "Tagmore, it is, isn't it? You, sir, are breakers of your holy fidelity vow and invaders of peaceful people." He quickly pointed at Blackwood. "And, Bishop, don't start the devil bullshit again; we already danced that dance." He then crossed his arms, looked at Gismore and, with a tilted head, silently repeated his first question.

John Macabe leaned over the table and placed his hands on it. "The only way we could have lost the number of men you just mentioned is if you captured our unit we sent up the road on a scouting mission."

Rupert stepped over to stand across the table from Macabe. "Really?" He looked back at his son and raised his hand in a gesture that said, "Well, that is clear." With a tightly controlled smile, he stepped back in front of Gismore and looked at him. After a minute of silence, Rupert spoke again. "Gismore, nothing new has been raised at this meeting, so again, what is the purpose?"

Gismore looked over at Tagmore who nodded his head. The knight turned to Rupert, "What has happened to the unit we sent up that small road?"

Rupert pointed at Michael to give the answer. "My lord, they are all dead."

All of Gismore's commanders shouted denials, but Gismore dropped back into his seat. It was Tagmore's voice that finally cut through. "That is a lie; you are trying to mislead us."

"Sir Knight, do you want proof?"

Several knights yelled, "Yes!"

Turning his head over his shoulder, Rupert said, "Michael, signal the archer commander to come here." He walked to the tent's edge and made hand signals. Rupert leaned over the table and grabbed Gismore's wine glass. "I know this one will not contain poison."

More comments were made as Rupert walked to the tent's edge and put his hand on Michael's shoulder. Together, they watched a horse and rider leave the woods. When the horse arrived, one of Gismore's squires held the reins. Rupert waited until the rider dismounted and then held the arm of the archer commander. When they reached the table,

Rupert said, "I know you have met Countess Sara. She commands our archers."

The shock existed at two levels. First, Sara wore brown-colored leggings, short skirt, shirt, and tunic. She and all the women archers wore tight leather skullcaps to keep their hair from interfering with their work. A strap tied under the chin kept the cap in place. Second, although rumors long circulated about Northdale women, no one had actually seen a female fighter before. Not a sound occurred for over a minute.

Sara looked at her husband. "I should be introduced." Rupert took her by the arm and walked up to each of Gismore's commanders.

"Countess Sara, this is …"

At each introduction, she made the correct courtly curtsy and with a voice encrusted with sweetness said to each, "I am pleased to meet you." Only Sir Harry Bristol and Sir Ranulf followed exact protocol when meeting a countess. All the rest mumbled their names and repeated the greeting.

When she stood in front of Gismore and repeated her greeting, he refused to stand or speak. With a flat voice, Gismore said, "You had no manners when we met years ago, and you have none now."

She turned to Rupert, shrugged her shoulders, and said with a smile, "I guess that should be expected from a low-class land grabber."

Before she could speak to Blackwood, Gismore jumped to his feet and almost yelled, "Do you have proof that the wine contingent was captured or killed?"

Still looking at her husband, Sara said, "My lord husband, do I have to respond to such a crude man?" Gismore slammed his fist on the table.

"Unfortunately, yes, my dear."

Sara turned to the table, reached inside her tunic, and drew out a folded piece of cloth. It wrapped around another piece of cloth that she took out and dropped on the table like it was filthy.

It was Macabe who, with a fierce voice, said, "What is that?"

Sara looked at him and said in a completely flat voice, "It is the neck scarf the unit's commander wore; the blood is his." An uproar of voices occurred and Gismore again dropped into his seat.

Macabe yelled again, "How could that have happened?"

Sara took a step toward the table. Her face projected disgust. "A great military leader like Gismore here knows a group of soldiers who have been in the field a long time are extremely eager to consume wine. So when the men seek a supply, the good commander always sends along a trusted group of provost men to both secure the wine and dispense it by the cupful. Otherwise, the men will become vulnerable to a very old trick by becoming piss drunk." Her face changed to a look of surprise. "Did you forget to do so?"

Gismore pounded his clenched fists on the chair's arms. The others all started talking at once.

Blackwood stepped to the table and raised his hands over his head. "Silence, silence!" When the group complied, he looked at Sara. "It is against God's law for women to take up arms, and you can be condemned for this." The men sounded their approval.

"Well, my dear bishop, is it not against God's laws to despoil helpless, poor people or to break a fealty vow? It does not appear that you stand in a place from whence to dispense God's judgment." More comments from the men followed.

Before Blackwood could respond, Rupert pushed out his hand, palm out, to demand silence from the bishop. While still making a squint-eyed stare at the bishop, Rupert said, "Gismore, I don't want to argue with this hypocritical bastard bishop. The answer to your question: no, I will not give up Richard. I made a vow, and in Northdale, we know the sacredness of holy vows."

Gismore still sat in his chair, but stared at Rupert with hate-filled eyes.

"Furthermore, I already told you that unless you leave now, none of you will live." Shouts from Gismore's commanders now rained down.

Rupert again took up Sara's arm and made a pointing gesture at Michael to leave. They walked out. As they mounted their horses, one of the commanders yelled, "Where are the bodies?"

Michael turned. "Northdale always throws invader's bodies into the ocean." They heard cursing and yelling as they rode away.

As they rode out, Michael exclaimed, "That was incredible. You two are great!"

LADY SARA

—

As they sat eating dinner together with Michael, Mary, Alfred, King Richard and the king's two knights, Sara explained, "We are not striking them as in the past. Now, they have surrounded themselves with brush. Our shots are constantly deflected by the thin branches." It was the night after the second conference with Gismore. "Last night, only one arrow hit anyone, and we fired at least two dozen." She hit her hand on the table. "We must develop methods to overcome that damn brush."

Richard asked, "Can you climb a tree?"

"We could, Your Majesty, but then we would be trapped by any countermoves by the enemy."

Rupert looked concerned. "Sara, do not succumb to the temptation to move your archers even closer than now. Gismore's commanders are anticipating that move."

"Dear, we cannot see our targets unless we get closer."

"Sara, I've heard from some of the archers that you are beginning to take increased risks when scouting the bastards."

She walked over to where Rupert sat and put her hands on his cheeks. "I love you, our children, and the people of Northdale. We must take risks."

"We must be bold, but risks should be kept to the minimum."

After taking several backward steps, Sara said, "Look, dear, you know the consequences if Gismore wins. You and our sons will be executed. Mary and I will get chained to the wall in a convent someplace and somehow be found dead. All of our captains will be executed, and some form of painful penance will be imposed on our people. I could envision that hypocrite Blackwood demanding one child from each family be given to the church."

She raised both hands up to her shoulders, pointed at Rupert, and increased the force if her words. "You know that *you and I cannot let that happen*! You and I must be prepared to pay the cost!"

"Sara, your archers have been very effective. You command them. Their continued success depends on your leadership. Reasonable, aggressive scouting can be performed by most of your people. You do not have to take all of the risks."

She put her hands on his shoulders, and looked directly into his eyes. "Do you think I could ask my ladies to take chances while I stayed behind? Leadership demands they see me in the thick of everything. My love, you know me, and you know I feel obligated to risk as much as any other trooper."

Rupert looked at the floor and then rubbed his forehead with one hand. Looking up at Sara, he said, "If you get killed, our whole effort will be dramatically injured and Gismore could succeed."

With a mild laugh, she responded, "I don't plan to get killed."

He smiled. "Sara, I want you to help me raise our grandchildren."

She again shook his shoulders. "I want to do two things. First, also play with our grandchildren, and second, I plan to correct everything you do wrong for many more years." They both laughed.

Rupert stood then, hugged and kissed her. Then, looking at the others he said, "Excuse us, but the thought of losing her makes me emotional." Mary and Michael had averted their eyes, Alfred said 'yuck', the others just smiled.

The king put his elbows on the table. "What do you think is their next move?" No longer the center of the conversation, Sara sat down.

"Sire, it is rather simple. We harass them at all times and wait until they make a mistake, like the wine excursion. Then we hit them. We have gained experience with this method of fighting after resisting the Vikings raids. It's Northdale's approach."

The king leaned over the table's edge. "Compared to us, they still have great strength?"

"Well, we estimate they have lost at least one third of their manpower. Our hidden advantage is that Gismore and his commanders don't recognize the trouble they are walking into. Lady Sara's archers slow Gismore's movement; he must fortify each night. He is consuming his food supply, and we stopped giving them any!"

Sir Benedict put down his wine cup and commented. "Please describe for the king your overall strategy."

"Well, sire, we continue to do the same. Gismore will certainly take the village, but it will cost him. He will not find you, food, or treasure, and I believe the food may end up being the most important."

The king shook his head. "I'm learning about Northdale's tactics."

Rupert looked down to the end of the table at which his children sat. "Anything to add?"

Michael said, "Your Majesty, Gismore told my father that none of us will be allowed to live. I guess stupid Bishop Blackwood will demand contrition for trafficking with the devil. Gismore will be free to extract any penance he chooses. Our women, children, and any other assets may be forfeited. So you see, besides your protection, we must resist at all costs."

"One more thing, Your Majesty." Rupert looked very serious. "Gismore has let it be known he wants you dead to remove an obstacle from his ambitions. That means you cannot personally participate in any of the fighting. That bastard and his men will be looking for you. If he kills you in battle, then no blame or accusations can be leveled at him. He probably already placed a huge gold reward on your royal neck. You will sacrifice England's future prosperity and stability if that asshole and his immediate associates get their hands on the crown and royal treasury after your death."

The king nodded in agreement. "If you will excuse me, I'm tired."

He rose and, as required, so did everyone else. Rupert asked his children to leave them alone, and then he escorted Sara to the front door of the keep.

"Sara, did you hear what I said? Don't get too close—*please*." He turned her and put both hands on her shoulders. "I don't want to lose you." He hugged her.

Sara smiled and then kissed him. "I never get too close."

That night, Sara moved her archer patrol into the brush overlooking Gismore's forces. She motioned Sophia to crawl over. Whispering, Sara said, "I don't see any targets from this angle. I'm going to get a little closer."

Sophia grabbed her arm and vigorously shook her head. She whispered, "Too close already."

Sara gave her a stay-down hand signal and then crawled toward the defenses.

Macabe had, the night before, sent ten of Gismore's trusted hard-fighting bodyguards out to set up an ambush. The men were to creep at night, one by one, into a camouflaged blind and then wait all the next day and not move or make sounds. These directions were intended to prevent detection by Northdale's archers entering the woods in the early afternoon.

The bodyguards heard Northdale's archers move in but only saw one crawling. In fact, she had moved directly in front of the hidden men.

She had no forewarning of the blow to her head that knocked her out.

Cold water thrown on her face awoke Sara. Two of the bodyguards held her by her arms with her hands tied behind her back. Gismore, Blackwood, and several of his commanders stood around her. They were all grinning.

With as much victory as he could cram into his voice, Gismore said, "Put Lady Sara in irons, get her a smock dress from one of the servants, and toss her into the stable; no need to mind what she sits on." He waved at his companions. "I'm serving wine in my tent. We must discuss this opportunity." Sara remained silent as she tried to orientate herself to this new situation.

When Sir Adam entered the tent, he said, "Gismore, you old fox, you caught the bitch countess!" Most of the commanders were present, and they all cheered. "She leads the archers who have been killing our men. How can we make her scream as we rip her apart?" More cheers erupted.

Gismore raised his hand. "What to do with her will take a little consideration. So everyone drink up—tonight we celebrate. Tomorrow we will deliberate." More cheers followed.

The next day at breakfast, many of the knights and captains had suggestions. In fact, the conversation lasted almost an hour, and each succeeding idea became more bizarre. When it got to using her skin as a cart cover, Gismore stood up.

"I think it's obvious. We send a herald to Rupert and offer to exchange her for his surrender. I know that does not sound like sufficient revenge, but once we have him, we can ignore any exchange agreements. Only a little mopping up will be required, and then we can extract anything we want. We might even be able to grab this whore again and give her the punishment she richly deserves! Agreed?"

The group shouted concurrence. Except Sir Henry. He just observed the goings-on. Sara remained chained to the stable stall and received bread and water.

The herald arrived in Northdale's command center at mid-morning and found Rupert, Oloff, Eleanor, Squire, and Michael sitting together. Much apprehension existed, as the whole Northdale force knew Sara had not returned. He delivered the ultimatum in a professional and objective manner. The message ended with, "I am directed to wait for your response."

Rupert jumped to his feet. "Shit, I told her not to get too close." His chair contained a pillow, and Rupert threw it across the main hall and then reached down and flipped the chair onto its back. "Who was with her? I want to ask questions."

Michael said, "I'll get someone who can answer questions."

Rupert stomped around the room while waiting. Michael entered the hall with his arm around Sophia's waist. She had obviously been crying.

She looked up. "My lord, I tried to stop her, but she would not listen. She crawled right in front of an ambush that we never knew existed." She started to cry again, and Michael placed both arms around her.

Eleanor added, "I think, my lord, that you were already aware of the risks she was taking. She just wanted to pierce those bushes."

Oloff threw his cup across the hall. "I know you talked to her about this, and so did I. But she felt she had to do it."

Rupert walked over to the unlit fireplace, placed his hand on the mantle, and stared at the ashes. No one made any noise for at least three minutes. With a large sigh, he faced the group. His eyes were red. "Let's meet in mid-afternoon and determine how we are going to react. I want to be alone."

Mary had arrived and took a step forward. "Father?" He shook his head while looking at the floor and waved them all away. He walked to the Downs' shore, picked up a bunch of smaller stones, and then sat in the grass. Every few minutes. he threw one with much force into the river.

The mid-afternoon gathering included their three children, Oloff, Eleanor, Squire, the king, and Sophia. Rupert invited all to sit and then passed the wine pitcher around the table. He waited until all glasses were filled.

"This is a very black time, but I don't think any alternatives exist." He swirled some wine in his glass. "I, of course, will listen to your ideas, but I see no honor in letting that horse's ass tear the shit out of Northdale. And with the holy approval of the church, I anticipate he will be absolutely brutal on devil traders. There will be no mercy of any sort."

Most of the group fixed their eyes on the wine glasses. No one spoke for several moments. Mary sat up. "Cannot we find a way to attack?"

Oloff put both forearms on the table. "I've been out looking at their camp construction. They expect an attack, so they built a fortified camp and keep their men stationed for one. It would be suicide." He slumped back in his chair and looked at Rupert.

Rupert leaned into the table and put his folded hands on it. Then with hard eyes he looked at each individual. "Do you understand what this means?" He took a deep breath. "We either let Northdale and its people be trampled by assholes, or we let them kill Sara." He now slumped back into his chair.

No one looked at each other for at least two minutes. Finally, Alfred said, "Father, I thought you said we were winning this fight."

With a pained expression, Rupert said, "There is a big difference between us knowing we are winning and them knowing that they are losing. They really think they now have the upper hand." Heads nodded in agreement. "Listen, I love your mother and would do anything I could to save her. But even if I offered a direct exchange, me for her, that bastard will want the king's life, and he will take revenge on our people."

With great sadness in his voice, Rupert added, "He already plans to kill all of you. Your mother would never forgive you or me for making such an exchange."

"In fact," Oloff said, "I've known her longer than any of you; she is very strong, but she knows what is right. It would kill her if we gave everything just for her." Everyone remained silent and unmoving.

Eleanor cleared her throat. "If you please, my lord, I would like to expand Oloff's comment." Rupert gave her a welcome gesture. "I've known Sara for twenty-some years. I've seen the fire of love she has for you and for Northdale's people. Together we gave birth to eight children. Together, we mourned over the deaths of two. We have assisted each other succeed with many projects. We have helped Northdale grow. And as a final seal between us, we have fought together. To get her out of a death sentence by surrendering the people of Northdale or yourself to the ravages of Gismore and Blackwood would really hurt her. She knows your fierce love of her, and her facing death, in an odd way, will make her love you more because she knows how much the correct decision will personally hurt you. But, if you kneel to those walking piles of shit by surrendering yourself and the people or by ordering a suicidal attack, it would break her spirit. She would be so disappointed she might not be able to face the people or you again."

Rupert rose and again walked to the fireplace. The others looked at the table or their hands in their laps. The silence seemed endless. After a long pause, he took a deep breath, returned to the conference, and placed his forearms on the back of his chair. Tears streamed from his eyes.

"It is obvious we all know what must be done. I love Sara and will desperately need your support as this plays out, but they will kill her." He then tipped over the chair.

Oloff stood. "I swear they will pay for this, even if it takes the rest of my life to do it."

Sorrow radiated from Rupert's face when, with a quiet voice, he said, "Squire, tell the herald there will be no response."

The herald returned to Gismore's camp after dark. Word of the herald's approach flashed through the camp, and the commanders came running. They were all smiles and laughter when the herald entered. Gismore stood and waved for all to be quiet. "Herald, what is the response?"

The herald walked to the middle of the tent and, in a clear voice, said, "There is no response." Considerable and loud comment occurred.

Gismore yelled for quiet. "What say you, herald? Lord Rupert did not write a response?"

"No, my lord, I waited almost all day until his man, Squire, told me to leave without any response."

The tent burst into another round of conversation. Gismore even turned his back on the others in order to exchange ideas with Blackwood. "Leave us, herald, but do not leave camp. We will have a message for you tomorrow."

After the herald left, again the commanders' proffered suggestions varied widely, but they settled on sending the herald again with a message stating if Rupert did not surrender, Sara would be tried then executed after being found guilty.

Blackwood rose, "Lords and captains, we might choose an alternative trial." The group fell silent. "We can put the woman on trial for treason for disobeying a direct and lawful order from a church sanctioned lord, or we can try her for witchcraft." This comment drew out considerable comment from the group.

When the hubbub died down, Blackwood continued. "You see, that woman has profited from exchanging gold with pagan devils, and despite church directions, she has personally engaged in armed fighting; she probably killed Christian soldiers.".

Again the Bishop stopped to let his words be clearly understood. "Either of these proves the person is following the dictates of some powers other than the true God. She clearly follows the devil's direction and, thus, is one of his followers."

The tent now filled with righteous yells condemning the devil worshiper. Blackwood raised his hand for quiet.

"If—and I say if—we try her for witchcraft, and if she is found guilty, then the church rules she is no longer a Christian woman." His voice rose to almost a yell, "We are free to do anything we want to her, including burning her at the stake!"

The men jumped to their feet and started yelling "Burn her, burn her!"

As the ruckus continued, Blackwood turned his back on the men and faced Gismore. He made a devious smile, and Gismore returned it with a slight nod of his head.

Sara asked her guard what caused the obvious uproar. "You husband sent the herald back without any response." With a twinkle in her eyes, Sara smiled.

At the back flap of the tent stood Sir Harry Bristol and Sir Ranulf of Alnwick. Neither participated in the clamoring. As the yells to "burn her' started, they looked at each other, and Harry made a slight nod toward the exit.

As they walked toward their encampment area, Harry said, "Two days ago, two boys took knighthood vows. I don't understand how our fellows could have heard the sacred words and now be screaming to burn Lady Sara."

Ranulf responded, "Something is clearly wrong here." They walked on in silence until they reached their own units.

"Look, Ranulf, we should talk again tonight on this subject." Ranulf nodded in agreement.

The next morning, after the herald left, Gismore directed that a fifty-man scout party should move down the road to find a large clearing on which a very strong defensive fort could be built. They did so and found one only two miles toward the village of Northdale. Its center rose above its outer edges, and a creek with clean water ran through a depressed bed. Plenty of timber for fortification grew nearby. While waiting for Rupert's response, a flurry of construction activity occurred. The men even dragged the defensive brush with them to ensure a solid fortification. Orders came down to leave a space large enough for a big fire near the center of the camp.

Gismore's personal guards bore responsibility for Sara and chained her hand and foot. When moving her to the new encampment, they used spear handles to prod her along. Many of the prods were much heavier than necessary, and her back was bruised from their blows. Sara resolved not to show irritation or fear, and she kept that resolution. Several of the knights rode their horses back to toss insults at Sara. She responded by giving them her sweetest smile.

The Trial

It took two days of frantic fortress-building before Gismore deemed it appropriate to hold Sara's trial. He set it for midmorning and sent written invitations to all of his knights. The invitation informed them they would decide the verdict.

Gismore's bodyguard had given over the guard duties to others because it was beneath their status as the earl's toughest warriors. Sara remained pleasant with her captors, and the new ones responded in kind. She had been told nothing about the trial, but when the guards presented her with a decent breakfast, she became suspicious.

"This is the nicest meal I have received since being captured. Thank you, but why are you giving it to me?" One of the guards told her the trial would start that morning.

Sara made a small laughing grunt and shook her head. "Trial."

Expecting an attack, Gismore ordered the entire force to stand alert at their defensive posts. At the four corners of the fortress, men built circular ramparts. Captains specifically told the ramparts' watchmen of their responsibility to warn the main body if an attack materialized. Anyone caught sleeping would be executed. This last pronouncement generated considerable bad feelings among the troops.

Tables placed in the main meeting tent were arranged in an L shape. One lone chair sat inside the table's angle and faced the corner at about a fifteen-foot distance. Gismore, Blackwood, and two scribes sat at the table's short end and the knights at the long side. The two newest, Theobald and Gilbert, sat at the very end as was fitting their seniority. The two seats reserved for Harry and Ranulf remained unoccupied.

Because of the pending public spectacle, Gismore's guards reasserted control over Sara. They removed her ankle shackles but left her wrists cuffed. They had exchanged her war garments for a peasant's shift dress made of a coarse tan material that covered her from wrists to ankles; the neckline almost squeezed her neck. Her hair hung loosely to her shoulders. Sara appeared relaxed and smiled, even after being roughly pushed into her seat.

The bishop presided as judge. Once everyone settled down, he pointed to one scribe. The man rose. "Countess

Sara of Northdale, you are hereby formally charged with witchcraft."

Leaning forward, Sara, with a smile, interrupted. "Witchcraft! Gismore or Blackwood, which of you two is responsible for that fabrication?"

Gismore slammed his fist on the table, leaned in, and said with unhidden disgust on his face, "Lady Sara, you are on trial for your life! *This is not a joke.*"

"Gismore, everything you have ever done is a joke."

"I am Earl of Denton. You shall address me by proper title."

"I am the Countess of Northdale. You and I are of equal rank; therefore, I can call you anything I like. Gismore, when I look at you, chamber pots always come to mind."

Gismore, whose face was now bright red, began to rise. Blackwood grabbed his arm and pulled him back to his seat.

Blackwood cleared his throat in order to sound more formal. "Lady Sara, you have been charged with witchcraft, so I must ask you some questions to establish your guilt or innocence." Sara's face clearly registered her low esteem of the bishop. "Have you ever killed a Christian warrior?"

Sara looked at the tent roof for a moment as she said, "Killed a Christian warrior?" She then looked directly at Blackwood. "I've shot my arrows at invaders of my country. I may have hit some of them, but I cannot answer about Christians. Some of them may have been, but some may have been atheists, or maybe even hypocrites. But I must defer that matter to this distinguished group of gentlemen because they know more about hypocrites than I do."

Loud comments could be heard from the knight's table.

Blackwood gave a victorious smile, "Thank you, Lady Sara. Have you ever exchanged services or materials for Viking gold?"

"Of course we have."

"Did you not know this gold came from despoiling church property?'

"I know Northdale faced yearly invasions from Vikings who made a habit of taking our children and property. The only way to stop these invasions was to negotiate peace with the invaders. No one, and I repeat no one, offered to help Northdale repel these intrusions. None of you sitting here offered to send assistance to the smallest earldom in England, so we faced the invaders alone. I know we took gold from them, but they never told its source, and it always came in unidentifiable small chunks."

"You expect us to believe that?"

"Well, my dear bishop, I did not travel with them, so I relied on their claim that the gold was theirs." The bishop raised his hand in a "there-it-is" gesture while looking at the knights.

Tapping his right-hand finger tips on the table, Blackwood then asked, "Do you know that God does not sanction women warriors? In fact, it is forbidden?"

"I have read the New Testament in Latin and it says no such thing. In the Old Testament, several ladies cut off enemies' heads. So, if not so declared in the Bible, then you must be referring to a church law." She faced the knights. "We all know the church adopted many such private laws only revealed to the faithful when the church's bishops or priests decide it serves their purposes."

The knights sat silent and with unmoving faces. The younger knights were squirming in their seats.

"The prosecution ends its case, and as we all can see, she is guilty of witchcraft."

Sara sat quietly looking at the ground for almost a minute. "You may proceed with your defense," said the Bishop.

"The only question is the futility of bothering to offer a defense." She then looked straight at each knight, one at a time. The new knights did not make eye contact. "I'm obviously not a witch. I have worked very hard to bring prosperity to the people who live in my county and have fought very hard against hypocritical invaders. There is simply nothing more to say."

Blackwood rose to his feet. "Is this lady guilty or not?" He asked each knight in the order they sat at the table. All said guilty. The young knights had looked at Gismore for direction. Gismore nodded his head, so both also answered yes. Sara just sat smiling with a slight shaking of her head.

The bishop pointed at one of the scribes, who pulled an already prepared death warrant from under the papers sitting on the desk. The bishop handed the document to Gismore. "Because you have been found guilty of witchcraft by a fair tribunal, I now sign this death warrant. You will be burned at the stake tomorrow morning."

Sara's face turned white as she rose. When Gismore finished signing, she said in a clear and commanding voice, "You think you signed my death warrant, but in fact it is your own." She looked at the table of knights. "It is your own. Lord Rupert will see to that."

Mocking snickers responded.

As the guards grabbed her arms in preparation of leading her out, Blackwood added, "The guilty verdict means that you are no longer noble or even a Christian." Sara turned her head to face him and spat on the ground.

While the trial continued, Sir Harry and Sir Ranulf met in the latter's tent. They discussed the current situation with Gismore and the trial. Both expressed their rising apprehension over Gismore's increasingly erratic behavior. They discussed the options.

Taking their men, if they would come, and retreating posed considerable risk. The group would be too small to fight off a full Northdale attack. Surrendering would mean a year of captivity and possible retribution from Gismore if Rupert actually lost Northdale. Staying meant continued participation in Gismore's activities. Their sworn knightly vows weighed heavily on them; they were obligated to honorably help the downtrodden. The campaign had changed from punishing a king who broke formal and informal covenants to one of personal aggrandizement. They would leave a final decision until the trial verdict and its ramifications became known.

Later that afternoon, responding to a summons from Gismore, Harry and Ranulf walked into the meeting tent as

Gismore gave instructions to a herald. Harry stepped over to the refreshment table and took a glass of wine.

"Who invited you to drink my wine?" It was Gismore, looking very unpleasant.

Harry smiled and said, "What the hell's the matter with you Gismore?"

"My problem is I have two knights who did not show up for their duty this morning." Both knights walked over to the table's edge.

Ranulf put his hand on his sword hilt. "Well, I can say you ordered increased security, and I was taking care of duty. But in reality, neither of us were quite comfortable with the trial."

Gismore, as usual, slammed both hands down on the table and stood up.

"Look, you two, that whore's daughter is now a condemned witch, by order of your peers. I demand you support the decision."

Harry put his hand out to Gismore, palm up. "Come on, Gismore. Capturing her makes a good bargaining chip when negotiations start. You should be able to wedge a considerable concession out of Rupert. But burning her at the stake as a witch is just not strategic or rational. You might argue that the threat is a good tactic to squeeze a last minute deal with Rupert. But it makes no sense to actually execute her; she is much too valuable alive."

Gismore leaned over the table's edge, and with mild yell, said, "The witch is burning tomorrow. And either you two cooperate or you get out, and I mean tonight!"

Ranulf put his other hand on his waist and, tipping his head slightly to the side, said, "Gismore, you are losing control of yourself."

Now yelling, Gismore continued. "You are a knight, and I am an earl! You will address me by my correct title!"

Harry said, "You and I have been fighting together for ten years. We don't need titles to talk man to man."

"You, sir, will be out of camp by tonight, or I will unleash the corps on you. And take any who think like you."

"This wine has lost its taste." Harry poured his cupful on the ground and then flipped the glass toward the side flap.

About halfway to their compound, the two stopped and faced each other. Ranulf raised his eyebrows, "Decision is forced upon us."

"You know, Ranulf, I don't relish the idea of being a prisoner for a year, but there is absolutely no honor in dying for or because of Gismore. I think we should surrender; it might cleanse us a little from this dirt."

"I agree."

Word quickly spread through camp that Harry and Ranulf were being kicked out because they refused to support Sara's burning. It also became known that anyone could leave with them. At evening mealtime, interested men would meet at the main entrance. Fifty men showed up.

Custom held that persons interested in surrendering would signify the fact by walking with their weapons over their shoulders and both arms draped over them. The two knights and the soldiers marched toward Northdale. The watching archers could not believe what they saw. Marta commanded the squad, and she signaled not to shoot.

About a mile from the camp, Marta stepped out on to the road. "Your business?"

One of the knights said, "Madam archer, two knights and fifty soldiers do not agree with the treatment of Lady Sara. Therefore, we must surrender."

Marta had already dispatched a runner to headquarters. "I will walk with you, but sirs, you are completely covered by archers; any tricks and they will riddle you."

"Please tell Lord Rupert that I am Sir Harry and this is Sir Ranulf, and we, by our honor, intend no tricks."

The runner's message surprised Northdale's commanders, and Eleanor, Michael, and Oloff grimly waited in the main square for the procession to arrive. The herald had delivered his ultimatum earlier, and Northdale's people showed extreme depression. Once disarmed, Oloff ordered the arrivals taken to the North House area. When he discovered that they had not eaten a decent meal in three days, food was ordered. Shortly after they'd all settled, Marta and two archers approached; one was male, the other female.

"My name is Marta, and I am an archer squad leader. For obvious reasons, Lord Rupert will not see you. However, I carry his intentions. You are now prisoners, and you have one simple choice. You agree to remain for one year or you die—that is all. If you choose to be prisoners, you agree to stay—no sneaky plans to run-off at your first opportunity. We have no intention of interning you in some prison. Opportunities to leave will be many. But if you choose to stay, remember: the term is one year, and we will kill any who tries to leave. Lord Rupert expects you two knights to give your word of honor on this point. He also expects that you will keep your men following the rules. Do you give your word as knights?"

She turned and motioned her two companions to stand next to her. She pointed at a dark stain on the wall of the North House located near the roofline. The two shot arrows at the spot; each came within an inch of the target's center. "Thank you," Marta said.

She again faced the group of prisoners. "Do you give your word for a year's service?"

Harry and Ranulf stepped forward. "Squad leader, my men have discussed this, and we agree to one year's service. Tell Lord Rupert that the two knights give their word, and so do the others who refused to stay with Gismore."

Marta nodded her head and then asked her two archers to produce the two swords attached to their backs that were the personal swords of Harry and Ranulf. They walked over and handed them to the knights.

Marta said, "We accept your word of honor." The three then started to walk back toward the keep.

Marta stopped. "We are very busy convincing Gismore that he is beaten, so you may have nothing to do for a few days. Once we are rid of that horse's ass, we will assign you duties." With a smile, she added, "You may enjoy the rest."

Gismore, Tagmore, and John sat eating dinner, discussing the betrayal by the two departed knights and plans for tomorrow's fire ceremony. Celebratory described the mood and wine flowed. One of the infantry captains walked in. "Excuse me, my lord. The cowards have departed."

Tagmore raised his glass. "Good, I bet very few went with them; it was either death on the trail or a year as a prisoner."

The food flew out of Gismore's mouth as he exclaimed, "When we take Northdale, those bastards will really feel pain, right across their necks." He signaled cutting off a head. The three laughed and toasted.

Smiling, John inquired of the captain, "How many went with them?"

"Sir, I counted fifty."

Gismore shot to his feet. "Fifty!" he shouted. "You mean fifty left because I'm about to burn that bitch?" He faced each of his two companions. "She is a devil's whore, first my son and his troop and now another fifty. Retribution will come tonight! A simple burning is way too easy for her." The other two knights grinned as they made eye contact.

Earlier in the day, Gismore ordered one of the infantry captains to find men who wished to take revenge on Sara for an arrow that caused death to one of their close fellow soldiers. Twenty volunteered. When assembled, Gismore told them Sara was no longer a Christian woman, therefore, after dark, they could go to the stable and do whatever they wanted to her.

Sara did not seem surprised when the men entered the stable. She seemed almost expecting them. Neither her hands nor feet were now chained. She stood and walked right up to them.

She said, "Men, you have seen war. You have seen the injury caused to non-fighting ordinary people. I think you know that you would fight hard to protect wives, daughters, sisters and mothers from any invading army. I have done nothing more than you would have done. Now, you have been sent here to punish me. Considering what I assume you were sent here to do, would you wish the same treatment for your women?"

One of the men almost began to cry when he said his only brother had been killed. Sara responded by listing the Northdale men and women who had already died in this totally unnecessary conflict. She also named their children, husbands, or wives. Limited talk changed into a flow of conversation. The men eventually sat down, and Sara sat on the table the guards earlier brought into the stable.

Gismore, already extremely angry over the departure of fifty men, became furious when one of his bodyguards told him the punishment party apparently had not touched Sara. He ordered his bodyguard to follow him to the stable. When he saw the men and Sara sitting down, he drew his sword and with the flat side began to strike the men. They ran out. He then announced each bodyguard member would take a turn with Sara after him.

Men grabbed her arms and legs then lifted her onto the table. Without making any sound, she wrinkled her face into a disgusted expression while Gismore raped her. When he stood up, she said, "You're not a very big man."

That did it. Gismore slugged her face and bellowed, "Devil whore!" Then he hit her hard again and shouted, "Witch!"

The bodyguard had arranged itself in a line by seniority. The next man stepped up to the table and, following Gismore's example, hit Sara in the face twice before raping her. The pattern repeated for the next three men. Sara's bruised and bleeding face clearly showed that she now was only semiconscious. The restraining men had dropped her arms and legs because she did not seem to have any strength to resist.

The sixth man opened his codpiece without taking off his belt on which a dagger hung. Just before starting, he shouted,

"I've always wanted to have sex with a countess! This will be my only chance, ever."

Somehow his yelling temporarily cleared Sara's eyes. As the man pumped, she reached down and pulled his dagger and thrust it into his rib cage. He screamed, stood up, and then fell dead on the floor. The bodyguards first bellowed and then began to beat any part of her body they could reach.

After a few moments, Gismore howled, "Stop! Stop! We have been too easy on her. Someone get a rake in here and we'll use the handle."

In the morning, the bodyguard could not stand her at the pole in the middle of the pyre because she was completely limp. They had to hang her on it with ropes around her armpits, waist, thighs, and calves. Even her head required lashing to keep it up. Her smock showed much blood from the beating, and blood soaked the garment from the waist down. One of the bishop's priests read the formal death warrant, and members of the bodyguard threw several torches. Sara's body never moved. Witnesses would later state Sara was obviously dead before they dragged her out.

Only a small part of the army watched the fire. Most of the men hunkered down in their defensive positions. The captains did not need to motivate them. They assumed an attack would be forthcoming, and they also expected a fight to the death.

Oloff, Eleanor, Squire, Michael, Mary, and Alfred stayed in the keep's residence with Rupert. He kept walking to the window and saying things like "God," "shit," "those filthy bastards," and the like. When mid-morning came, he sat in the chair with his palms over his eyes and wept. The others joined him. Once he jumped up and yelled he was getting his weapons, but Alfred and Michael tackled him. By noon, he just sat in a chair facing a window and looked out. Oloff sat on the floor in one corner and, with blank eyes, just stared.

After an hour, Rupert stood and faced the group. "I swear before you and God that not one of those bastards will ever leave Northdale alive. I will die carrying out this vow."

He then walked to the window and yelled at the top of his lungs, "Gismore, I will kill you and feed your nuts to the pigs." He slammed his hand on the window's edges, turned his back to the wall, and slid down to the floor.

Oloff now stood and yelled, "With all due respect, Lord Rupert, you will have to beat me to him, because I plan to tear him apart with my bare hands."

Gismore threw a party for his knights, even the boys. They consumed a great deal of wine. Congratulations flowed as fast as the wine. They all believed Rupert and his troops could not recover from the humiliation of Sara's death.

Macabe asserted, "Once you mop up the remaining rabble, and Richard happens to die fighting, you will be king!" Loud cheers rang out. "In fact, I will make sure he dies fighting you!" More cheers erupted.

However, the troops under the command of captains remained at their posts. They only received a small, cold meal; their celebration of the witch's death remained considerably less energetic than the commanders' revelry.

At Gismore's meeting with commanders the next morning, everyone agreed to stay in the fort. It was argued that the army faced its highest risk of attack during movement. Therefore, it would stay behind its defensive fortifications for two days. They asserted the time spent waiting would illustrate Northdale's resolve. If no attack occurred, then Gismore's estimate of weakness would be confirmed, and the army could make careful advances towards the village of Northdale. They also warned that the food would only last two days, so capture of the village soon was imperative.

Retaliation Raid

Rupert did not leave the residence on the day of Sara's death or the day after. He did not respond to anyone who tried to engage him in conversation, even the king. He would wave then away, even his three children. He just sat and gazed out the window. Servers brought food, but he only nibbled. His children found that he did not even drink wine. They wished to share in his mourning, but Rupert chose to face it alone.

Michael, Mary, and Alfred directed their emotions in a different direction. They intensely felt the need for revenge. They told each other that mourning could come later. They began to search for methods to extract retribution. None of them paid attention to regular military duties. They wanted to find a way.

Oloff and Eleanor took command of military operations. They posted a careful watch, and archers unleashed arrows at available targets. They also studied Gismore's schedule. The guards in the redoubts rotated every six hours. During the night, one shift change occurred at midnight. They also observed that Gismore had not set any forward observation posts other than the four circular redoubts located at the camp's corners.

On the second day, Michael and Sophia came into headquarters with a rolled-up paper. They asked to see the commanders because they had found a crack in Gismore's defenses. When Oloff, Eleanor, Rodger Cartwright, the king and his knights, and Squire assembled, they unrolled the paper that outlined the plan.

First, the dense bushes kept out arrows, but they also kept the defenders from seeing through them. They formed a visual blockade. Second, the deep creek bed could easily hide a large number of troops. Third, the defenders raised a brush line along the creek's bank for about two hundred feet from the outer defense lines but no farther.

This was the key opening. No watchmen patrolled the end of the brush line. Command only assigned guards to stay within the circular lookout posts. If Northdale could get fifty or so fighters into the depressed creek bed without being noticed by the watchers, they could launch a raid right into the heart of Gismore's camp.

Oloff pointed at the drawing of the plan and then at its proposers. "Tomorrow will be the last sliver of moonlight, a very good time to sneak around."

"After almost four days of standing on alert, I bet some of those guards will fall asleep on the midnight shift," Eleanor surmised.

Michael started to roll up the drawing. "If you agree, I think this might stir my father to abandon wallowing in sorrow and get him to take some action." Without saying anything, Oloff started walking to the stairs; he motioned the others to follow.

Rupert looked at the group and then away; he remained slouched in his chair near the window. Sorrow and lack of sleep had etched dark circles below his eyes.

Oloff walked directly in front of Rupert. "Michael and Sophia made a good plan to launch a surprise raid tomorrow night. You better get your ass out of that chair and look it over."

Everyone took in a breath and waited. Rupert peered at Oloff for a few moments, and then slowly rose. He looked clearly irritated to be disturbed. Sophia rolled out the drawing, and Michael made the presentation.

Oloff added, "If we get into the center, they will not know what hit them or how to respond. Great confusion will occur. We should be able to kill a bunch of them, but we cannot stay long. It must be a quick, hard hit and then get the hell out."

Rupert took a moment, and with almost reluctant eyes looked at each person. Then he studied the drawing without comment for almost a whole minute. When he looked up, his facial expression clearly began to show interest. He asked, "Fifty swordsmen will do it?"

Sophia straightened up. "No, my lord, thirty-five swordsmen and fifteen archers."

Rupert looked at her. "You know what those assholes did to my wife. I cannot let them capture any more women. No women will go."

Sophia put her hands on her hips. "I love you, my lord, and normally do what you wish, but you have no choice. The lady archers wish for retribution just as you men do. We will follow you in even if you order us not to. We are well-trained sneaks."

Oloff, Michael, and Eleanor stood smiling. Rupert looked at Eleanor. "You agree?"

"My plan is to either shoot that bastard Gismore or to stick my bow up his ass. The archers who are going know the danger, but are quite willing to risk it for the chance to pay back those murderers."

Rupert began to look energized. Some color even returned to his face. He evaluated the determination shown in both women's faces. "All right, fifteen archers, but your job is to shoot and not fight with swords."

Simultaneously, both answered, "Agreed."

"Everyone, grab a chair. We need to work out the details. I'm hungry and I think a glass of wine will help us all."

The final plan called for Rupert and Oloff, each accompanied by two men, to seek out the two main tents, Gismore's and Blackwood's. They would be the spearhead of the attack. The others would divide in half. One group under Michael's command would attack the camp on one side of the creek, and the other under the command of Thomas Lancaster, one of the king's knights, would attack the other side. The plan anticipated that the darkness would help create considerable confusion. This would allow two things to occur. First, the Northdale attackers would be unimpeded as they withdrew into the creek bed. Second, if the timing worked, the soldiers on one side of the creek would begin fighting others from the other side.

Michael asked, "What about them trying to run down our people as we retreat? Will they charge?"

Rupert had a dry pen in his hand. He tossed it on the paper with the attack plan. "What resources do we have?"

Oloff looked at Eleanor, who said, "Reassign Rodger Cartwright's squad from border protection to the woods across from the creek entrance. If any pursuit develops, his archers could hold them until the raiders get away." Oloff's forehead wrinkled while his head nodded approval.

Rodger tapped his hand on the table. "It could be a risk to leave the border undefended, but I think the raid is more important. My men will ensure the bastards do not follow you even one inch." Rupert looked at Rodger, and a small smile developed.

After concluding the planning, Rupert stood. "I'll let you choose the men and women who will come. Make sure to have several of our best knife men in front to silence the guard posts."

Eleanor stood up. "This will be the hard part."

Rupert looked a question at her.

"My lord, we'll have to select who goes and the ones not included will be unhappy. They all want revenge!" Rupert smiled and then walked to the window.

The next midday's meeting hashed out last-minute details including the list of troopers, routes, and meals. All commanders attended, as well as Richard and his two knights. A strong, but subtle confidence permeated the group. At mid-afternoon, the fifty selected to go would practice their roles. They would divide in half and each attack a different side of the creek bed. The return of Rupert and Oloff after they sought out Gismore and Blackwood would signal the withdrawal. The need for silent movement dominated the venture, so the combatants would muffle any metal weapons to avoid any noise.

As they spoke, Mary came into the main hall. As an assistant squad leader, she often carried messages. After normal greetings, she walked over to the table and placed a handmade box constructed of crudely cut sticks. Its rough shape and protruding stick pieces suggested its fabrication by a one-arm basket weaver. "Daughter, what is it and why have you brought it?"

"Marta Posley, my captain, told me to bring it; it's a squirrel trap that we found near Gismore's camp."

Squire crinkled his face. "So?"

"Marta guesses Gismore's men are beginning to starve. They are eating squirrels."

All the commanders stopped and faced Mary. Their faces projected contemplation. After a moment, they faced each other and almost simultaneously started to throw out ideas on how to exploit the hunger angle. After a few minutes, the ideas stopped flowing, but no decision was reached.

Mary, still standing at the food table, chirped in. "From what I've seen, soldiers who eat a big meal seem to fall asleep." For the second time, all of the commanders looked at her while thinking over the possibilities.

Later in the afternoon, two oxen still constrained by the double wood-yoke around their necks walked down the road toward the main entrance to Gismore's fortress. Torn leather harness dragged from their yoke. The men in one guard redoubt called their captain, and he decided food availability sanctioned a quick dash out of the fortification. He gathered twenty men, and with shields raised, they ran to the oxen and then escorted them into camp. No arrows came. Within one-half hour, the oxen provided considerable meat for hungry soldiers.

Gismore, holding the torn harness in his hand, smiled and looked at Tagmore. "Good fortune. An omen, I think. Tomorrow we will advance on Northdale."

Tagmore slapped him on the shoulder. "I cannot wait."

The Northdale contingent made almost no noise approaching the creek bed. Enough rain had fallen that the sound of water rushing in the creek covered any footfall noises. At an hour past midnight, Gismore's camp dramatically quieted down. Rupert gave the signal to advance.

The four men assigned to silence the guard redoubt nearest the creek crawled on their bellies up to the lip of the structure. Hearing no noise, one peered into the post. Three of the guards slept on the ground, and the one sitting at the alert position nodded his head in sleep. Northdale's men eased over the wall and, within a minute, signaled the guards would never warn anyone again.

All of the fifty attackers crept up the creek bed without any incident or sound. If anyone happened to stumble on the rocky creek bottom, others would steady him or her. The unit moved up to the opening in the brush line where Rupert and Oloff looked in. After noting no movement occurring within the fortress, Rupert stood and made the first signal, starting the assault. The plan called for all fifty raiders to get inside the brush line before springing the attack. Rupert put his hand on Oloff's shoulder, and the spearhead group began a quick, crouched advancement toward the two biggest tents.

Rupert's threesome, by chance, had taken the spearhead's right side, thus lined up with Blackwood's tent. Oloff's group headed for Gismore's tent. Rupert's eyes became more focused as he approached the bishop's quarters. Knuckles holding his sword turned completely white. The faces of all three clearly showed no intention of giving quarter.

No guards stood outside of the tent, so with a quick slash of his sword, Rupert cut the door's closing laces and entered the tent. Blackwood and his two assistant priests sat around the center table, playing a board game. They looked with disbelief at the three entering men. Despite the mud spread on their faces to lower the glare of skin, Blackwood immediately recognized Rupert.

"What in God's name are you doing here?" His state of total surprise kept him from speaking above a normal voice.

"In God's name, I am going to send a hypocritical sinner to hell."

Blackwood dropped his game pieces, stood up, and began to step back. In a trembling voice, he said, "God will not forgive you for attacking His emissary."

"God will not forgive me if I don't remove you from this world." He drove his sword's hilt all the way to the bishop's chest. The look of horror on Blackwood's face formed a reward Rupert carried the rest of his life. After the bishop's body hit the ground, Rupert started kicking it. "You pile of pig shit, you killed Sara!" A good dozen hard kicks landed, and each was accompanied by damning expletives.

Rupert's companions had quickly dispatched the two assistant priests. However, one of the assistants had screamed before dying. A very quick scan of the tent showed that the bishop had placed a large bag of coins on the table next to his bed. One man grabbed the bag, and then they picked up the candles lighting the tent.

The two men moved to each side of Rupert and then gently took an arm. One said, "My lord, we have many other things to do tonight." Rupert looked at him for a moment and then landed one more kick to the bishop's corpse. He then pointed to the door. They left the two dead assistants on the floor, threw one candle on the bed, and the other on a pile of clothes.

The scream triggered the attack. Northdale's troops launched themselves on Gismore's men. The sleeping men had been lulled into complacency, so they were caught completely unprepared to fight. Weapons were scattered. No one wore any armor, and in the dark, no command structure existed. A true melee started. The defenders found enemies all around them. They became disorientated, and the fighting followed an every-man-for-himself instinct.

The archers greatly enhanced the confusion; they stayed behind the swordsmen and loosed arrows. The arrows struck fewer targets than would have occurred in daylight, but their zinging sound added to the defender's fright. Some men simply ran away instead of assisting their fellows.

Oloff ripped into Gismore's tent. Only two of his bodyguard sat inside. Oloff let out a curse and charged one.

When the spear point on top of his ax's head entered the bodyguard's body, Oloff, holding the ax's handle, lifted him off the ground and carried him across the tent to its far wall. Oloff put his foot on the man's chest and pulled out the point and then thrust it in again.

One of his two companions used his sword hilt to knock out the other bodyguard. Oloff took one look at him and said, "Hold his arms." He then buried the ax head six inches into the ground after it severed the man's neck. He walked over to the other dead man, kicked him onto his back, and decapitated him with one ax stroke. No bag of gold could be found. As they left, Oloff and his men also threw in lit candles. They ran toward the creek bed fighting and killing anyone who came into view. It took too much time to decapitate enemies so Oloff stopped.

Gismore had been walking rounds when the fighting started. He raced to what he perceived to be the middle of the fight and started screaming orders while waving his sword above his head. He found a tree stump and jumped on it so his troopers could readily see a rallying point.

Eleanor, Sophia, and Marta made a covenant before the assault without telling Rupert. They avowed it their duty to find and kill Gismore. They did not stay behind the swordsmen. They also did not waste time engaging regular soldiers. The three, in a crouched position, moved behind the soldier's sleeping tents in order to avoid detection. They ran across only one man urinating behind his tent, and he died on the spot.

The three found Gismore by the sound of his yelling. He made a perfect target by standing on a stump and bellowing. All three exchanged glances and then took aim. One arrow passed through his open mouth and lodged in his brain. He stopped yelling and simply fell over backward. In the future, the three ladies would never tell anyone whose shot hit the mark.

The whole raid lasted just about twenty minutes. The command to withdraw was the word "crust." After meeting with each other and engaging in some of the fighting, Oloff signaled to Rupert by pointing at the exit. They both started to repeatedly shout, "Crust!" Sir Thomas and Sir Michael North followed suit, and most of their troops made it out of Gismore's camp. The bodies of two men and one woman had to be left behind. The surviving attackers carried out five wounded men.

It had been assumed that Gismore's men might, in the passion of fighting and in the dark, not recognize each other. It so occurred. The men on one side of the creek mixed in the melee with those on the other.

Macabe and Tagmore ran into each other. "Tagmore, have you seen a large group of Rupert's men?"

"John, I haven't seen any, and the light from the burning tents shows only our men. This must have been a raid."

Macabe shot a glance at the fighting occurring all around them. "Then who in God's name are we fighting?"

The two looked at each other. "Shit, Tagmore, we are fighting ourselves." Tagmore nodded his head in agreement.

The two raised their swords into the air, and both started yelling, "Stop fighting!" They found other knights and captains who also began shouting to stop fighting. It took almost half an hour to restore order.

Aftermath

THE RAID'S SUCCESS COULD BE measured in the utter disbelief Gismore's army experienced the next day. But an even more fundamental shock occurred with the discovery of the two top commander's bodies. The men and nobles walked around the fortress as if they were numb. John Macabe could not organize a command meeting until mid-afternoon.

John de Bristol, Tagmore, Adam de Yealand, and Thomas Travers met with Macabe. They chose not to involve the two recently knighted boys due to the death of one's father.

The group sullenly sat around the table in the command tent. Travers broke the brooding silence. "How in God's name did they get in here?"

Adam pointed out that all of the guards in the redoubt nearest the creek were killed, so the assaulters must have utilized it.

Macabe put his hand on his forehead and rubbed. "I agree, based on the location of most of the bodies."

Tagmore threw one of his gloves hard on the tabletop. "Shit, our own men probably caused most of the causalities. The captains estimate one hundred fifty dead and another fifty wounded."

They sat without speaking for more than a minute. Macabe sat up, again leaned his forearms on the table, "They killed Gismore and Blackwood. It had to be Rupert himself." The others just grunted an agreement.

Tagmore stood and walked to the refreshment table. He returned with a pitcher of wine and glasses for everyone. Once he filled the glasses, Tagmore spoke. "Well, we need to make some decisions."

John de Bristol, with much disgust, said, "I have heard Northdale throws all enemy bodies into the ocean. That is not a Catholic burial. So first thing, our men should dig a burial pit." A discussion occurred on how to quickly accomplish the task. They also decided to put Gismore's and Blackwood's formal clothing on two ordinary trooper's bodies, thus disguising the real ones. They speculated that Rupert might exhibit these as trophies.

Adam de Yealand said, "Let's drop the unimportant subjects and concentrate on the most important. What is our next step, advance or retreat?"

Macabe let opinions fly for a few moments and then stood up. In a commanding voice, he said, "We really have no choice. If we try and retreat, we will be shot to pieces by arrows all along the road back to Hollingsbrook. No matter what happened last night, Rupert still has not demonstrated the ability to stand up to our organized troops. He obviously does not have the manpower to do so." The others sullenly made slight head nods.

"If we move on to Northdale, chances are we will find some food. I think I remember they find fish in the river Downs. I want to burn everything in this cursed place to the ground, even any crops! I understand Rupert lives in a keep. After I throw his body off its top, I want to make it permanently useless." He leaned over and pounded his fist on the table. The men made approving grunts.

Tagmore reached for his glass. "I agree. We must keep fortifying every night, because to not do so is suicide. To save troops, we must maintain tight formations while marching. We have to beat this Northdale rabble into submission before we can leave." More grunted agreement followed this statement.

"As the appointed marshal, I will command the final disposition of Rupert and Northdale. We make one more day's march and camp. The following one, we take the village. Agree?'

One at a time, he looked each commander in the eyes. They all did.

Two different Northdale reactions existed. The fighters and the people celebrated the defeat they had laid on the invaders. They were tired of being hammered around and definitely mad about Sara's murder. To the people, the raid seemed like a great battle victory, and it should be commemorated.

Squire set up a cow roasting pit in the central square and opened several barrels of wine. Music played and everyone ate, drank, and danced their fill. The captains circulated to make sure troopers knew their next day's duties, but for the night, no authority stopped the party.

Rupert met briefly with the commanders. He thanked them for the great raid and made sure all knew that both Gismore and Blackwood were killed. Congratulations seemed out of place, so the reaction to the news came in short, quiet comments. Rupert then ordered them to all get some rest after drinking at least one glass of wine. Tight smiles occurred. He set the commanders' meeting for the following midday. He then started walking to the keep.

Michael stopped Rupert before he reached the stairs. Rupert put his hand on his shoulder. "Look, son, I struggle with the need to postpone mourning and take up the pending fight. It proves very hard for me, so you must let me cope with the situation on my own." Michael shot a quick look at Oloff, who nodded his head.

Mary North and Ann Watcher climbed to the keep's roof. It offered a quiet place where the two friends could talk over the recent events. They had spent many days and nights in the archer ranks, an experience that both physically and emotionally drained them. When they reached the roof, it held an occupant. King Richard sat against one of the parapet walls. His knees were drawn up, his elbows were on them, and his hands held his slumped head. When he heard them coming, he gave them a fast look and then returned his head to his hands.

Ann stepped close to the king. "Richard, what is the matter?"

He looked up at both of their faces and then down at the roof again.

Mary now stepped next to Ann. "Richard, we know you have to be king around this place, but sometimes you require an ear to listen to what you are feeling. We are two sets of ears that will not betray you in any way."

He slowly shook his head from side to side and then pointed for them to sit. With a very stressed voice, the king said, "Well, there are two things."

He went on to describe how, after giving permission to one of his knights, Thomas Lancaster, to join the raid, he felt like a coward for not joining himself. He knew Rupert would never give permission, so he watched the preparations and privately prepared clothes that matched the raiding party's. After dark, he'd snuck into the raider's ranks and joined the fight. After the raiders returned he'd become very tired, so he'd sat down and leaned against the wall that surrounded the keep.

Mary suggested, "You did nothing unlike what a small number of others did."

"Yes, but I sat there and reminisced on the raid. I did not notice Rupert walk up. He stopped to give some comfort to me because he is always concerned for his men. I wore my raiding cloths and had spread mud on my face, so you can imagine Rupert's face when he recognized me. He asked me in an angry voice if I had gone on the raid, and became enraged when I said yes. He picked me up off the ground by my tunic, raised me into the air, and shook me. When he put me down, he started yelling about how Northdale risked everything and

Sara had died fighting for me. He told me I had no right, after all of this sacrifice, to take the chance of getting killed or captured. He then told me that despite the fact that I was king, he would personally beat the shit out of me if I ever took such a risk again." He looked down at his feet.

Ann looked at Mary's troubled face and then turned to the king. "Look, Richard, Rupert and all of us are in mourning. Mary lost her wonderful mother who was also my beloved aunt. Lord Rupert loved Lady Sara so much you could feel it when they were in a room together. We are all expressing our mourning in different ways. Most of us are now focused on killing the bastards who hurt her. I assume traditional mourning will hit us all after we get revenge. My uncle Rupert is very torn up by Sara's death. You just hit his very raw nerve."

They sat quietly which, in Mary's case, confirmed Ann's words. After a few moments, Mary asked in a low voice, "What is the second item?"

Richard kicked his legs straight out on the roof surface and then picked up a stone and threw it. His voice very stressed, Richard continued. "I killed a man. I stood with the first wave out of the creek bed. We came upon a group of sleeping men. We all stood next to a victim and upon the captain's signal struck them with our swords. My man happened to roll over just before my sword hit. After that, the general battle started, and I exchanged many thrusts with other men and I probably killed others. But I saw the first man's face. I cannot forget it." He put his elbows on his knees and again buried his face in his hands.

Both women leaned back against the wall. They had talked to each other about this subject. As skilled archers, they could not point to any bodies, but both knew they had killed. At first, stopping invaders had provided motivation. Then it had become repaying the murders. Together, they had decided to do the obvious necessary killing. They also had agreed not to think about the individual men or the simple fact of killing other people.

Mary leaned forward and put her hand on Richard's back. "Look, this conversation is between the three of us, so no one will ever know what we say here. To me, being in combat the first time made me feel like drinking wine. I remained excited until after I returned to camp. Then it hit me, just like it's hitting you. I slipped into some nearby bushes and threw up. It proved hard even to go on my second mission, but once the action started, I shot my arrows as true as I could. Now, I know those bastards were all given a chance to walk away from killing my mother. They made the choice to stay, and now they face punishment. Maybe I've become hard, but I have become accustomed to the fighting and its consequences." She looked at Ann. "You agree?"

Ann nodded her head. "I absolutely agree, with one exception." Both Mary and Richard looked at her. "I threw up the first three times." She smiled. Mary grinned and even Richard made a small crack of a smile.

Ann added, "Richard, you have done something you should never do again, but you now understand what your future troops will endure. All sorts of knights will brag and bluster about combat, but you now will be able to see the truth through the noise. You will be a better king for knowing this."

Richard pulled his knees back up and sat straight, looking at the sky.

Mary stood up and signaled for Ann to do the same. "Think about it, Richard. The soldier you killed would have killed you if given a chance, or turned you over to others who'd gladly planned to kill you. I don't think you owe them anything except the tip of your sword. The thing is, no matter what anyone says, it's something you yourself must come to terms with."

Mary looked at Ann and, with a smile at him, said, "King Richard of England, you also should remember the Earl of Northdale will never hesitate about beating the shit out of you." Both ladies laughed, and Richard, finally, really smiled.

At midday, Rupert and the commanders gathered in the main hall. The mood was somber. The king and his two knights, Sir Thomas Lancaster and Sir Benedict of Caton, joined the deliberations. Professor Hazelwood also attended. It was agreed that despite the raid's success, not enough damage had been caused to compel the invaders to quit. The surrendered men now at North House had described Macabe as the appointed marshal. The two knights knew John Macabe and described him as fiercely devoted to promoting his own valorous glories. Neither believed he could or would consider anything but a victory. They all agreed that Macabe planned to continue the invasion.

Rupert rose at the table's end. "Your Majesty, gentlemen, and ladies, we cannot kill them unless they are here. We can trap them in the village because from numerous window openings our archers will have endless opportunities to pick them off. They will march in here very proud and then have to dig in to survive. We will encourage this movement by placing a cow near their likely camp for tonight, and then another in the square the day after."

Oloff pounded his hand on the table. "I like it. Feed them so as to lead them to slaughter, just like the pigs they really are." Smiles occurred around the table.

Benedict suggested the key would be to somehow motivate the invaders to divide themselves into smaller groups and then defeat them one group at a time. He asked for time to formulate a plan after he'd roughly investigated the keep, square, and abutting buildings. Rupert assigned Squire to serve as escort and information source.

The group then discussed a number of details about monitoring Macabe's movements, identifying the defensive positions they occupied, and evaluating their level of alert. Supplies and weapons required carful distribution. They agreed no major strategic loss would occur if Rodger Cartwright's squad joined the main fight. Eleanor mentioned that Ann would take the message to Rodger. At meeting's end, Rupert asked for other subjects.

Hazelwood spoke. "Gentle persons, I have a Latin text describing the battle of Thermopolis. Great story of a small number beating a larger one. Might be good reading for you." They all looked at him without speaking.

Michael snorted. "Shut up, Hazelwood."

Eleanor pulled out and then unrolled a piece of paper. "Rodger Cartwright gave this to my daughter, Ann, and she to me. It is a list of the knights still alive in the invading army. A small number of Macabe's troops keep trying to desert Gismore's army and sneak out of Northdale. Rodger catches most, and if they still can speak, he questions them. Thus, he made the list. His questioning allowed him to reconstruct the events surrounding Sara's death. This list contains the names of the surviving knights, all of whom voted to execute Sara."

The room went completely quiet. People's eyes moved from the paper to Rupert and back several times. Even the king watched to see his reaction.

Rupert again rose, slowly. He leaned over the table and placed both hands on it. "Everyone in that army had the chance to leave before they killed Sara. Only Sir Harry and Sir Ranulf plus fifty soldiers choose to do so. That means the remaining men are all guilty of the great injustice. The penalty for murder is death, and I plan to kill them all."

He motioned for the paper to be handed to him. "But these seven swore a holy oath to act correctly and protect the helpless. Before God, they swore not to act unjustly. So as an earl of a district, I have the authority to sign death warrants. Your Majesty, I would like your scribe to write one each for the seven. I will sign them."

Everyone faced the king. "Lord Rupert, these men did violate their oaths. You may use my scribe, and I will also sign them." Approving nods occurred all around the table.

Rupert nodded to the king and then straightened up. "I believe just retribution awaits, and I sincerely believe they are going to walk right into it.

Into Northdale

—

THE COMMANDERS' MEETING OCCURRED AT noon on the next day. Scouts reported the invaders were already setting up camp less than a half-day's march from the square. Tomorrow, Macabe would be in Northdale. They also reported scrupulously prepared defensive works; this fact obviously precluded another surprise raid.

Rupert asked for Benedict's report.

Just as he was about to speak, the hall door opened and in walked the Viking sea captain, Estrid. "Don't your guards know no one closes doors to a Viking?"

Surprise kept everyone in his and her seats. "Judging by your stony manner, you have a little problem brewing."

With a smile, Rupert stood, walked over to Estrid, and extended his arm. The Norseman vigorously shook it.

"My friend," Rupert said, "you know I'm always glad to receive you, even though you smell of dried fish."

Estrid place both of his hands on Rupert's shoulders. "The dock hands told me about Sara. I cannot explain how much I admired her. I can assure you that she now resides in Valhalla." Several Englishmen's eyebrows rose at this comment.

Rupert waved his hand at the table and introduced everyone. Estrid bowed to the king.

Looking his friend in the eyes, Rupert shook his head. "We are being invaded by an army that hates Northdale, King Richard, and, absolutely, Vikings. It might prove wise for you to shove off as soon as you're resupplied."

Estrid, with a smiling but surprised face, looked at each individual. "It has long proven to be very unhealthy to hate Vikings. And if an old friend needs some help, I'll be glad to split some heads." The king's two knights shifted in their seats.

Rupert first looked at the men sitting around the table and then back at Estrid. "If these people win, they will confiscate your boat and kill all of you."

Estrid's smile grew even bigger. "Rupert, Englishmen have tried to kill me many times, always to their own detriment." He now faced the table. "I may have even fought some of you. But if Rupert requires assistance, I gladly volunteer, unless you object."

No one said anything for a moment. King Richard leaned forward. "Sir Viking, we can use the talents of a well-intentioned man." Sir Benedict and Sir Thomas did not look enthusiastic.

Rupert resumed his seat, and Estrid joined the group. "Benedict, you were about to discuss your plans."

Benedict cleared his throat and asked, "How many men do they have left?"

Rupert looked at Oloff, who said, "It is very hard to make an accurate estimate. We counted about twelve hundred troops crossing the Ibix. We obviously must make informed guesses, because we never get an opportunity to count the enemy's dead. However, I think the causality count reaches about half."

Nodding, Benedict unrolled a large piece of cloth on which he had drawn his battle plan. In short, he assumed that the most esteemed personality would take the biggest building; therefore, Macabe would claim the keep. He commanded his own small troop and would probably take the remaining members of Gismore's bodyguard. He also assumed that the other four knights would also take up residence in the keep. He doubted the two boy knights would impact anything, but assumed they also would move into the keep. That translated into about sixty men and five knights in the building. He guessed that Tagmore also commanded a small personal troop, which could add a few numbers to the keep's occupants.

Tapping the drawing, Benedict said, "That is our opportunity. They will be divided. Possibly one hundred people moving into the keep and maybe four hundred to five hundred someplace else. The only shelter would be in the village's buildings, so I assume they would be assigned to them."

He proposed Northdale's troops divide the attackers by inserting themselves between the keep and the village. The wall outside that circles the keep offered the best strategic location. The enemy forces in the keep would have to climb the wall in order to attack, and such a maneuver would lead to causalities. With concentrated arrow fire, they, in effect, could trap the one hundred in the keep. With continued arrow shooting, the remaining five hundred in the village's buildings would, in all likelihood, become defensive.

Oloff tapped his hand on the table. "Sir Benedict, how would our men be protected when their backs are to the wall? They will be open to attack from both sides."

Benedict raised his hand and nodded, "Here is the part that requires all of Northdale to get into action tonight.

Movable, wooden, wall–like shields must be manufactured. The troops who form the separation force will all have to carry them out with them and basically set up a wooden fortification to repulse the five hundred's counterattack while the circle-wall protects them from the troops inside the keep."

Everyone remained quiet. The proposal contained many points to consider. Oloff and Eleanor pulled the drawing across the table to give it closer scrutiny.

Finally, Rupert addressed Benedict. "I appreciate the plan, but it is based on many assumptions."

Benedict stood straight up and faced the question. "Lord Rupert, one of the basic military failures is to assume you know what your opponent is thinking. I've considered that point and made this proposal because I have fought with Macabe, Tagmore, and Adam de Yealand. I am not assuming when I say they have always been contemptuous of enemies whom they deem inferior. It is my informed guess that they evaluate you so."

Michael asked, "Sir Benedict, what happens if they don't act the way you expect?"

Benedict held up both hands with palms toward the assembled commanders. "Northdale monitors every move they make. If I am wrong, and I think I am reasonable enough to admit I could be wrong, then we don't implement my plan and revert to the alternative."

All faces asked a question. "You resume your harassment until Macabe and his gang get tired and decide to declare victory, burn down the village, and go home. This could take months and leave you unprepared for winter's food storage and possibly without any buildings to give shelter."

He looked at the king. "And Your Majesty will have to stay hiding in Northdale until a relief can be organized, if ever."

People sat back in their chairs. Some looked at the table and others at the ceiling.

Sir Thomas Lancaster cleared his throat. "I'm a little older that the rest of you, and I've seen conflicts. In the end, fewer people are killed and much less useless destruction occurs if the fighting ends quickly. In the short run, it may cause more soldiers' deaths, but in the long run, a quick, hard fight proves less damaging to everyone."

After a few moments, the king said, "Lord Rupert, these are your people."

Rupert put both forearms on the table. "If we prolong this situation, only more and more injury and disaster will occur. We should move to end this as soon as possible."

He looked around the table at each of the commanders' faces. One by one all nodded their heads in agreement.

Rupert stood up. "We shall adopt Sir Benedict's plan, and if Macabe follows his own stupidity, he will fall into the trap. Oloff, Eleanor, and Sir Thomas, you select the troops and explain their functions. Michael and Squire, you make the wooded shields. Take every board or beam you need out of the village's buildings. Your Majesty certainly can help organize the construction. Oh, also, Squire, make sure a cow is available to the larger number of troops and a fat sheep to the keep. Someone wake up Hazelwood. He will set up and service the command tent."

A flurry of activity followed. People almost ran to their assignments. When everyone had gone, Rupert walked over to Benedict and quietly asked, "What are our chances?"

Benedict turned to Rupert and put one hand on his shoulder. "It certainly is a risk, but those assholes are very overconfident. Even after the raid, I bet you they still consider you as rabble. That is the key: they underestimate you and your people's commitment."

Rupert now put his hand on Benedict's shoulder and said with a small shake, "Thank you. Now I've got to find that scribe to see if the warrants are ready."

Estrid stood near the hall's door. "Uh ... Rupert, I command a knarr, and it only has ten men. Only five of them are Viking fighters. One other is a slave, and the last four are hired seamen."

Rupert asked, "What?"

Estrid pointed both hands at Rupert. "Our trading operations grew so big that we simply do not have enough fighting men to sail the boats. So all captains take a few fighters in case of trouble and then grab what is available."

Rupert gazed at the floor for a moment and then looked up. "I once dressed non-fighters to look like experienced men. Could we not dress up your ordinary sailors to look like fierce Vikings? You could teach them how to stand in battle readiness and assure them they can run off once fighting starts."

Laughing, Estrid said, "If you could dig up some of the old armor we've left here over the years, I'll deliver ten hard Vikings."

Rupert slapped him on the arm as they left the hall.

Separations

Just before dinner, Ann found Rodger walking across the square. They smiled at each other, and Rodger nodded toward one of the now-empty buildings. Once inside the door, he made a quick glance outside to make sure no one could see them. Then they embraced in a long hug followed by several long kisses. Breathing was fast, and each placed his and her hands on the other's cheeks. Ann pointed at two chairs; they pulled them together and sat down, still holding hands.

Ann rubbed Rodger's back. "It looks like the big fight will happen tomorrow or the next day. Sophia, my captain for this round, is assigned to put all of her archers in shooting positions behind the first ring of buildings touching the square, this one included. She will later rotate to guard the road to prevent reinforcements or escape, and I will be reassigned someplace."

Rodger looked out the window. "My men are to form a special squad assigned to seal off the keep's doors. We are going to use some wood walls. I will captain the force that faces the square behind these walls, and Michael will lead the group that faces the keep. Your father will be in overall command. We are to sleep until two hours past midnight and then go and pick up the wall sections. We expect to fight off counterattacks from the keep and from the buildings on the square. I believe it's your company's job to shoot arrows into the troops that attack my position."

Ann got up and walked over to a window and gazed at the square. She turned and her faced showed concern and fear. "This is going to be the big fight. We are not playing skirmish with Vikings anymore."

Rodger stood, walked over to her, and took her hands. "You are right. We will not play anymore." They stared into each other's eyes without speaking. The kiss that followed contained real passion.

When it was over, Ann pushed away a half-arm's length. "You know this house not only has two chairs, it also has a bed."

Rodgers eyes widened, and he immediately looked out the window and scanned the whole square. He looked back. "Your father scares me; he would kill me."

"Not if we are married and seeing how Squire is a little busy tonight, I am perfectly willing to declare our marriage." She walked over and picked up her bow. "I'll meet anyone who says otherwise, even my father. And besides, you are one of the church's knights. It will be your job to tell Oloff!" She smiled.

Rodger walked over, took the bow from her hands, and tossed it on the floor. He then picked her up. "I, Rodger Cartwright, declare to be your husband for now and always."

With a smile, Ann responded. "I, Ann, declare to be your wife for now and forever."

It was a short trip to the bed. No one disturbed them. Neither got any sleep before reporting for duty.

Sophia waited for Michael outside the commanders meeting. His face projected worry. They walked for a while before she said, "You look concerned. What is your assignment?"

Michael explained the plan and his particular responsibilities. "Sophia, this will be a hard fight. People who have never been in a battle usually vastly underestimate the reality of one. I'm sure you have witnessed this attitude. I want to provide the leadership that gives courage to my men. It is important that my company hold its ground." He kicked a stone.

Mary pointed to the empty barn, and they walked into it. They sat on a bench that allowed them to lean against the wall. Straw covered the floor. "Look, my love, you have never done a poor job of leading your men. In fact, I think they would fight at your side anyplace you directed them. "

In silence, he looked out the barn's door at the night sky. After a few moments, he sat up straight and looked at her. "What about you?"

"I have two jobs. First, while you boys play behind the wood walls, I'm to organize a shooting attack on the backs of any soldier group that advances on you. Eleanor plans to rotate assignments, so my following job will be closing the road out of the village and capturing or killing any escapees. It will be exciting fun in either position."

Michael looked up at her and then down at his hand again. "Exciting? Exciting? We must do a good job. My mother deserves our success. That is what is important. I want to pay those bastards back so bad I can taste it." He spat on the floor and sat quietly.

Mary watched him for a minute, and then she stood up and stepped in front of him. She slipped off her boots and then removed her leggings. Michael raised his eyebrows as he watched.

"It's too cold in here for you to see any more of me tonight. This is all you get." She then straddled his lap. It only took two kisses for him to unfasten his leggings. They would discover it truly does take time to pick the straw out of a lover's hair before returning to public view.

Fight in the Village

―――

Macabe's preparations to assault the village of Northdale took some time. He directed that every piece of necessary equipment be carefully packed in six wagons. "I want every weapon available to counter whatever those Northdale peasants try."

Troop movement required extraordinary organization. The knights planned to ride horses; the men would march four abreast. The constant threat from Northdale's archers required extra precaution, especially as the army approached the village's center square. The invading army's safety measures slowed its movement.

At about mid-afternoon, the column reached Northdale's square. The keep and its ring wall occupied one side with houses and other buildings lining the remaining three sides. Roads at each of its four corners provided access. Early architects placed the water well near the buildings opposite the keep. Large, flat, dark gray stones covered the ground of the square. The central part of the square, near where Sara long ago encountered Eleanor's whipping, had always been free of any structures; it provided a gathering place.

Adam de Yealand rode next to Macabe. "No one is here; it's completely deserted."

Macabe turned around in his saddle as he studied the buildings. "Don't think for a moment they are not watching every move."

Thomas Travers rode up. "'Who goes to the keep?"

Macabe grinned. "I'm going to sleep in Rupert's bed tonight!" They all laughed. "You gentlemen can divide up the children's and servant's beds."

He started pointing at the buildings ringing the square. "Adam, tell the captains to move their men into those buildings. Pack them in. We don't what them spreading all over town offering easy targets."

He then looked at the keep. "Knights, Gismore's bodyguard, and any personal troops will occupy the keep."

He circled his horse and said with another big grin, "We will save the window on the north side for us to piss out. Rupert and his stupid people will certainly see that!" Laughter again followed.

Tagmore arrived and he was smiling. "They left two large sheep inside the keep's circle-wall and one good size cow behind that first house over there. We eat! And it won't be nasty fish."

Macabe made a signal to advance to the keep. They rode their horses into the main hall.

After staking out their sleeping quarters, the commanders met in the main hall. They decided to make the buildings facing the square into the outer ring of a fortress. The troops were to barricade any the back windows and doors of the buildings, leaving access only through the front doors. It was also decided to send out three twenty- to forty-men patrols the next day. Their goals would be to gather intelligence and scrounge up food. The day after that, the whole army would commence its building-burning campaign.

The men required no great speeches to get them motivated to erect a fortress. Numerous incidents with arrows provided the necessary construction energy. Just as night fell, the commanders released wine to the men. Although the men appreciated the wine, more than just a few noted that the big shots moved into the safest place to sleep.

Just before dark, Macabe ordered that one knight spend each night with the men in the village buildings. The need to remain watchful caused the corresponding need for a commander to supervise an effective defensive guard. The invading command sensed something must be afoot because the Northdale forces had ceased harassing them. The assignment would rotate; Tagmore took the first night's command.

The forces housed in the village posted guards on the roofs, facing the square, and on each road entering the square. The keep force placed one in each of the four second-story windows. About two hours after midnight, they all heard activity but could not identify it.

At two hours past midnight, Oloff, Eleanor, and Sir Thomas began the mobile fortress movement. Success depended on moving quickly and not making much noise. Four men carried each wooden fortress section by means of two poles slipped under it. A sortie from either the keep or village could have disrupted the entire plan. None occurred. The soldiers installed the wooden fortress without incident. By very early dawn, troops manned the fortress separating the invaders into two groups.

The keep's guards were the first to notice the wooden wall. They aroused their captains who in turn awoke the commanding knights. They all met at the window overlooking the square; the temporary wood walls could easily be seen. Macabe, John de Burghton, Adam de Yealand, and Thomas Travers stood and evaluated the strategic situation.

Macabe gestured that they step away from the window opening. "Well, what do you suggest, although I think the next step is obvious."

Adam said, "I think it is great. Rupert stupidly put his forces in a position to be attacked from two different directions!" The other two made affirming grunts.

"Then you agree: we should take the initiative and strike at the rabble?" The three knights nodded their heads.

Macabe turned to the window. He picked up a sand-filled hourglass that sat on a near table, walked to the window facing the courtyard and yelled for Tagmore.

Tagmore came to one of the windows facing the square. "What?"

Macabe quickly lifted and then pointed at the hourglass. He indicated two hours from the present time by raising two fingers. He then quickly dropped the hourglass from sight. "Tagmore, did you get the meaning?"

Tagmore raised his hand and made gesture that indicated he understood. Then he shouted back, "Who?"

Making a circular gesture with his left hand, Macabe indicated, "Your whole troop." Tagmore made another signal that indicated his understanding.

The Northdale men watching this exchange now knew that something was up and it would involve the whole troop. One hundred and fifty men formed the wooden-wall force, of which one hundred were swordsmen and fifty archers. Commanders ordered them to eat and then rest, as the coming battle would tax their physical and mental resources. Northdale's remaining fifty archers and fifty swordsmen waited behind the now-fortified buildings located on the square.

Two hours after dawn, a signal horn blew in the keep. The keep's main double doors flew open, and soldiers charged out. Only six men at a time could pass through the doorway. A shower of arrows descended on them. The charging men's armor and shields provided some protection, but by the end of the first encounter with Northdale's arrows, twenty would be dead. The door acted like a funnel: only a fraction of the insiders could get out, thus offering a perfectly condensed target for the archers.

The width of the surrounding circle-wall's gate matched that of the double main doors. Only six soldiers could confront an equal number of Northdale swordsmen. Although warned by the other commanders not to do so, Rupert stood right in the gate and, with great emotion, fought hand to hand. His vengeance took a toll on the invaders.

Macabe observed the inability of his whole force to engage Northdale's troops. He ordered his men to climb the six-foot high circle-wall. Not having scaling ladders, his men improvised by using any available furniture or wood objects. In the end, they even started lifting each other over the wall.

Northdale's soldiers took full advantage of the wall. As Macabe's men struggled to climb over it, they became easy targets for arrows or swords. Those who did make it over the wall perished immediately.

As the fight started, Tagmore ordered his men into the square. They formed ranks and began to move forward.

A skilled archer can shoot three to four arrows a minute, especially if the shots did not require careful aim. A phalanx of moving troops provides a target requiring little aim by archers; they simply shoot at the moving mass and not at individual men.

Michael, Squire, and Sophia directed their troops to move to the edge of the square as soon as Tagmore's men moved. Not fearing a rear attack, Tagmore did not post a rear guard. Soldiers' backs were the least protected by armor. Arrows fired with a low trajectory could and would penetrate chain mail or leather vests. The first volley took down thirty men and the second another thirty.

Hearing yells, Tagmore stopped his forward movement and directed the rear ranks to face backward. Due to the armor and shields, now only a few of the arrows hit, but their volume caused Tagmore's unit to pull together in a defensive square and, more importantly, hesitate to move toward the wooden wall.

Even though Sir Adam and Sir Thomas continued to yell at their men to cross the keep's circle-wall and break out of the gate, Macabe stepped back from the fight to evaluate the situation. He screamed at Adam and Thomas to come over.

When they arrived, the conversation was brief. Macabe pointed at the gate. "This is not going well. I don't know why Tagmore did not hit that flimsy wooden wall from the other side. We need to make a new plan."

The other two knights looked for a moment at the fighting, and then they both said, "You are right."

"Adam, you stay here. Thomas and I will take the signal-horn man into the keep in order to see what happened to

Tagmore. If I blow the horn, then you retreat." The three ran into the keep.

Once Tagmore stopped his men, Michael ordered his fifty swordsmen and the archers to move into plain sight into the square. The archers now took time to aim and scored some hits, but mostly kept the men hunkered down and not moving.

It became Tagmore's turn to make a decision. He faced a wooden wall behind which he could not estimate the enemy's strength, or he faced a relatively small number of soldiers and an array of archers who did not wear armor. It was obvious the one thing he could not do was to stay put—he had to charge one way or the other. He expected Macabe to have broken out of the keep's yard, but he could see that had not happened. He chose the easy target, the small number of troops and archers exposed in the square.

Tagmore's men, in general, wore chain mail and carried armor that protected them from the waist up. This fact caused considerable vulnerability to the Northdale archers who started aiming at the unprotected body parts from the waist down. Numerous men had received nonfatal wounds that required them to be carried or otherwise assisted off the field. His force consisting of the still-able men and the injured walked back to the building fortress. The Northdale force, as planned, withdrew.

From the keep's window, Macabe witnessed the retreat. "That horse's ass Tagmore cannot take some casualties. He could have broken through the wooden wall! Damn him!" He shouted for Adam to blow retreat. His men made a hasty run into the keep and slammed its large double doors.

Macabe's causalities were high. The keep's force lost forty-five men. The square's force lost about one hundred and twenty-five, or about one quarter of its strength. Northdale lost no archers and ten swordsmen.

The respective commanders held strategy meetings. Tagmore's consisted of two captains. They were not happy with the situation. One pointed out, "We should try again to break out of these buildings and get into the keep and join forces."

Tagmore dropped his sword on the table around which the meeting was being held. "Or we could make a breakout from this square, just take all able men and charge up one of the two adjacent roads and get the hell out of this place."

The second captain pointed out, "If we did that, Lord Rupert's archers would just kill us one at a time."

Tagmore dropped himself into a chair. He rubbed his head with both hands. Looking at his captains, Tagmore said, "Shit, I know we will be targets. The question is which alternative will result in less lost men. I'm leaning to joining with the keep. We should be able to quietly stand at these doors then dash across the square. This will surprise the bitch's archers so they won't get organized fast enough to do us great damage."

The others nodded their heads.

Tagmore continued. "I suggest we wait through the night to see if Sir John Macabe can get a plan to us. If nothing comes, then we decide which direction looks best and then make a break for it. Agreed?"

One captain asked, "What about the wounded?"

The question stopped Tagmore as he stood up. He leaned over the table and, with a very cold face, said, "We leave them."

After setting the troop's positions for the night and making sure Squire set up a watch detail, Michael sought out Sophia. He only had glanced at her as the day's fight progressed; her face expressed deep unhappiness. He found her sitting alone behind a fence. She now looked sick.

Kneeling in front of her, Michael asked, "How are you?"

She had been crying. "I thought kicking those murderers' asses would be enjoyable. It is not at all so. The wounded men yelled for help and relief from the pain. I put an arrow through a man's back, and it protruded from his stomach. He spun around, screaming."

She put her hands on Michael's shoulders and lowered her head to his chest and commenced crying again. Michael put his arms around her.

"You did ... hell, we all did what had to be done today."

"I know they deserve it and that we had to win this fight, but Michael, it was horrible. When we snuck up and shot arrows, I never really saw the results. The other enemy soldiers always jumped in and carried off the wounded. Today, I clearly saw the blood and pain." She put her head down again.

Michael shifted his body to sit beside her, and he put his arm around her shoulders. He waited about five minutes before saying, "Sophia, you and I are captains. We must continue tomorrow."

Sophia stared at her knees. "I will be ready. I have guard duty at the road tomorrow, and none of those bastards will get away." She leaned over and kissed Michael. "You cannot stay with me; you must stay awake to monitor any developments. I will see you tomorrow night." They kissed again, stood, and walked to their respective duty stations.

Thinking about what Sophia had said, Michael walked to his soldiers' camp. He quietly asked everyone to gather around the biggest fire. "How do you feel about what is going on here?"

No one spoke, but a lot of foot shuffling occurred. "Come on, you all know that I'm not one of those commanders who will get mad if you tell the truth."

Agnes Longpath said, "Well, Sir Michael, I've fought the Vikings on several occasions. This is just harder. It's longer getting to the end. I'm a farmer and an arrow-fisher woman; I'm tired of hunting men. It seems like we have to kill a lot more now than we ever did of the Vikings."

Emma Malton added, "This is my first time, and it is not a good feeling. I mean, I know the enemy will try and wreck Northdale and the rats murdered Lady Sara, but some of the men I shot are just like us. Can't we just punish their leaders?" Mumbling could be heard throughout the gathering.

Michael moved next to Emma. "I know it is hard, but those men will follow their lord's orders, and it will be very hard on you as women and who knows what they will do to the children. It is sad, but we have no choice but to beat them down until they quit."

She said, "I've told several people that I got sick after the first fights, and they tell me the same." Some small laughs occurred.

Michael put his arm around Emma. "I truly think it will only be a few more days."

Macabe and others sat around the table in the main hall. "Can we get a message to Tagmore?"

Adam nodded. "I have one champion archer. He could hit the front door on Tagmore's building."

Macabe raised his wine glass. "Ideas?"

Thomas put his glass down. "Two prongs. We take every movable piece of wood in this keep and construct ladders. Then we split the troop. Send thirty men as a diversion against the main gate and the rest around behind the stables. They can use the ladders or the stable roof to cross the wall and then, as a group, sweep up behind the rabble."

John de Burghton added, "If Adam's man can get the message over to Tagmore, he can rush the wood wall. We must tell him that no choice exists, staying put is fatal." They made a toast and then departed to organize their men. Within ten minutes, the sound of construction begun.

Adam called for his archer. He wrapped tomorrow's plan, written in Latin, around the shaft. The archer chose the roof of the keep as the most advantageous shooting position, and the arrow hit Tagmore's front door. One of the men inside heard the thump and yelled to Tagmore. Curious, Tagmore walked to the door, and then he heard Adam yell his name. He went to the window and responded. In Latin, Adam said, "Get the arrow." None of the on-duty Northdale soldiers could speak Latin; all they could report was that a message had been passed.

Macabe signaled to the captain of his personal corps. "Get our men up to my room in fifteen minutes and do not attract any attention doing it."

When his personal twenty-man troop squeezed into Rupert's bedroom, Macabe made a hand signal to be quiet. "Listen, men, I suspect we are really trapped here. We just adopted a plan to climb the wall tomorrow morning, but unless the rabble is asleep, they will catch on real fast. Tomorrow's fight could end like today's."

The men's shifting of their bodies gave a clear statement of their discomfort.

"I want to make a private plan for just our escape, but we cannot tell any others. Agree?" He looked at their faces, and to a man, they eagerly nodded their affirmation.

"Tomorrow, about an hour before dawn, we will all sneak up to the wall right next to the gate. Then we will make a surprise hit on the few Northdale soldiers watching the gate from the other side. No matter what size of unit they stationed at the gate, we will be able to push right through before they can react. I'll bring my horse and act like a battering ram. I will also put on my armor, and the horse will be covered in chain mail. We can cover your escape."

The men started looking at each other and their faces were positive.

One raised his voice, "Where do we go after breaking through?"

"The only way out is down the road we came in on. If we stick to the brush, I don't think Rupert's men will have time to search for us. They will be busy with our other forces. Got it?"

Heads nodded in the affirmative.

"Remember, this will get us out, but if you mention this to anyone, the other members of this ill-fated army will protest, and we'll be stuck here. Do you understand this point? It is very important." He stood up and the men all whispered their approval.

Oloff slapped Rupert on the back as the commanders met. "I smashed one guy's face in and cut off another's arm. After that, I lost count. My troops made sure no one got over the wall. I just wish I could have gotten more of those bastards."

Rupert smiled. "I did not count the dogs I killed, but I could not see any of the command knights. They are too scared to face you and me." He slapped Oloff back. "I want so bad to kill every one of Gismore's bodyguard. You better not beat me to them."

"If we can keep this up, we will kill all of those shits and the rest of their army!"

"Oloff, I want to send them all to hell. We can do it now!"

Eleanor, Squire, King Richard his two knights, Estrid, and Michael stood listening and watching.

When all sat down and Rupert had called for ideas, it was Sir Benedict who spoke first. "Lord Rupert, a quicker end may come if the opposition is not afraid of being executed."

Oloff's and Rupert's faces froze.

"If the opposition know they are all going to die, why would they do anything except take the biggest toll from you and your people?" The others at the table inhaled.

Rupert slowly stood up, and he leaned as far as possible over the table, "Those bastards burnt my wife at the stake after raping her. Oloff and I will gladly behead them one at a time even if it takes a whole week."

Oloff yelled, "I will sharpen my ax every night."

Michael cleared his throat, "Father, my archers and soldiers are getting worn out. It has been weeks. They would like it to end and soon."

Rupert's eyes blazed as he stood straight up. He pulled out his sword and threw it on the table and shouted, "As long as my arm can swing that sword, I will take retribution." Oloff stood up and tossed his ax on the table.

Eleanor's eyes projected major concern, "Excuse me, gentlemen. I think we should be focusing on what Macabe and his thugs are planning. What can they do and how do we react?" Her question seemed to let some of the steam out of the room. Rupert and Oloff sat down.

After a few moments, Sir Thomas started to tap his fingers on the table. 'Two things are obvious. First, they cannot stay where they are. Second, that circle-wall prevents them from effectively deploying their whole force. A small number of men fighting an equally small number is our advantage. They need to get their entire force fighting our smaller one."

King Richard said, "It then is important for them to get out of the circle-wall."

This comment initiated a lively discussion. Numerous alternatives were discussed along with their countermeasures. In the end, they settled on some main points. The attack would not come at the main gate because Northdale stationed too many men there. Macabe could not spread his men along the wall because they could be picked off and would not be a fighting unit once on the other side. They had to pick a spot then and, en masse, breach the wall.

The group agreed on the countermeasures. They would divide the Northdale men into three groups and place them around the wall. One group would be stationed at the gate and the two others at intervals of one third of the circle-wall's circumference. The goal for each group would be to delay any breach attempt until one or both of the other groups reinforced them. They understood the first group to confront the breaching effort would suffer heavy, but necessary causalities.

Michael's force would be divided into two segments. The swordsmen would join the wooden-wall forces and be used to face Tagmore's, who they all assumed would attempt to connect with Macabe. Michaels's archers would continue to follow and harass Tagmore.

Estrid interjected. "My guess, the men inside the wall will use the roof of any building located against the wall as a jump off point. I want to station my Norsemen near that spot." Rupert agreed.

Sir Benedict stood. "Sir Thomas and I have watched you folks take on the fight for King Richard. We have not experienced the grave risk and valor that you have. So we wish to make one addition to the plans."

Everyone at the table listened with great interest.

"We both brought all of our armor and our horses' chain-mail coverings. Tomorrow, when Tagmore places his troops in formation on the square, we plan to be totally suited up and waiting on the road that leads up behind him. When he positions his men in the square, we will charge. Mounted knights carry a lot of momentum; we should bash through Tagmore without much trouble. That will give your archers many targets as his men scramble to avert our charge."

King Richard looking very concerned. "Gentleman, I've heard foot infantry can and will eventually pull down mounted knights. You two will not survive."

Sir Thomas placed his hands on the table. "Your Majesty, they will not react at first. Charging mounted knights are very intimidating. So we should get two and, if lucky, three charges completed before Tagmore can get his men organized to pull us down."

Benedict began to laugh. "Your Majesty, Sir Michael's archers better be good shots, otherwise it will get a little ugly for us."

The king now stood up. "You two have been my trusted advisors and protectors. I cannot let you go."

Thomas now stood. "Your Majesty, our knightly vows require us to sacrifice for justice, no matter what the personal costs. We love and serve you, but you cannot expect us to sit on the side. This fight could save your life. We must join it. Do not ask us to stop being knights."

The king looked at Rupert. "Your Majesty, that charge could really disrupt Tagmore. It is a good idea. You should approve. But more importantly, these two knights feel obligated to try it. They will charge tomorrow; you might as well approve it now." The king dropped into his chair and waved his hand in acceptance.

Rupert waited until the two knights had sat, and then he rose. "Oloff, you command one of the squads. Eleanor and Michael, you oversee the main gate, and we will get Rodger Cartwright to direct the other group. If the main-gate force must be split, Michael, you take half to react to any wall breach. I will remain in overall command. Sophia will command Michael's archers and function as a floating force to be applied where necessary.

King Richard, Professor Hazelwood, and Squire will organize a command post and keep all units informed with runners.

Michael cleared his throat. "Sophia already left to take a post guarding the road to prevent anyone from getting out. She uses her considerable hiding skills so I don't think we will have time to find her and get her back. I suggest Marta and my sister handle the floating archers; both are capable."

Rupert looked quizzically at Michael for a moment, and then he said, "Done. How will we get word to Sir Rodger?"

Eleanor said, smiling, "Ann seems to know where he is at all times."

Now both Oloff's and Rupert's faces expressed questions. Eleanor reached over and patted Oloff's leg. "I'll explain when this is over."

Rupert, using his commanding voice, said, "We are fighting for justice and our homeland—justice for the true king, justice for the murder of Sara, and finally for Northdale's future. I normally make such speeches with a toast, but somehow, tonight, it does not seem proper. Tomorrow, we will drink." He reached for his sword and then looked individually at each commander.

They filed out without speaking. Michael walked over to Rupert. "Father, please think about the killing. Only the knights and the bodyguards deserve to be executed."

Rupert looked at his son with very hard, slit eyes. He then turned without speaking and walked away.

Sir Thomas Travers made his decision after realizing the situation resembled a trap and his peers still did not grasp the seriousness. He expected decapitation if captured; therefore, escaping made much more sense. The distance between the third-floor window and the ground could be reached if he fabricated a rope out of bed clothes and curtains. He waited until about the second hour after midnight and then tied the rope to a bed-frame board and swung out the window.

Sir Thomas overlooked one important fact. Even the starlight gave the keep's stones a slightly lighter color than the clothes worn by a descending knight. He could clearly be observed. Two of the on-duty guards were fisher-women archers. They put two arrows into his body before it hit the ground.

About an hour later, Macabe's men began to organize. They had volunteered for the second watch on the main door, so they all slipped out unnoticed. Macabe draped a blanket over his armor so it did not make any sounds. The men successfully crept up to the gate without being noticed. Macabe and four men snuck to the stable.

They placed a blanket over the horse's head, and it remained quiet while the men put on its chain mail and saddle. Macabe cut up his blanket to make quieting boots for the hooves. When ready, they slowly walked to the wall. It took four men to lift Macabe into the saddle and one to hold the blanketed horse's head. When mounted, he waved his men to their feet, flipped down his visor, and pointed his sword at the gate.

Macabe's plan worked. Only five guards stood watch on the gate, two of them female archers. Expecting trouble on the following day, Oloff gave his unit a night of sleep and planned to have them back at the gate by dawn. The swordsmen quickly scattered the Northdale troops and pushed aside the wooden wall sections. Macabe spurred his horse and charged into the square, across it, and onto the road leading from it. The on-duty archers were so surprised by the mounted knight that they did not get off a shot.

One of his men yelled, "That bastard is leaving us!" The others lowered their swords and just stared at the horse's rear end. Several shouted for Macabe to return, but he could not hear. They started to look at each other. One man said, "Shit! That asshole left us, and we are now targets." Another man screamed,

"I'm for the keep!" He started to run, and the rest followed. They did not hold back on cursing Sir John Macabe.

Once inside the keep, the yelling really started. "That asshole used us to make his getaway."

Shields were thrown on the floor. "If I ever see that bastard again, he is dead!" The remaining men just walked around in the main hall and voiced their hate.

Then one shouted, "Are we going to get paid?" That stopped all noise and movement.

One man standing near the stairs said, "I'll check his room." Two others joined him.

They returned, slowly, down the stairs. "He took all of his valuables." Again, general yelling occurred.

"I've fought for him for over five years, and he dumped me here?"

"We're not getting paid?"

"Someone get the other knights down here!" By this time. the racket awoke Sirs Adam and John.

When they came down the steps, all of the soldiers left in the keep filled the hall. One off the captains stepped forward, "With all due respect, we have checked, and only you two are left. Sir Thomas died trying to climb out the window, and Macabe just ran away."

Adam and John shot each other worried looks.

"The men want to know if they will be paid."

Adam climbed on top of the table. "Men, we always find our pay in the gold of those we capture. Northdale holds gold because they traded with Vikings for years. And who knows what else they have that we can sell? Remember: Bishop Blackwood declared they are not Christians; we can sell them!"

Laughter filled the room.

"So we have to whip them today or tomorrow, and then it will all be available." Halfhearted cheers went up from the men.

Looking at John, Adam said, "I speak for Sir John, and I'm sure for Tagmore, that you will be paid first before the knights divide up their shares."

The men really cheered then. Adam moved to John, looked at the ceiling, and slightly shook his head.

Oloff was the first commander responding to the gate fight. He immediately called up off-duty fighters and prepared to lead the counterattack himself.

One of Oloff's men reported to him. "A man on a horse broke through the wall. He wore Macabe's tunic."

Oloff sprung out onto the square and yelled at the top of his voice, "You filthy coward. Kill Lady Sara, cause all of this shit, and then flee when things get hot! You better leave England because if you stay, I'll kill you."

He shook his ax at the empty road. Turning to his men, he shouted, "A knight! Ha! A walking pile of pig shit!"

Directing his attention to the gate area, Oloff could see the men who had made the breakout raid running back into the keep. His troops quickly restored the wooden wall.

The faces on Sirs Adam and John spoke volumes. Two of their peers had tried to flee; only one seemed to have made it. They sat at the main hall table and did not speak. The other men of the keep sat around the walls. No one spoke.

Adam finally said, "Look, we must combine our force with Tagmore's. If not, we are trapped."

John replied, "This keep is strong, too strong for Rupert to take by force. But, and this is the big but, it is also a prison. We need to combine with Tagmore and then, together, make a fighting retreat out of Northdale."

"Let's ask Tagmore to get his men out into the square, en masse. This will draw the attention of most of Rupert's force. We will assemble in the stable buildings and then jump the back wall when Tagmore is in place. We can combine with him and then either beat Northdale or begin a retreat out of this hell hole."

John added, "When we send over the message, tell him to surround themselves with shields. They also need to fashion a shield roof to protect from lobbed shots."

While the scribe wrote out the directions in Latin, Adam added, "Tell Tagmore to wave a flag side-to-side if he understands." The message wrapped around an arrow shaft hit Tagmore's front door.

Two hours after sunrise, Tagmore's men piled out of their buildings and quickly formed a circle shield-wall. With small steps to prevent tripping, the formation moved about two hundred feet into the square. Penetration beyond that point seemed strategically inappropriate because their job was to make a demonstration and then retreat back into the buildings once the keep forces joined them. They waited.

As the Northdale commanders met to organize the day's reaction to an almost assured outbreak of some sort, a runner arrived. He reported that Tagmore's force had just formed a tight, protective circle in the square and left a large number of wounded without a protecting force.

Rupert took a small piece of paper, wrote a short instruction, and told the messenger to deliver it to Marta.

Michael stood. "Father, what did you tell her?"

"Kill all of the wounded who are left behind." Oloff grunted.

"Father—"

Rupert leaped to his feet and interrupted. "There is no discussion on this point." He and Oloff walked out of the meeting.

Marta sat with Mary North when the runner arrived. Her mouth dropped open when she read the note. Her hand started to shake. "I cannot do this."

Mary reached over and read the note. "My father hurts over the death of my mother. He wants to punish the offenders." She took a deep breath. "But I cannot help you do it either." The two looked at each other.

"Mary, I obey and love your father, but to kill wounded men ..." She stopped. "I just can't."

"Marta, I will tell him I received the note because you were out surveying the situation. I will tell him I never showed it to you."

Both faces showed considerable stress. Marta looked into the square and then back at Mary. Marta said, "Yes." She stood. "Let's get everyone ready. We have business with those bastards out there."

Macabe knew a horse could not run at full speed for long distances, especially uphill and carrying a knight in armor and a full draping of its own defensive chain mail. When the road reached the crest of the Downs' valley, he stopped the horse. Its heavy panting showed the necessity of pausing. He removed his helmet to listen for possible Northdale guards. Hearing none, he turned his horse to watch the situation in the village; the sun had risen high enough to provide light. He could not dismount because it took four men or a hoist to put him into the saddle. He sat for almost half an hour to give the animal time to recover.

Sophia and another archer, Jutta, watched Macabe the whole time. Sophia whispered, "Before we do anything, we should wait to see if another joins him."

Jutta raised their eyebrows. "Do what?'

Sophia smiled and patted her assistant on the shoulder. "We must prevent him from leaving." Doubt radiated from Jutta's face.

After it seemed clear that no one would join the knight, Sophia pointed at the road. "I'll stand in the road and shoot when he charges. You shoot at any opening when he passes." They quietly stood and notched arrows. Sophia also held a second arrow in the hand holding the bow.

She stepped into the middle of the road and yelled, "Surrender, Sir Knight, you cannot leave Northdale."

Macabe's face first registered concern and then melted into humor. Utilizing his most commanding voice, Macabe shouted, "Girl, what do you think you are doing? I will pass over or through you, but pass I will!"

Sophia did not move. He put on his helmet, drew his sword, and spurred the horse. It charged.

Sophia could see the connecting strings that closed the horse's chain mail at its chest. Someone had not tied them tightly, so the horse's skin could be seen. She drew carful aim and the first arrow hit the horse's upper chest between its front legs. It did not stop. Macabe started to yell and swing his sword over his head. Jutta had her opening. She aimed at his armpit but missed low by about an inch: it bounced off his body armor. Sophia's second shot entered the horse's chest on the side containing its heart. The horse took two more strides and then collapsed. Macabe's momentum did not stop with the horse's fall. He flew over the falling head and landed on his own. He never moved again.

Sophia stared at the man and then began to shake all over. Jutta stepped out of the bushes. "My God, you got the bastard! What a great shot!" She ran over to Sophia and gave her a hug. "My shot hit his armor plate just below his armpit, but it bounced off."

Sophia faced Jutta, "I don't think we are quite done. This is a chance to make a statement about ending this fight."

She directed Jutta to pull off Macabe's helmet and roll back any chain-mail head covering. She retrieved his sword.

"It is simple. We need to cut off his head and take it back to the village."

Jutta expressed surprise then amusement. Each lady had to take several whacks with the sword because that instrument was not designed for the task. When done, they spent almost fifteen minutes taking off his armor in order to reach Macabe's tunic on which his crest was embroidered.

"We must make an obvious entrance to the square." They cut a sapling tree to make a pole and hung Macabe's tunic over it, thus forming a sling into which they placed the head.

Sophia said, "I'll take one end, and you the other. We must get to the square quickly. Can you run?'

Jutta began to vigorously nod her head in the affirmative. With a smile, Jutta said, "I can outlast you any day."

Sophia slapped her on the back. They picked up the pole ends and then began to jog toward the village.

Tagmore advanced only partially through the square and then stopped to await the keep's soldiers. He did not want to advance all the way across the open space because then no retreat would be possible. The shield walls seemed to protect his men. Hostilities actually stopped as both sides watched for the other's maneuvers.

Oloff had one of the women archers sit on the shoulders of a swordsman and peer over the circle-wall. The two walked around almost the whole circle-wall. No assembly activity could be seen. Oloff signaled for Eleanor.

"We heard some type of preparation noise last night," Oloff said to her, "but no movement is detected in the yard. That leaves only the cluster of stable buildings against the back wall. Let's take a chance and combine our forces across the wall from those buildings. Make sure the Vikings are there."

Eleanor agreed.

Rupert and the Northdale commanders approached one side of the square to observe the situation and formulate necessary reaction. They wanted to correctly coordinate the knights' charge, position archers, and prepare the swordsmen. King Richard came with them. A discussion of alternatives started when a signal horn sounded from the road.

Attached to Macabe's saddle had been this signal horn. Jutta blew it as they entered the square, and the sound produced the desired effect. The combatants stopped any activity and stared at them. The sight of Macabe's bloody tunic hanging from a pole seemed to freeze everyone.

After placing the pole on the ground, Sophia reached into the sling, pulled the severed head out by its hair, and held it up at arm's length. She yelled as loud as she could, "Invaders, here is your Marshal's head!"

She walked toward the wooden wall, stopped, and repeated in a loud voice, "Soldiers of the keep, here is Macabe."

Stunned silence followed. She then walked over near Tagmore and made the same announcement. This time, she began to swing the head in a circle and then released the head so it flew right into Tagmore's formation. The men quickly jumped out of the way to avoid touching it. They also remained silent. Tagmore, seeing the impact on his men, loudly cursed and kicked the head out of his formation.

Sophia returned to the middle of the square. "Men of the invading army, this conflict is over."

The surprise also registered on Northdale's commanders. They remained stationary with the exception of their faces that clearly showed active contemplation.

After a few moments, Rupert stepped forward. "How did this happen?" Jutta immediately explained how Sophia faced down Macabe and killed his horse. She deliberately projected her voice so that everyone could hear it. The invaders were struck by the fact that a woman archer had killed their army's fearsome marshal.

With a broad smile, Rupert turned to the king. "Your Majesty, can a woman be knighted?"

With surprise on his face and, after clearing his throat, the king said, "Well, not really. However, she can be a lady if she marries a noble."

"My eldest, Sir Michael, will someday inherit this earldom. Could you not make him a baron today?"

With the same reaction to the last question, the king replied, "Why, yes, I can."

Rupert yelled, "Get Michael over here."

Michael had been organizing troops on the opposite side of the square. He walked across its middle with his sword drawn and staring at Tagmore's men.

The king stood next to Rupert as Michael walked up. "Kneel, Sir Michael of Northdale." When he did, Richard continued. "I now grant to you the title of Baron of Northdale. Rise, Baron Michael." The Northdale forces all started to cheer.

Rupert signaled Squire to come forward. "Please marry these two if they will have it." He waved Sophia to walk over.

Squire said with a solemn, but joyful tone, "Baron Michael, will you take Sophia Harness as your wife?"

Michael faced her. "Absolutely."

"Sophia, will you take this man as your husband?"

She turned away from Michael and looked at Rupert. "Before I say yes, my lord—and I certainly will say yes—will you give me a wedding present?"

An audible gasp could be heard. Smiling, but very curious, Rupert asked, "What is it, Sophia?"

"Can you stop the killing of these foot soldiers and only execute the guilty parties? I don't think Lady Sara would ever ask for all of this blood. In fact, I know she would not."

Rupert staggered back. The commanders reached for him to keep him from falling. Deep concern showed on all their faces. Michael put his arm around Sophia's shoulders. Rupert pulled out his sword and threw it on the ground, then turned, and walked a few steps.

Sophia added, "I don't care if you pin the guilty ones to a wall and give a gold coin to each archer who shoots off one of their balls, but you know the foot soldiers really have no choice in what their commanders do."

Oloff moved over and stood in front of Rupert. The two men looked into each other's eyes. Rupert took hold of one of Oloff's arms, and together they walked off ten feet. A conversation that no one could hear and lasting almost five minutes occurred between the two. By facial expressions and arm movements, it was clear that both men injected emotion into the talk. Oloff put one hand on Rupert's shoulder, and in a moment, Rupert did the same to Oloff. The two then placed their heads on the shoulder of the other. The invading and defending armies watched, fascinated by the pending answer.

With a bowed head, Rupert walked back to the gathering. He looked up and had tears in his eyes. "Your request is granted."

Northdale troops, many of Tagmore's men, and a few of the forces in the keep, let out a cheer. All of the Northdale commanders also cheered. The only ones not cheering were Rupert and Oloff. Showing horrified faces, three others did not cheer: Sirs Tagmore, Adam, and John.

When things quieted down, Sophia, with a big smile, faced Michael. "Squire, my answer is yes!" Michael lifted Sophia off her feet and kissed her. Cheers resounded again.

This exchange completely extinguished any remaining fighting spirit in Tagmore's men. Their arms went limp. The men hidden in the stable stopped moving.

Rupert held a quick huddle with the commanders, including the king, and then he asked Lord Michael to make the announcement. Michael walked from the commander group and stood in the middle of the square. "The knights who unjustly condemned my mother to death and Gismore's horrible bodyguard will be executed. We will accept the surrender of the rest of you on terms previously established."

The men standing on Tagmore's outer ring began dropping their weapons. Tagmore yelled, "Bullshit!" and, grabbing Gismore's son's hand, began pushing out of the circle. His own men quickly disarmed him and shoved both toward Northdale's commanders.

The men in the keep's stable were already anxious because they could see Estrid's men. As one said, "Shit, they want us to fight Vikings! Not me!" They began to retreat into the keep. The remaining members of Gismore's bodyguard placed themselves at the keep's doors and drew their swords. Sirs Adam and John and Adam's son joined them.

One yelled, "No one is going to agree to this bullshit!" The door slammed shut. After a few minutes, yelling could be heard and then the sounds of an intense fight.

After five minutes, the keep doors opened and a group of soldiers led Sir John and Sir Theobald, Adam's son, out. One of the captains shouted that Gismore's bodyguard and Sir

Adam were now all dead. He pushed the two captives toward the square.

Events moved quickly. Men carried a large log into the center of the square, and the four condemned were led to it. Oloff, with ax in hand, stood next to it.

Rupert strode forward to speak, but just as he was about to begin, Squire stepped in front of him.

"My lord, you cannot execute the two boy knights."

"Squire, they swore the knightly oath about justice, and subsequently agreed to Sara's death. End of the story!" He took a step sideways to face the prisoners.

Squire stepped in front of Rupert again. "My lord, if you execute these two boys, that fact will be the only thing remembered about this invasion. No one will remember what these assholes did to Lady Sara. No one will consider the justice of our cause. They will only remember and condemn you for the execution of boys. Please, ask yourself if Lady Sara would want the retribution taken on two whose fathers intimidated them into voting as they did."

Rupert, without looking at Squire, took another side step. Squire again matched his move. "My lord, you lost one daughter and I my whole family. The pain is awful—no one should have to experience the loss of a child." He took a deep breath. "Therefore, Rupert, I have no choice. You will have to go through me to do this."

Rupert grabbed Squire by his tunic, pulled him close, and glowered at him. He then stepped back, shoved Squire, and exchanged a look with Oloff. The sword previously thrown on the ground had been sheathed. Rupert now slowly pulled it out. He took a step backward.

"Squire, kneel down." With a face full of resolution, Squire did so. Michael, Mary, and the other commanders looked on with fearful anticipation.

"You have continually shown that you understand the concept of knighthood, better than the bastards we recently fought." Lifting his sword and touching each of the squire's shoulders, Rupert continued. "Therefore, you are now Sir Squire." The crowd cheered. King Richard put his hand on Rupert's shoulder and gave it a slight shake. They smiled at each other.

Rupert then pointed at Oloff and then at the log. Only Sir Tagmore and Sir John de Burghton lost their heads.

Lord Michael and Lady Sophia stood in front of the assembled invaders who had surrendered. "Northdale's rules are simple. You make a choice. My wife just saved your lives, but you must choose: death or surrender." He waved for

Oloff, who carried his ax and stood next to Michael. "This is Oloff. He will gladly cut off the head of anyone who requests it or who pretends to surrender. Any attempt to leave will result in your death, no questions asked. We always have people stationed in the woods along the road. Any questions?"

Most of the men made slight headshakes.

Rodger Cartwright and Ann stood near the edge of the crowd. She leaned close to his ear. "Who is on guard on the road? Everyone is here."

While keeping his face toward the square, he whispered out of the side of his mouth, "No one." He smiled. "Shush."

"Good, because I need your sword and now!" She grabbed his arm and half pulled him into one of the still-empty buildings.

Once the invaders' arms had been turned in, a great party began. Cow-roasting and wine-drinking started almost immediately. The men who had previously surrendered were invited and a huge bonfire was built. Northdale families who had lost loved ones did not participate. Most of the invaders remained subdued as they drank and ate, but a good number celebrated the end of the fighting.

Michael and Sophia politely took their leave after a few hours. The two boy knights stayed in one of the buildings and only ate dinner. Rupert, after sharing some wine with Oloff and Eleanor, retired to his room in the keep. Oloff and Eleanor's children joined the festivities as did Rupert's other two children.

The ale servers rolled barrels up onto a table. They then filled mugs and placed them on a structure which consisted to two posts driven into the ground and planks nailed across their tops. Jutta was leaning her back to the bar with her elbows on it when Richard walked up.

He looked at her. "Weren't you the person who helped Lady Sophia kill Macabe?"

Jutta, turning her head to reply, said, "Yes, I am."

"Well, it seems you should receive some credit. After all, you helped Lady Sophia."

"No, she is the one who stood in the path and blocked it. My arrow bounced off his armor."

"Well, if you helped her get to the position, then you assisted in the outcome."

Jutta now turned her body to face Richard and just one elbow remained on the bar. With a big smile, she said, "Thank you for seeing me like that."

"Well, Jutta, it is only fair. The Crown issues red sashes to persons who provided great service to it. I will issue you a red sash in honor of your contribution and include in the decree that from this day forward, you will be entitled to be addressed as Lady.'" They raised their mugs and clinked them together.

After a drink, Jutta turned toward the bar and placed her mug near Richard's cup. "Now, tell me about being a king."

King Richard and Jutta acted very egalitarian that night. Lady Jutta would always have a small smirk on her face when she told people she had earned the sash by serving the king.

Next Day

The next noon, Rupert called a commander's meeting. He told them many tasks required attention. The biggest of these concerned how to feed and house the surrendered troops, followed by organization of their work service. Responsibilities would be assigned, and he asked for everyone except King Richard and his two knights to select which duty they would supervise.

After the routine matters, Rupert rose and, in his most commanding voice, said, "But one thing must be accomplished first, the bodies of the assholes must be thrown into the sea."

The Northdale commanders accepted this as routine, but the king and his two knights looked shocked.

"Lord Rupert, should we not give these men Christian burial?"

"Your Majesty, Northdale always consigns the bodies of invaders to the sea. We will not let their filthy carcasses poison our scarce soil. We never have. The men responsible for Sara's death and the recent invasion cannot rest here. I will not allow it nor accept questions on the subject." He pointed his finger as his eldest, Michael. "This will be your task."

"Oh, and one last thing: no one will ever mention those men's names in Northdale again. Let it be known that anyone who does will discuss the matter with Oloff's ax."

Oloff smiled and made a satisfying grunt.

Turning to the king, Rupert continued. "Your Majesty, this applies to you and your men. I mean no disrespect. But the incredible sins those men committed denies them any further recognition. I hope you understand."

Michael undertook the grisly task. The corpses found in the keep had been piled outside. They were the first to go, and the group included Gismore's bodyguard, the two beheaded knights, the one who died fighting in the keep, and the one shot trying to climb out the back window. The task also included exhuming Gismore, Blackwood, and their soldiers killed in the raid.

Michael used Northdale workers because he could not predict the reaction of the surrendered troops to digging up their former commanders. The digging party moved to the site of the camp raid. It only took a short inspection to find the pit containing the bodies. They found one dressed in the commander's tunic and one in the bishop's robe. Based on the fatal wounds on each, it became clear they were not the commanders. The baron called for Northdale's best hunter to investigate. It took him almost one day to finally locate the carefully camouflaged burial site. One was stabbed through the chest and the outer still had the stub of an arrow sticking out of his mouth.

At dinner that night Michael reported, "We found the two hidden commanders, and we tossed them into a watery hell. We took four wagons full of bodies, about forty, and also put them in the sea."

Rupert leaned forward on the table and grasped his glass so tightly that his hand slightly shook. "How long to finish?'

"Father, the task is absolutely disgusting. The bodies in the lower layers decomposed more than the ones at the top. Everyone is getting sick. Considering the guilty knights and the bodyguard have gone to the sea, cannot we just bury the rest?"

Rupert slowly rose.

"Father, those soldiers simply obeyed their lords when they came here; you know most really had no choice, and they certainly did not have a choice about what their cursed commander did. This task is actually punishment to our people."

The last point stopped the sound from coming out of Rupert's opened mouth. He slumped into his chair and stared at his hands on the table. The others attending did not make any sound at all.

Mary cleared her throat. "Father, I cannot believe Mother would demand such work."

His eyes showed great sadness as he stood up. He looked at Michael, nodded his head, waved his hand, and then walked to his room.

Rupert called Sir Ranulf and Sir Harry Bristol, the two who had refused to participate in Sara's death, to a meeting. "Gentlemen, we now have too many surrendered to feed. My captains suggest the men who surrendered with you should be freed. I agree, but we require someone to help supervise the other men until their year is up. I will free your men if you two agree to finish your year of service."

Their faces registered resignation and not resentment. Ranulf looked at Harry and then Ranulf said, "We agreed with you for one year's service. We will hold to our word."

Harry took a small step forward. "The men were never paid anything. They will need some money to pay for their trips home; otherwise, they will be forced to become thieves and, thus, hunted men."

Rupert turned to Sir Squire. "Did we retrieve enough gold from the recent assholes to pay the men some money?"

"Lord Rupert, half pay is available."

Harry, after looking at Ranulf, said, "That amount would give them enough travel funds to make it home." Harry smiled. "Although I cannot swear to the thieving part."

Rupert smiled too. "Agreed." By the year's end, Harry and Rupert would become friends for life.

Northdale used some of the captured gold to purchase beef from Hollingsbrook and other lands farther south. The surrendered troops would be fed. The prisoners' main tasks revolved around carving out stone blocks. The blocks would be used in all future projects and could be trimmed to fit a stonemason's requirements. Workers who demonstrated stone carving skill worked on Sara's monument.

When finished, the Lady Sara's monument consisted of a flat stone platform large enough to hold forty people. In the middle of it, a square pillar rose twenty feet. Masons carved a stone plaque stating, "Here is the site where Lady Sara was cruelly and unjustly burned to death after being raped by unchristian men. May her beauty and grace be remembered by all and seen again in Heaven."

The manufactured stone blocks would be used to build harbor improvements, including a solid wharf. Workers also used them to build two guard towers located on either side of the road leading from the Ibix.

An additional, unexpected, and positive impact occurred with the prisoners. Due to its loose immigration policies, Northdale supported more women than men. Ten marriages would eventually occur between the surrendered troopers and local ladies. It quickly became a Northdale social norm never to mention how these men arrived.

Three days after the battle, Oloff asked Sir Squire the location of his daughter, Ann. He had not seen her since the fight. The squire made excuses that she drew several duties and magnanimously volunteered for others so they could celebrate. Oloff departed, saying, "I'll talk to Eleanor."

Squire sought out Rupert. "My lord, you might have a small situation to deal with." He placed the marriage register on the table and pointed to the entry before Michael and Sophia's entry.

"So Rodger married Ann. It's a good match." He then looked at Squire's face and saw the strain. "You are not telling me that Oloff doesn't know?" For the first time in days and days, he roared with laughter.

The plot was simple. The next day, Rupert invited Oloff for breakfast. Michael, Lady Mary, Lady Sophia, Alfred North, and Sir Squire attended. They suppressed the humorous overtone of the meeting. Oloff came in with Eleanor. As was his habit, he placed his ax against one of the far walls before sitting. Rupert snuck down the stairs and quietly took the ax back up him. When Rupert joined them, Squire announced he wanted to read the latest marriage records. Everyone worked hard not to smile.

When it came to Rodger and Ann's names, Oloff jumped to his feet and yelled, "What!" He immediately went to the wall for his ax. Again he yelled, "Where is it?"

Rupert said, holding a tight face, "I did not see you bring it in today."

Oloff made a quick reconnoiter of the room's walls and then yelled again, "Shit, I'm going home to get it!"

He ran for the door and Eleanor, quite concerned, ran after him. Laughter erupted around the table. Someone said, "It is a good thing that Rodger is one of God's knights. He will need the protection!"

More laughter followed the comment. Rupert smiled. "I will go after him, but he knows Rodger's qualities and when the smoke clears, things will be smooth."

Oloff found a wood ax and then found the two as they walked across the square hand-in-hand. He shouted, "You got married to my daughter without my permission!" He raised his ax, and Eleanor put both hands on his arm.

Ann stepped in front of Rodger. "Father, we did so during the battle. We did not want to wait because we both faced fighting and possible death. I did not think your command responsibilities would have allowed for time to consider formalities."

Rodger put his arm in front of Ann and stepped in front of her. "Oloff, I love your daughter, and I will be an excellent husband for her." Eleanor's whole weight hung from Oloff's arm and it began to lower.

Rupert walked up, carrying Oloff's battle-ax. "Oloff, he is right. His value is well known."

Oloff looked at Rupert. "You had my ax?"

"Old friend, I didn't want you to get hasty."

Oloff stared at Rupert and then his face began to soften and a slight smile formed. He looked at Eleanor's slight smile and dropped his arm. Rodger and Ann stood with arms around each other. He looked at them. "He is a good man. I'm glad you picked him." A round of hugs occurred.

Standing next to Rupert, Oloff said softly, "Don't ever take my ax again."

Rupert smiled. "Don't have another attractive daughter."

―――

The celebration in the main hall that night became a raucous affair. It would be an understatement that people just got drunk. More laughter filled the room than had in months. Oloff and Rupert ended the evening, sitting in a corner, leaning shoulder to shoulder.

Boy Knights

THE QUESTION OF WHAT TO do with the boy knights persisted. When the commanders discussed this topic, King Richard suggested a deal could be made with their families: exchange the boy's lives for a permanent nonaggression agreement. In short, if the boys' extended families agreed never to attempt revenge on Northdale and the boy knights themselves also agreed, they should be given back to their families.

A herald was dispatched. The tidings were received with joy. No news of the Northdale battles had reached the rest of England. The families, and especially the boys' mothers, had worried about them.

The Gismore and de Yealand families conferred and immediately sent a herald in response. They proposed to travel in the winter to negotiate. Rupert responded via herald that he would not receive anyone until spring. In addition, he required the boys' mothers and the two dead men's successors to attend the meetings. On May 15, the two families began their trip.

Nothing eventful happed before the visitors reached the Ibix. The guard patrols observed the assemblage and passed on an alert. Lady Sophia had drawn the day's captain duties; she waited on the north shore. She politely asked in a loud voice, "Who are you and what business do you seek in Northdale?"

It was Gismore's youngest brother who spoke out. "We are the families of Lord Gismore and Sir de Yealand; we are responding to the summons of your Lord Rupert. Whom, may I ask, am I addressing?"

Adjusting her bow over her shoulders, she replied, "Lady Sophia, Baroness of Northdale and today's guard captain."

That simple statement held so much unfamiliar information that all of the visitors sat quietly. A young woman addressing men, as an archer, a guard captain, and a baroness: staggering.

Gismore's wife broke the silence. "Is my son, Gilbert, all right? And the same question for Theobald de Yealand."

With a big smile, Sophia announced, "Lady, we of Northdale do not hurt children. You are welcome, but please remember our guards will be watching you. Drawing a weapon, even in jest, will result in your death. Also, Northdale has one more rule that cannot be broken under any circumstances; you may never mention the names of your dead relatives or other members of that damned invading army. Do you understand this last point?"

She waited until the group members agreed and then waved then across the river.

The party stopped at Sara's site. The prisoners had finished its clearing and leveling. Mary explained that everyone must dismount or get out of wagons and stand with her. When all were standing in a semicircle around her, Sophia looked at each with very level eyes. She proceeded to tell them of the site's significance. Lady de Yealand dramatically fainted when Sophia described the rape and burning at the stake. The visitors did not speak until they reached the keep.

The two mothers were given separate rooms, and the rest of the party accepted whatever accommodations were available. The lack of refined living accommodations would, of course, be transmitted all over the kingdom.

Rupert did not allow the boy knights to attend the first dinner. He explained that despite their knightly vows, the two had, in fact, voted to unjustly burn Lady Sara. He pointed out that only the intervention of Sir Squire and King Richard had saved their lives. The boys had committed a serious crime, and he would have been totally within his rights to behead both of them. Lady de Yealand repeated her fainting act.

Rupert then outlined the agreement's terms. The boys could leave Northdale without any further retribution. In exchange, the extended families and successors to the dead men's titles and estates must irrevocably agree to never seek revenge on Northdale or any of its people, both now and the future. No Northdale property would ever be confiscated, and Northdale's people would be allowed permanent free passage through any of the families' lands with hospitality extended to them.

Gismore's brother rose and said in a clear voice, "We will accept these terms." Although this seemed like a simple statement, it had taken hard discussion to produce. Several family members demanded a chance to organize another invasion of Northdale. Others pointed out the futility of sending another army, the last one having been crushed. In the end, the choice to retrieve a son outweighed any other alternative.

Raising a glass, Rupert told them that he would direct Professor Hazelwood and lawyers to produce the required document within two days. All parties would sign and seal it.

Eleanor stood. "Lord Rupert, are you satisfied?"

He nodded.

"Then may the boys enter?"

Rupert nodded again. She pointed at a door, and a servant opened it. The two boys came bounding through. Lady de Yealand woke right up. Gismore's wife cried as she hugged her son.

Lady Mary sat at the breakfast table when the two mothers came to eat. Gismore's wife stood next to Lady de Yealand. "We noted that the two boys seem very well cared for. Please pass on our thanks to Lord Rupert."

Mary smiled. "Northdale's air is rumored to be very healthy. I believe my father will never forgive your two sons, but he did not allow any mistreatment of them."

Four days later, the boys and their families departed. Visitors passing Sara's site on the way out were not required to stop. This group hurried past the site. No violation of the agreement ever occurred.

King's Departure

Heralds organized themselves into what amounted to a guild. Its rules dictated faithful and accurate transmission of messages without any personal interpretation. The guild adopted as its symbol a flying griffon carrying a scroll in one claw. The guild also chose blue for the background color and yellow for the griffon. The banner, attached to a six-foot pole set into a slot in a stirrup, served one major practical service—it identified a herald and provided safe passage between disagreeing parties.

As occurs in all ages, the behavior of a support team reflected on its leaders. Thus, the herald's deportment, manners, speech, and attire must broadcast the leader's status. The herald who approached Hollingsbrook made a clear statement of having powerful bosses. His tunic showed no wear, fading, or dirt, and real gold had been intertwined in its embroidery. Gold thread rimmed his hat, and his belt was made of gold chain. Leggings were spotless, without any sign of repair. His boot shine almost reflected light.

With the herald came ten knights who dressed with the same quality as the herald. The two men riding at the front of the knight's column wore helmets to which earls' crowns had been affixed. Behind the knights, a considerable number of support staff and servants rode on a variety of horses and in wagons.

Of the two approaching earls, Lord Matthew of Cornish represented the southern coalition of nobles and Lord Jacob of Manchester, the middle group. After the news of Gismore's defeat reached London, the northern, middle, and southern nobles held a conference. In the end, none of the three wanted to see one of the other's candidate ascend to the throne. Because they all lost enthusiasm for Gismore's thinly veiled ambitions, a strong motivation to settle issues existed. The conference resolved to restore Richard to the throne for the time being, and to cooperate with each other, at least on the paper agreement. The biggest concession came from the southern nobles who finally accepted the practical limits of French alliances.

As the august party approached, Hollingsbrook's Lord David and his wife, Gyrid, began a frantic effort to arrange rank-sensitive sleeping quarters and a high-quality banquet. Lady Gyrid almost experienced a nervous breakdown trying to perform as a perfect hostess for such a distinguished group of guests.

At the banquet, David asked the purpose of the trip to Northdale.

Lord Matthew put down his food and drink. "Lord David, you are a northern noble, but from what we understand made little contribution to Gismore's recent attempt on King Richard. Therefore, we, and I mean the vast majority of England's earls, expect you to cooperate with us. If you do so, then no retribution will occur."

Lord David responded, "I was never comfortable with Gismore's strong attitudes."

Several quiet, doubting comments came from the knights and Lord Jacob said, "The majority of England's earls have decided to again have Richard assume his throne. We here are his escort. You will cooperate."

David raised his eyebrows in a look of innocence. "Of course, of course. You know that Gismore and Blackwood arrived here with an army. I had no choice."

After several people expressed understanding, the conversation moved off Hollingsbrook's position and took up the practical details of getting into Northdale.

David described Northdale's accommodations. "Most of you will be sleeping on the floor."

As the banquet continued, many men made comments about Northdale and most were not complimentary. David became somewhat irritated at this blatant disrespect. "You know that Lord Rupert, with only about three hundred fighters, half of them women, defended the king against about twelve hundred men. And he defeated them."

This comment did redirect the conversation to expression of limited appreciation, but never nudged the disrespect.

The lords decided to send an assistant herald to Northdale with a message for Richard to come to Hollingsbrook. The return trip would begin from here.

Lord David said, "I tell you, gentlemen, Rupert will never agree to that. He lost his beloved wife defending the king. He will never let him travel with you until he evaluates your credentials and any written agreement you carry."

One of the retinue's knights chipped in, "She is the one they burned at the stake." A moderate amount of laughter was heard.

David slowly stood up. "Sir Knight, Rupert would eviscerate you, with maximum pain, if you ever show disrespect to Lady Sara. In fact, Lady Sara's guardian, Oloff would split you in two with his huge ax even if you wore armor."

The banquet's remaining conversation avoided any hint of insult. At its conclusion, the two lords decided to proceed into Northdale.

The king had sent Sir Benjamin to London to proclaim the victory. He returned with the cavalcade. He left Hollingsbrook before the banquet in order to carry the news of the overall attitude and the earls' change of heart.

After receiving the information, Rupert sent Michael to receive them at the Ibix's banks. He and Sir Squire stopped their horses on the north bank and introduced themselves when the delegation reached the southern shore. The immaculate herald made his formal introduction and explanation of his mission. Michael welcomed all of them.

When the procession reached Sara's death site, a confrontation occurred. The herald and the two earls refused to stop. Michael signaled for an arrow to be shot over their heads and then, in no uncertain terms, explained moving forward without stopping would result in their deaths.

Lord Jacob decided to smooth over the situation. "Is this important to Lord Rupert and the people of Northdale?"

"It is."

Jacob dismounted and faced Michael. "Both Gismore and Blackwood were asses." The others dismounted. Only the herald remained in his saddle.

"Sir Herald, the requirement applies to you as does the penalty for trying to ride another step."

After looking behind himself and seeing no support, the herald dismounted. The long-term consequence of this act would be the herald guild's endless, widespread decrying of Northdale's uncivilized, backward habits.

When the delegation reached the square, it found Rupert, Oloff, King Richard, and his two knights waiting for them. Due to the demands of battle, none of them, except Benjamin, looked well-dressed at all. Benjamin had used the trip to London as an opportunity to restore his wardrobe.

After the requisite formal introductions, all entered the main hall. Gismore's troops had trashed the furniture, so a table consisting of planks occupied the room's center. Only simple benches provided seating. The recently captured armaments lined all of the room's walls.

When all found socially correct seating, the herald began, using his most formal voice, an invitation for the king to resume his duties. He emphasized the point that the majority of all England's earls extended this offer. He blathered on with fancy compliments and a strong vow to end useless conflict.

It took almost fifteen minutes for the herald to finish. Rupert held up his hand. "Before the king responds, do you bring written testimony to the statements just made?"

Lord Jacob said yes. He then signaled to his squire to bring forth a document. Once unrolled, it was seen that the Latin declaration was signed and sealed by forty-eight of the fifty-two recognized earls. Rupert gave it a quick glance. The status of the king prevented him from becoming entangled in the interpretation of legal wording, so the document passed to Sir Benjamin.

"We will review your proposal and respond at tonight's banquet." Rupert rose and his retinue, including the king, climbed the stairs to the second floor. This abrupt departure caused angry, but muted, comments from the delegation's members.

Northdale's contingent broke out into smiles and congratulated themselves when they'd reached the second floor, out of the hearing range of the delegation. The king, in particular, received many slaps on the back.

The king pointed at Rupert. "They were very surprised at being left down there."

Sir Thomas slapped Rupert on the back. "Proper way to receive those smug attitudes. They act like they are doing Your Majesty a favor instead of recognizing they were in the wrong and should be asking forgiveness."

The king smiled as he looked each of his companions in the eye. "Gentlemen and ladies, you fought and suffered grievous losses for justice and myself. I owe all of you. But the facts are facts, and I must agree to their invitation because it will settle discord and bring England peace for years to come." He started shaking his fist. "I don't mind making those lords damn uncomfortable for now and a long time to come."

He walked over to the table and poured glasses of wine. Then, acting like a humble servant, he handed a glass to each person in the room. He said, "To peace and prosperity for England and for Northdale."

All raised their glasses. "Hear, hear."

They sat and talked for almost an hour about the king's future challenges and who among the signatories he could really trust. By this time, Thomas, Benjamin, and Hazelwood had made a reasonable translation of the document. Everyone gathered around the table, and they made a simplified, condensed summation of its stipulations. In short, it stated in writing what had been stated aloud. Rupert, the king, Mary, and Ann followed the translation and confirmed its accuracy.

Rupert sent a servant to the main hall and he announced a banquet would convene at an hour past dusk. The king would respond then. The man then invited the delegation to sit outside and refresh themselves in the courtyard's water trough. More muttering occurred.

When everyone gathered, the head table held Rupert, the king, the two earls, Baron Michael, and Baroness Sophia. The rest grabbed bench seats along the long rectangular plank table. Rank was ignored. Wine flowed and roasted pig was served, a very plain meal.

One of the visiting knights whispered a question about Lady Sophia's background. When he heard she herself killed Macabe, a respect exuded from the nearby knights.

Toward the end of the meal, King Richard arose. "My lords, ladies, knights, and other distinguished guests, I accept your proposal to return to London. The document states that all earls will renew their fealty vow to me as king, and you two will do so right now."

A servant brought out a small pillow and placed it on the floor in front of Richard.

With surprise clearly registered, the two lords slowly rose and approached. Jacob made his vow with a voice and manner clearly showing pleasure. Matthew stiffly and, without a smile, also swore his allegiance.

The king then announced the return trip would begin the next day, then turned, and walked up the stairs. The Northdale men struggled to contain smiles.

When the king was gone, one of the knights asked, "Where do we sleep?"

With a large grin, Michael pointed to Eleanor. She, also smiling, said, "The grass is soft, but the dew makes it wet. The main hall's floor is hard but dry. Gentlemen, it's your choice. The circle-wall gate will be closed so your animals will not wander off." She made a slight curtsy, and then all of the Northdale members left the room.

The complaints from the knights became quite loud. Lord Jacob silenced them with a hand gesture. "I think the king has been quite inconvenienced by the last year's events. I will take the floor." Unhappy people sorted themselves out.

When they arrived upstairs, King Richard stood in front of Rupert. "I know I'm going to be caught up in court life. It's quite different than here. I just want you to know that despite how I will be required to act, I will never be able to give all the gratitude you personally and your Northdale people deserve."

"Richard, I was one of your father's trusted friends, not one of his polite ones. It is a reward to help you resist the bastards, even the ones downstairs."

"Rupert, you gave your word to my father to help his child. I now give you the same word in regards to your three.

Tell them to feel free to call on me whenever necessary, and I will do all in my power to protect them."

He stopped and then put both hands on Rupert's shoulders. "Also, I want to pass on my sincere condolences for the loss of Sara. I always enjoyed our time together and understand why you so enjoyed her presence."

The two grasped each other's wrists in a gesture that advanced quickly into a sincere hug.

After the next day's breakfast, the now-royal party departed Northdale. Most would never visit it again. When Lord Matthew made a disparaging remark about Northdale within the king's hearing, he stopped his horse. "Matthew, you will refrain from making any negative comments about Northdale, both now and in the future. Do you understand?"

The responding "Yes, Your Majesty" spoke for all of them.

Lord Papal Legate Rossi's Second Visit

After spending nearly ten years as a prisoner in a locked monastery because of the papal dispensation he gave to Northdale, the former Papal Legate Rossi was freed. The Rossi family interests using bribery, favors, and promises of lucrative positions had wrestled the vacant pope's seat away from its last holders the Gambino coalition. His nephew had been elevated to the papal thrown and offered Rossi the opportunity to either resume the positon of abbot of the Fourth Cross Monastery or the chance to again take the Papal Legate position and launch a new investigation of the renegade Northdale. The exile years had given him plenty of time to review how that earldom had generated his abuse. His hatred of Northdale had grown.

After arriving in England, Rossi's first appointment was with the archbishop of Canterbury. The later had become tired of Northdale's policies and wanted the legate to write a report that provided justification for him to impose strict church rules. Rossi assured the archbishop his work would easily produce the desired result. The archbishop assigned two assistant priests to act as scribes.

Remembering his last visit, Rossi was not surprised by a very informal reception. Sir Squire assigned him food and lodging without any ceremony. It proved, however, very irritating when informed that Rupert's cow herding duties would prevent a meeting for two days.

When they met, Rupert's attitude had not changed from the one shown at their last meetings. Rupert showed no deference to the legate's rank and actually refused to discuss business at their first meeting. After breakfast the next morning, Rupert ordered everyone out of the main hall so he and Rossi could talk.

The legate, with a firm voice, said, "I always keep my assistants with me during formal occasions."

With a pleasant smile and with his hands folded on the table, Rupert said, "Papal Legate Rossi, I am the lord here. Everyone, except you, leaves." He then sat without moving and gazed at Rossi.

The legate glared back and then looked at papers he had placed on the table. He shuffled them around then waved his assistants out. When alone, he first stared at Rupert and then began to explain of the reasons for the investigation ordered by Canterbury. Rupert did not try and hide his amusement.

"I first want to protest the actions of your Guard Captain Sir Cartwright. He drew his sword and required me to leave my carriage for a visit to your wife's still-under construction memorial site. As a Church Lord, I am immune from local regulations; the Guard Captain, in fact, sinned by stopping me."

Rupert laughed, "I guess you don't remember that Cartwright is a knight you appointed by use of papal authority. Maybe you should have been more carful in whom you picked." He laughed again.

With a very angry voice, Rossi picked up a paper and read the list of Northdale policies he was sent to investigate. Rupert just smiled as he listened. The legate ended with, "I am directed by the pope himself to chronical the fate of Bishop Blackwood. What happened to him?"

Rupert now put both hands flat on the table and leaned into its edge. "Rossi, rules exist in Northdale that you should know. No one is allowed to speak the names of those murdering assholes who invaded this district, raped Lady Sara, and then killed her."

The legate opened his mouth to speak, but Rupert raised his hand and voice. "Did you hear what I just said? No mention of those names, period. Punishments will be imposed on any who break that rule, and I mean any." He pounded his fist on the table to emphasize the last point.

Rossi, with wide eyes, sat back in his chair.

"As for your question about that individual, during a battle I personally killed him."

"By what authority do you kill ..." He took a moment to collect his thoughts. "A consecrated member of the church's hierarchy?"

"Rossi, have you ever been in a battle? No one goes around checking credentials before engaging in swordplay. Besides, the invading army's two leaders directed the atrocities, so my marshal—Oloff, by name—and I decided that we would each seek out one of them. By circumstance, I found the person we are talking about."

"So you admit killing this person?"

With a voice colored by emotion Rupert said, "An army invaded Northdale and murdered my wife. By doing so, its leaders signed their own death warrants. They were served on all of them."

The legate wrote notes for a few moments and then looked up. "May I see their graves?"

Rupert's voice returned to normal. "Fall work must be performed so livestock will survive the winter. We hold only one banquet a month, and it will be held three days from now. Sir Squire can arrange a tour for you tomorrow." Rupert stood up. "I will next see you at banquet."

Rossi did not like the fact that two women, Sophia and Ann, had been assigned to lead the tour. Their weapons, unusual clothes, and totally relaxed manners toward him would be placed into his report.

When mounted, Sophia asked, "We are to give you a tour. Is there anything you particularly wish to see?"

Holding himself as straight as possible, Rossi said, "The grave of Bishop Blackwood."

Ann slowly pulled an arrow out of her quiver and strung her bow. She stopped and half turned her head to Sophia while keeping her eyes on the legate. "Baroness?"

"Lord Legate, I believe you have already been told about not repeating any of the invaders' names. By the orders of

Lord Rupert, either of us should put an arrow into anyone who speaks one of the names. As baroness, I hold the authority to let this one breach pass, but there will be no others. Is that clear?"

The two assistants did not look comfortable.

Rossi flushed because two women had threatened his life while enforcing an abhorrent local law. Such a situation laid completely outside of accepted social norms. With a very cold face, he said, "I am prepared for the tour."

The tour included some of the nearby farms and then progressed to the school at which the bishop received another surprise—children of both sexes took lessons. At North House, the nurse admitted him on the permission of the baroness. Ann described the salmon harvesting at the rapids. At the harbor, Sophia showed the stone wharf constructed by the prisoners.

The last stop was the lookout on the Downs River. Sophia pointed with her bow at the ocean. "Here are the graves of the invaders."

With almost a shout, Rossi said, "What?"

Ann turned her back to the ocean and looked directly at the legate. "Northdale, for years, has fought off invaders. The rule was long established that their bodies would not poison its soil. Therefore, the bodies are placed on the shore at low tide, and the sea takes them."

Yelling now, Rossi said, "That is not Christian!"

Sophia, with a pleasant smile and in Latin, said, "Invading peaceful people and committing atrocities puts one outside the teachings of the Lord Jesus."

Compacted blasphemy from a woman completely overwhelmed the legate's ability to speak. His face assumed a scarlet color. His two assistants looked as if they had seen the devil himself. The two ladies walked to their horses and waited for almost ten minutes for the clerics. They could hear loud, heated comments above the sound of the waves. The three men oozed anger when they returned to the horses. Sophia and Ann chatted the whole of the return ride. The men rode in stony silence.

The monthly banquet took the atmosphere of a party. Guests, commanders, extended families, and common folks attended. Rupert made an introductory speech, which usually included business matters and upcoming projects' schedules. Lady Sophia presented a short report on women's matters. Other commanders gave operation announcements, and then, as the last formal activity, guests were introduced.

During this agenda, wine flowed and ample amounts of food were served. When the servants had filled the tables and wine pitchers, they also sat for the meal.

Standing at the head of the big table, Rupert raised a glass. "Let us give a toast to our guest, Lord Papal Legate Rossi from Canterbury and Rome." All toasted. "Would you like to say something, Lord Legate Rossi?"

If the legate held any intention of restraining his comments, the fact that the servants not only sat at a meal with a lord, but had also toasted him released the necessity to control his following comments. Holding a piece of paper in his hand, he rose and fixed his body ramrod straight.

"Lord Rupert, you are a Christian, a knight who took holy vows, and a noble elevated by the king himself. God, through his holy church, established laws that govern behavior. Giving Christian burial to Christians is required. No such law applies to pagans, but I have never heard of a Christian not properly burying dead Christians."

The main hall fell immediately quiet at the first sentence of this statement. Rupert put down his glass and stood with a somber face. Rossi slammed the paper on the table and started to point at the list it contained. Slowly, he began. "What have you done with the body of Bishop Blackwood, the body of Lord Gismore, the body of Sir John Macabe ..."

While the bishop started reading, Rupert's face broke into a huge smile as he moved to a position across the table from the legate. As he passed Oloff, he picked up his ax and then landed it between Rossi's hands. The stroke cut the paper in half.

"Rossi, you hypocritical bastard, Christian nobles and knights who had sworn a vow to the king came here to kill him! Christian nobles and knights judged a perfectly Christian and beautiful woman to be a pagan because she fought to save her homeland. Christian nobles and knights allowed this wonderful woman to be raped by a platoon of Christian men. And these same Christian men condemned Lady Sara to be burned at the stake. I cannot tell the difference between your tongue and the devil's tail."

When the ax fell, Rossi jumped back as far as his chair would allow.

Rupert continued. "You were told twice that no one can speak those names in Northdale; and you were told that punishment exists for all offenders!" His hands began to finger the ax, and the legate's eyes reflected true terror.

By this time, Oloff, Eleanor, Michael, Sophia, Mary, Rodger, Ann, and Squire had stood up. Issuing a hiss, Rupert turned and looked at them. Other than Oloff, whose face registered anger over not holding his ax at the moment, the other's held controlled smiles.

Lady Mary North, in Latin, said, "Father, this bishop shows no Christian understanding, but being an ignorant hypocrite is not a reason to kill him. Serious consequences would occur if you did."

Rupert continued to look at them while his hands began to clutch the ax so hard that his arms began to shake. After about a half-minute, Rupert took a deep breath, dropped the ax, and regained his smile.

As Rupert's body relaxed, everybody's in the room, except the three clerics, also loosened. "Marshal Oloff, who is today's guard captain?"

"Marta Posley, archer."

Seeing Marta in the crowd, Rupert said, "Captain Marta, get three other on-duty guards here immediately."

The people in the room began to talk quietly; snickers could be heard. The three clerics stood without moving. When the three guards ran into the Hall, Rupert said, "Captain, take these three to the door and strip them naked."

Marta and her guards, with big smiles, did so. The room now filled with laughter and shouts.

"Send a guard to the stable and find some rags for these bastards," Rupert said.

More laughter and shouts occurred, accompanied by raised cups. When they were dressed, Rupert commanded, "Sir Squire, give each of these persons a half gold crown for their trip back to Canterbury." The laughter continued.

"Rupert, this is an outrage," screamed Rossi.

"My dear Lord Legate, one more word out of you, and it will be your last." At least three archers picked up bows.

"Captain, walk these three out of Northdale. Take some whips with you; if they stop, use them." The crowd cheered and threw food waste at them.

As Rossi walked, he outlined the condemnation he would write. But as the hours wore on and several whip strokes landed, he realized that revenge should be more thorough and long lasting. When they reached Hollingsbrook, food, clothes, shoes, and horses were provided. The trip to Canterbury took a week and gave the legate plenty of time to structure his response.

Rossi's long document spelled out a very one-sided view of Northdale's uncivilized lifestyle. He, of course, started with unchristian burial and then described the school to teach all children, no matter social class or sex. He decried women fighters. He described the complete abandonment of proper etiquette, particularly the disrespect women showed for their proper role and clothes. He manufactured descriptions of the benefits from trading with the pagan Vikings for stolen gold. Finally, he proclaimed the number of blond children produced by dark-haired mothers proved that Christian Northdale women engaged in intercourse with pagans.

The archbishop wrote a blistering letter to King Richard demanding retribution; and the king made sure the court's bureaucracy buried it. The archbishop ordered numerous monasteries to prepare hand-produced copies of the document. He then widely circulated it. The report's numerous readers, of course, would never know of the attempt on the king's life, the rape, or burning at the stake.

A formal and an informal reaction to Rossi's report occurred. Formally, King Richard announced that Northdale was under his personal protection and, therefore, he would not tolerate any interference with its affairs. After learning of the king's position, the Archbishop of Canterbury decided that Northdale's low significance, compared to his other responsibilities, required no more attention.

Informally, the document cemented English society's attitude toward Northdale. It became the butt of political and social conversations that relegated Northdale to the level of a joke. The educated and political classes adopted an informal norm that assigned Northdale's nobles and people to complete low-class status. Polite society simply would never consider anyone from Northdale as acceptable and rejected the distasteful policies it followed.

Epilogue

Rupert, Oloff, Squire, and Eleanor aged gracefully. Northdale received no additional frontal attacks, thus its leaders settled into a routine of trying to improve the resident's life quality and economic vitality.

Every three years the king organized grand councils that all earls were expected to attend. Fashions in clothes, weapons, and even horse attire changed as economic stability continued. The amount of gold draped on women and men increased. Rupert never attempted to keep up with the latest outfits because he did not see the value of wasting valuable money on fancy clothes. Michael and Sophia followed suit, and toward the end of Rupert's life, they represented Northdale, wearing modest apparel at these great conferences. More than once, someone mistook them for servants.

The king always scheduled at least one exclusive dinner with Rupert. The servants knew to keep a flood of wine flowing and to never repeat anything they heard. He remained one of the very few men who could address the king, in private, by his given name.

A similar gathering occurred at York. Its duke also scheduled a great meeting one year before the king's. Its basic purpose revolved around writing a unified list of demands for the king's review. Rupert had no interest, so Michael and Sophia attended.

When the carriage pulled to York Castle's front door, a uniformed servant announced in a loud voice the names of the passengers. "Baron Michael and Baroness Sophia of Northdale!"

As they stepped out, the Duke's official greeter met them. Lady Adela Radcliff said, "Welcome to York." She then looked at them and asked, "My lady, did you not spend a few months here?"

"Yes, Lady Radcliff, I did."

The lady waved her hand at the main door. "Please proceed."

Sophia stopped. "When here, I was taught a person of lesser rank must curtsy when joining with and departing from a person of higher rank."

Lady Radcliff stood stiff and evaluated Sophia though squinted eyes. Sophia just stood still.

Lady Radcliff then made a curtsy. "If I remember your wild ways, it is a surprise someone elevated you to baroness."

As Sophia turned to walk in, she replied. "No one elevated me. I earned the position through combat."

Smiling, she walked away and never again spoke to Lady Radcliff. However, this last bit of information shot through the gossip channels.

Four trends began to formulate Northdale's future. First, Northdale's small size began to impact its residents. Geography limited the amount of tillable land and grazing pastures. Rupert's initial efforts to improve output produced results. One consequence of increased food supply was an increase in the number of children born. Unfortunately, the increased population could not find reasonable economic opportunities in Northdale. To prosper, young families began moving to other locations.

Second, the shipping market abandoned the Downs River port because other harbors eclipsed its size and quantity of trade activity. Only small coastal ships visited, particularly to haul out dried salmon. Agricultural efforts did produce a small surplus that fit easily into the coastal ships.

Third, no matter what efforts the people put into it, Northdale's daily life became very routine. Its children became bored and began leaving to experience larger towns, society life, and entertainments. Once gone, they rarely ever returned.

Fourth, English society never accepted Northdale. Its sins, described by Legate Rossi, stained the place and its people. In short, despite noble titles and knighthoods, the country assigned low-class stature to everything associated with Northdale. Noble families preferred the ignominy of marrying their children off to rich merchants rather than accepting a Northdale noble or knight. "They are all part Viking," was a frequent comment.

Northdale did begin to export a completely unique asset—young men and women who could read and write English and Latin and who could converse in French. In the general society, such skills usually could only be found in the high nobility and religious institutions. However, the expanding merchant and guild classes discovered that only their family members could be trusted to protect operational assets. The educated, young people's skills quickly overcame any lingering questions about Northdale. Marriage opportunities in the merchant class abounded.

Michael and Sophia had two children, a boy and a girl. Unfortunately, both were taken by a sweeping illness. They closely modeled their administration on the example that Rupert and Sara had established.

When studying polite social manners at York, Mary had met the third son of a distant earl, Heescome. He became enamored with her, and the feeling was mutual. After he spent six months in Northdale, as Mary insisted, they married. His father disinherited him. One son and two daughters came from the union. The boy, Simon, would become the third earl of Northdale.

Rupert and Sara's second son, Alfred, pursued an interest in Northdale's trading enterprise. Norsemen trained him to be a sailing master. Vikings were known for their longboats, but they also transported their goods in supply ships called knarrs. Rupert obtained one knarr through his trading, and Alfred became its master. He became motivated to seek a better location in which to expand his operations after gaining experience in the wine trade and observing potential increases in all types of commercial activity. Chester, a developing large harbor, became his choice.

He remained in contact with Northdale, but his increasing economic status made him focus on the new location and expanded operations. His success resulted in wealth that far exceeded anything the earldom could ever generate. As a knight, Alfred could have passed on the honor to his three sons; however, they declined in order to concentrate on shipping and to avoid the periodic draft for military service. Their wealth did allow a few quality families to ignore their background when offering sons and daughters for marriage.

The earldom would come to an end with the fourth earl, Mary's grandson. The king he served began demanding great fiscal contributions and troops for a standing army from all earls. Northdale could provide neither. So the fourth earl made a deal with the king. He would relinquish his title and allow the king to redistribute the land to other nobles. In exchange, he would be made a baron and given a commission in the army.

General Lord North spent years serving in king's campaigns in Spain, France, and in the remnants of the Holy Roman Empire. He never married, but a child with the last name of North was born in Spain and another in Vienna. Both children claimed noble status, but the English social structure ignored these assertions.

In the end, the name of Northdale simply stopped being used. The people who lived on its land would identify with the new earldom into which the king assigned them. Due to its low social stature, formal historians never recognized it as a place. Over the years, Sara's monument completely deteriorated. Eventually some architect used its stones for another building.

Northdale's most lasting note concerned the falls at the head of the Downs River. The people began to call them Sara's Falls, and the name remained.

About the Author

Robert L. Nelis began his writing career as he commuted to and from his job as a municipal official in Chicago suburbs, creating characters and laying out plots as he drove and sketching them out later. Now retired, he enjoys having time to write the stories he planned over his twenty-five years of commuting.

Robert has a Masters degree in urban planning and policy from the University of Illinois at Chicago where he also served as adjunct faculty. He lives with his wife of forty-one years in a 110-year-old house in Chicago where they raised their three children. Robert and his wife have four grandchildren, all of whom they love to spoil.

Made in the USA
Lexington, KY
15 April 2017